About the author

Harlan Coben is one of the most exciting talents in crime writing. His recent novels, *Caught*, *Long Lost* and *Hold Tight* were all international bestsellers, hitting the charts[1] of the *Sunday Times*, the *New York Times*, *Le Monde* and many others throughout the world. His books are published in 41 languages and there are more than 60 million of his novels in print worldwide. He was the first ever[2] author to win all three major US crime awards[3], and established a best-selling series of crime novels starring[4] his powerful creation, Myron Bolitar, before turning to stand-alone[5] books. Harlan lives in New Jersey with his wife and four children.

Visit his website at www.harlancoben.com.

1. dans les meilleures ventes
2. tout premier
3. prix
4. avec pour personnage principal
5. qui ne font pas partie d'une série

DIRECTION DE LA PUBLICATION : Carine Girac-Marinier

DIRECTION ÉDITORIALE : Claude Nimmo

NOTES EN MARGE : Patricia Seixas

RÉVISION DES NOTES : Valérie Katzaros, Marie-Noëlle Tilliette

RELECTURE : Joëlle Narjollet

INFORMATIQUE ÉDITORIALE : Philippe Cazabet, Marie-Noëlle Tilliette

CONCEPTION GRAPHIQUE : Uli Meindl

MISE EN PAGES : Cynthia Savage

FABRICATION : Rebecca Dubois

Mot de l'Éditeur

Vous aimeriez lire en langue originale, mais le vocabulaire, les expressions figurées ou la syntaxe vous arrêtent parfois ?

Cette collection est faite pour vous !

Vous trouverez en effet, en note dans la marge, une traduction de certains mots et expressions qui vous permettra d'avancer facilement dans votre lecture.

Nous n'avons pas cherché à vous donner une traduction littéraire de l'ouvrage et nous nous sommes parfois écartés du sens littéral pour vous fournir le sens qui convient le mieux à l'histoire. Aussi les mots sont-ils traduits dans le contexte du texte original.

Les expressions figées anglaises sont, bien entendu, rendues par une expression équivalente en français.

Les allusions à des réalités culturelles du monde anglo-saxon sont expliquées également dans la marge, pour vous aider à mieux comprendre la trame de l'histoire.

Vous aurez ainsi, en regard du texte original, tout le savoir-faire d'un dictionnaire rien que pour vous et adapté à ce livre !

Notre objectif est de vous mener jusqu'au mot FIN en vous donnant les clés nécessaires à la compréhension du récit.

Laissez-vous gagner par l'angoisse, l'humour et le suspense qui règnent chez les maîtres de la littérature anglo-saxonne.

Lire en VO ? You can indeed!

This one is for

Alek Coben
Thomas Bradbeer
Annie van der Heide

The three joys I'm lucky enough to call my godchildren[1]

1. filleuls

Acknowledgments

I'm not an expert in much, so it's a good thing I know generous geniuses who are. This might sound like name-dropping[1], but I was helped by my friends and/or colleagues Dr. Michael Baden, Linda Fairstein, Dr. David Gold, Dr. Anne Armstrong-Coben, Christopher J. Christie, and the real Jeff Bedford.

1. Cela peut paraître de la vantardise de ma part

Thanks to Mitch Hoffman, Lisa Johnson, Brian Tart, Erika Imranyi, and everyone at Dutton. Thanks to Jon Wood at Orion and Françoise Triffaux at Belfond. Thanks to Aaron Priest and everyone at the creatively dubbed[2] Aaron Priest Literary Agency.

2. au nom très créatif de :

Lastly, I would like to give a special thanks to the brilliant Lisa Erbach Vance, who has learned over the past decade to deal splendidly with my moods[3] and insecurities. You rock[4], Lisa.

3. humeurs changeantes

4. Tu es sensass

Coup de pouce pour vous aider à bien comprendre le début de l'histoire...

Le père de Paul Copeland est sur son lit de mort et Paul se souvient : à 18 ans, il allait épier son père qui partait, soi-disant pour pêcher, en réalité pour creuser dans les bois. C'est l'heure où se révèlent les secrets de famille...

Prologue

I see my father with that shovel[1].

There are tears streaming down[2] his face. An awful, guttural sob[3] forces its way up from deep in his lungs[4] and out through his lips[5]. He raises the shovel up and strikes[6] the ground. The blade rips into the earth[7] like it's wet flesh[8].

I am eighteen years old, and this is my most vivid memory[9] of my father – him, in the woods, with that shovel. He doesn't know I'm watching. I hide behind a tree while he digs[10]. He does it with a fury[11], as though the ground has angered him[12] and he is seeking vengeance[13].

I have never seen my father cry before – not when his own father died, not when my mother ran off and left us[14], not even when he first heard about[15] my sister, Camille. But he is crying now. He is crying without shame[16]. The tears cascade down his face in a free fall[17]. The sobs echo through the trees[18].

This is the first time I've spied on him[19] like this. Most Saturdays he would pretend[20] to be going on fishing trips[21], but I never really believed that. I think I always knew that this place, this horrible place, was his secret destination.

Because, sometimes, it is mine too.

1. pelle
2. Des larmes ruissellent le long de
3. sanglot
4. surgit du plus profond de ses poumons
5. s'échappe de ses lèvres
6. frappe
7. La lame éventre la terre
8. de la chair tendre
9. souvenir le plus marquant
10. creuse
11. fureur
12. comme si le sol l'avait mis en colère
13. qu'il cherchait à se venger
14. s'est enfuie en nous abandonnant
15. lorsqu'il a appris pour
16. sans honte
17. sans retenue
18. résonnent au cœur de la forêt
19. que je l'espionne
20. prétextait
21. partir à la pêche

I stand behind the tree and watch him. I will do this eight more times. I never interrupt him. I never reveal myself[1]. I think he doesn't know that I am there. I am sure of it, in fact. And then one day, as he heads to[2] his car, my father looks at me with dry eyes and says, "Not today, Paul. Today I go alone."

I watch him drive off[3]. He goes to those woods for the last time.

On his deathbed[4] nearly two decades later[5], my father takes my hand. He is heavily medicated[6]. His hands are rough and callused[7]. He used them his whole life – even in the flusher years[8] in a country that no longer exists. He has one of those tough exteriors[9] where all the skin looks baked[10] and hard, almost like his own tortoise shell[11]. He has been in immense physical pain[12], but there are no tears.

He just closes his eyes and rides it out[13].

My father has always made me feel safe, even now, even though I am now an adult with a child of my own[14]. We went to a bar three months ago, when he was still strong enough. A fight broke out.[15] My father stood in front of me, readying to take on anyone[16] who came near me. Still. That is how it is.

I look at him in the bed. I think about those days in the woods. I think about how he dug[17], how he finally stopped, how I thought he had given up[18] after my mother left.

"Paul?"

My father is suddenly agitated.

I want to beg him[19] not to die, but that wouldn't be right. I had been here before.[20] It doesn't get better – not for anyone.

"It's okay, Dad," I tell him. "It's all going to be okay."

He does not calm down. He tries to sit up[21]. I want to help him, but he shakes me off[22]. He looks deep into my eyes[23] and I see clarity[24], or maybe that is one of those things that we make ourselves believe at the end. A final false comfort.[25]

1. ne me montre jamais
2. alors qu'il se dirige vers
3. s'éloigner en voiture
4. lit de mort
5. presque 20 ans plus tard
6. assommé par les médicaments
7. rêches et pleines de callosités
8. au cours des années plus fastes
9. traits rugueux
10. tannée
11. carapace de tortue
12. Il a énormément souffert
13. supporte
14. et père d'un enfant
15. Une bagarre avait éclaté.
16. prêt à se battre contre le premier
17. il creusait
18. renoncé
19. le supplier
20. J'ai déjà vécu ça.
21. de se redresser
22. me repousse
23. me regarde droit dans les yeux
24. de la lucidité
25. Illusoire réconfort des derniers instants.

One tear escapes his eye. I watch it slowly slide down[1] his cheek.

"Paul," my father says to me, his voice still thick with a Russian accent[2]. "We still need to find her.[3]"

"We will, Dad."

He checks[4] my face again. I nod, assure him[5]. But I don't think that he is looking for assurance. I think, for the first time, he is looking for guilt[6].

"Did you know?" he asks, his voice barely[7] audible.

I feel my entire body quake[8], but I don't blink[9], don't look away[10]. I wonder what he sees, what he believes. But I will never know.

Because then, right then[11], my father closes his eyes and dies.

1. glisser le long de
2. d'une voix où persiste un fort accent russe
3. Il faut qu'on la retrouve.
4. inspecte
5. hoche la tête, le lui assure
6. de la culpabilité
7. à peine
8. tout mon corps frémir
9. je ne cille pas
10. ne détourne pas le regard
11. à ce moment précis

Chapter 1

Three Months Later

I was sitting in an elementary school gymnasium, watching my six-year-old daughter, Cara, nervously navigate across[1] a balance beam[2] that hovered[3] maybe four inches off the floor[4], but in less than an hour, I would be looking at the face of a man who'd been viciously[5] murdered.

That should not shock anyone.

I have learned over the years[6] – in the most horrible ways imaginable – that the wall[7] between life and death, between extraordinary beauty and mind-boggling ugliness[8], between the most innocent setting[9] and a frightening bloodbath[10], is flimsy[11]. It takes a second to tear through it.[12] One moment, life appears idyllic. You are in a place as chaste[13] as an elementary school gymnasium. Your little girl is twirling[14]. Her voice is giddy[15]. Her eyes are closed. You see her mother's face there, the way her mother used to close her eyes and smile, and you remember how flimsy that wall really is[16].

"Cope?"

1. avancer sur
2. poutre de gymnastique
3. fixée à
4. 10 cm du sol
5. sauvagement
6. au fil des années
7. la frontière
8. une laideur effrayante
9. cadre
10. bain de sang
11. ténue
12. Cette frontière se franchit en une seconde.
13. endroit aussi pur
14. est en train de virevolter
15. espiègle
16. à quel point cette frontière est ténue

It was my sister-in-law, Greta. I turned to her. Greta looked at me with her normal concern[1]. I smiled through it.[2]

"What are you thinking about?" she whispered[3].

She knew. I lied anyway[4].

"Handheld video cameras[5]," I said.

"What?"

The folding[6] chairs had all been taken by the other parents. I stood in the back, arms crossed, leaning against[7] the cement wall. There were rules posted above the doorway[8] and those annoyingly cute inspirational aphorisms[9] like "Don't Tell Me the Sky's the Limit When There Are Footprints on the Moon"[10] scattered throughout[11]. The lunch tables were folded in[12]. I leaned against that, feeling the cool of the steel[13] and metal. Elementary school gyms never change as we age[14]. They just seem to grow smaller[15].

I gestured at the parents. "There are more video cameras here than kids."

Greta nodded.

"And the parents, they film everything. I mean, everything. What do they do with all that? Does anybody really watch this again from beginning to end?"

"You don't?"

"I'd rather give birth.[16]"

She smiled at that. "No," she said, "you wouldn't."

"Okay, yeah, maybe not, but didn't we all grow up in the MTV generation? Quick cuts.[17] Lots of angles. But to just film this straight out[18] like this, to subject[19] an unsuspecting[20] friend or family member to that..."

The door opened. The moment the two men stepped into[21] the gym I could tell that they were cops[22]. Even if I didn't have a fair amount of experience[23] – I am the county prosecutor[24] for Essex County, which includes the rather violent city of Newark – I would know. Television does indeed get some stuff right[25]. The way most cops dressed, for example – fa-

1. avec son air soucieux habituel
2. Je lui souris.
3. chuchota-t-elle
4. mentis quand même
5. Aux Caméscopes
6. pliantes
7. appuyé contre
8. un règlement affiché au-dessus de la porte
9. aphorismes inspirés à la fois attendrissants et agaçants
10. « On ne peut plus dire que le ciel est inatteignable puisque l'homme a marché sur la Lune »
11. placardés partout
12. repliées
13. la fraîcheur de l'acier
14. ne changent pas à mesure qu'on vieillit
15. rétrécir
16. Je préférerais accoucher.
17. Des séquences rapides.
18. tel quel
19. infliger ça à
20. qui ne se doute de rien
21. entrèrent dans
22. c'était des flics
23. Même si je n'avais pas beaucoup d'expérience
24. procureur du comté
25. voit juste parfois

thers in the lush suburb[1] of Ridgewood[2] don't dress that way. We don't don suits[3] when we come to see our kids perform quasi-gymnastics. We wear corduroys[4] or jeans with a V-neck[5] over a T-shirt. These two guys wore ill-fitted[6] suits in a brown hue[7] that reminded me of wood chips[8] after a rainstorm.

They were not smiling. Their eyes scanned the room. I know most of the cops in the area, but I didn't know these guys. That troubled me. Something felt wrong[9]. I knew that I hadn't done anything, of course, but there was still a little I'm-innocent-but-I-still-feel-guilty[10] flutter in my stomach[11].

My sister-in-law, Greta, and her husband, Bob, have three kids of their own. Their youngest daughter, Madison, was six years old and in the same class as my Cara. Greta and Bob have been a tremendous help[12]. After my wife, Jane – Greta's sister – died, they moved to[13] Ridgewood. Greta claims[14] that they had planned on doing that anyway. I doubt it. But I am so grateful[15] that I don't question it much. I can't imagine what it would be like without them.

Usually the other fathers stand in the back[16] with me, but since this was a daytime event[17], there were very few here. The mothers – except for the one now glaring at me[18] over her video camera because she overheard my anti-video-cam rant[19] – adore me. It is not me, of course, but my story. My wife died five years ago, and I raise[20] my daughter alone. There are other single parents[21] in town, mostly divorced mothers, but I get a ton of slack[22]. If I forget to write a note or pick up my daughter late or leave her lunch on the counter, the other mothers or the staff in the school office chip in[23] and help. They think my male helplessness is cute[24]. When a single mother does any of those things, she is neglectful and on the receiving end of the superior moms' scorn[25].

The kids continued to tumble or stumble[26], depending on how you wanted to look at it[27]. I watched

1. banlieue cossue
2. [dans le New Jersey]
3. ne portons pas de costumes
4. pantalons en velours côtelé
5. pull à col en V
6. mal coupés
7. teinte
8. des brisures de bois
9. ne tournait pas rond
10. me sens quand même coupable
11. inquiétude
12. m'ont beaucoup aidé
13. ont déménagé à
14. prétend
15. reconnaissant
16. au fond de la salle
17. le spectacle avait lieu pendant la journée
18. celle qui me jette un regard noir
19. ma tirade contre les Caméscopes
20. j'élève
21. familles monoparentales
22. ils sont super indulgents envers moi
23. viennent à la rescousse
24. sont touchées par mon inaptitude masculine
25. subit le mépris des mères parfaites
26. à faire leurs figures ou à s'étaler
27. selon le point de vue qu'on veut avoir

Cara. She was big on concentration[1] and did just fine[2], but I suspected she had inherited her father's lack[3] of coordination. There were high school[4] girls from the gymnastics team helping. The girls were seniors[5], probably seventeen or eighteen. The one who spotted[6] Cara during her attempted somersault[7] reminded me of my sister. My sister, Camille, died when she was about this teen's age[8], and the media never lets me forget it. But maybe that was a good thing.

My sister would be in her late thirties now, at least as old as most of these mothers. Weird[9] to think of it that way. I see Camille forever as a teen[10]. It is hard to imagine where she would be now – where she *should* be now, sitting in one of those chairs, the doofy-happy-concerned-I'm-a-mom-first smile[11] on her face, overfilming[12] her own offspring[13]. I wonder what she would look like today, but again all I see is the teenager who died.

It may appear that I'm somewhat[14] obsessed with death, but there is a huge difference between my sister's murder and my wife's premature passing[15]. The first, my sister's, led me to my current[16] job and career trajectory. I can fight that injustice in the courtroom[17]. And I do. I try to make the world safer, try to put those who would harm others behind bars[18], try to bring other families something my family never really had – closure[19].

With the second death – my wife's – I was helpless[20] and screwed up[21] and no matter what I do now, I will never be able to make amends[22].

The school principal[23] strapped that faux-concerned smile[24] onto her over-lipsticked[25] mouth and headed in the direction of[26] the two cops. She engaged them in conversation, but neither one of them so much as glanced at her[27]. I watched their eyes. When the taller cop, the lead cop[28] for certain, hit my face[29], he stopped. Neither of us moved for a moment. He gave his head the slightest tilt[30], beckoning

1. très concentrée
2. se débrouillait bien
3. manque
4. du lycée
5. en terminale
6. assurait
7. tentative de saut périlleux
8. à peu près à l'âge de cette ado
9. Bizarre
10. toujours ado
11. sourire à la fois béat et soucieux de la maman qui assure
12. filmant à outrance
13. sa propre progéniture
14. quelque peu
15. le décès prématuré
16. actuel
17. au tribunal
18. derrière les barreaux
19. la possibilité de tourner la page
20. je m'étais senti impuissant
21. paumé
22. me racheter
23. directrice
24. afficha ce sourire faussement préoccupé
25. peinturlurée
26. se dirigea vers
27. ne prit la peine de la regarder
28. le chef
29. aperçut ma bobine
30. me fit un léger signe de tête

me outside this safe haven[1] of laughter and tumbling. I made my nod equally slight[2].

"Where are you going?" Greta asked me.

I don't want to sound unkind, but Greta was the ugly sister. They looked alike, she and my lovely dead bride[3]. You could tell that they were from the same parents. But everything that worked physically with[4] my Jane just doesn't quite make it[5] on Greta. My wife had a prominent nose that somehow made her sexier. Greta has a prominent nose that looks, well, big. My wife's eyes, set far apart[6], gave her an exotic appeal[7]. On Greta, the wide spacing[8] makes her look somewhat reptilian.

"I'm not sure," I said.

"Business?[9]"

"Could be."

She glanced over at[10] the two probable-cops, then back at me. "I was going to take Madison to Friendly's for lunch. Do you want me to bring Cara?"

"Sure, that'd be great."

"I could also pick her up after school."

I nodded. "That might help."

Greta kissed my cheek gently then – something she rarely does. I headed off.[11] The peals of children's laughter[12] rolled with me[13]. I opened the door and stepped into the corridor. The two policemen followed me. School corridors never change much either. They have an almost haunted-house echo to them[14], a strange sort of semisilence and a faint but distinct smell[15] that both soothed and agitated[16].

"Are you Paul Copeland?" the taller one asked.

"Yes."

He looked at his shorter[17] partner. The shorter guy was meaty[18] with no neck. His head was shaped like a cinder block[19]. His skin was coarse[20] too, adding to the illusion. From around the corner came a class of maybe fourth graders[21]. They were all red-faced from exertion[22]. Probably had just come from the

1. m'invitant à quitter ce havre
2. répondis d'un hochement de tête tout aussi discret
3. épouse
4. embellissait
5. n'a pas le même effet
6. très écartés
7. charme exotique
8. cet écart assez large
9. Le boulot ?
10. jeta un regard vers
11. Je partis.
12. éclats de rire enfantins
13. m'accompagnèrent
14. résonnent un peu comme les maisons hantées
15. odeur légère mais nette
16. à la fois apaisante et troublante
17. plus petit
18. grassouillet
19. était carrée et faisait penser à un parpaing
20. rugueuse
21. [élèves de CM1]
22. avaient tous le visage rougi par l'effort

playground[1]. They made their way past us[2], trailed by their harried teacher[3]. She gave us a strained smile[4].

"Maybe we should talk outside," the taller one said.

I shrugged[5]. I had no idea what this was about. I had the guile[6] of the innocent, but the experience to know that nothing with cops is what it appears to be. This was not about the big, headline-splashing case[7] I was working on. If it had been, they'd have called my office. I'd have gotten word[8] on my cell[9] or BlackBerry.

No, they were here for something else – something personal.

Again I knew that I had done nothing wrong. But I have seen all kinds of suspects in my time[10] and all kinds of reactions. It might surprise you. For example, when the police have a major[11] suspect in custody[12] they often keep them locked in the interrogation[13] room for hours on end[14]. You would think the guilty ones[15] would be climbing walls[16], but for the most part, it is the opposite. The innocent ones get the most antsy[17] and nervous. They have no idea why they are there or what the police mistakenly[18] think they've done. The guilty often go to sleep.

We stood outside. The sun blazed down[19]. The taller one squinted[20] and raised a hand to shade his eyes[21]. The Cinder Block[22] would not give anyone that satisfaction[23].

"My name is Detective Tucker York," the taller one said. He took out his badge and then motioned toward[24] the Cinder Block. "This is Detective Don Dillon."

Dillon took out his ID[25] too. They showed them to me. I don't know why they do that. How hard can it be to fake those[26]? "What can I do for you?" I asked.

"Do you mind telling us where you were last night?" York asked.

Sirens should have gone off[27] at a question like that[28]. I should have right away reminded them of

1. cour de récréation
2. passèrent devant nous
3. suivis de leur institutrice épuisée
4. sourire forcé
5. haussai les épaules
6. fourberie
7. l'énorme affaire qui faisait les gros titres
8. J'en aurais été informé
9. téléphone portable
10. dans ma vie
11. principal
12. en garde à vue
13. d'interrogatoire
14. pendant des heures
15. que ceux qui sont coupables
16. grimperaient aux rideaux
17. agités
18. à tort
19. tapait fort
20. plissa les yeux
21. se protégea les yeux avec la main
22. Son collègue à la tête de parpaing
23. n'allait pas s'abaisser à faire de même
24. désigna
25. son badge
26. de falsifier ces trucs
27. Des signaux auraient dû s'allumer dans ma tête
28. à l'énoncé de cette question

who I was and that I wouldn't answer any questions without an attorney[1] present. But I am an attorney. A damned good one. And that, of course, just makes you more foolish when you represent yourself, not less so[2]. I was also human. When you are rousted[3] by the police, even with all my experience, you want to please. You can't help that feeling.[4]

"I was home."

"Anyone who can verify[5] that?"

"My daughter."

York and Dillon looked back at the school. "That's the girl who was tumbling in there?"

"Yes."

"Anyone else?"

"I don't think so. What's this about?[6]"

York was the one who was doing all the talking. He ignored my question. "Do you know a man named Manolo Santiago?"

"No."

"Are you sure?"

"Pretty sure.[7]"

"Why only pretty sure?"

"Do you know who I am?"

"Yep[8]," York said. He coughed into his fist.[9] "You want us to maybe take a knee or kiss your ring[10] or something?"

"That's not what I meant."

"Good, then we're on the same page[11]." I did not like his attitude, but I let it slide[12]. "So why are you only 'pretty sure' you don't know Manolo Santiago?"

"I mean, the name isn't familiar[13]. I don't think I know him. But maybe it's someone I prosecuted[14] or was a witness[15] in one of my cases, or hell[16], maybe I met him at a fund-raiser[17] ten years ago."

York nodded, encouraging me to blabber more[18]. I didn't.

"Do you mind coming with us?"

"Where?"

1. avocat
2. et non l'inverse
3. malmené
4. C'est instinctif.
5. confirmer
6. De quoi s'agit-il ?
7. À peu près certain.
8. Ouais
9. Il toussota en portant sa main fermée à sa bouche.
10. qu'on s'agenouille ou qu'on embrasse votre bague
11. sur la même longueur d'ondes
12. je ne relevai pas
13. ne me dit rien
14. contre qui j'ai engagé des poursuites
15. témoin
16. ou bien, je ne sais pas,
17. soirée de charité
18. à continuer à en dire plus

"It won't take long."

"Won't take long," I repeated. "That doesn't sound like a place.[1]"

The two cops exchanged a glance[2]. I tried to look as if I would hold my ground.[3]

"A man named Manolo Santiago was murdered last night."

"Where?"

"His body was in Manhattan. Washington Heights area."

"And what does this have to do with me?"

"We think you might be able to help."

"Help how? I already told you. I don't know him."

"You said" – York actually referred to his pad[4], but it was only for effect[5]; he hadn't written anything while I was talking – "that you were 'pretty sure' you didn't know him."

"I'm sure then. Okay? I'm sure."

He snapped the pad closed[6] with dramatic flair[7]. "Mr. Santiago knew you."

"How do you know that?"

"We'd prefer to show you."

"And I'd prefer you tell me."

"Mr. Santiago" – York hesitated as though choosing his next words by hand[8] – "had certain items[9] on him."

"Items?"

"Yes."

"Could you be more specific[10]?"

"Items," he said, "that point to you[11]."

"Point to me as what[12]?"

"Yo[13], Mr. DA[14]?"

Dillon – the Cinder Block – had finally spoken.

"It's County Prosecutor," I said.

"Whatever.[15]" He cracked[16] his neck and pointed at my chest[17]. "You're really starting to itch my ass[18]."

"Excuse me?"

1. Ça ne me dit rien, comme endroit !
2. un regard
3. J'essayai d'avoir l'air sûr de moi.
4. consulta son bloc-notes
5. pour m'impressionner
6. ferma son bloc d'un coup sec
7. d'un geste théâtral
8. choisissant ses mots avec précaution
9. objets
10. précis
11. qui vous désignent
12. en tant que quoi
13. Hé !
14. le Procureur
15. Peu importe.
16. fit craquer
17. me pointa du doigt
18. à me gonfler

Dillon stepped into my face[1]. "Do we look like we're here for a goddamn semantics lesson[2]?"

I thought the question was rhetorical[3], but he waited. Finally I said, "No."

"Then listen up[4]. We got a dead body. The guy is linked to you in a big way[5]. Do you want to come and help clear this up[6], or do you want to play more word games[7] that make you look suspicious as hell?"

"Who exactly do you think you're talking to, Detective?"

"A guy running for office[8] who wouldn't want us to take this directly to the press."

"Are you threatening me?"

York stepped in[9]. "Nobody is threatening anything."

But Dillon had hit me where I lived[10]. The truth was, my appointment was still only temporary. My friend, the current governor of the Garden State[11], had made me acting[12] county prosecutor. There was also serious talk[13] of my running for Congress[14], maybe even the vacant Senate seat[15]. I would be lying if I said I didn't have political ambitions. A scandal, even the fake whiff of one, would not play well.[16]

"I can't see how I can help," I said.

"Maybe you can't, maybe you can." Dillon rotated the cinder block[17]. "But you want to help if you can, don't you?"

"Of course," I said. "I mean, I don't want your ass itching any more than it has to[18]."

He almost smiled at that one. "Then get in the car."

"I have an important meeting this afternoon."

"We'll have you back by then.[19]"

I expected a beat-up[20] Chevy[21] Caprice, but the car was a clean Ford. I sat in the back. My two new friends sat in the front. We did not speak during the ride[22]. There was traffic at the George Washington Bridge, but we just hit[23] our siren and sliced through it[24]. When we were on the Manhattan side, York spoke.

1. s'approcha de moi
2. pour un cours de langue à la con
3. de pure forme
4. écoutez bien
5. a un lien évident avec vous
6. contribuer à éclaircir tout ça
7. continuer à jouer sur les mots
8. qui se présente aux élections
9. s'interposa
10. avait mis le doigt là où ça fait mal
11. [surnom de l'État du New Jersey]
12. par intérim
13. sérieusement question
14. que je me présente aux législatives
15. aux partielles de renouvellement du Sénat
16. La moindre rumeur de scandale, même infondée, ferait désordre.
17. fit pivoter sa tête carrée
18. vous gonfler plus que nécessaire
19. Vous serez rentré d'ici là.
20. délabrée
21. Chevrolet
22. trajet
23. ils déclenchèrent
24. la voiture fila à travers les embouteillages

"We think Manolo Santiago might be an alias."

I said, "Uh-huh[1]," because I didn't know what else to say.

"You see, we don't have a positive ID[2] on the victim. We found him last night. His driver's license reads[3] Manolo Santiago. We checked it out.[4] It doesn't appear to be his real name. We ran his prints.[5] No hits.[6] So we don't know who he is."

"And you think I will?"

They did not bother answering[7].

York's voice was as casual as a spring day[8]. "You're a widower[9], Mr. Copeland, right?"

"Right," I said.

"Must be tough.[10] Raising a kid on your own.[11]"

I said nothing.

"Your wife had cancer, we understand. You're very involved[12] in some organization to find a cure[13]."

"Uh-huh."

"Admirable."

They should only know.[14]

"This must be weird for you," York said.

"How's that?[15]"

"Being on the other side. You're usually the one asking the questions, not answering them. That's gotta be[16] a little strange."

He smiled at me in the rearview mirror[17].

"Hey, York?" I said.

"What?"

"Do you have a playbill or a program[18]?" I asked.

"A what?"

"A playbill," I said. "So I can see your past credits[19], you know – before you landed the coveted role of Good Cop[20]."

York chuckled at that[21]. "I'm just saying, it's weird is all[22]. I mean, have you ever been questioned[23] by the police before?"

It was a setup[24] question. They had to know. When I was eighteen years old, I worked as a

1. ah bon
2. identification formelle
3. permis de conduire est au nom de
4. On a vérifié.
5. On a vérifié ses empreintes.
6. Aucune correspondance.
7. ne prirent pas la peine de répondre
8. était naturelle et posée
9. veuf
10. Ça doit être dur.
11. D'élever seul un enfant.
12. Vous êtes très impliqué
13. remède
14. Si seulement ils savaient.
15. Comment ça ?
16. Ça doit être
17. rétroviseur
18. programme du spectacle
19. votre répertoire
20. vous ne décrochiez le rôle si convoité du flic sympa
21. salua le trait d'un petit rire
22. que c'est bizarre, c'est tout
23. interrogé
24. piège

counselor[1] at a summer camp[2]. Four campers – Gil Perez and his girlfriend, Margot Green, Doug Billingham and his girlfriend, Camille Copeland (aka[3] my sister) – sneaked[4] into the woods late one night.

They were never seen again.

Only two of the bodies have ever been found. Margot Green, age seventeen, was found with her throat slit within a hundred yards[5] of the campsite[6]. Doug Billingham, also seventeen, was found half a mile away[7]. He had several stab wounds[8], but cause of death was also a slit throat. The bodies of the other two – Gil Perez and my sister, Camille – have never been found.

The case made headlines.[9] Wayne Steubens, a rich-kid[10] counselor at the camp, was caught two years later – after his third summer of terror – but not until he murdered at least four more teens. He was dubbed[11] the Summer Slasher[12] – an all-too-obvious moniker[13]. Wayne's next two victims were found near a Boy Scout camp in Muncie, Indiana. Another victim was attending one of those all-around[14] camps in Vienna, Virginia. His last victim had been at a sports camp in the Poconos[15]. Most had their throats slit. All had been buried out in the woods[16], some before death. Yes, as in buried alive.[17] It took a fair amount[18] of time to locate[19] the bodies. The Poconos kid, for example, took six months to be found. Most experts believe that there are others still out there, still underground, deep in the[20] woods.

Like my sister.

Wayne has never confessed, and despite being[21] in a supermaximum-security facility[22] for the past eighteen years, he insists that he had nothing to do with the four murders that started it all.

I don't believe him. The fact that at least two bodies were still out there led to[23] speculation and mystery. It gave Wayne more attention. I think he likes

1. moniteur
2. colonie de vacances
3. alias
4. étaient partis en douce
5. la gorge tranchée, à moins de 100 m
6. campement
7. à moins d'un kilomètre
8. avait reçu plusieurs coups de couteau
9. L'affaire avait fait les gros titres.
10. gosse de riches
11. surnommé
12. l'Égorgeur de l'été
13. surnom un peu facile
14. sans thème particulier
15. [montagnes de Pennsylvanie]
16. quelque part dans les bois
17. Oui, enterrés vivants.
18. Il avait fallu pas mal
19. pour trouver
20. au fond des
21. bien qu'il soit
22. quartier de haute sécurité
23. a suscité

that. But that unknown[1] – that glimmer[2] – still hurts like hell[3].

I loved my sister. We all did. Most people believe death is the cruelest thing. Not so. After a while, hope is a far more abusive mistress[4]. When you live with it as long as I have, your neck constantly on the chopping block, the ax raised above you[5] for days, then months, then years, you long for it to fall[6] and lop off your[7] head. Most believed that my mother ran off because my sister was murdered. But the truth is the opposite. My mother left us because we could never prove it.

I wished Wayne Steubens would tell us what he did with her. Not to give her a proper burial[8] or any of that. That would be nice, but beside the point[9]. Death is pure, wrecking-ball[10] destructive. It hits, you're crushed, you start to rebuild. But not knowing – that doubt, that glimmer – makes death work more like termites or some sort of relentless germ[11]. It eats away from the inside[12]. You cannot stop the rot[13]. You cannot rebuild because that doubt will just keep gnawing away[14].

It still does, I think.

That part of my life, much as I want to keep it private[15], was always picked up by the[16] media. Even the quickest Google search would have brought up my name in connection with the mystery of the Vanished[17] Campers, as they were quickly dubbed. Heck[18], the story still played on[19] those "real crime" shows[20] on Discovery or Court TV[21]. I was there that night, in those woods. My name was out there for the finding[22]. I was questioned by the police. Interrogated. Under suspicion even.

So they had to know.

I chose not to answer. York and Dillon didn't push it[23].

When we arrived at the morgue, they led me down a long corridor. No one spoke. I wasn't sure what

1. cette inconnue
2. lueur d'espoir
3. me fait encore très mal
4. bien pire qu'une maîtresse qui vous maltraite
5. avec cette épée de Damoclès au-dessus de la tête en permanence
6. il vous tarde qu'elle retombe
7. vous tranche la
8. enterrement en bonne et due forme
9. hors de propos
10. comme une boule de démolition
11. microbe persistant
12. mine de l'intérieur
13. empêcher la gangrène de gagner
14. continue à vous ronger
15. que je m'efforce pourtant de garder secrète
16. connue des
17. disparus
18. Bon sang
19. était encore diffusée dans
20. émissions sur les faits divers
21. [chaîne filmant les procès]
22. était facile à trouver
23. n'insistèrent pas

to make[1] of this. What York said made sense now. I was on the other side. I had watched plenty of witnesses make walks like this[2]. I had seen every sort of reaction in the morgue. The identifiers usually start off stoic[3]. I'm not sure why. Are they bracing themselves?[4] Or does a smidgen[5] of hope – that word again – still exist? I'm not sure. Whatever[6], the hope quickly vanishes. We never make a mistake on the ID. If we think it's your loved one, it is. The morgue is not a place of last-minute miracles. Not ever.

I knew that they were watching me, studying my responses[7]. I became aware[8] of my steps, my posture, my facial expression. I aimed for neutral[9] and then wondered why I bothered[10].

They brought me to the window. You don't go into the room. You stay behind glass. The room was tiled[11] so that you could just hose it down[12] – no need to get fancy[13] with decor or cleaners[14]. All the gurneys save one[15] were empty. The body was covered with a sheet, but I could see the toe tag[16]. They really used those. I looked at the big toe sticking out[17] from under the sheet – it was wholly unfamiliar[18]. That was what I thought. I do not recognize the man's[19] toe.

The mind does funny things under stress.

A woman wearing a mask rolled the gurney closer to[20] the window. I flashed back to, of all things[21], the day my daughter was born. I remember the nursery[22]. The window was much the same, with those thin strips of foil[23] forming diamonds[24]. The nurse, a woman about the size of the woman in the morgue, rolled the little cart[25] with my little daughter in it close to the window. Just like this. I guess I would normally have seen something poignant in this – the beginning of life, the end of it – but today I didn't.

She pulled back[26] the top of the sheet. I looked down at the face. All eyes were on me. I knew that. The dead man was about my age, late thirties. He had a beard[27]. His head looked shaved[28]. He wore a

1. que penser
2. témoins faire ce parcours
3. sont stoïques au début
4. Se préparent-ils au pire ?
5. un tout petit peu
6. En tout cas
7. réactions
8. Je pris conscience
9. J'essayai de ne rien laisser paraître
10. je m'en préoccupais
11. carrelée
12. la passer au jet d'eau
13. de faire des fantaisies
14. les produits d'entretien
15. Tous les lits [roulants] d'hôpital, sauf un
16. l'étiquette à son orteil
17. qui dépassait
18. il ne me disait rien du tout
19. de ce type
20. plus près de
21. Cela me rappela, de façon assez singulière
22. pouponnière
23. fines lamelles métalliques
24. en losanges
25. berceau à roulettes
26. souleva
27. barbe
28. rasée

shower cap[1]. I thought that looked pretty goofy[2], the shower cap, but I knew why it was there.

"Shot in the head?" I asked.

"Yes."

"How many times?"

"Twice."

"Caliber?"

York cleared his throat[3], as if trying to remind me that this wasn't my case. "Do you know him?"

I took another look. "No," I said.

"Are you sure?"

I started to nod. But something made me stop.

"What?" York said

"Why am I here?"

"We want to see if you know – "

"Right, but what made you think I would know him?"

I slid my eyes to the side[4], saw York and Dillon exchange a glance. Dillon shrugged and York picked up the ball[5]. "He had your address in his pocket," York said. "And he had a bunch of clippings[6] about you."

"I'm a public figure[7]."

"Yes, we know."

He stopped talking. I turned toward him. "What else?"

"The clippings weren't about you. Not really."

"What were they about?"

"Your sister," he said. "And about what happened in those woods."

The room dropped[8] ten degrees, but hey, we were in a morgue. I tried to sound nonchalant[9]. "Maybe he's a real-crime nut[10]. There are lots of them."

He hesitated. I saw him exchange a glance with his partner.

"What else?" I asked.

"What do you mean?"

"What else did he have on him?"

1. bonnet de douche
2. idiot
3. se racla la gorge
4. Je jetai un coup d'œil sur le côté
5. prit le relais
6. liasse de coupures de presse
7. personnage
8. Il me sembla que la température de la pièce avait chuté de
9. paraître détaché
10. fana

York turned toward a subordinate[1] I hadn't even noticed was standing there[2]. "Can we show Mr. Copeland here the personal effects?"

I kept my eye on the dead man's face. There were pockmarks and lines.[3] I tried to smooth them out[4]. I didn't know him. Manolo Santiago was a stranger to me[5].

Someone pulled out a red plastic evidence bag[6]. They emptied it out onto a table. From the distance I could see a pair of blue jeans and a flannel shirt. There was a wallet[7] and a cell phone.

"You check the cell phone?" I asked.

"Yep. It's a throwaway[8]. The phone log[9] is empty."

I wrested my gaze away from the[10] dead man's face and walked over to the table. My legs quaked[11].

There were folded sheets of paper[12]. I carefully opened one up. The article from *Newsweek*. The picture of the four dead teens was there – the Summer Slasher's first victims. They always started with Margot Green because her body was found right away[13]. It took another day to locate Doug Billingham. But the real interest lay in the other two[14]. Blood had been found and torn clothes belonging to[15] both Gil Perez and my sister – but no bodies.

Why not?

Simple. The woods were massive[16]. Wayne Steubens had hidden them well. But some people, those who loved a good conspiracy[17], didn't buy that[18]. Why had just those two not been found? How could Steubens have moved and buried bodies so quickly? Did he have an accomplice[19]? How had he pulled it off[20]? What were those four doing in those woods in the first place[21]?

Even today, eighteen years after Wayne's arrest, people talk about the "ghosts" in those woods – or maybe there is a secret cult living in[22] an abandoned cabin[23] or escaped mental patients or men with hook arms[24] or bizarre medical experiments[25]

1. auxiliaire
2. dont la présence m'avait échappé
3. Il avait la peau grêlée et des rides.
4. les gommer
5. m'était inconnu
6. sachet de pièces à conviction
7. portefeuille
8. jetable
9. historique des appels
10. Je détachai mon regard du
11. se mirent à trembler
12. feuilles de papier pliées
13. tout de suite
14. c'était les deux autres qui suscitaient l'intérêt
15. des vêtements déchirés appartenant à
16. gigantesques
17. les amateurs de complot
18. n'y croyaient pas
19. complice
20. réussi
21. d'ailleurs, hein
22. culte pratiqué en secret dans
23. cabane
24. les bras armés de crochets
25. expériences

gone wrong[1]. They talk about the bogeyman[2], finding the remnants[3] of his burned-out campfire[4], still surrounded by the bones of children he'd eaten. They say how at night they can still hear Gil Perez and my sister, Camille, howl for vengeance[5].

I spent a lot of nights out there, alone in those woods. I never heard anyone howl.

My eyes moved past Margot Green's picture and Doug Billingham's. The photograph of my sister was next[6]. I had seen this same shot[7] a million times. The media loved it because she looked so wonderfully ordinary. She was the girl next door[8], your favorite babysitter, the sweet teen[9] who lived down the block[10]. That wasn't Camille at all. She was mischievous[11], with lively[12] eyes and a sideways devil-may-care grin[13] that knocked the boys back a step[14]. This picture was so not her[15]. She was more than this. And maybe that had cost her her life.

I was about to head over to[16] the final picture, the one of Gil Perez, but something made me pull up[17].

My heart stopped.

I know that sounds dramatic, but that was how it felt[18]. I looked at the pile of coins from Manolo Santiago's pocket and saw it, and it was as if a hand reached into my chest[19] and squeezed[20] my heart so hard it couldn't beat[21] anymore.

I stepped back.

"Mr. Copeland?"

My hand went out as if it were acting on its own[22]. I watched my fingers pluck it up[23] and bring it to my eye level.

It was a ring. A girl's ring.

I looked at the picture of Gil Perez, the boy who'd been murdered with my sister in the woods. I flashed back[24] twenty years. And I remembered the scar[25].

"Mr. Copeland?"

"Show me his arm," I said.

"Excuse me?"

1. ayant mal tourné
2. croque-mitaine
3. vestiges
4. feu de camp éteint
5. hurler vengeance
6. suivait
7. ce cliché-là
8. d'à côté
9. l'adorable ado
10. en bas de la rue
11. espiègle
12. vifs
13. un petit sourire insouciant
14. séduisait les garçons
15. lui ressemblait si peu
16. passer à
17. m'arrêta dans mon élan
18. ce que je ressentis
19. me déchirait la poitrine
20. comprimait
21. battre
22. comme si elle agissait de son propre gré
23. la récupérer
24. Je fis un bond en arrière de
25. cicatrice

1. cadavre
2. foutu
3. fit un signe à
4. bouton de l'Interphone
5. perplexes
6. velue
7. plus corpulent
8. 15 kg de plus
9. qu'à l'époque
10. cicatrice en dents de scie
11. Je ne sursautai pas
12. ni n'eus aucune réaction de la sorte
13. venait de se détacher
14. trop pétrifié
15. Je désignai la photo

"His arm." I turned back to the window and pointed to the corpse[1]. "Show me his goddamn[2] arm."

York signaled to[3] Dillon. Dillon pressed the intercom button[4]. "He wants to the see the guy's arm."

"Which one?" the woman in the morgue asked.

They looked at me.

"I don't know," I said. "Both, I guess."

They looked puzzled[5], but the woman obeyed. The sheet was pulled back.

The chest was hairy[6] now. He was bigger[7], at least thirty pounds more[8] than he was back in those days[9], but that wasn't surprising. He had changed. We all had. But that wasn't what I was looking for. I was looking at the arm, for the ragged scar[10].

It was there.

On his left arm. I did not gasp[11] or any of that[12]. It was as if part of my reality had just been pulled away[13] and I was too numb[14] to do anything about it. I just stood there.

"Mr. Copeland?"

"I know him," I said.

"Who is he?"

I pointed to the picture[15] in the magazine. "His name is Gil Perez."

Chapter 2

There was a time when Professor Lucy Gold, PhD[1] in both English and psychology, loved office hours[2].

It was a chance to sit one-on-one with[3] students and really get to know them[4]. She loved when the quiet ones who sat in the back with their heads down, taking notes as though it were dictation[5], the ones who had their hair hanging[6] in front of their faces like a protective curtain[7] – when they arrived at her door and raised their eyes and told her what was in their hearts.

But most of the time, like now, the students who showed up[8] were the brownnosers[9], the ones who felt[10] that their grade[11] should depend solely[12] on their outward[13] enthusiasm, that the more face time they got[14], the higher the grade[15], as though being an extrovert[16] was not rewarded enough[17] in this country.

"Professor Gold," the girl named Sylvia Potter said. Lucy imagined her a little younger, in middle school[18]. She would have been the annoying girl who arrived the morning of a big test whining[19] that she was going to fail[20] and then ended up being the first one done[21], smugly handing in[22] her A-plus paper[23]

1. titulaire d'un doctorat
2. aimait les heures de permanence
3. de voir en tête-à-tête
4. d'apprendre à bien les connaître
5. c'était une dictée
6. qui retombaient
7. un rideau protecteur
8. se pointaient
9. lèche-bottes
10. pensaient
11. note
12. uniquement
13. apparent
14. plus ils avaient de tête-à-tête
15. meilleure serait la note
16. extraverti
17. pas déjà assez récompensé
18. au collège
19. en se plaignant
20. le rater
21. la première à avoir fini
22. tendant d'un air suffisant
23. excellente copie

early, and using the rest of the class time to put reinforcements in her notebook[1].

"Yes, Sylvia?"

"When you were reading that passage from Yeats in class today, I mean, I was so moved[2]. Between the actual words[3] and the way you can use your voice, you know, like a professional actress..."

Lucy Gold was tempted to say, "Do me a favor[4] – just bake me some brownies[5]," but she kept the smile on instead. No easy task.[6] She glanced at her watch and then felt like crap[7] for doing that. Sylvia was a student trying her best. That was all. We all find our ways to cope[8], to adapt and survive. Sylvia's way was probably wiser[9] and less self-destructive than most.

"I loved writing that journal piece[10] too," she said.

"I'm glad."

"Mine was about[11]... well, my first time, if you know what I mean[12]...."

Lucy nodded. "We're keeping them confidential and anonymous[13], remember?"

"Oh, right." She glanced down now. Lucy wondered about that[14]. Sylvia never looked down.

"Maybe after I read them all," Lucy said, "if you want, we can talk about yours. In private."

Her head was still down.

"Sylvia?"

The girl's voice was very soft. "Okay."

Office hours were over. Lucy wanted to get home. She tried not to sound halfhearted[15] when she asked, "Do you want to talk about it now?"

"No."

Sylvia's head was still down.

"Okay then," Lucy said, making a production of looking at[16] her watch. "I have a staff meeting[17] in ten minutes."

Sylvia stood. "Thank you for meeting with me."

"My pleasure[18], Sylvia."

1. pour coller des œillets dans son classeur
2. si émue
3. ces mots
4. Fais-moi plaisir
5. va voir ailleurs si j'y suis
6. Pas facile.
7. se sentit minable
8. essayer de s'en sortir
9. plus sensée
10. extrait de journal intime
11. Le mien évoquait
12. si vous voyez ce que je veux dire
13. Ils resteront confidentiels et anonymes
14. se demanda pourquoi
15. essaya de cacher son peu d'enthousiasme
16. en regardant ostensiblement
17. réunion du personnel
18. Je t'en prie

Sylvia looked as if she wanted to say something more. But she didn't. Five minutes later, Lucy stood at her window and looked down at the quad[1]. Sylvia walked out the door, wiped her face[2], set the head high[3], forced up a smile. She started walk-skipping[4] across campus. Lucy watched her wave at[5] her fellow students, fall in with[6] a group, and blend with[7] the others until Sylvia became an indistinct part of the mass.

Lucy turned away. She caught her reflection[8] in the mirror and did not like what she saw. Had that girl been calling out for help?

Probably, Luce, and you didn't answer. Nice work, superstar.

She sat at her desk and opened the bottom drawer[9]. The vodka was there. Vodka was good. You didn't smell vodka.

Her office door opened. The guy who entered had long black hair tucked[10] behind his ears and several earrings. He was unshaven, fashionably so[11], handsome in an aging-boy-band way[12]. He had the silver stud[13] in his chin, a look that always detracted[14], low pants[15] barely held up by a studded[16] belt, and a tattoo on the neck that said, "Breed Often[17]."

"You," the guy said, gunning[18] his best smile in her direction, "look immensely doable[19]."

"Thanks, Lonnie."

"Nah, I mean it.[20] Immensely doable."

Lonnie Berger was her TA[21], though he was her age. He was permanently caught in that education trap[22], getting a new degree[23], hanging on campus, the telltale sign[24] of age around the eyes. Lonnie was getting tired of the PC sexual crap[25] on campus, so he was going out of his way[26] to push that boundary[27] and hit on[28] every woman he could.

"You should wear something that shows a little more cleavage[29], maybe one of those new push-

1. cour intérieure
2. s'essuya le visage
3. releva la tête bien haut
4. marcher en sautillant
5. saluer de la main
6. aborder
7. se mêler à
8. aperçut son reflet
9. tiroir du bas
10. ramenés
11. avait le look mal rasé à la mode
12. façon boys band vieillissant
13. clou en argent
14. air toujours critique
15. un pantalon taille basse
16. cloutée
17. baisez souvent
18. en décochant
19. baisable
20. Nan, je suis sincère.
21. [teaching assistant] assitant
22. piège des études
23. diplôme
24. signes révélateurs
25. rapports sexuels politiquement corrects
26. faisait tout
27. pour repousser cette limite
28. draguer
29. de plus décolleté

up bras[1]," Lonnie added. "Might make the boys pay more attention in class."

"Yeah, that's what I want."

"Seriously, chief, when was the last time you got some[2]?"

"It's been eight months, six days, and about" – Lucy checked her watch – "four hours."

He laughed. "You're playing me[3], right?"

She just stared at him.

"I printed out the journals," he said.

The confidential, anonymous journals.

She was teaching a class that the university had dubbed Creative Reasoning, a combination of cutting-edge psychological trauma[4] with creative writing[5] and philosophy. Truth be told[6], Lucy loved it. Current assignment[7]: Each student was supposed to write on a traumatic event in their lives – something that they would not normally share with anyone[8]. No names were to be used. No grades given.[9] If the anonymous student gave permission on the bottom of the page, Lucy might read a few out loud[10] to the class for the purpose of discussion[11] – again keeping the author anonymous.

"Did you start reading them?" she asked.

Lonnie nodded and sat in the seat that Sylvia had occupied a few minutes ago. He threw his feet up on[12] the desk. "The usual," he said.

"Bad erotica[13]?"

"I'd say more like soft porn[14]."

"What's the difference?"

"Damned if I know.[15] Did I tell you about my new chick[16]?"

"No."

"Delectable.[17]"

"Uh-huh."

"I'm serious. A waitress.[18] Hottest piece of ass[19] I've ever dated[20]."

"And I want to hear this because[21]?"

1. soutiens-gorge qui remontent la poitrine
2. que tu as couché avec quelqu'un
3. Tu me fais marcher
4. mêlant de manière avant-gardiste traumatisme psychologique
5. et écriture créative
6. À dire vrai
7. Le travail du moment
8. dont ils n'auraient normalement parlé à personne
9. Ce ne serait pas noté.
10. à haute voix
11. dans le but d'en débattre
12. balança ses pieds sur
13. littérature érotique
14. du porno soft
15. J'en sais rien.
16. nana
17. Délicieuse.
18. Une serveuse.
19. La nana la plus sexy
20. avec laquelle je sois sorti
21. en quoi ça me regarde

"Jealous?"

"Yeah," Lucy said. "That must be it.[1] Give me the journals, will you[2]?"

Lonnie handed her a few[3]. They both started digging in[4]. Five minutes later, Lonnie shook his head.

Lucy said, "What?"

"How old are most of these kids?" Lonnie asked. "Maybe twenty, right?"

"Right."

"And their sexual escapades always last, like[5], two hours?"

Lucy smiled. "Active[6] imagination."

"Did guys last that long[7] when you were young?"

"They don't last that long now," she said.

Lonnie arched an eyebrow[8]. "That's because you're so hot[9]. They can't control themselves. It's your fault, really."

"Hmm." She tapped the pencil's eraser against her lower lip[10]. "That's not the first time you've used that line[11], is it?"

"You think I need a new one? How about: "This has never happened to me before, I swear[12]'?"

Lucy made a buzzing sound[13]. "Sorry, try again[14]."

"Damn."

They went back to reading. Lonnie whistled[15] and shook his head. "Maybe we just grew up in the wrong era[16]."

"Definitely.[17]"

"Luce?" He looked over the paper. "You really need to get some."

"Uh-huh."

"I'm willing to help[18], you know. No strings attached.[19]"

"What about Ms. Delectable Waitress?[20]"

"We're not exclusive.[21]"

"I see."

1. Ça doit être ça.
2. tu veux
3. lui en tendit quelques-uns
4. se plongèrent dans les copies
5. durent toujours, disons
6. fertile
7. aussi longtemps
8. haussa un sourcil
9. sexy
10. se tapota la lèvre inférieure avec la gomme du crayon
11. que tu me sors ça
12. je le jure
13. imita le buzz des jeux télévisés
14. mauvaise réponse
15. siffla
16. à la mauvaise époque
17. Aucun doute.
18. Je ne demande qu'à t'aider
19. Sans aucun engagement.
20. Et la super serveuse ?
21. Ça ne nous empêche pas d'aller voir ailleurs.

"So what I'm suggesting here is purely a physical thing. A mutual pipe cleaning[1], if you catch my drift[2]."

"Shush[3], I'm reading."

He caught the hint.[4] Half an hour later, Lonnie sat forward and looked at her.

"What?"

"Read this one," he said.

"Why?"

"Just read it, okay?"

She shrugged, put down the journal she'd been reading – yet another[5] story of a girl who'd gotten drunk[6] with her new boyfriend and ended up in a threesome[7]. Lucy had read lots of stories of threesomes. None seemed to happen without alcoholic involvement[8].

But a minute later she forgot all about that. She forgot that she lived alone or that she had no real family left[9] and that she was a college professor[10] or that she was in her office overlooking[11] the quad or that Lonnie was still sitting in front of her. Lucy Gold was gone[12]. And in her place was a younger woman, a girl really, with a different name, a girl on the verge of adulthood[13] but still so very much a girl[14]:

This happened when I was seventeen. I was at summer camp. I worked there as a CIT. That stands for Counselor In Training.[15] It wasn't hard for me to get the job because my dad owned[16] the place...

Lucy stopped. She looked at the front sheet[17]. There was no name, of course. The students e-mailed the papers in[18]. Lonnie had printed them out. There was supposed to be no way[19] to know who sent what paper. It was part of the comfort[20]. You didn't even have to risk having your fingerprints[21] on it. You just hit[22] the anonymous Send[23] button:

1. nettoyage de tuyauterie
2. tu vois où je veux en venir
3. Chut
4. Il reçut le message.
5. encore une
6. s'était saoulée
7. s'était retrouvée dans un plan à trois
8. sans influence de l'alcool
9. qu'il ne lui restait plus vraiment de famille
10. professeur d'université
11. donnant sur
12. ailleurs
13. sur le point de devenir adulte
14. si jeune encore
15. Cela signifie « monitrice stagiaire ».
16. était propriétaire de
17. première page
18. transmettaient les devoirs par mail
19. Il ne devait y avoir aucun moyen
20. un des points qui rassurait les étudiants
21. empreintes digitales
22. Il suffisait de cliquer sur
23. Envoyer

It was the best summer of my life. At least it was until that final night. Even now I know I will never know a time like it. Weird, right? But I know. I know that I will never, ever, be that happy[1] *again. Not ever. My smile is different now. It is sadder*[2]*, like it is broken and can't be fixed*[3]*.*

I loved a boy that summer. I will call him P for this story. He was a year older than me and a junior counselor. His whole family was at the camp. His sister worked there and his father was the camp doctor. But I barely noticed them[4] *because the moment I met P, I felt my stomach clench*[5]*.*

I know what you're thinking. It was just a dumb[6] *summer romance. But it wasn't. And now I'm scared I will never love someone like I loved him. That sounds silly. That is what everyone thinks. Maybe they are right. I don't know. I am still so young. But it doesn't feel like that*[7]*. It feels like I had one chance at happiness and I blew it*[8]*.*

A hole[9] in Lucy's heart started opening, expanding.

One night, we went into the woods. We weren't supposed to[10]*. There were strict rules about it. Nobody knew those rules better than me. I had been spending summers here since I was nine. That was when my dad bought the camp. But P was on "night" duty. And because my dad owned the camp, I had full access. Smart, right? Two kids in love who were supposed to guard the other campers? Give me a break!*[11]

He didn't want to go because he thought he should keep watch[12]*, but hey, I knew how to entice him*[13]*. I regret that now, of course. But I did it. So we headed into*[14] *the woods, just the two of us. Alone. The woods are huge. If you make a wrong turn*[15]*, you can get lost in there forever*[16]*. I had heard tales*[17] *of children going out*

1. aussi heureuse
2. plus triste
3. n'est pas réparable
4. les avais à peine remarqués
5. mon estomac s'était noué
6. stupide
7. ce n'est pas ce que je ressens
8. que je l'ai gâchée
9. blessure
10. n'étions pas censés le faire
11. À d'autres !
12. qu'il devait monter la garde
13. l'attirer
14. nous nous aventurâmes dans
15. Si on se trompe de chemin
16. on peut carrément se perdre
17. des histoires

there and never coming back. Some say they still wander around[1], living like animals. Some say they died or worse. Well, you know how it is with camp-fire stories.

I used to laugh at stories like that. I never got scared of them. Now I shudder at the thought[2].

We kept walking. I knew the way. P was holding my hand. The woods were so dark. You couldn't see more than ten feet[3] in front of you. We heard a rustling noise[4] and realized that someone was in the woods. I froze[5], but I remember P smiling in the dark and shaking his head in a funny way. You see, the only reason campers met up in the woods was, well, it was a coed[6] camp. There was a boys' side[7] and a girls' side and this finger of the woods stood between them[8]. You figure it out.[9] P sighed[10]. "We better check it out[11]," he said. Or something like that. I don't remember his exact words.

But I didn't want to. I wanted to be alone with him.

My flashlight was out of batteries.[12] I can still remember how fast my heart was beating as we stepped into the trees. There I was, in the dark, holding hands with the guy I loved. He would touch me[13] and I would just melt[14]. You know that feeling? When you can't stand to[15] be away from[16] a guy for even five minutes. When you put everything in context of him[17]. You do something, anything really, and you wonder, "What would he think about that?" It is a crazy feeling. It is wonderful but it also hurts. You are so vulnerable and raw that it's scary[18].

"Shh," he whispers. "Just stop."

We do. We stop.

P pulls me[19] behind a tree. He cups my face in both of his hands.[20] He has big hands and I love the way that feels[21]. He tilts my face up[22] and then

1. qu'ils y errent encore
2. je frémis rien que d'y songer
3. à plus de 3 m
4. bruissement
5. Je m'arrêtai net
6. mixte
7. le côté des garçons
8. bande de forêt était entre les deux
9. Vous voyez le truc.
10. soupira
11. On devrait aller voir
12. Les piles de ma lampe torche étaient déchargées.
13. Il suffisait qu'il me touche
14. moi, je fondais
15. ne pouvez supporter
16. d'être séparée d'
17. tout votre univers tourne autour de lui
18. et à vif que ça fait peur
19. m'attire
20. Il prend mon visage entre ses mains.
21. cette sensation
22. tourne mon visage vers lui

he kisses me. I feel it everywhere, a fluttering[1] *that begins in the center of my heart and then spreads*[2]. *He takes his hand away from my face. He puts it on my rib cage*[3], *right next to my breast*[4]. *I start to anticipate. I groan out loud.*[5]

We kept kissing. It was so passionate. We couldn't get close enough to each other.[6] *Every part of me felt on fire. He moved his hand under my shirt. I won't say more about that. I forgot about the rustling in the woods. But now I know. We should have contacted someone. We should have stopped them from going deeper in the woods. But we didn't. We made love instead.*

I was so lost in us[7], *in what we were doing, that at first I didn't even hear the screams. I don't think P did either.*

But the screams kept coming and you know how people describe near-death[8] *experiences? That was what it was like, but kinda in reverse*[9]. *It was like we were both headed for*[10] *some wonderful light and the screams were like a rope that was trying to pull us back*[11], *even though we didn't want to go back.*

He stopped kissing me. And here is the terrible thing.

He never kissed me again.

Lucy turned the page, but there were no more. She snapped her head up[12]. "Where's the rest?"

"That's it.[13] You said to send it in parts, remember? That's all there is."

She looked at the pages again.

"You okay, Luce?"

"You're good[14] with computers, aren't you, Lonnie?"

He arched the eyebrow again. "I'm better with da[15] ladies."

"Do I look like I'm in the mood?[16]"

"Okay, okay, yeah, I'm good with computers. Why?"

1. frémissement
2. se diffuse
3. torse
4. tout près de mes seins
5. Un gémissement m'échappe.
6. Nos corps étaient de plus en plus attirés l'un vers l'autre.
7. en émoi
8. de mort imminente
9. à l'envers
10. avancions tous deux vers
11. nous retenir
12. redressa la tête d'un coup
13. C'est tout ce qu'il y a.
14. doué
15. [façon de prononcer « the »]
16. Ai-je l'air d'être d'humeur à ça ?

"I need to find out who wrote this."

"But – "

"I need," she repeated, "to find out who wrote this."

He met her eye.[1] He studied her face for a second. She knew what he wanted to say. It betrayed everything that they were about.[2] They had read horrible stories in here, one this year about father-daughter incest even, and they had never tried to track the person down[3].

Lonnie said, "Do you want to tell me what this is about[4]?"

"No."

"But you want me to break all the confidences[5] we've ever set up[6] here?"

"Yes."

"That bad?[7]"

She just looked at him.

"Ah, what the hell[8]," Lonnie said. "I'll see what I can do."

1. Il croisa son regard.
2. C'était contraire à toute leur démarche.
3. retrouver la personne
4. de quoi il s'agit
5. que je trahisse le rapport de confiance
6. toujours établi
7. C'est si grave ?
8. et puis merde

Chapter 3

"I'm telling you[1]," I said yet again. "It's Gil Perez."

"The guy who died with your sister twenty years ago."

"Obviously[2]," I said, "he didn't die."

I don't think they believed me.

"Maybe it's his brother," York tried.

"With my sister's ring?"

Dillon added, "That ring isn't unusual[3]. Twenty years ago they were all the rage[4]. I think my sister had the same one. Got it for her sweet sixteen[5], I think. Was your sister's engraved[6]?"

"No."

"So we don't know for sure[7]."

We talked for a while, but there was not much to add. I really didn't know anything. They would be in touch[8], they said. They'd find Gil Perez's family, see if they could make a positive ID[9]. I didn't know what to do. I felt lost and numb and confused[10].

My BlackBerry and cell phone were going nuts[11]. I was late now for an appointment with the defense team[12] in the biggest case[13] of my career. Two wealthy[14] collegiate tennis players[15] from the ritzy suburb[16] of Short Hills stood accused of raping[17] a

1. Je vous assure
2. Manifestement
3. n'a rien d'exceptionnel
4. très à la mode
5. ses 16 ans
6. gravée
7. on ne peut en avoir la certitude
8. me recontacteraient
9. l'identifier avec certitude
10. tétanisé et désorienté
11. n'arrêtaient pas de sonner
12. la défense
13. plus grosse affaire
14. riches
15. joueurs de tennis universitaires
16. banlieue chic
17. étaient accusés d'avoir violé

sixteen-year-old African-American girl from Irvington named – and no, her name didn't help – Chamique[1] Johnson. The trial[2] had already started, had hit a delay[3], and now I hoped to cut a jail-time deal[4] before we had to start up again.

The cops gave me a lift[5] to my office in Newark. I knew that opposing counsel[6] would think my tardiness[7] was a ploy[8], but there wasn't much to be done about that. When I entered my office, the two lead defense lawyers[9] were already seated.

One, Mort Pubin, stood and started bellowing[10]. "You son of a bitch![11] Do you know what time it is? Do you?"

"Mort, did you lose weight[12]?"

"Don't start that crap with me.[13]"

"Wait, no, that's not it[14]. You're taller, right? You grew. Just like a real boy."

"Up yours[15], Cope. We've been sitting here for an hour!"

The other lawyer, Flair Hickory, just sat there, legs crossed, not a care in the world[16]. Flair was the one I paid attention to. Mort was loud and obnoxious[17] and showy[18]. Flair was the defense attorney I feared like no other[19]. He was not what anyone expected. In the first place, Flair – he swore it was his real name but I had my doubts – was gay. Okay, that wasn't a big deal. Plenty of attorneys are gay, but Flair was *gay* gay, like the love child[20] of Liberace[21] and Liza Minnelli, who'd been brought up on nothing but[22] Streisand and show tunes[23].

Flair did not tone it down[24] for the courtroom[25] – he intentionally ratcheted it up[26].

He let Mort rant[27] another minute or two. Flair flexed his fingers and studied his manicure. He seemed pleased by it. Then he raised his hand and silenced Mort with a fluttery wave[28].

"Enough," Flair said.

1. [allusion à Chamique Holdsclaw, joueuse de basket-ball]
2. procès
3. pris du retard
4. passer un accord sur la durée de la peine
5. me déposèrent
6. l'avocat de la partie adverse
7. retard
8. calculé
9. principaux avocats de la défense
10. à beugler
11. Espèce de salaud !
12. t'as maigri, non
13. Fais pas chier avec ça.
14. c'est pas tout
15. Va te faire foutre
16. l'air de s'en foutre royalement
17. grande gueule, insupportable
18. m'as-tu-vu
19. le plus
20. l'enfant naturel
21. [comique américain, homosexuel]
22. élevé uniquement aux chansons de [Barbra]
23. aux tubes de comédies musicales
24. ne se modérait pas
25. au tribunal
26. forçait le trait
27. déblatérer
28. geste vif

He wore a purple suit. Or maybe it was eggplant[1] or periwinkle, some such hue[2]. I'm not good with colors. The shirt was the same color as the suit. So was the solid[3] tie. So was the pocket hanky[4]. So were – good Lord – the shoes. Flair noticed me noticing the clothes.

"You like it?" Flair asked me.

"Barney[5] joins the Village People," I said.

Flair frowned at me[6].

"What?"

"Barney, the Village People," he said, pursing his[7] lips. "Could you possibly come up with[8] two more dated, overused[9] pop references?"

"I was going to say the purple Teletubby, but I couldn't remember his name."

"Tinky Winky. And that's still dated." He crossed his arms and sighed. "So now that we are all together in this clearly hetero-decorated[10] office, can we just let our clients walk[11] and be done with this[12]?"

I met his eye. "They did it, Flair."

He wouldn't deny it. "Are you really going to put[13] that deranged stripper-cum-prostitute[14] on the stand[15]?"

I was going to defend her, but he already knew the facts. "I am."

Flair tried not to smile. "I will," he said, "destroy her."

I said nothing.

He would. I knew that. And that was the thing about his act[16]. He could slice and dice[17] and still make you like him. I'd seen him do it before. You'd think at least some of the jury would consist of[18] homophobes and that they'd hate or fear him. But that wasn't how it worked with Flair. The female jurists wanted to go shopping with him and tell him about their husbands' inadequacies[19]. The men found him so nonthreatening[20] that they thought there was no way he could put anything over on them[21].

It made for a lethal defense.[22]

1. aubergine
2. pervenche, une teinte de ce ton-là
3. unie
4. pochette
5. [tyrannosaure de dessin animé, violet]
6. me regarda en fronçant les sourcils
7. en se pinçant les
8. Tu ne pouvais pas trouver
9. plus démodées et plus bateau
10. au décor nettement hétéro
11. relâcher nos clients
12. en finir
13. appeler
14. strip-teaseuse et par ailleurs prostituée
15. à la barre
16. c'était ça, son truc
17. vous réduire en charpie
18. qu'au moins quelques membres du jury seraient
19. défauts
20. inoffensif
21. qu'il ne pourrait jamais leur jouer un tour
22. Cela donnait une défense implacable.

"What are you looking for?" I asked.

Flair grinned[1]. "You're nervous, aren't you?"

"I'm just hoping to spare[2] a rape victim from your bullying[3]."

"Moi?" He put a hand to his chest. "I'm insulted."

I just looked at him. As I did, the door opened. Loren Muse, my chief investigator[4], walked in[5]. Muse was my age, midthirties[6], and had been a homicide[7] investigator under[8] my predecessor, Ed Steinberg.

Muse sat down without a word or even a wave[9].

I turned back to Flair. "What do you want?" I asked again.

"For starters[10]," Flair said, "I want Ms. Chamique Johnson to apologize[11] for destroying the reputation of two fine, upstanding[12] boys."

I looked at him some more.

"But we'll settle for[13] an immediate dropping of all charges[14]."

"Dream on.[15]"

"Cope, Cope, Cope." Flair shook his head and tsk-tsked[16].

"I said no."

"You're adorable when you're macho, but you know that already, don't you?" Flair looked over at Loren Muse. A stricken[17] expression crossed[18] his face. "Dear God[19], what are you wearing?"

Muse sat up[20]. "What?"

"Your wardrobe[21]. It's like a frightening new Fox reality show[22]: *When Policewomen Dress Themselves.* Dear God. And those shoes..."

"They're practical[23]," Muse said.

"Sweetheart,[24] fashion rule one[25]: The words *shoes* and *practical* should never be in the same sentence[26]." Without blinking an eye[27], Flair turned back to me: "Our clients cop to a misdemeanor[28] and you give them probation[29]."

"No."

"Can I just say two words to you?"

1. sourit
2. éviter à
3. que tu la malmènes
4. enquêtrice principale
5. entra
6. la trentaine
7. de la brigade criminelle
8. sous les ordres de
9. sans dire un mot ni saluer
10. Pour commencer
11. s'excuse
12. respectables
13. on se contentera d'
14. abandon de toutes les accusations
15. Tu peux toujours rêver.
16. fit « tss-tss »
17. accablée
18. parcourut
19. Grand Dieu
20. se redressa
21. tenue
22. émission de télé-réalité
23. confortables
24. Chérie,
25. règle n° 1 en matière de mode
26. phrase
27. Sans cligner des yeux
28. plaident coupable pour un simple délit
29. la liberté conditionnelle

"Those two words wouldn't be *shoes* and *practical*, would they?"

"No, something far more dire[1] for you, I'm afraid: Cal and Jim."

He paused. I glanced at Muse. She shifted[2] in her seat.

"Those two little names," Flair went on, a lilt[3] in his voice. "Cal and Jim. Music to my ears.[4] Do you know what I'm saying, Cope?"

I didn't take the bait.[5]

"In your alleged[6] victim's statement[7]... you read her statement, didn't you?... in her statement she clearly says that her rapists[8] were named Cal and Jim."

"It means nothing," I said.

"Well, see, sweetie[9] – and try to pay attention here[10] because I think this could be very important to your case – our clients are named Barry Marantz and Edward Jenrette. Not Cal and Jim. Barry and Edward. Say them out loud[11] with me. Come on, you can do it. Barry and Edward. Now, do those two names sound at all like[12] Cal and Jim?"

Mort Pubin answered that one. He grinned and said, "No, they don't, Flair."

I kept still.[13]

"And, you see, that's *your* victim's statement," Flair went on. "It really is so wonderful, don't you think? Hold on[14], let me find it. I just love reading it. Mort, do you have it? Wait, here it is." Flair had on half-moon reading glasses[15]. He cleared his throat and changed voices[16]. "'The two boys who did this. Their names were Cal and Jim.'"

He lowered the paper and looked up as if expecting applause[17].

I said, "Barry Marantz's semen[18] was found in her."

"Ah, yes, but young Barry – a handsome boy, by the way, and we both know that matters[19] – admits to a consensual sex act[20] with your eager[21], young Ms. Johnson earlier in the evening. We all know that

1. de bien plus terrible
2. changea de position
3. certaine intonation
4. Ces noms me ravissent.
5. Je ne mordis pas à l'hameçon.
6. présumée
7. déclaration
8. violeurs
9. tu vois, mon chéri
10. essaie d'être attentif, là
11. Répète à haute voix
12. ont quelque chose à voir avec
13. Je ne bougeai pas.
14. Attends
15. portait des lunettes en demi-lune
16. prit une autre voix
17. comme s'il s'attendait à des applaudissements
18. sperme
19. que ça compte
20. acte sexuel consenti
21. empressée

Chamique was at their fraternity house[1] – that's not in dispute[2], is it?"

I didn't like it, but I said, "No, that's not in dispute."

"In fact, we both agree that Chamique Johnson had worked there the week before as a stripper."

"Exotic dancer[3]," I corrected.

He just looked at me. "And so she returned. Without the benefit of money being exchanged.[4] We can agree on that too, can't we?" He didn't bother waiting for me. "And I can get five, six boys to say she was acting very friendly[5] with Barry. Come on, Cope. You've been around this block before.[6] She's a stripper. She's underage[7]. She sneaked[8] into a college fraternity party. She got nailed[9] by the handsome rich kid. He, what, blew her off[10] or didn't call or whatever. She got upset.[11]"

"And plenty of bruises[12]," I said.

Mort pounded[13] the table with a fist that looked like roadkill[14]. "She's just looking for[15] a big payday[16]," Mort said.

Flair said, "Not now, Mort."

"Screw that.[17] We all know the deal.[18] She's going after them[19] because they're loaded[20]." Mort gave me his best flinty-eyed stare[21]. "You do know the whore[22] has a record[23], right? Chamique" – he stretched out[24] her name in a mocking way that pissed me off[25] – "has already got a lawyer too. Going to shake our boys down[26]. This is just a big payday for that cow[27]. That's all. A big friggin[28]' payday."

"Mort?" I said.

"What?"

"Shh, the grown-ups are talking now."

Mort sneered[29]. "You're no better, Cope."

I waited.

"The only reason you're prosecuting them is because they're wealthy. And you know it. You're playing that rich-versus-poor crap[30] in the media too.

1. résidence universitaire
2. contesté
3. Effeuilleuse
4. Sans contrepartie financière.
5. qui diront qu'elle avait l'air d'être amie
6. Tu connais la chanson.
7. mineure
8. est entrée en douce
9. s'est fait sauter
10. Disons qu'il l'a plaquée
11. Elle a eu les boules.
12. plein de bleus
13. tapa sur la table
14. d'un poing mou
15. cherche juste
16. à se faire un paquet de fric
17. Rien à battre.
18. On sait tous ce que c'est.
19. Elle s'en prend à eux
20. pleins aux as
21. regard le plus dur
22. que cette pute
23. un casier [judiciaire]
24. s'attarda sur
25. m'énerva
26. plumer nos petits gars
27. conne
28. foutu
29. ricana
30. connerie

Don't pretend you aren't. You know what sucks[1] about that? You know what really burns my butt[2]?"

I had itched an ass this morning and now I had burned a butt. A big day for me.

"Tell me, Mort."

"It's accepted in our society," he said.

"What is?"

"Hating rich people." Mort threw his hands up[3], outraged. "You hear it all the time. 'I hate him, he's so rich.' Look at Enron and those other scandals. It is now an encouraged prejudice[4] – to hate rich people. If I ever said, 'Hey, I hate poor people,' I'd be strung up[5]. But call the rich names[6]? Well, you have a free pass[7]. Everyone is allowed to hate the rich."

I looked at him. "Maybe they should form a support group[8]."

"Up yours, Cope."

"No, I mean it. Trump, the Halliburton guys. I mean, the world hasn't been fair to them[9]. A support group. That's what they should have. Maybe hold a telethon or something."

Flair Hickory rose. Theatrically, of course. I half-expected him to curtsy[10]. "I think we're done here[11]. See you tomorrow, handsome[12]. And you" – he looked at Loren Muse, opened his mouth, closed it, shuddered[13].

"Flair?"

He looked at me.

"That Cal and Jim thing," I said. "It just proves she's telling the truth."

Flair smiled. "How's that, exactly?"

"Your boys were smart[14]. They called themselves Cal and Jim, so she'd say that."

He raised an eyebrow. "You think that will fly[15]?"

"Why else would she say that, Flair?"

"Pardon?"

"I mean, if Chamique wanted to set your clients up[16], why wouldn't she use their correct names? Why

1. ce qui craint
2. me fout vraiment en rogne
3. leva les mains au ciel
4. préjugé
5. on me pendrait
6. insulter les riches
7. carte blanche
8. groupe de soutien
9. n'est pas juste envers eux
10. m'attendais presque à ce qu'il fasse la révérence
11. qu'on a fini, là
12. beau gosse
13. frémit
14. malins
15. que cela marchera
16. piéger tes clients

would she make up[1] all that dialogue with Cal and Jim? You read the statement. 'Turn her this way[2], Cal.' 'Bend her over[3], Jim.' 'Whoa, Cal, she's loving this.' Why would she make that all up?"

Mort took that one.[4] "Because she's a money-hungry[5] whore who is dumber than dirt[6]?"

But I could see that I'd scored[7] a point with Flair.

"It doesn't make sense," I said to him.

Flair leaned in[8] toward me. "Here's the thing[9], Cope: It doesn't have to. You know that. Perhaps you're right. Perhaps it doesn't make sense. But see, that leads to[10] confusion. And confusion has the major hots for my favorite hunk[11], Mr. Reasonable Doubt[12]." He smiled. "You might have some physical evidence[13]. But, well, you put that girl on the stand[14], I will not hold back[15]. It will be game, set, match. We both know that."

They headed to the door.

"Toodles[16], my friend. See you in court.[17]"

1. inventerait-elle
2. Tourne-la par là
3. Penche-la en avant
4. C'est Mort qui répondit.
5. vénale
6. bête comme ses pieds
7. marqué
8. se pencha
9. Je vais te dire
10. sème la
11. apporte de l'eau au moulin de mon atout préféré
12. le doute raisonnable
13. des preuves matérielles
14. si tu appelles cette fille à la barre
15. je vais me lâcher
16. À plus
17. On se voit au procès.

Chapter 4

Muse and I said nothing for a few moments. Cal and Jim. The names deflated us[1].

The position[2] of chief investigator was almost always held[3] by some male lifer[4], a gruff[5] guy slightly burned out[6] by what he'd seen over the years, with a big belly[7] and a heavy sigh[8] and a well-worn trench coat[9]. It would be that man's job to maneuver[10] the guileless[11] county prosecutor, a political appointee[12] like me, through the rings[13] of the Essex County legal[14] system.

Loren Muse was maybe five feet tall[15] and weighed about as much as your average fourth grader[16]. My choosing Muse had caused some nasty ripples[17] among the veterans, but here was my own private prejudice[18]: I prefer hiring single women[19] of a certain age. They work harder and are more loyal. I know, I know, but I have found this to be true in almost every case. You find a single woman over the age of, say, thirty-three, and she lives for her career and will give you hours and devotion[20] the married ones with kids will never give you.

To be fair[21], Muse was also an incredibly gifted[22] investigator. I liked talking things out[23] with her. I would say "muse"-ing them over[24], but then you'd

1. nous avaient fichu un coup
2. poste
3. occupé
4. un type au look de condamné à perpète
5. bourru
6. un peu usé
7. bedaine
8. poussant de gros soupirs
9. une vieille gabardine
10. de piloter
11. candide
12. dont la nomination est politique
13. à travers les rouages
14. judiciaire
15. devait faire 1,53 m
16. ne pesait pas plus qu'un gosse de CM1
17. remous
18. voilà, j'ai mes propres préjugés
19. embaucher des femmes célibataires
20. du temps et un dévouement
21. Il faut reconnaître que
22. douée
23. débattre des dossiers
24. Je dirais bien « m'a-Muser à discuter »

understandably groan[1]. Right now she was staring down at the floor.

"What's on your mind?" I asked her.

"Are these shoes really that ugly[2]?"

I looked at her and waited.

"Put simply[3]," she said, "if we don't find a way to explain Cal and Jim, we're screwed[4]."

I stared at the ceiling.[5]

"What?" Muse said.

"Those two names."

"What about them?"

"Why?" I asked for the umpteenth time[6]. "Why Cal and Jim?"

"Don't know."

"You questioned[7] Chamique again?"

"I did. Her story is frighteningly consistent[8]. They used those two names. I think you're right. They simply did that as a cover[9] – so her story would sound idiotic."

"But why those two names?"

"Probably just random[10]."

I frowned. "We're missing something[11], Muse."

She nodded. "I know."

I have always been pretty good about partitioning[12] my life. We all are[13], but I am especially good at it. I can create separate universes in my own world. I can deal with[14] one aspect of my life and not have it interfere[15] with another in any way. Some people watch a gangster movie and wonder how the mobster[16] can be so violent on the streets and so loving[17] at home. I get that.[18] I have that ability[19].

I'm not proud of this.[20] It is not necessarily a great attribute[21]. It protects, yes, but I have seen what actions it can justify.

So for the past half hour I had been pushing away[22] the obvious questions: If Gil Perez had been alive this whole time[23], where had he been? What had happened that night in the woods? And of course,

1. vous auriez raison de grogner
2. si moches que ça
3. Pour faire court
4. on est foutus
5. Je levai les yeux au ciel.
6. énième fois
7. as interrogé
8. terriblement cohérente
9. pour se protéger
10. choisis au hasard
11. Quelque chose nous échappe
12. assez bien su compartimenter
13. Comme tout le monde, certes
14. m'occuper d'
15. faire en sorte qu'il n'interfère pas
16. truand
17. affectueux
18. Moi, je comprends très bien.
19. cette faculté
20. Je n'en suis pas fier.
21. forcément une qualité
22. depuis une demi-heure, j'évitais
23. vivant tout ce temps

the biggest question: If Gil Perez had survived that awful night...

Had my sister survived too?

"Cope?"

It was Muse.

"What's going on?"

I wanted to tell her. But now was not the time[1]. I needed to sort it through myself first.[2] Figure out what was what.[3] Make sure that body really did belong to[4] Gil Perez. I stood and walked toward her.

"Cal and Jim," I said. "We have to figure out what the hell that's all about[5] – and fast."

My wife's sister, Greta, and her husband, Bob, lived in a McMansion[6] on a new cul-de-sac that looks almost precisely the same as every other new cul-de-sac in North America. The lots[7] are too small for the ginormous brick edifices[8] that stretch across them[9]. The houses have a variety of shapes and shades but somehow still look exactly the same. Everything is a little too brushed[10], trying to look aged[11] and only looking more faux.

I had met Greta first, before my wife. My mother ran away[12] before I turned twenty[13], but I remember something she told me a few months before Camille went into those woods. We were the poorest citizens[14] in our rather mixed town. We were immigrants who had come over from the old Soviet Union when I was four. We had started out okay[15] – we had arrived in the USA as heroes – but things turned very bad[16] very quickly.

We were living on the top floor of a three-family dwelling[17] in Newark, though we went to school at Columbia High in Maplewood. My father, Vladimir Copinsky (he anglicized it to Copeland), who had once been a doctor in Leningrad, couldn't get a license to practice[18] in this country. He ended up working as a house painter[19]. My mother, a frail[20]

1. ce n'était pas le moment
2. Je devais d'abord faire le point moi-même.
3. Y voir plus clair.
4. était bien celui de
5. trouver ce que ça veut dire, bon sang
6. grande baraque de nouveaux riches
7. parcelles
8. énormes constructions en brique
9. qui en occupent pratiquement toute la surface
10. patiné
11. faire ancien
12. s'est enfuie
13. mes 20 ans
14. les habitants les plus pauvres
15. On avait bien commencé
16. se sont gâtées
17. logement
18. obtenir l'autorisation d'exercer
19. peintre en bâtiment
20. fragile

beauty named Natasha, the once-proud[1], well-educated[2] daughter of aristocratic college professors, took on a variety of cleaning jobs[3] for the wealthier families[4] in Short Hills and Livingston but could never hold on to one[5] for very long.

On this particular day, my sister, Camille, came home from school and announced in a teasing[6] voice that the town rich girl had a crush on me[7]. My mother was excited by this.

"You should ask her out[8]," my mother said to me.

I made a face[9]. "Have you seen her?"

"I have."

"Then you know," I said, speaking as a seventeen-year-old would. "She's a beast[10]."

"There is an old Russian expression," my mother countered[11], raising a finger to clarify her point[12]. "A rich girl is beautiful when she stands on her money[13]."

That was the first thought that came through my mind when I met Greta. Her parents – my former in-laws[14], I guess, still the grandparents of my Cara – are loaded. My wife came from money[15]. It is all in trust[16] for Cara. I'm the executor[17]. Jane and I discussed long and hard[18] the age at which she should get the bulk of the estate[19]. You don't want someone too young inheriting that kind of money, but hey, on the other hand, it is hers.

My Jane was so practical after the doctors had announced her death sentence[20]. I couldn't listen. You learn a lot when someone you love goes down for the count[21]. I learned that my wife had amazing strength and bravery I would have thought unfathomable[22] before her illness. And I found that I had neither.

Cara and Madison, my niece, were playing in the driveway[23]. The days were starting to get longer now. Madison sat on the asphalt and drew with pieces of chalk[24] that resembled cigars. My own daughter rode one of those motorized, slow-moving minicars that are all the rage with today's under-six crowd[25]. The

1. naguère fière
2. cultivée
3. faisait des travaux de ménage
4. dans les familles plus aisées
5. conserver un poste
6. moqueuse
7. était amoureuse de moi
8. sortir avec elle
9. fis la grimace
10. hideuse
11. rétorqua
12. pour bien se faire comprendre
13. est assise sur son argent
14. ex-beaux-parents
15. venait d'une famille riche
16. Tout est placé sous tutelle
17. exécuteur testamentaire
18. avions longuement réfléchi à
19. toucher l'essentiel de l'héritage
20. qu'elle était condamnée
21. un être aimé est touché
22. que je n'aurais pas soupçonnés
23. allée
24. des craies
25. les moins de 6 ans

kids who own them never play on them. Only visitors on playdates[1] do. Playdates. Man, I hated that term.

I stepped out of the car and shouted, "Hey, kiddos.[2]"

I waited for the two six-year-old girls to stop what they were doing and sprint over to me[3] and wrap me in big hugs[4]. Yeah, right. Madison glanced my way[5], but she couldn't have looked less interested without some sort of surgical cerebral disconnect[6]. My own daughter pretended[7] not to hear. Cara steered[8] the Barbie Jeep in a circle. The battery was fading fast[9], the electric vehicle churning at a speed slower[10] than my uncle Morris reaching for the check[11].

Greta pushed open the screen door[12]. "Hey."

"Hey," I said. "So how was the rest of the gymnastics show?"

"Don't worry," Greta said, shading her eyes with her hand in a pseudosalute. "I have the whole thing on video."

"Cute.[13]"

"So what was up with[14] those two cops?"

I shrugged. "Just work."

She didn't buy it[15] but she didn't press[16]. "I have Cara's backpack[17] inside."

She let the door close behind her. There were workers coming around back.[18] Bob and Greta were putting in[19] a swimming pool with matching landscaping[20]. They'd been thinking about it for several years but wanted to wait until Madison and Cara were old enough to be safe.

"Come on," I said to my daughter, "we need to go."

Cara ignored me again, pretending that the whir[21] of the pink Barbie Jeep was overwhelming her aural faculties[22]. I frowned and started toward her[23]. Cara was ridiculously stubborn[24]. I would like to say, "like her mother," but my Jane was the most patient and understanding woman you ever met[25]. It was amazing. You see qualities both good and bad in your chil-

1. les enfants invités pour jouer avec eux
2. Salut, les enfants
3. courent vers moi
4. se jettent à mon cou
5. jeta bien un regard dans ma direction
6. aurait difficilement pu avoir l'air plus indifférent
7. fit semblant de
8. conduisait
9. était presque à plat
10. se traînant encore plus lentement
11. que l'oncle Morris pour payer l'addition
12. porte moustiquaire
13. Super.
14. qu'est-ce qu'ils voulaient
15. ne me crut pas
16. n'insista pas
17. sac à dos
18. Des ouvriers arrivaient de l'arrière de la maison.
19. faisaient ajouter
20. et réaménager le jardin en fonction
21. ronronnement
22. l'empêchait d'entendre
23. me dirigeai vers elle
24. entêtée
25. du monde

dren. In the case of Cara, all the negative qualities seemed to emanate from her father.

Madison put down the chalk. "Come on, Cara."

Cara ignored her too. Madison shrugged at me and gave me that kid-world-weary sigh[1]. "Hi, Uncle Cope."

"Hey, sweetie. Have a good playdate?"

"No," Madison said with her fists on her hips. "Cara never plays with me. She just plays with my toys."

I tried to look understanding[2].

Greta came out with the backpack. "We already did the homework[3]," she said.

"Thank you."

She waved it off[4]. "Cara, sweetheart? Your father is here."

Cara ignored her too. I knew that a tantrum[5] was coming. That too, I guess, she gets from her father. In our Disney-inspired worldview[6], the widowed father-daughter relationship is a magic one. Witness[7] pretty much every kid film[8] – *The Little Mermaid*[9], *Beauty and the Beast, A Little Princess, Aladdin* – you get the point[10]. In movies, not having a mother seems to be a pretty nifty thing[11], which, when you think about it, is really perverse. In real life, not having a mother was just about the worst thing that could happen to a little girl.

I made my voice firm. "Cara, we're going now."

Her face was set[12] – I braced for[13] the confrontation – but fortunately the gods interceded. The Barbie battery went totally dead[14]. The pink Jeep stopped. Cara tried to body-language[15] the vehicle another foot or two[16], but Barbie wouldn't budge[17]. Cara sighed, stepped out of the Jeep, and started for[18] the car.

"Say good-bye to Aunt Greta and your cousin."

She did so[19] in a voice sullen enough to make a teenager envious[20].

When we got home, Cara snapped on[21] the TV without asking permission and settled in for[22] an episode of *SpongeBob*[23]. It seems as though *SpongeBob* is

1. soupir d'enfant blasé
2. compatissant
3. les devoirs
4. balaya le remerciement d'un geste
5. crise de colère
6. vision du monde très Disney
7. J'en veux pour preuve
8. presque tous les films pour enfants
9. Sirène
10. vous voyez ce que je veux dire
11. ça a l'air chouette
12. fermé
13. je me préparai à
14. s'arrêta, complètement à plat
15. de gigoter pour faire avancer
16. encore un tout petit peu
17. ne voulut rien savoir
18. partit vers
19. s'exécuta
20. maussade à faire pâlir d'envie un ado
21. alluma
22. s'installa devant
23. Bob l'Éponge

on[1] all the time. I wonder if there is an all[2]-*Sponge-Bob* station[3]. There also only seems to be maybe three different episodes of the show. That does not seem to deter[4] kids, though.

I was going to say something, but I let it go[5]. Right now I just wanted her distracted[6]. I was still trying to put together[7] what was going on with both the Chamique Johnson rape case[8] and now the sudden reemergence[9] and murder of Gil Perez. I confess that my big case, the biggest of my career, was getting the short end of the stick[10].

I started preparing dinner. We eat out most nights[11] or order in[12]. I do have a nanny-housekeeper[13], but today was her day off[14]. "Hot dogs sound good[15]?"

"Whatever.[16]"

The phone rang. I picked it up.

"Mr. Copeland? This is Detective Tucker York."

"Yes, Detective, what can I do for you?"

"We located[17] Gil Perez's parents."

I felt my grip tighten on the phone[18]. "Did they identify the body?"

"Not yet."

"What did you tell them?"

"Look, no offense[19], Mr. Copeland, but this isn't the kind of thing you just say over the phone[20], you know? 'Your dead child might have been alive this whole time – and oh yeah[21], he's just been murdered'?"

"I understand."

"So we were pretty[22] vague. We're going to bring them in[23] and see if we can get an ID. But here's the other thing: How sure are you that it's Gil Perez?"

"Pretty sure."

"You understand that's not really good enough[24]."

"I do."

"And anyway, it's late. My partner and I are off duty[25]. So we're going to have one of our men drive the Perezes down[26] tomorrow morning."

"So this is, what, a courtesy call[27]?"

1. diffusé
2. cent pour cent
3. chaîne
4. n'a pas l'air de décourager
5. me ravisai
6. qu'elle soit occupée
7. comprendre
8. l'affaire du viol
9. réapparition
10. en faisait les frais
11. En général, on dîne dehors
12. on se fait livrer
13. nounou-femme de ménage
14. de congé
15. ça te dit
16. Je m'en fiche.
17. avons retrouvé
18. serrai le combiné
19. ne le prenez pas mal
20. annoncez, comme ça, au téléphone
21. au fait
22. on est restés assez
23. les faire venir
24. que ce n'est pas suffisant
25. on n'est plus de service
26. c'est un collègue qui amènera les Perez
27. vous m'appelez comme ça, juste par politesse

"Something like that. I understand your interest. And maybe you should be here in the morning, you know, in case any weird questions come up."

"Where?"

"The morgue again. You need a ride[1]?"

"No, I know my way[2]."

1. qu'on vous y conduise
2. je connais le chemin

Chapter 5

A few hours later I tucked my daughter into bed[1]. Cara never gives me trouble at bedtime[2]. We have a wonderful routine[3]. I read to her. I do not do it because all the parenting[4] magazines tell me to. I do it because she adores it. It never puts her to sleep[5]. I read to her every night and not once has she done as much as doze[6]. I have.[7] Some of the books are awful. I fall asleep right in her bed. She lets me.

I couldn't keep up with[8] her voracious desire for books to be read to her, so I started getting books on audio[9]. I read to her and then she can listen to one side of a tape[10] – usually forty-five minutes – before it is time to close her eyes and go to sleep. Cara understands and likes this rule[11].

I am reading Roald Dahl to her right now. Her eyes are wide.[12] Last year, when I took her to see the stage production[13] of *The Lion King*, I bought her a terribly overpriced[14] Timon[15] doll[16]. She has it gripped[17] in her right arm. Timon is a pretty avid listener[18] too.

I finished reading and gave Cara a kiss on the cheek. She smelled like baby shampoo. "Good night, Daddy," she said.

"Good night, Pumpkin[19]."

1. je bordais ma fille
2. au moment de se coucher
3. rituel
4. pour parents
5. ne l'endort jamais
6. pas une fois elle ne s'est assoupie
7. Moi, oui.
8. J'avais du mal à alimenter
9. des livres audio
10. une face de la cassette
11. cette règle
12. Elle a les yeux grands ouverts.
13. comédie musicale
14. bien trop chère
15. [le suricate, dans le Roi Lion]
16. peluche
17. Elle la serre
18. auditeur très attentif
19. ma puce

1. Médée
2. un accès de mauvaise humeur
3. l'instant d'après
4. bénis des dieux
5. lecteur de cassette
6. éteignis
7. J'ai accès à mes dossiers professionnels.
8. à l'étudier
9. du genre à s'attirer la sympathie du jury
10. était mère célibataire
11. racolage
12. dans les soirées
13. le politiquement correct
14. ma passion, ma vraie passion, c'est la justice
15. d'une association étudiante
16. pour Blancs de blancs
17. vous me suivez
18. coincer ces salauds
19. repris tout depuis le début
20. résidence universitaire
21. luxueuse, avec colonnes en marbre
22. moquette
23. les relevés
24. des textos
25. était remonté à la source de
26. d'appels sortants
27. rien de singulier
28. les sommes dues

Kids. One moment they're like Medea[1] having a bad mood swing[2], the next[3] they are God-kissed[4] angels.

I snapped on the tape player[5] and snapped off[6] her light. I headed down to my home office and turned on the computer. I have a hookup to my work files.[7] I opened up the rape case of Chamique Johnson and started poring over it[8].

Cal and Jim.

My victim wasn't what we call jury-pool sympathetic[9]. Chamique was sixteen and had a child out of wedlock[10]. She had been arrested twice for solicitation[11], once for possession of marijuana. She worked parties[12] as an exotic dancer, and yes, that is a euphemism for stripper. People would wonder what she was doing at that party. That sort of thing does not discourage me. It makes me fight harder. Not because I care about political correctness[13], but because I am into – very into – justice[14]. If Chamique had been a blond student council[15] vice-president from lily-white[16] Livingston and the boys were black, I mean, come on[17].

Chamique was a person, a human being. She did not deserve what Barry Marantz and Edward Jenrette did to her.

And I was going to nail their asses to the wall[18].

I went back to the beginning of the case and sifted through it again[19]. The frat house[20] was a ritzy affair with marble columns[21] and Greek letters and fresh paint and carpeting[22]. I checked telephone records[23]. There was a massive amount of them, each kid having his own private line, not to mention cell phones, text messaging[24], e-mails, BlackBerrys. One of Muse's investigators had backtracked[25] every outgoing[26] phone number from that night. There were more than a hundred, but nothing that stuck out[27]. The rest of the bills were ordinary – electric, water, their account[28] at the local liquor store[1], janitorial[2] services, cable TV, online services, Netflix, pizza ordered via the Internet...

Hold up.[3]

I thought about that. I thought about my victim's statement – I didn't have to read it again. It was disgusting and rather specific[4]. The two boys had made[5] Chamique do things, had put her in different positions, had talked the whole time. But something about it all, the way they moved her around[6], positioned her[7]....

My phone rang. It was Loren Muse.

"Good news?" I asked.

"Only if the expression 'No news is good news' is really true."

"It's not," I said.

"Damn.[8]"

"Anything on your end[9]?" she asked.

Cal and Jim. What the hell was I missing?[10] It was there, just out of reach[11]. You know that feeling, when something you know is right around the corner[12], like the name of the dog on *Petticoat Junction*[13] or what was the name of the boxer Mr. T played in *Rocky III?* It was like that. Right out of reach.

Cal and Jim.

The answer was here somewhere, just hiding, just around that mental corner[14]. Damned if I wasn't going to keep running[15] until I caught that sumbitch[16] and nailed him to the wall.

"Not yet," I said. "But let's keep working on it."

Early the next morning, Detective York sat across from[17] Mr. and Mrs. Perez.

"Thank you for coming in," he said.

Twenty years ago, Mrs. Perez had worked in the camp's laundry[18], but I'd only seen her once since the tragedy. There had been a meeting of the victims' families – the wealthy Greens, the wealthier Billinghams, the poor Copelands, the poorer Perezes – in a

1. chez le caviste du coin
2. de gardiennage
3. Tiens.
4. explicite
5. forcé
6. la faisaient bouger
7. la plaçaient
8. Zut alors.
9. de ton côté
10. Qu'est-ce qui m'échappait, nom d'un chien ?
11. mais insaisissable
12. vous avez un mot sur le bout de la langue
13. [série TV américaine des années 1960-1970]
14. dans un recoin de mon esprit
15. Je n'allais sûrement pas arrêter de chercher
16. [son of a bitch]
17. en face de
18. buanderie

big fancy law office[1] not far from where we now were. The case had gone class action with the four families[2] against the camp owner. The Perezes had barely spoken that day. They'd sat and listened and let the others rant[3] and take the lead[4]. I remember Mrs. Perez had kept her purse on her lap[5] and clutched it[6]. Now she had it on the table, but both hands were still bolted to its sides[7].

They were in an interrogation room. At the suggestion of Detective York, I watched from behind one-way glass[8]. He didn't want them to see me yet. That made sense.[9]

"Why are we here?" Mr. Perez asked.

Perez was heavyset[10], his button-down shirt[11] a size too small[12] so that his gut strained[13] the buttons.

"This isn't easy to say." Detective York glanced at the mirror and while his gaze was off[14], I knew that he was seeking me out[15]. "So I'm just going to come out with it[16]."

Mr. Perez's eyes narrowed[17]. Mrs. Perez tightened her grip on[18] the purse. I wondered idly[19] if it was the same purse from fifteen years ago. Weird where the mind goes[20] at times like this.

"There was a murder yesterday in the Washington Heights section of Manhattan," York said. "We found the body in an alley near 157th Street."

I kept my eyes on their faces. The Perezes gave away nothing[21].

"The victim is male and appears to be between the ages of thirty-five and forty years old. He is five-ten and weighs one hundred seventy pounds[22]." Detective York's voice had fallen into[23] a professional rhythm. "The man was using an alias[24], so we are having trouble identifying him."

York stopped. Classic technique. See if they end up saying something. Mr. Perez did. "I don't understand what that has to do with us."

1. prestigieux cabinet d'avocats
2. faisait l'objet d'une plainte collective des quatre familles
3. exprimer leur colère
4. mener la danse
5. son sac à main sur les genoux
6. ne l'avait pas lâché
7. le tenait toujours fermement
8. une vitre sans tain
9. Cela se comprenait.
10. costaud
11. chemise à boutons
12. une taille trop petite
13. sa bedaine tirait sur
14. bien qu'il ait l'air de regarder au loin
15. qu'il me cherchait du regard
16. le dire sans détour
17. se plissèrent
18. serra plus fort
19. distraitement
20. C'est drôle, les idées qu'on a
21. restaient imperturbables
22. fait environ 1,78 m et dans les 80 kg
23. avait pris
24. faux nom

Mrs. Perez's eyes slid toward[1] her husband, but the rest of her did not move.

"I'm getting to that.[2]"

I could almost see York's wheels spinning[3], wondering what approach to take[4], start talking about the clippings in the pocket, the ring, what[5]. I could almost imagine him rehearsing[6] the words in his head and realizing how idiotic they sounded. Clippings, rings – they don't really prove anything. Suddenly even I had my doubts. Here we were, at the moment when the Perezes' world was about to be gut-torn open[7] like a slaughtered calf[8]. I was glad that I was behind glass.

"We brought in a witness[9] to identify the body," York went on. "This witness seems to feel that the victim could be your son Gil."

Mrs. Perez closed her eyes. Mr. Perez stiffened[10]. For a few moments no one spoke, no one moved. Perez did not look at his wife. She did not look at him. They just stood there, frozen, the words still hanging in the air[11].

"Our son was killed twenty years ago," Mr. Perez said at last.

York nodded[12], not sure what to say.

"Are you saying that you've finally found his body?"

"No, I don't think so. Your son was eighteen when he vanished, correct?"

"Almost nineteen," Mr. Perez said.

"This man – the victim – as I mentioned before, he was probably in his late thirties[13]."

Perez's father sat back. The mother still hadn't moved.

York dove in[14]. "Your son's body was never found, isn't that correct?"

"Are you trying to tell us...?"

Mr. Perez's voice died off there[15]. No one jumped in and said[16], "Yes, that's exactly what we are suggesting – that your son Gil has been alive this whole

1. glissèrent vers
2. J'y viens.
3. cogiter
4. comment aborder ça
5. ou quoi
6. se répéter
7. éventré
8. veau à l'abattoir
9. témoin
10. se raidit
11. résonnant encore dans l'atmosphère
12. acquiesça de la tête
13. proche de la quarantaine
14. se lança
15. ne finit pas sa phrase
16. n'intervint pour dire

time, twenty years, and didn't tell you or anyone else, and now, when you finally have the chance to be reunited with your missing child[1], he's been murdered. Life's a gas, ain't it?[2]"

Mr. Perez said, "This is crazy."

"I know what it must sound like – "

"Why do you think it's our son?"

"Like I said before. We have a witness."

"Who?"

It was the first time that I had heard Mrs. Perez speak. I almost ducked.[3]

York tried to sound reassuring. "Look, I understand you're upset[4] – "

"Upset?"

The father again.

"Do you know what it's like... can you imagine...?" His voice died off again. His wife put her hand on his forearm[5]. She sat up a little straighter[6]. For a second she turned to the window and I was sure she could see me through it. Then she met York's eye and said, "I assume[7] you have a body."

"Yes, ma'am."

"And that's why you brought us here. You want us to look at it and see if it's our son."

"Yes."

Mrs. Perez stood. Her husband watched her, looking small and helpless[8].

"Okay," she said. "Why don't we do that?"

Mr. and Mrs. Perez started down the corridor.

I followed at a discreet[9] distance. Dillon was with me. York stayed with the parents. Mrs. Perez held her head high[10]. She still gripped the purse tight against her[11] as though she feared a snatcher[12]. She stayed a step ahead of[13] her husband. So sexist to think it should be the other way around[14] – that the mother should collapse while the father pushed on[15]. Mr. Perez had been the strong one for the "show"

1. enfant disparu
2. Quelle rigolade, la vie, pas vrai ?
3. Je baissai presque la tête instinctivement.
4. que vous soyez bouleversés
5. avant-bras
6. se redressa légèrement
7. suppose
8. déboussolé
9. certaine
10. marchait la tête haute
11. serré contre elle
12. qu'on le lui arrache
13. juste devant
14. l'inverse
15. s'effondre et que le père tienne le coup

part[1]. Now that the grenade had exploded, Mrs. Perez took the lead while her husband seemed to shrink farther back[2] with every step.

With its worn[3] floor of linoleum and walls of scrape-the-skin concrete[4], the corridor couldn't have looked more institutional with[5] a bored[6] bureaucrat leaning against it on a coffee break[7]. I could hear the echo of the footsteps. Mrs. Perez wore heavy gold bracelets. I could hear them clank[8] in rhythm with the walking.

When they turned right at the same window I had stood in front of[9] yesterday, Dillon stuck out his hand[10] in front of me, almost in a protective way, as if I were a kid in the front seat[11] and he'd just stopped short[12]. We stayed a good ten yards back[13], maneuvering so that we stayed out of their line of vision.

It was hard to see their faces. Mr. and Mrs. Perez stood next to each other[14]. They did not touch. I could see Mr. Perez lower[15] his head. He was wearing a blue blazer. Mrs. Perez had on a dark blouse[16] almost the color of dried blood[17]. She wore a lot of gold. I watched a different person – a tall man with a beard[18] this time – wheel the gurney toward the window. The sheet covered the body.

When it was in place, the man with the beard glanced toward York. York nodded. The man carefully lifted[19] the sheet, as if there were something fragile underneath[20]. I was afraid to make a sound, but I still tilted my body[21] a little to the left[22]. I wanted to see some of Mrs. Perez's face, at least a sliver of profile[23].

I remember reading about torture victims who want to control something, anything, and so they fight hard not to cry out[24], not to twist up their face[25], not to show anything, not to give their tormenters any satisfaction whatsoever[26]. Something in Mrs. Perez's face reminded me of that. She had braced herself[27]. She took the blow[28] with a small shudder[29], nothing more.

1. avait fait bonne figure jusqu'ici
2. se ratatiner un peu plus
3. usé
4. béton crépi
5. s'il y avait eu
6. assommé d'ennui
7. appuyé contre le mur pendant sa pause-café
8. s'entrechoquer
9. devant laquelle je m'étais tenu
10. mit un bras
11. siège du passager
12. qu'il venait de piler
13. une bonne dizaine de mètres en retrait
14. se tenaient l'un à côté de l'autre
15. baisser
16. chemisier
17. sang séché
18. barbu
19. souleva délicatement
20. dessous
21. je me penchai tout de même
22. vers la gauche
23. ne serait-ce qu'apercevoir son profil
24. luttent pour ne laisser échapper aucun cri
25. aucune grimace
26. aucune satisfaction à leurs tortionnaires
27. s'était armée de courage
28. encaissa le coup
29. frisson

She stared a little while. Nobody spoke. I realized that I was holding my breath[1]. I turned my attention toward Mr. Perez. His eyes were on the floor. They were wet[2]. I could see the quake cross his lips.[3]

Without looking away, Mrs. Perez said, "That's not our son."

Silence. I had not expected that.

York said, "Are you sure, Mrs. Perez?"

She did not reply.

"He was a teenager when you last saw him[4]," York continued. "I understand[5] he had long hair."

"He did."

"This man's head is shaven. And he has a beard. It's been a lot of years, Mrs. Perez. Please take your time."

Mrs. Perez finally wrested her eyes[6] from the body. She turned her gaze toward York. York stopped speaking.

"That's not Gil," she said again.

York swallowed[7], looked toward the father. "Mr. Perez?"

He managed a nod[8], cleared his throat. "There's not even much of a resemblance." His eyes closed and another quake ran across[9] his face. "It's just..."

"It's the right age," Mrs. Perez finished for him.

York said, "I'm not sure I follow[10]."

"When you lose a son like that, you always wonder[11]. For us, he'll be forever a teenager. But if he had lived, he would be, yes, the same age as this husky[12] man. So you wonder what he'd be like. Would he be married? Have children? What would he look like?"

"And you're certain this man isn't your son?"

She smiled the saddest[13] smile I had ever seen. "Yes, Detective, I am certain."

York nodded. "I'm sorry to bring you out here."

They began to turn away[14] when I said, "Show them the arm."

1. retenais mon souffle
2. humides
3. Je vis ses lèvres trembler.
4. la dernière fois que vous l'avez vu
5. Si j'ai bien compris,
6. détacha péniblement son regard
7. avala sa salive
8. parvint à hocher la tête
9. parcourut
10. de comprendre
11. vous vous demandez toujours
12. costaud
13. le plus triste
14. tourner les talons

Everyone turned in my direction. Mrs. Perez's laser gaze zeroed in on me[1]. There was something there, a strange sense of cunning[2], a challenge maybe. Mr. Perez spoke first.

"Who are you?" he asked.

I had my eyes on Mrs. Perez. Her sad smile returned. "You're the Copeland boy[3], aren't you?"

"Yes, ma'am."

"Camille Copeland's brother."

"Yes."

"Are you the one who made the identification?"

I wanted to explain about the clippings and the ring, but it felt as though I was running out of time[4]. "The arm," I said. "Gil had that awful scar on his arm."

She nodded. "One of our neighbors kept llamas[5]. He had a barbed-wire fence[6]. Gil was always a good climber[7]. He tried to get into the pen[8] when he was eight years old. He slipped[9] and the wire dug deep[10] into his shoulder." She turned to her husband. "How many stitches[11] did he need, Jorge?"

Jorge Perez had the sad smile now too. "Twenty-two."

That was not the story Gil had told us. He had weaved a tale[12] about a knife fight[13] that sounded like something out of a bad production[14] of *West Side Story*. I hadn't believed him then, even as a kid, so this inconsistency[15] hardly[16] surprised me.

"I remembered it from camp," I said. I gestured with my chin back toward[17] the glass. "Look at his arm."

Mr. Perez shook his head. "But we already said – "

His wife put a hand up, quieting him[18]. No question about it. She was the leader here.[19] She nodded in my direction before turning back to the glass.

"Show me," she said.

Her husband looked confused[20], but he joined her at the window. This time she took his hand and held it. The bearded man had already wheeled the gurney away. York knocked on the glass. The bearded

1. me fixa de son regard perçant
2. une expression curieusement rusée
3. le fils Copeland
4. j'avais l'impression d'être à court de temps
5. avait des lamas
6. clôture de barbelés
7. adorait l'escalade
8. l'enclos
9. a glissé
10. a pénétré en profondeur
11. points de suture
12. concocté une histoire
13. bagarre au couteau
14. mauvaise reprise
15. incohérence
16. guère
17. du menton, j'indiquai à nouveau
18. pour le faire taire
19. C'était elle qui commandait.
20. désorienté

man startled upright[1]. York beckoned him to bring the gurney back[2] toward the window. He did.

I moved closer to Mrs. Perez. I could smell her perfume. It was vaguely familiar, but I didn't remember from where[3]. I stood maybe a foot[4] behind them, looking between their heads.

York hit the white intercom button. "Please show them his arms."

The bearded man pulled back the sheet, again using that gentle, respectful[5] technique. The scar was there, an angry slash[6]. A smile returned to[7] Mrs. Perez's face, but what type – sad, happy, confused, fake, practiced[8], spontaneous? – I couldn't say.

"The left," she said.

"What?"

She turned to me. "This scar is on the left arm," she said. "Gil's was on the right. And Gil's wasn't that long or deep[9]."

Mrs. Perez turned to me and put a hand on my arm. "It's not him, Mr. Copeland. I understand why you'd so much want it to be[10] Gil. But it's not. He isn't coming back to us.[11] And neither is your sister."

1. tressaillit et se redressa
2. lui fit signe de ramener le brancard
3. d'où cela venait
4. juste
5. délicate et respectueuse
6. une vilaine lacération
7. réapparut sur
8. faux, étudié
9. n'était ni aussi longue ni aussi profonde
10. vous aimeriez tant que ce soit
11. On ne va pas nous le rendre.

Chapter 6

When I got back to my house, Loren Muse was pacing[1] like a lion near a wounded[2] gazelle. Cara was in the backseat. She had dance class in an hour. I wasn't taking her.[3] Our nanny, Estelle, was back today. She drove. I overpay[4] Estelle and don't care. You find someone good[5] who also drives? You pay them whatever they want.

I pulled into[6] my driveway. The house was a three-bedroom split-level[7] that had all the personality of[8] that morgue corridor. It was supposed to be our "starter[9]" house. Jane had wanted to upgrade to[10] a McMansion, maybe in Franklin Lakes. I didn't care much where we lived. I'm not into[11] houses or cars and would pretty much let Jane have her way[12] on that kind of stuff[13].

I missed my wife.

Loren Muse had a something-eating grin[14] locked onto[15] her face. No poker player was[16] Muse, that was for certain. "I got all the bills. Computer records[17] too. The works.[18]" Then she turned to my daughter. "Hi, Cara."

"Loren!" Cara shouted. She jumped out of the car. Cara liked Muse. Muse was good[19] with kids. Muse had never been married, never had any of her own[20].

1. faisait les cent pas
2. blessée
3. Ce n'était pas moi qui l'y conduirais.
4. paie trop
5. de compétent
6. Je me garai dans
7. à deux niveaux
8. autant de cachet que
9. pour commencer
10. passer à quelque chose de mieux comme
11. Je me fiche des
12. laisser faire Jane
13. ce genre de choses
14. sourire révélateur
15. affiché sur
16. Pas le style impassible [du joueur de poker],
17. Les fichiers informatiques
18. La totale.
19. savait y faire
20. n'avait pas d'enfants

A few weeks ago I met her most recent boyfriend. The guy wasn't in her league[1], but that again seemed to be the norm for[2] single women of a certain age.

Muse and I spread everything out on the den floor[3] – witness statements, police reports, phone records, all the fraternity's bills[4]. We started with the frat bills, and man[5], there were a ton. Every cell phone. Every beer order. Every online purchase[6].

"So," Muse said, "what are we looking for?"

"Damned if I know.[7]"

"I thought you had something."

"Just a feeling."

"Oh, gag me.[8] Please don't tell me you're playing a hunch[9]."

"I would never," I said.

We kept looking.

"So," she said, "basically[10] we're going through these papers looking for a sign[11] saying, 'Big Clue This Way[12]'?"

"We are looking," I said, "for a catalyst[13]."

"Good word. In what way?"

"I don't know, Muse. But the answer is here. I can almost see it."

"Ooookay," she said, managing with great effort not to roll her eyes[14].

So we searched. They ordered pizza pretty much every night, eight pies, from Pizza-To-Go, directly billed to[15] their credit card. They had Netflix so that they could rent regular DVD movies[16], three at a time delivered to your door[17], and something called Hot-Flixxx, so they could do the same with dirty ones[18]. They ordered fraternity frat-logo golf shirts[19]. The frat logo was also on golf balls, tons of them.

We tried to put them in some kind of order. I don't have a clue why.[20]

I lifted the HotFlixxx bill and showed it to Muse. "Cheap[21]," I said.

1. ne lui arrivait pas à la cheville
2. c'était la règle, apparemment, chez
3. par terre dans le salon
4. factures de la résidence
5. mon vieux
6. achat sur Internet
7. Je voudrais bien le savoir.
8. Ah non, pitié !
9. que tu suis une intuition
10. en gros
11. un panneau
12. Pour le super indice, c'est par là
13. catalyseur
14. lever les yeux au ciel
15. débitées sur
16. louer des DVD classiques
17. livrés à domicile
18. les films pornos
19. des tee-shirts de golf avec le logo de la résidence
20. Je ne sais pas pourquoi.
21. C'est pas cher

"The Internet makes porn readily accessible[1] and thus affordable to the masses[2]."

"Good to know," I said.

"But this might be an opening[3]," Muse said.

"What is?"

"Young boys, hot women. Or in this case, woman."

"Explain," I said.

"I want to hire[4] someone outside the office."

"Who?"

"A private eye[5] named Cingle Shaker. Have you heard of her?"

I nodded. I had.

"Forget heard," she said. "Have you seen her?"

"No."

"But you've heard?"

"Yeah," I said. "I've heard."

"Well, it's no exaggeration. Cingle Shaker has a body that not only stops traffic[6] – it pulls up the road and bulldozes highway dividers[7]. And she's very good. If anyone can get lawyered-up frat boys to spill[8], it's Cingle."

"Okay," I said.

Hours later – I can't even tell you how many – Muse started to rise. "There's nothing here, Cope."

"Seems that way[9], doesn't it?"

"You have Chamique's direct[10] first thing in the morning[11]?"

"Yes."

She stood over me. "Your time would be better spent[12] working on that."

I did a mock "yes, sir" salute[13] in her direction. Chamique and I had worked on her testimony[14] already, but not as hard as one might imagine. I didn't want her to sound practiced[15]. I had another strategy in mind.

"I'll get you what I can," Muse said.

She stomped out the door[16] in her best lick-da-world mode[17].

1. rend le porno facilement accessible
2. donc à la portée de tous
3. un début
4. engager
5. détective privé
6. pas juste beau à provoquer un embouteillage
7. mais carrément à faire exploser le bitume et à mettre en accordéon les glissières de sécurité
8. faire cracher le morceau à des étudiants surprotégés par leurs avocats
9. On dirait bien
10. l'interrogatoire principal [au procès]
11. en début de matinée
12. mieux employé
13. Je mimai un « oui, mon commandant »
14. témoignage
15. qu'elle donne l'impression de s'être entraînée
16. sortit d'un pas déterminé
17. et conquérant

1. des boulettes de viande
2. ça passait
3. pour lui faire plaisir
4. plus bavarde
5. attachée sur
6. être majeur [avoir l'âge légal pour boire de l'alcool]
7. autorisé
8. babillait
9. méchante avec
10. avait lancé une gomme
11. pourquoi
12. faire de la balançoire
13. à la récré,
14. si Kiera n'y allait pas
15. le nez froncé
16. sentiment irrépressible
17. Ça m'a pris par surprise.
18. sans que l'enfant soit sur scène
19. en train de marquer dans un match
20. vous chamboule
21. j'avais pu me relever
22. dont je ne me relèverais pas
23. Mais plus si souvent.
24. qu'elle avait dû endurer

Estelle made us all dinner – spaghetti and meatballs[1]. Estelle is not a great cook, but it went down[2]. I took Cara out for Van Dyke's ice cream afterward, a special treat[3]. She was chattier[4] now. In the rearview mirror, I could see her strapped into[5] the car seat. When I was a kid, we were allowed to sit in the front seat. Now you had to be of drinking age[6] before that was permissible[7].

I tried to listen to what she was saying but Cara was just yakking pure nonsense[8] the way kids do. It seems Brittany had been mean to[9] Morgan so Kyle threw an eraser[10] and how come[11] Kylie, not Kylie G, Kylie N – there were two Kylies in her class – how come Kylie N didn't want to go on the swings[12] at recess[13] unless Kiera was on one[14] too? I kept glancing at her animated face, scrunched up[15] as though imitating an adult. I got hit with that overwhelming feeling[16]. It sneaked up on me.[17] Parents get it from time to time. You are looking at your child and it is an ordinary moment, not like they are onstage[18] or hitting a winning shot[19], just sitting there and you look at them and you know that they are your whole life and that moves you[20] and scares you and makes you want to stop time.

I had lost a sister. I had lost a wife. And most recently, I had lost my father. In all three cases I had gotten off the canvas[21]. But as I looked at Cara, at the way she talked with her hands and widened her eyes, I knew that there was indeed one blow from which I could never rise[22].

I thought about my father. In the woods. With that shovel. His heart broken. Searching for his little girl. I thought about my mother. She had run away. I didn't know where she was. Sometimes I still think about searching her out. But not that often anymore.[23] For years I had hated her. Maybe I still do. Or maybe now that I have a child I understand a little better about the pain she must have been going through[24].

When we walked back into the house, the phone rang. Estelle took Cara from me. I picked it up[1] and said hello.

"We got a problem, Cope."

It was my brother-in-law, Bob, Greta's husband. He was chairman of the charitable fund[2] JaneCare. Greta, Bob and I had founded it[3] after my wife's death. I had gotten lots of wonderful press[4] for it. My living memorial[5] to my lovely, beautiful, gentle wife.

My[6], what a wonderful husband I must have been.

"What's the matter?" I asked.

"Your rape case is costing us big-time[7]. Edward Jenrette's father has gotten[8] several of his friends to back out of their commitments[9]."

I closed my eyes. "Classy.[10]"

"Worse, he's making noises[11] that we've embezzled funds[12]. EJ Jenrette is a well-connected[13] son of a bitch. I'm already getting calls."

"So we open our books[14]," I said. "They won't find anything."

"Don't be naive, Cope. We compete with[15] other charities[16] for the giving dollar[17]. If there is even a whiff[18] of a scandal, we're finished[19]."

"Not much we can do about it, Bob."

"I know. It's just that... we're doing a lot of good here, Cope."

"I know."

"But funding is always tough[20]."

"So what are you suggesting?"

"Nothing." Bob hesitated and I could tell he had more to say. So I waited. "But come on, Cope, you guys plea-bargain all the time[21], right?"

"We do."

"You let a lesser injustice slide[22] so you can nail[23] someone for a bigger one."

"When we have to."

"These two boys. I hear[24] they're good kids."

"You hear wrong.[25]"

1. décrochai
2. fonds caritatif
3. l'avions créé
4. plein d'éloges de la presse
5. C'était mon hommage à la mémoire
6. Mon Dieu
7. nous coûte très cher
8. a poussé
9. à revenir sur leurs engagements
10. La classe !
11. il fait courir le bruit
12. détourné de l'argent
13. qui a des relations
14. on donne accès à nos comptes
15. On est en concurrence avec
16. associations caritatives
17. pour savoir qui remportera les sous
18. le moindre soupçon
19. fichus
20. c'est toujours dur d'avoir des financements
21. négociez souvent
22. fermez les yeux sur une petite injustice
23. épingler
24. J'ai entendu dire
25. Tu as mal entendu.

"Look, I'm not saying that they don't deserve to be punished, but sometimes you have to trade[1]. The greater good.[2] JaneCare is making big strides[3]. It might be the greater good. That's all I'm saying."

"Good night, Bob."

"No offense[4], Cope. I'm just trying to help."

"I know. Good night, Bob."

I hung up[5]. My hands were shaking. Jenrette, that son of a bitch, hadn't gone after me[6]. He had gone after my wife's memory. I started upstairs. Rage consumed me.[7] I would channel it.[8] I sat at my desk. There were only two pictures on it. One was the current school photo[9] of my daughter, Cara. It had a prized spot[10], dead center[11].

The second photograph was a grainy[12] picture of my Noni and Popi from the old country, Russia – or, as it was called when they died in that gulag[13], the Soviet Union. They died when I was very young, when we still lived in Leningrad, but I have vague recollections[14] of them, especially my Popi's big shock of white hair[15].

Why, I often wondered, do I keep this picture out[16]?

Their daughter, my mother, had abandoned me, right? Dumb[17] when you thought about it. But somehow[18], despite the obvious pain intertwined[19], I find the picture oddly relevant[20]. I would look at it, at my Noni and Popi, and I would wonder about ripples[21] and family curses[22] and where it all might have started.

I used to keep out pictures of Jane and Camille. I liked having them in view. They brought me comfort. But just because I found comfort in the dead, that didn't mean my daughter did. It was a hard balance[23] with a six-year-old. You want to talk about her mother. You want her to know about Jane, her wonderful spirit, how much she would have loved her little girl. You want to offer some kind of comfort, too, that her mother was up in heaven looking down on her[24].

1. accepter un compromis
2. Un mal pour un bien.
3. progresse à grands pas
4. Ne le prends pas mal
5. raccrochai
6. ne s'en prenait pas à moi
7. J'enrageais.
8. J'allais canaliser ça.
9. photo de classe récente
10. emplacement privilégié
11. pile au milieu
12. toute piquée
13. goulag
14. souvenirs
15. l'épaisse chevelure blanche
16. en évidence
17. C'était idiot
18. je ne sais trop pourquoi
19. que cette photo provoquait
20. étrangement appropriée
21. les remous
22. les épreuves que traversait notre famille
23. un équilibre compliqué
24. veillait sur elle de là-haut

But I didn't believe in that. I want to. I want to believe that there is a glorious afterlife[1] and that above us, my wife, my sister and my father are all smiling down. But I can't make myself believe it. And when I peddle it[2] to my daughter, I feel as though I'm lying to her. I do it anyway. For now it feels like[3] Santa Claus[4] or the Easter Bunny[5], something temporary and soothing[6], but in the end, she, like all children, will learn it is yet another parental lie with minimum justification[7]. Or maybe I'm wrong and they are up there looking down on us. Maybe that is what Cara will conclude someday.

At midnight I finally allowed my mind to go where it wanted to – my sister, Camille, Gil Perez, that awful, magical summer. I flashed back to camp.[8] I thought about Camille. I thought about that night. And for the first time in several years, I let myself think about Lucy.

A sad smile crossed my face. Lucy Silverstein had been my first real girlfriend. We'd had it so good[9], a fairytale summer romance[10], until that night. We never had the chance to break up[11] – we were, instead, ripped apart[12] by bloody murders. We were torn away while still enmeshed in each other[13], at a point where[14] our love – as silly and immature as it was supposed to have been – was still rising and growing[15].

Lucy was the past[16]. I had given myself an ultimatum and shut her out[17]. But the heart doesn't really know from[18] ultimatums. Over the years, I have tried to see what Lucy is up to[19], harmlessly Googling[20] her name and stuff[21], though I doubt I would ever have the courage to contact her. I never found anything. My bet is[22], after all that happened, she'd wisely changed her[23] name. Lucy was probably married now – like I had been. She was probably happy. I hoped so.

1. vie merveilleuse après la mort
2. je récite cette litanie
3. Pour l'instant, c'est comme
4. le père Noël
5. lapin de Pâques
6. d'apaisant
7. un mensonge parental de plus, peu justifiable
8. Je me remémorais cette colo.
9. Tout allait tellement bien
10. un flirt d'été, un véritable conte de fées
11. n'avons même pas pu rompre
12. arrachés l'un à l'autre
13. alors que nous étions encore fusionnels
14. à un moment où
15. était en plein épanouissement
16. appartenait au passé
17. avais décidé de l'oublier
18. n'obéit pas vraiment aux
19. est devenue
20. en regardant, comme ça, sur Google,
21. et tout ça
22. Je parierais
23. qu'elle a eu la sagesse de changer de

I pushed that all away. Right now I needed to think about Gil Perez. I closed my eyes and went back. I thought about him at camp, how we horsed around[1], how I used to fun-punch him in the arm[2], the way he'd say, "Wimp![3] I didn't even feel that[4]...."

I could see him now, with the skinny torso[5], his shorts too baggy[6] before that was a fashionable look[7], the smile that needed major orthodontia[8], the...

My eyes opened. Something felt wrong[9].

I headed into the basement[10]. I found the cardboard box right away. Jane had been good about marking everything. I saw her extraneat handwriting[11] on the side of the box. It made me pause. Handwriting is so damn personal. My fingertips drifted over it.[12] I touched her lettering and pictured her with the big Magic Marker in her hand, the top in her mouth[13] as she wrote boldly[14]: PHOTOGRAPHS – COPELANDS.

I had made many mistakes in my life. But Jane... it was my one great break[15]. Her good[16] transformed me, made me better and stronger in every way. Yes, I loved her and there was passion, but more than that, she had the ability to make me my best[17]. I was neurotic and insecure[18], the financial-aid kid[19] at a school with very few of them, and there she was, this nearly perfect creature who saw something in me. How? How could I be so awful and worthless[20] if a creature this magnificent[21] loved me?

Jane was my rock. And then she got sick. My rock crumbled[22]. And so did I.

I found the photographs from that long-ago[23] summer. There were none of Lucy. I had wisely thrown them all away years ago. Lucy and I had our songs too – Cat Stevens, James Taylor – stuff that was syrupy enough to be gag worthy[24]. I have trouble listening to them. Still. To this day. I make sure that they are nowhere near[25] my iPod. If they come on the radio, I switch stations at a dizzying speed[26].

1. nous chahutions
2. lui cognais le bras pour rire
3. Mauviette !
4. J'ai rien senti
5. son torse tout maigre
6. trop large
7. à la mode
8. de sérieux soins dentaires
9. ne collait pas
10. sous-sol
11. écriture hyper soignée
12. Je l'effleurai du bout des doigts.
13. le capuchon à la bouche
14. en grosses lettres
15. la grande chance de ma vie
16. Ses bienfaits
17. le pouvoir de faire ressortir le meilleur de moi
18. névrosé et peu sûr de moi
19. l'enfant boursier
20. incapable
21. d'une telle beauté
22. s'est écroulé
23. lointain
24. des trucs sirupeux à vomir
25. qu'elles ne puissent jamais se trouver sur
26. je change de fréquence en vitesse

I sifted through a stack[1] of pictures from that summer. Most of them were of my sister. I pushed through them[2] until I found one that was taken three days before she died. Doug Billingham was in the picture – her boyfriend. A rich kid. Mom had approved, of course. The camp was an odd social mix[3] of privileged and poor. Inside that camp, the upper and lower classes mingled on about as level a playing field as you could find[4]. That was how the hippie who ran[5] the camp, Lucy's fun-loving hippie dad, Ira, wanted it.

Margot Green, another rich kid, was smack in the middle[6]. She always was. She had been the camp hottie[7] and knew it. She was blond and busty[8] and worked it[9] constantly. She always dated older guys, until Gil anyway, and to the mere mortals[10] around her, Margot's life was like something on TV, a melodrama we all watched with fascination. I looked at her now and pictured her throat slit[11]. I closed my eyes for a second.

Gil Perez was in the photograph too. And that was why I was here.

I pointed my desk light[12] and took a closer look[13].

Upstairs, I'd remembered something. I am right-handed[14], but when I fun-punched Gil on the arm, I used my left hand. I did this to avoid touching that awful scar. True, it was healed up[15], but I was afraid to go near it. Like it might tear open anew[16] and start spewing blood[17]. So I used my left hand and hit his right arm. I squinted[18] and moved closer.

I could see the bottom of the scar peeking out[19] beneath the T-shirt.

The room began to spin.[20]

Mrs. Perez had said that her son's scar was on his right arm. But then I would have punched him with my right hand, ergo[21], hitting his left shoulder. But I hadn't done that. I had punched him with my left hand – on his right shoulder.

1. Je fouillai dans une pile
2. Je les passai en revue
3. un curieux melting-pot
4. se mélangeaient de sorte que les différences sociales étaient complètement gommées
5. dirigeait
6. au beau milieu de la photo
7. belle nana
8. avait une belle poitrine
9. en jouait
10. simples mortels
11. l'imaginai la gorge tranchée
12. Je braquai dessus ma lampe de bureau
13. regardai de plus près
14. droitier
15. bien cicatrisée
16. se rouvrir
17. à pisser le sang
18. plissai les yeux
19. qui dépassait
20. Le tournis me prit.
21. donc

Now I had the proof[1].
Gil Perez's scar was on his left arm.
Mrs. Perez had lied[2].
And now I had to wonder why.

1. je détenais la preuve
2. menti

Chapter 7

I arrived in my office early the next morning. In half an hour, I would have[1] Chamique Johnson, the victim, on the stand[2]. I was going over[3] my notes. When the clock struck nine, I had enough. So I called Detective York.

"Mrs. Perez lied," I said.

He listened to my explanation.

"Lied," York repeated when I finished. "Don't you think that's a little strong[4]?"

"What would you call it?"

"Maybe she just made a mistake?"

"A mistake about which one of her son's arms was scarred[5]?"

"Sure, why not. She knew it wasn't him already. Natural."

I wasn't buying it. "Have you got anything new on the case?"

"We think Santiago was living in New Jersey."

"You have an address?"

"Nope.[6] But we have a girlfriend. Or at least we think she's a girlfriend. A friend anyway."

"How did you find her?"

"That empty cell phone[7]. She called it looking for him."

1. j'appellerais
2. à la barre
3. Je relisais
4. que vous y allez un peu fort
5. portait la cicatrice
6. Nan.
7. téléphone dont l'historique des appels a été effacé

"So who is he really? Manolo Santiago, I mean?"

"Don't know."

"The girlfriend won't tell you[1]?"

"The girlfriend only knew him as Santiago. Oh, something else important."

"What?"

"His body was moved[2]. I mean, we were sure of that in the first place[3]. But now we have it confirmed. And our ME[4] says, based on the bleeding out[5] and some other nonsense[6] I don't quite understand or care to[7], Santiago was probably dead an hour before he got dumped[8]. There are some carpet fibers, stuff like that. Preliminary shows that[9] they're from a car."

"So Santiago was murdered, stuck in a trunk[10], and then dumped in Washington Heights?"

"That's our working theory[11]."

"Do you have a make on[12] the car?"

"Not yet. But our guy says it's something old. That's all he knows. But they're working on it."

"How old?"

"I don't know. Not new. Come on, Copeland, give me a break here[13]."

"I have a pretty big personal interest in this case."

"Speaking of which.[14]"

"What?"

"Why don't you jump in and help?[15]"

"Meaning?[16]"

"Meaning I have a psychotic caseload[17]. We now have a possible New Jersey connection – Santiago probably lived there. Or at least his girlfriend does. And that's where she saw him exclusively – in New Jersey."

"My county?"

"No, I think it's Hudson. Or maybe Bergen. Hell[18], I don't know. But it's close enough[19]. But let me add something else into the mix[20]."

"I'm listening."

"Your sister lived in New Jersey, right?"

1. ne veut pas vous le dire
2. a été déplacé
3. dès le départ
4. médecin légiste
5. vu le sang qu'il a perdu
6. d'autres inepties
7. ou dont je me fiche
8. qu'il soit abandonné
9. D'après les premières analyses,
10. balancé dans un coffre
11. hypothèse de travail
12. une marque pour
13. lâchez-moi un peu
14. À ce propos.
15. Vous ne voulez pas nous donner un coup de main ?
16. C'est-à-dire ?
17. un nombre dingue de dossiers sur les bras
18. Merde
19. c'est dans le coin
20. j'ai encore un truc à dire

"Yes."

"That's not my jurisdiction[1]. You can probably claim it as your own[2], even if it's out of your county. Open up the old case[3] – it's not like anybody else wants it[4]."

I thought about that. I was being played[5], in part. He was hoping I'd do some of his legwork[6] and hand off the glory[7] – all of which was fine with me[8].

"This girlfriend," I said. "Do you have a name?"

"Raya Singh."

"How about an address?"

"You're going to talk to her?"

"You mind?[9]"

"As long as you don't screw up my case[10], you can do whatever you want. But can I give you a piece of friendly advice[11]?"

"Sure."

"That lunatic[12], the Summer Slasher. I forget his real name."

"Wayne Steubens," I said.

"You knew him, didn't you?"

"Have you read the case file[13]?" I asked.

"Yep.[14] They looked at you hard for it[15], didn't they?"

I still remember that Sheriff Lowell, that look of skepticism. Understandable, of course.

"What's your point?"

"Just this: Steubens is still looking to[16] overturn his conviction[17]."

"He was never tried[18] for those first four murders," I said. "They didn't need them – they had better evidence[19] in the other cases."

"I know. But still. He was linked.[20] If it really is Gil Perez and Steubens was to hear[21], well, it would help him. You know what I'm saying?"

He was saying to keep it quiet[22] until I knew something for sure. I got that.[23] The last thing I wanted to do was help Wayne Steubens.

1. secteur
2. invoquer que vous, si
3. Faites rouvrir le dossier
4. qu'il y ait beaucoup d'amateurs
5. Il me manipulait
6. travail de terrain
7. que je lui laisserais toute la gloire
8. me convenait très bien
9. Ça vous dérange ?
10. Du moment que vous ne bousillez pas mon affaire
11. conseil d'ami
12. Ce dingue
13. dossier
14. Ouais.
15. Ils vous ont soupçonné
16. s'efforce toujours de
17. faire casser sa condamnation
18. jugé
19. des preuves plus solides
20. Il y avait un lien avec lui.
21. venait à l'apprendre
22. de ne rien révéler
23. Je compris le message.

We hung up. Loren Muse stuck her head[1] in my office.

"You got anything new for me?" I asked.

"Nope. Sorry." She checked her watch. "You ready for your big direct?"

"I am."

"Then come on. It's showtime.[2]"

"The People[3] call Chamique Johnson."

Chamique was dressed on the conservative side[4] but not ridiculously so. You could still see the street.[5] You could still see the curves[6]. I even had her wear[7] high heels[8]. There are times you try to obstruct the jury's view[9]. And there are times, like this, when you know that your only chance is for them to see the entire picture[10], warts and all[11].

Chamique kept her head high. Her eyes shifted right and left[12], not in a dishonest-Nixon way[13] but in a where-is-the-next-blow-coming-from way[14]. Her makeup was a little heavy[15]. But that was okay too. It made her look like a girl trying to look like a grown-up[16].

There were those in my office who disagreed with this strategy. But I believed that if you are going to go down[17], go down with the truth. So that was what I was prepared to do now.

Chamique stated her name and swore on[18] the Bible and sat down. I smiled at her and met her eye. Chamique offered me a little nod, giving me the okay to go ahead.

"You work as a stripper, isn't that right?"

Opening up with a question like that – without any preliminaries – surprised the gallery[19]. There were a few gasps[20]. Chamique blinked[21]. She had some idea of what I was going to do here, but I had intentionally not been specific[22].

"Part time[23]," she said.

I didn't like that answer. It seemed too wary[24].

1. passa la tête
2. Que le spectacle commence.
3. Le ministère public
4. de façon classique
5. On voyait quand même le trottoir.
6. ses formes
7. Je lui avais même demander de mettre
8. des talons hauts
9. où mieux vaut essayer de brouiller la vue du jury
10. c'est qu'ils voient tout le tableau
11. tout, même les défauts
12. Elle regardait de tous côtés
13. pas d'un air louche, à la Nixon
14. d'un air très craintif
15. un peu chargé
16. vraie femme
17. quitte à perdre
18. déclina son nom, jura sur
19. l'assistance
20. exclamations étouffées
21. cligna des yeux
22. j'étais volontairement resté vague
23. À mi-temps
24. méfiante

"But you do take off your clothes for money[1], right?"
"Yeah."
That was more like it.[2] No hesitation.
"Do you strip in clubs or at private parties?"
"Both."
"What club do you strip out of?[3]"
"Pink Tail. It's in Newark."
"How old are you?" I asked.
"Sixteen."
"Don't you have to be eighteen to strip?"
"Yeah."
"So how do you get around that[4]?"
Chamique shrugged. "I got a fake ID[5], says I'm twenty-one."
"So you break the law[6]?"
"Guess so.[7]"
"Do you break the law or not?" I asked. There was a hint of steel[8] in my voice. Chamique understood. I wanted her to be honest. I wanted her to – pardon the pun[9], her being a stripper and all[10] – expose herself totally[11]. The steel was a reminder.
"Yeah. I break the law."
I looked over at the defense table. Mort Pubin stared at me as if I were out of my mind[12]. Flair Hickory had his palms pressed together[13], his index finger resting on his lips[14]. Their two clients, Barry Marantz and Edward Jenrette, wore blue blazers and pale faces[15]. They did not look smug or confident[16] or evil[17]. They looked contrite[18] and scared and very young. The cynic would say that this was intentional – that their lawyers had told them how to sit and what expressions to wear on their faces[19]. But I knew better[20]. I just didn't let it matter to me.
I smiled at my witness. "You're not the only one, Chamique. We found a bunch[21] of fake IDs at your rapists' frat house[22] – so that they could all go out and do a little underage partying[23]. At least you broke the law to make a living[24]."

1. en échange d'argent
2. Là, c'était beaucoup mieux.
3. Dans quel club faites-vous du strip-tease ?
4. contournez-vous cela
5. fausse carte d'identité
6. vous enfreignez la loi
7. Je suppose.
8. une pointe de dureté
9. excusez le jeu de mots
10. s'agissant d'une strip-teaseuse
11. se mette à nu
12. devenu fou
13. les mains jointes
14. l'index posé sur les lèvres
15. étaient pâles
16. trop sûrs d'eux
17. méchants
18. avaient l'air contrits
19. arborer
20. je savais que ce n'était pas le cas ici
21. un tas
22. dans la résidence de vos violeurs
23. faire la fête, même s'ils sont mineurs
24. pour gagner votre vie

Mort was on his feet[1]. "Objection!"

"Sustained.[2]"

But it was in[3]. As the old saw goes[4], "You can't unring a bell[5]."

"Miss Johnson," I continued, "you're not a virgin[6], are you?"

"No."

"In fact, you have a son out of wedlock."

"I do."

"How old is he?"

"Fifteen months."

"Tell me, Miss Johnson. Does the fact that you're not a virgin and have a son out of marriage make you less of a human being[7]?"

"Objection!"

"Sustained." The judge, a bushy-eyed[8] man named Arnold Pierce, frowned at me.

"I'm just pointing out the obvious[9], Your Honor[10]. If Miss Johnson were an upper-class[11] blonde from Short Hills or Livingston – "

"Save it for the summation[12], Mr. Copeland."

I would. And I had used it in the opening[13]. I turned back to my victim.

"Do you enjoy stripping, Chamique?"

"Objection!" Mort Pubin was up again. "Irrelevant.[14] Who cares if she likes stripping or not?"

Judge Pierce looked at me. "Well?"

"Tell you what[15]," I said, looking at Pubin. "I won't ask about her stripping if you don't."

Pubin went still[16]. Flair Hickory still had not spoken. He did not like to object. By and large[17], juries don't like objections. They think you're hiding something from them. Flair wanted to stay liked[18]. So he had[19] Mort do the hatchet work[20]. It was the attorney version of good cop, bad cop.

I turned back to Chamique. "You weren't stripping the night you were raped, were you?"

"Objection!"

1. se leva
2. Accordée.
3. c'était dit
4. Comme dit l'adage
5. Ce qui est dit est dit
6. vierge
7. feraient que vous ne devriez pas être considérée comme un être humain
8. aux sourcils broussailleux
9. ne fais que souligner l'évidence
10. M. le Juge
11. de la haute société
12. Gardez cela pour le réquisitoire
13. dès l'ouverture
14. C'est hors de propos.
15. Vous savez quoi
16. se figea
17. De manière générale
18. rester sympathique
19. laissait
20. faire la sale besogne

"Alleged rape[1]," I corrected.

"No," Chamique said. "I was invited."

"You were invited to a party at the frat house where Mr. Marantz and Mr. Jenrette live?"

"That's right."

"Did either Mr. Marantz or Mr. Jenrette invite you?"

"No."

"Who did?"

"Another boy who lived there."

"What's his name?"

"Jerry Flynn."

"I see. How did you meet Mr. Flynn?"

"I worked the frat[2] the week before."

"When you say you worked the frat – "

"I stripped for them," Chamique finished for me[3]. I liked that. We were getting a rhythm.[4]

"And Mr. Flynn was there?"

"They all were."

"When you say 'they all' – "

She pointed at the two defendants[5]. "They were there too. A bunch[6] of other guys."

"How many would you say[7]?"

"Twenty, twenty-five maybe."

"Okay, but it was Mr. Flynn who invited you to the party a week later?"

"Yes."

"And you accepted the invitation?"

Her eyes were wet now, but she held her head high. "Yes."

"Why did you choose to go?"

Chamique thought about that. "It would be like a billionaire[8] inviting you on his yacht."

"You were impressed with them?"

"Yeah. 'Course.[9]"

"And their money?"

"That too," she said.

I loved her for that answer.

1. Où vous auriez subi un viol
2. J'avais bossé à la résidence
3. à ma place
4. On commençait à être en phase.
5. accusés
6. Une bande
7. à votre avis
8. milliardaire
9. Ben bien sûr.

"And," she went on, "Jerry was sweet to me[1] when I was stripping."

"Mr. Flynn treated you nicely[2]?"

"Yeah."

I nodded. I was entering trickier territory[3] now, but I went for it[4]. "By the way, Chamique, going back to[5] the night you were hired to strip..." I felt my breath go a little shallow.[6] "Did you perform other services[7] on any of the men in attendance[8]?"

I met her eye. She swallowed, but she held it together[9]. Her voice was soft. The edges were gone[10] now. "Yeah."

"Were these favors of a sexual nature?"

"Yeah."

She lowered her head.

"Don't be ashamed[11]," I said. "You needed the money." I gestured toward the defense table. "What's their excuse?"

"Objection!"

"Sustained."

But Mort Pubin wasn't done[12]. "Your Honor, that statement was an outrage[13]!"

"It is an outrage," I agreed[14]. "You should castigate[15] your clients immediately."

Mort Pubin turned red. His voice was a whine[16]. "Your Honor!"

"Mr. Copeland."

I held my palm up to the[17] judge, signaling he was right and I would cease[18]. I am a firm believer in getting out[19] all the bad news during direct, albeit in my own way[20]. You take the wind out of their cross.[21]

"Were you interested in Mr. Flynn as a potential[22] boyfriend?"

Mort Pubin again: "Objection! Relevance?[23]"

"Mr. Copeland?"

"Of course it's relevant. They are going to say that Miss Johnson is making up these charges[24] to shake

1. avait été gentil avec moi
2. avec égard
3. m'engageais sur un terrain plus délicat
4. je fonçai
5. pour revenir à
6. Je sentais que j'avais le souffle court.
7. Avez-vous effectué d'autres prestations
8. présents
9. elle tint bon
10. La tension avait disparu
11. N'ayez pas honte
12. n'avait pas terminé
13. scandale
14. approuvai-je
15. punir
16. tourna au gémissement
17. Je levai la main, la paume face au
18. que j'allais m'en tenir là
19. J'ai la ferme conviction qu'il vaut mieux livrer
20. mais à ma façon
21. Cela affaiblit d'avance leur contre-interrogatoire.
22. éventuel
23. En quoi est-ce pertinent ?
24. invente ces accusations

down their clients financially[1]. I'm trying to establish her frame of mind[2] on that night."

"I'll allow it[3]," Judge Pierce said.

I repeated the question.

Chamique squirmed[4] a little and it made her look her age. "Jerry was out of my league[5]."

"But?"

"But, I mean, yeah, I don't know. I never met anyone like him. He held a door for me.[6] He was so nice. I'm not used to that.[7]"

"And he's rich. I mean, compared with you."

"Yeah."

"Did that mean something to you?"

"Sure."

I loved the honesty.

Chamique's eyes darted toward the jury box[8]. The defiant expression was back. "I got dreams too.[9]"

I let that echo a few moments[10] before following up[11]. "And what was your dream that night, Chamique?"

Mort was about to object again but Flair Hickory put his hand on Mort's forearm.

Chamique shrugged. "It's stupid."

"Tell me anyway[12]."

"I thought maybe... it was stupid... I thought maybe he'd like me, you know?"

"I do," I said. "How did you get to the party?"

"Took a bus from Irvington and then I walked."

"And when you arrived at the frat house, Mr. Flynn was there?"

"Yes."

"Was he still sweet[13]?"

"At first, yeah." Now a tear escaped.[14] "He was real[15] sweet. It was – "

She stopped.

"It was what, Chamique?"

"In the beginning" – another tear ran down her cheek – "it was the best night of my life."

1. pour plumer leurs clients
2. état d'esprit
3. Autorisé !
4. se tortilla
5. n'était pas de mon monde
6. Il m'a tenu la porte.
7. Je n'ai pas l'habitude.
8. fusèrent en direction de la tribune du jury
9. Moi aussi, j'ai des rêves.
10. Je laissai ces mots résonner quelques instants
11. d'enchaîner
12. quand même
13. toujours gentil
14. Cette fois elle ne put retenir une larme.
15. vraiment

I let the words hang[1] and echo. A third tear escaped.

"Are you okay?" I asked.

Chamique wiped the tear. "I'm fine."

"You sure?"

Her voice was hard again. "Ask your question, Mr. Copeland," she said.

She was wonderful. The jury[2] all had their heads up, listening to – and believing, I thought – every word.

"Was there a time when Mr. Flynn's behavior[3] toward you changed?"

"Yeah."

"When?"

"I saw him whispering with that one over there[4]." She pointed toward Edward Jenrette.

"Mr. Jenrette?"

"Yeah. Him."

Jenrette tried not to shrink from[5] Chamique's gaze[6]. He was half successful.[7]

"You saw Mr. Jenrette whisper something to Mr. Flynn?"

"Yeah."

"And then what happened?"

"Jerry asked me if I wanted to take a walk[8]."

"By Jerry, you mean Jerry Flynn?"

"Yeah."

"Okay, tell us what happened."

"We walked outside. They had a keg[9]. He asked me if I wanted a beer. I said no. He was acting all jumpy and stuff[10]."

Mort Pubin was up. "Objection."

I spread my arm[11] and looked exasperated. "Your Honor."

"I'll allow it," the judge said.

"Go on," I said.

"Jerry got a beer from the keg and he kept looking at it."

"Looking at his beer?"

1. planer
2. Les jurés
3. comportement
4. chuchoter avec celui-là, là-bas
5. essaya de ne pas détourner les yeux du
6. regard
7. Il n'y parvint qu'à moitié.
8. me promener
9. un fût de bière
10. nerveux et tout
11. Je levai les bras au ciel

"Yeah, a little, I guess. He wouldn't look at me no more.[1] Something was different. I asked him if he was okay. He said, sure, everything was great. And then" – her voice didn't catch, but it came awfully close[2] – "he said I had a hot bod[3] and that he liked watching me take off my clothes."

"Did that surprise you?"

"Yeah. I mean, he never talked like that before. His voice was all rough[4] now." She swallowed. "Like the others."

"Go on."

"He said, 'You wanna go upstairs and[5] see my room?'"

"What did you say?"

"I said okay."

"Did you want to go to his room?"

Chamique closed her eyes. Another tear leaked out[6]. She shook her head.

"You need to answer out loud[7]."

"No," she said.

"Why did you go?"

"I wanted him to like me."

"And you thought he would like you if you went upstairs with him?"

Chamique's voice was soft. "I knew he wouldn't if I said no."

I turned away and moved back to my table. I pretended to look at notes. I just wanted to give the jury time to digest[8]. Chamique had her back straight[9]. She kept her chin high.[10] She tried to show nothing, but you could feel the hurt[11] emanating from her.

"What happened when you got upstairs?"

"I walked past[12] a door." She turned her eyes back to Jenrette. "And then he grabbed me[13]."

Again I made her point out Edward Jenrette and identify him by name.

"Was anyone else in the room?"

"Yeah. Him."

1. Il me regardait plus.
2. sa voix ne se brisa pas mais il s'en fallut de peu
3. un corps sexy
4. rauque
5. Tu veux pas monter
6. s'échappa
7. à haute voix
8. le temps de digérer ça
9. se tenait toute droite
10. Le menton relevé.
11. la douleur
12. devant
13. il m'a attrapée

She pointed to Barry Marantz. I noticed the two families behind the defendants. The parents had those death-mask[1] faces, where the skin looks as if it were being pulled from behind, the cheekbones appear too prominent[2], the eyes sunken and shattered[3]. They were the sentinels, lined up to shelter their offspring[4]. They were devastated. I felt bad[5] for them. But too bad[6]. Edward Jenrette and Barry Marantz had people to protect them.

Chamique Johnson had no one.

Yet part of me understood[7] what really had happened there. You start drinking, you get out of control[8], you forget about the[9] consequences. Maybe they would never do this again. Maybe they had indeed learned their[10] lesson. But again too bad.

There were some people who were bad to the bone[11], who would always be cruel and nasty[12] and hurt others. There were others, maybe most that came through my office[13], who just messed up[14]. It is not my job to differentiate[15]. I leave that to the judge during sentencing[16].

"Okay," I said, "what happened next[17]?"

"He closed the door."

"Which one?"

She pointed to Marantz.

"Chamique, to make this easier[18], could you call him Mr. Marantz and the other one Mr. Jenrette?"

She nodded.

"So Mr. Marantz closed the door. And then what happened?"

"Mr. Jenrette told me to get on my knees[19]."

"Where was Mr. Flynn at this point[20]?"

"I don't know."

"You don't know?" I feigned surprise. "Hadn't he walked up the stairs with you?"

"Yeah."

"Hadn't he been standing next to you[21] when Mr. Jenrette grabbed you?"

1. de masque mortuaire
2. les pommettes ont l'air trop saillantes
3. cernés et abattus
4. au garde-à-vous afin de protéger leur progéniture
5. J'avais de la peine
6. tant pis
7. Pourtant, je comprenais en partie
8. on perd les pédales
9. ne pense pas aux
10. effectivement retenu la
11. pourris jusqu'à la moelle
12. méchants
13. la plupart de ceux qui passaient par mon bureau
14. avaient simplement merdé
15. de faire la distinction
16. quand il prononce la condamnation
17. ensuite
18. pour faciliter les choses
19. de m'agenouiller
20. à ce moment-là
21. N'était-il pas à vos côtés

"Yeah."

"And then?"

"I don't know. He didn't come in the room. He just let the door close."

"Did you see him again?"

"Not till later.[1]"

I took a deep breath[2] and dove in[3]. I asked Chamique what happened next. I walked her through the assault.[4] The testimony was graphic[5]. She spoke matter-of-factly[6] – a total disconnect[7]. There was much to get in[8], what they had said, how they had laughed, what they had done to her. I needed specifics[9]. I don't think the jury wanted to hear it. I understood that. But I needed her to try to be as specific as possible, to remember every position, who had been where, who had done what.

It was numbing.[10]

When we finished the testimony on the assault[11], I gave it a few seconds[12] and then approached our trickiest[13] problem. "In your testimony, you claimed[14] your attackers used the names Cal and Jim."

"Objection, Your Honor."

It was Flair Hickory, speaking up[15] for the first time. His voice was quiet, the kind of quiet that draws all ears[16].

"She did not claim they *used* the names Cal and Jim," Flair said. "She claimed, in both her testimony and prior statements[17], that they *were* Cal and Jim."

"I'll rephrase[18]," I said with a tone of exasperation, as if to say to the jury, Can you believe how picky he's being?[19] I turned back to Chamique. "Which one *was* Cal and which one *was* Jim?"

Chamique identified Barry Marantz as Cal and Edward Jenrette as Jim.

"Did they introduce themselves to you?[20]" I asked.

"No."

"So how did you know their names?"

"They used them with each other."

1. Plus tard seulement.
2. Je respirai un grand coup
3. me jetai à l'eau
4. Je lui fis raconter pas à pas l'agression.
5. explicite
6. d'un ton neutre
7. totalement détaché
8. Il y avait beaucoup de choses à préciser
9. de détails
10. Cela faisait froid dans le dos.
11. relatif à l'agression
12. je ne dis rien pendant quelques instants
13. le plus épineux
14. avez affirmé
15. qui intervenait
16. suscite toute l'attention
17. aussi bien dans son témoignage que dans ses précédentes déclarations
18. Je vais reformuler
19. Vous voyez comme il pinaille ?
20. Se sont-ils présentés ?

1. C'est dans
2. Penche-la en avant
3. Vous savez
4. qu'aucun

"Per[1] your testimony. For example, Mr. Marantz said, 'Bend her over[2], Jim.' Like that?"

"Yeah."

"You are aware[3]," I said, "that neither[4] of the defendants is named Cal or Jim."

"I know," she said.

"Can you explain that?"

"No. I'm just telling you what they said."

5. Je ne revins pas dessus.

No hesitation, no trying to make excuses – it was a good answer. I left it alone.[5]

"What happened after they raped you?"

6. m'ont forcée à me laver
7. m'ont savonnée
8. un de ces tuyaux flexibles
9. à me frotter

"They made me clean up[6]."

"How?"

"They stuck me in a shower. They used soap on me[7]. The shower had one of those hoses[8]. They made me scrub off[9]."

"Then what?"

"They took my clothes – they said they were going to burn them. Then they gave me a T-shirt and shorts."

"What happened next?"

10. m'a raccompagnée

"Jerry walked me[10] to the bus stop."

"Did Mr. Flynn say anything to you during the walk?"

"No."

"Not one word?"

"Not one word."

"Did you say anything to him?"

"No."

11. Là non plus, je ne renchéris pas.
12. passer à autre chose
13. pris un avocat
14. Si on veut.

Again I looked surprised. "You didn't tell him you were raped?"

She smiled for the first time. "You don't think he knew that?"

I let that go too.[11] I wanted to shift gears again[12].

"Have you hired a lawyer[13], Chamique?"

"Kinda.[14]"

"What do you mean, kinda?"

"I didn't really hire him. He found me."

"What's his name?"

"Horace Foley. He don't dress nice like[1] Mr. Hickory over there."

Flair smiled at that one[2].

"Are you suing[3] the defendants?"

"Yeah."

"Why are you suing them?"

"To make them pay," she said.

"Isn't that what we're doing here?" I asked. "Finding a way to punish them?"

"Yeah. But the lawsuit is about money[4]."

I made a face[5] as though I didn't understand. "But the defense is going to claim[6] that you made up these charges to extort[7] money. They're going to say that your lawsuit proves, in fact, that you're interested in money."

"I am interested in money," Chamique said. "Did I ever say I wasn't?"

I waited.

"Aren't you interested in money, Mr. Copeland?"

"I am," I said.

"So?"

"So," I said, "the defense is going to claim it's a motive to lie[8]."

"Can't do nothing about that[9]," she said. "See[10], if I say I don't care about money, that would be a lie." She looked at the jury. "If I sat here and told you, money means nothing to me[11], would you believe me? 'Course not. Same as if you told me you didn't care about money. I cared about money before they raped me. I care about it now. I'm not lying. They raped me. I want them to go to jail[12] for that. And if I can get some money from them too, why not? I could use it.[13]"

I stepped back. Candor[14] – real candor – smells like nothing else[15].

"Nothing further[16]," I said.

1. Il s'habille pas aussi bien que
2. en entendant ça
3. Intentez-vous une action contre
4. l'action en justice, c'est pour l'argent
5. Je fis la grimace
6. prétendre
7. extorquer
8. une bonne raison de mentir
9. J'y peux rien
10. Vous voyez
11. ne m'intéresse pas
12. qu'ils aillent en prison
13. J'en ai bien besoin.
14. La franchise
15. il n'y a que ça qui sonne vrai
16. Je n'ai rien à ajouter

Chapter 8

The trial broke[1] for lunch.

Lunch is usually a time to discuss strategy with my subordinates[2]. But I didn't want that right now. I wanted to be alone. I wanted to rework the direct[3] in my head, see what I missed, figure out[4] what Flair was going to do.

I ordered a cheeseburger and a beer from a waitress who looked as though she wanted to be in one of those want-to-get-away? commercials[5]. She called me hon[6]. I love when a waitress calls me hon.

A trial is two narratives competing for your attention[7]. You need to make your protagonist a real person. Real is much more important than pure. Attorneys forget that. They think they need to make their clients sweet and perfect. They don't. So I try to never dumb it down[8] for the jury. People are pretty good judges of character[9]. They are more likely to believe you if you show your foibles[10]. At least on my side – the prosecution's. When you're doing defense[11], you want to muddy up the waters[12]. As Flair Hickory had made abundantly clear[13], you want to bring forth[14] that beautiful mistress known as Reasonable Doubt. I was the opposite. I needed it clear.[15]

1. L'audience fut suspendue
2. collaborateurs
3. repasser l'interrogatoire
4. essayer de deviner
5. publicités du type « soif d'évasion ? »
6. chéri [honey]
7. ce sont deux histoires qui se disputent votre attention
8. j'essaie de ne jamais rien atténuer
9. d'assez fins psychologues
10. faiblesses
11. on est du côté de la défense
12. brouiller les cartes
13. l'avait très clairement exprimé
14. provoquer l'apparition de
15. Il fallait qu'il n'y ait pas l'ombre d'un doute.

The waitress reappeared and said, "Here, hon," as she dropped[1] the burger in front of me. I eyed it.[2] It looked so greasy[3] I almost ordered a side of angiogram[4]. But in truth, this mess[5] was just what I'd wanted. I put both hands on it and felt my fingers sink into the bun[6].

"Mr. Copeland?"

I didn't recognize the young man standing over me.

"You mind?[7]" I said. "I'm trying to eat here."

"This is for you."

He dropped a note on the table and left. It was a sheet from a legal yellow pad[8] folded into a small rectangle. I opened it up.

Please meet me in the back booth[9] on your right.
EJ Jenrette

It was Edward's father. I looked down at my beloved[10] burger. It looked back at me. I hate eating cold food or anything reheated[11]. So I ate it. I was starving[12]. I tried not to wolf it down.[13] The beer tasted damn good[14].

When I was done[15] I rose and headed toward the back booth on my right. EJ Jenrette was there. A glass of what looked like scotch[16] sat[17] on the table in front of him. He had both hands surrounding the glass[18], as if he were trying to protect it. His eyes were transfixed[19] by the liquor.

He did not look up as I slid into the booth. If he was upset by my tardiness[20] – heck[21], if he noticed it – EJ Jenrette was hiding it well.

"You wanted to see me?" I said.

EJ nodded. He was a big man, ex-athlete type, with designer[22] shirts that still looked as though the collar was strangling the neck[23]. I waited.

"You have a child," he said.

I waited some more.

"What would you do to protect her?"

1. en déposant
2. Je le regardai.
3. gras
4. une angiographie en accompagnement
5. saleté
6. s'enfoncer dans le pain
7. Vous permettez ?
8. feuille de bloc-notes jaune
9. dans le box du fond
10. cher
11. de réchauffé
12. affamé
13. de ne pas l'engloutir d'un coup.
14. était drôlement bonne
15. j'eus fini,
16. du whisky
17. était posé
18. Ses deux mains entouraient le verre
19. hypnotisés
20. S'il était contrarié que j'aie pris mon temps
21. tant pis
22. de marque
23. avait l'air d'avoir un col trop serré

"For one[1]," I said, "I'd never let her go to a party at your son's frat house."

He looked up. "That's not funny."

"Are we done here?[2]"

He took a long pull on his drink[3].

"I will give that girl a hundred thousand dollars," Jenrette said. "I will give your wife's charity another one hundred thousand."

"Great. Do you want to write the checks[4] now?"

"You'll drop the charges?[5]"

"No."

He met my eye.[6] "He's my son. Do you really want him to spend the next ten years in prison?"

"Yes. But the judge will decide the sentence[7]."

"He's just a kid. At worst, he got carried away[8]."

"You have a daughter, don't you, Mr. Jenrette?

Jenrette stared at his drink.

"If a couple of black kids from Irvington grabbed her, dragged her[9] into a room and did those things to her, would you want it swept under the rug[10]?"

"My daughter isn't a stripper."

"No, sir, she isn't. She has all the privileges in life. She has all the advantages. Why would she strip?"

"Do me a favor[11]," he said. "Don't hand me that socioeconomic crap.[12] Are you saying that because she was disadvantaged she had no choice but to choose whoredom[13]? Please. It's an insult to any disadvantaged person who ever worked their way out[14] of the ghetto."

I raised my eyebrows.[15] "Ghetto?"

He said nothing.

"You live in Short Hills, don't you, Mr. Jenrette?"

"So?"

"Tell me," I said, "how many of your neighbors choose stripping[16] or, to use your term, whoredom?"

"I don't know."

"What Chamique Johnson does or doesn't do is totally irrelevant to her being raped[17]. We don't get

1. Pour commencer
2. C'est bon, on a fini là ?
3. but une longue gorgée
4. faire les chèques
5. Vous abandonnerez les poursuites ?
6. Il me regarda dans les yeux.
7. déterminera la peine
8. est allé un peu loin
9. l'attrapait, la traînait
10. qu'on étouffe l'affaire
11. Je vous en prie
12. Épargnez-moi ces âneries socio-économiques.
13. d'autre choix que de se prostituer
14. qui ont réussi à se sortir
15. Je levai les sourcils.
16. de faire du strip-tease
17. n'a rien à voir avec le fait qu'elle ait été violée

to choose like that. Your son doesn't get to[1] decide who deserves to be raped or not. But either way[2], Chamique Johnson stripped because she had limited options[3]. Your daughter doesn't." I shook my head. "You really don't get it.[4]"

"Get what?"

"The fact that she's forced to strip and sell herself doesn't make Edward less culpable[5]. If anything[6], it makes him more so."

"My son didn't rape her."

"That's why we have trials," I said. "Are we done now?"

He finally lifted his head. "I can make it hard on you[7]."

"Seems like you're already trying that."

"The fund stoppage[8]?" He shrugged. "That was nothing. A muscle flex[9]."

He met my eye and held it. This had gone far enough.

"Good-bye, Mr. Jenrette."

He reached out and grabbed my forearm. "They're going to get off[10]."

"We'll see."

"You scored points[11] today, but that whore still needs to be crossed[12]. You can't explain away[13] the fact that she got their names wrong. That will be your downfall.[14] You know that. So listen to what I'm suggesting."

I waited.

"My son and the Marantz boy will plead to whatever charge you come up with[15] so long as[16] there is no jail time. They'll do community service[17]. They can be on strict probation[18] for as long as you want. That's fair.[19] But in addition, I will help support this troubled[20] woman and I will make sure that JaneCare gets the proper funding. It's a win-win-win.[21]"

"No," I said.

1. Ce n'est pas à votre fils de
2. en tout cas
3. elle n'avait pas beaucoup de choix
4. Vous ne comprenez pas.
5. coupable
6. Au contraire
7. vous créer des difficultés
8. gel des fonds
9. petite démonstration de force
10. s'en tirer
11. avez marqué des points
12. doit subir un contre-interrogatoire
13. n'avez pas d'explication pour
14. C'est ce qui vous perdra.
15. plaideront coupables de ce que vous voudrez
16. du moment que
17. des travaux d'intérêt général
18. placés sous stricte liberté conditionnelle
19. Ce n'est que justice.
20. dérangée
21. Tout le monde y gagne.

"Do you really think these boys will do something like this again?"

"Truth?[1]" I said. "Probably not."

"I thought prison was about[2] rehabilitation[3]."

"Yeah, but I'm not big on[4] rehabilitation," I said. "I'm big on justice."

"And you think my son going to prison is justice?"

"Yes," I said. "But again, that's why we have juries[5] and judges."

"Have you ever made a mistake, Mr. Copeland?"

I said nothing.

"Because I'm going to dig[6]. I'm going to dig until I find every mistake you ever made. And I'll use them. You got skeletons[7], Mr. Copeland. We both know that. If you keep up[8] this witch hunt[9], I'm going to drag them out for all the world to see[10]." He seemed to be gaining confidence[11] now. I didn't like that. "At worst, my son made a big mistake. We're trying to find a way to make amends for[12] what he did without destroying his life. Can you understand that?"

"I have nothing more to say to you," I said.

He kept hold of my arm.[13]

"Last warning[14], Mr. Copeland. I will do whatever I can to protect my child."

I looked at EJ Jenrette and then I did something that surprised him. I smiled.

"What?" he said.

"It's nice," I said.

"What is?"

"That your son has so many people who will fight[15] for him," I said. "In the courtroom too. Edward has so many people on his side."

"He is loved."

"Nice," I said again, pulling away[16] my arm. "But when I look at all those people sitting behind your son, you know what I can't help but notice[17]?"

"What?"

1. Honnêtement ?
2. que la prison c'était une question de
3. rééducation
4. ce n'est pas mon truc,
5. des jurys
6. creuser
7. Il y a des squelettes dans votre placard
8. persistez dans
9. chasse aux sorcières
10. je les exposerai au grand jour
11. prendre de l'assurance
12. une façon de réparer
13. Il me tenait toujours le bras.
14. Dernier avertissement
15. prêts à se battre
16. en dégageant
17. ce que je ne peux m'empêcher de remarquer

"Chamique Johnson," I said, "has no one sitting behind her."

"I would like to share[1] this journal entry[2] with the class," Lucy Gold said.

Lucy liked having her students form a big circle with their desks. She stood in the center of it. Sure[3], it was hokey[4], her stalking around the "ring of learning"[5] like the bad-guy wrestler[6], but she found it worked. When you put the students in a circle, no matter how large[7], they all had front-row seats[8]. There was no place to hide.

Lonnie was in the room. Lucy had considered[9] letting him read the entry so she could better study the faces, but the narrator was female. It wouldn't sound right[10]. Besides, whoever wrote this[11] *knew* that Lucy would be watching for a reaction[12]. Had to know.[13] Had to be screwing with her mind.[14] So Lucy decided that she would read it while Lonnie searched for reactions. And of course, Lucy would look up a lot, pausing during the reading, hoping something would give[15].

Sylvia Potter, the brownnoser[16], was directly[17] in front of her. Her hands were folded and her eyes were wide. Lucy met her eye and gave her a small smile. Sylvia brightened up.[18] Next to her was Alvin Renfro, a big-time slacker[19]. Renfro sat the way most students did, as though they had no bones[20] and might slide off[21] their chairs and become a puddle[22] on the floor.

"This happened when I was seventeen," Lucy read. "I was at summer camp. I worked there as a CIT. That stands for Counselor In Training..."

As she continued to read about the incident in the woods, the narrator and her boyfriend, "P", the kiss against the tree, the screams in the woods, she moved around the tight circle. She had read the piece at least a dozen times already, but now, reading out loud to others, she felt her throat start to constrict[23]. Her legs

1. partager
2. extrait de journal intime
3. D'accord
4. gnangnan
5. le fait d'arpenter ce « cercle du savoir »
6. le catcheur qui joue les méchants
7. quel que soit son diamètre
8. étaient tous assis au premier rang
9. envisagé de
10. ne sonnerait pas juste
11. l'auteur, quel qu'il soit,
12. guetterait les réactions
13. Il savait forcément.
14. Il se payait forcément sa tête.
15. que quelque chose transparaîtrait
16. lèche-bottes
17. juste
18. Le visage de Sylvia s'égaya.
19. un vrai fumiste
20. d'ossature
21. glisser de
22. se transformer en flaque
23. se serrer

turned rubbery[1]. She shot[2] a quick glance at Lonnie. He had heard something in her tone too, was looking at her. She gave him a look that said, "You're supposed to be watching them, not me," and he quickly turned away.

When she finished, Lucy asked for comments. This request pretty much always followed the same route[3]. The students knew that the author was right there, in this very room[4], but because the only way to build yourself up is to tear others down[5], they ripped into the work with a fury[6]. They raised their hands and always started with some sort of disclaimer[7], like, "Is it just me?" or "I could be wrong about this, but," and then it began:

"The writing is flat[8]...."

"I don't feel her passion for this P, do you?..."

"Hand under the shirt? Please..."

"Really, I thought it was just dreck[9]."

"The narrator says, 'We were kissing, it was so passionate.' Don't *tell* me it was passionate. *Show* me..."

Lucy moderated[10]. This was the most important part of the class. It was hard to teach students. She often thought back[11] to her own education, the hours of mind-numbing lectures[12], and could not remember one thing from any of them. The lessons she had truly learned, the ones she internalized and recalled and put to use[13], were the quick comments a teacher would make during discussion time. Teaching was about quality, not quantity. You talk too much, you become Muzak[14] – annoying[15] background[16] music. If you say very little, you can actually score[17].

Teachers also like attention. That can be a danger too. One of her early professors had given her sound[18] and simple advice[19] on this: It's not all about you.[20] She kept that front and center at all times.[21] On the other hand, students didn't want you floating above the fray[22]. So when she did tell the occasional anecdote, she tried to make it one where she

1. commencèrent à trembler
2. jeta
3. déclenchait presque toujours la même réaction
4. dans cette même salle
5. de se construire, c'est de démolir les autres
6. se déchaînaient sur le texte comme des enragés
7. une formule pour se dissocier de la critique
8. Le style est plat
9. de la merde
10. animait le débat
11. repensait
12. cours magistraux abrutissants
13. qu'elle avait assimilées, qu'elle se rappelait et avait utilisées
14. un fond sonore
15. pénible
16. d'ambiance
17. marquez vraiment des points
18. bon
19. conseil
20. Tout ne tourne pas autour de vous.
21. Elle gardait toujours ça en tête.
22. qu'on se place trop au-dessus de la mêlée

messed up[1] – there were plenty of those anyway – and how, despite that, she ended up okay[2].

Another problem was that students did not say what they truly believed as much as[3] what they hoped would impress[4]. Of course this was true at the faculty meetings[5] too – the priority was sounding good[6], not telling the truth.

But right now Lucy was being a bit more pointed than usual[7]. She wanted reactions. She wanted the author to reveal him- or herself. So she pushed[8].

"This was supposed to be memoir[9]," she said. "But does anybody really believe this happened?"

That quieted the room. There were unspoken rules[10] here. Lucy had pretty much called out the author[11], called her a liar. She backtracked[12]. "What I mean to say is, it reads like[13] fiction. That is usually a good thing, but does it make it difficult in this case? Do you start to question the veracity[14]?"

The discussion was lively[15]. Hands shot up[16]. Students debated one another. This was the high of the job[17]. Truth was, she had very little in her life. But she loved these kids. Every semester she fell in love all over again. They were her family, from either September through December or January through May. Then they left her. Some came back. Very few. And she was always glad to see them. But they were never her family again. Only the current[18] students achieved that status[19]. It was weird.

During some point[20], Lonnie headed out[21]. Lucy wondered where he was going, but she was lost[22] in the class. On some days, it ended too quickly. This was one of them. When time ran out and the students started packing their backpacks, she was no closer to knowing[23] who had sent her that anonymous journal.

"Don't forget," Lucy said. "Two more pages of the journals. I'd like them in by tomorrow[24]." Then she added, "Uh, you can send more than two pages, if you want. Whatever you have for me."

1. où elle avait raté
2. elle s'en était bien tirée
3. mais plutôt
4. ce avec quoi ils espéraient impressionner
5. réunions de professeurs
6. c'était d'avoir des propos qui plaisent
7. un peu plus directe que d'habitude
8. insista
9. autobiographique
10. des règles tacites
11. venait quasiment d'interpeller l'auteur
12. fit marche arrière
13. ressemble à
14. douter de sa véracité
15. animée
16. se levèrent d'un coup
17. le bon côté de ce métier
18. du moment
19. se voyaient accorder ce statut
20. À un moment donné
21. sortit
22. absorbée
23. ignorait toujours
24. que vous les remettiez d'ici demain

Ten minutes later, she arrived at her office. Lonnie was already there.

"You see anything in their faces?" she asked.

"No," he said.

Lucy started packing her stuff[1], jamming[2] papers into her laptop bag[3].

"Where are you going?" Lonnie asked.

"I have an appointment."

Her tone kept him from asking any more. Lucy kept this particular "appointment"[4] once a week, but she didn't trust anyone with that information[5]. Not even Lonnie.

"Oh," Lonnie said. His eyes were on the floor. She stopped.

"What is it, Lonnie?"

"Are you sure you want to know who sent the journal? I mean, I don't know, this whole thing is such a betrayal[6]."

"I need to know."

"Why?"

"I can't tell you."

He nodded. "Okay, then."

"Okay, what?"

"When will you be back?"

"An hour, maybe two."

Lonnie checked his watch. "By then[7]," he said, "I should know who sent it."

1. à mettre ses affaires dans son sac
2. fourrant
3. la sacoche de son ordinateur
4. allait à ce rendez-vous
5. personne n'était dans la confidence
6. représente une telle trahison
7. D'ici là

Chapter 9

The trial was postponed[1] for the afternoon.

There were those who would argue[2] that this made a difference in the case – that the jury would be left overnight with my direct and that it would settle in[3], blah, blah, blah. That sort of strategizing was nonsense[4]. It was the life cycle of a case. If there was a positive in this development[5], it would be offset[6] by the fact that Flair Hickory would now have more time to prepare his cross[7]. Trials work like that. You get hysterical about it[8], but stuff like this tends to even out[9].

I called Loren Muse on my cell. "You have anything yet?"

"Still working on it."

I hung up and saw there was a message from Detective York. I wasn't sure what to do anymore about Mrs. Perez lying about the scar on Gil's arm. If I confronted her with it, she would probably say she just got mixed up[10]. No harm, no foul.[11]

But why would she have said it in the first place?[12]

Was she, in fact, telling what she believed to be the truth[13] – that this body did not belong to her son? Were both Mr. and Mrs. Perez merely making a grievous[14] (but understandable) mistake here – that it

1. avait été ajourné
2. prétendaient
3. du coup, les jurés resteraient sur l'effet produit par mon interrogatoire
4. d'élucubration était absurde
5. S'il y avait vraiment un quelconque avantage à cet ajournement
6. pondéré
7. contre-interrogatoire
8. Ça peut être horripilant
9. ce genre de choses permet d'équilibrer les chances
10. qu'elle s'était trompée
11. Il n'y avait pas de mal à ça.
12. Mais alors pourquoi l'avoir affirmé ?
13. ce qu'elle croyait vrai
14. grave

was so hard to fathom[1] that their Gil had been alive this whole time[2] that they could not accept what their own eyes were showing them[3]?

Or were they lying?

And if they were lying, well, why?

Before I confronted them, I needed to have more facts on hand[4]. I would have to provide definitive proof[5] that the corpse in the morgue with the alias Manolo Santiago was really Gil Perez, the young man who had disappeared into the woods with my sister and Margot Green and Doug Billingham nearly twenty years ago.

York's message said: "Sorry it took me so long to get this. You asked about Raya Singh, the victim's girlfriend. We only had a cell on her[6], believe it or not. Anyway, we called up. She works at an Indian restaurant on Route 3 near the Lincoln Tunnel." He gave me the name and address. "She's supposed to be there all day. Hey, if you learn anything about Santiago's real name, let me know[7]. Far as we can tell[8], he's had the alias for a while[9]. We got some hits on him[10] out in the Los Angeles area from six years ago. Nothing heavy.[11] Talk to you later."

I wondered what to make of that[12]. Not much. I headed to my car, and as soon as I started to slide in, I knew something was very wrong.

There was a manila envelope sitting[13] on the driver's seat.

I knew it wasn't mine. I knew I hadn't left it here. And I knew that I had locked my car doors.

Someone had broken into[14] my car.

I stopped and picked up the envelope. No address, no postage[15]. The front was totally blank[16]. It felt thin.[17] I sat down in the front seat and closed the door behind me. The envelope was sealed[18]. I slit it open[19] with my index finger. I reached in[20] and plucked out the contents[21].

1. si pénible d'admettre
2. vivant tout ce temps
3. en croire leurs propres yeux
4. devais réunir davantage de faits
5. apporter la preuve formelle
6. n'avions que son portable
7. dites-le-moi
8. D'après nous
9. cela fait un moment qu'il utilisait ce faux nom
10. On a trouvé quelques délits qu'il a commis
11. Rien de très sérieux.
12. qu'en penser
13. Une enveloppe kraft était posée
14. s'était introduit dans
15. pas de timbre
16. vierge
17. Elle était toute plate.
18. cachetée
19. Je l'ouvris
20. Je mis la main dedans
21. en sortis le contenu

Ice poured in my veins[1] when I saw what it was: a photograph of my father.

I frowned. What the...?

On the bottom, neatly typed[2] on the white border[3], was his name: "Vladimir Copeland." That was all.

I didn't get it.[4]

I just sat there for a moment. I stared at the photograph of my beloved father. I thought about how he had been a young doctor in Leningrad, how so much had been taken away from him, how his life ended up being an endless series[5] of tragedies and disappointments. I remember him arguing[6] with my mother, both of them wounded[7] with no one to strike at but each other[8]. I remembered my mother crying by herself[9]. I remembered sitting some of those nights with Camille. She and I never fought[10] – weird for a brother and sister – but maybe we had seen enough. Sometimes she would take my hand or say that we should take a walk. But most of the time we would go into her room and Camille would put on one of her favorite dopey pop songs[11] and tell me about it, about why she liked it, as if it had hidden meanings[12], and then she'd tell me about some boy she liked at school. I would sit there and listen and feel the strangest contentment[13].

I didn't get it. Why was this photograph... ?

There was something else in the envelope.

I turned it upside down[14]. Nothing. I dug with my hand to the bottom[15]. It felt like an index card[16]. I pulled it into view.[17] Yep, an index card. White with red lines. That side – the lined side – was left blank. But on the other side – the side that was plain white[18] – someone had typed three words all in caps[19]:

THE FIRST SKELETON

"You know who sent the journal?" Lucy asked.

"Not yet," Lonnie said. "But I will."

1. Mon sang se glaça
2. En bas, soigneusement dactylographié
3. marge
4. Je n'y comprenais rien.
5. s'était soldée par une interminable série
6. se disputant
7. meurtris
8. et ne pouvant s'en prendre que l'un à l'autre
9. pleurant dans son coin
10. on ne se chamaillait jamais
11. chansons pop psychédéliques
12. un sens caché
13. une étrange sensation d'apaisement
14. la retournai vers le bas
15. mis ma main jusqu'au fond
16. fiche cartonnée
17. Je la sortis.
18. tout blanc
19. tout en majuscules

"How?"

Lonnie kept his head down. Gone was the confident swagger.[1] Lucy felt bad about that[2]. He didn't like what she was making him do. She didn't like it either. But there was no choice here. She had worked hard to conceal her past[3]. She had changed her name. She had not let Paul find her. She had gotten rid of her naturally blond hair – man, how many women her age had naturally blond hair? – and replaced it with this brown mess[4].

"Okay," she said. "You'll be here when I get back?"

He nodded. Lucy headed down the stairs to her car.

On TV it seems so easy to get a new identity. Maybe it was, but Lucy hadn't found that to be the case[5]. It was a slow process[6]. She started by changing her last name from Silverstein to Gold. Silver to Gold. Clever, no? She didn't think so, but somehow it worked for her, still gave her a link to[7] the father she had so loved.

She had moved around the country. The camp was long gone[8]. So were[9] all her father's assets[10]. And so, in the end, was most of her father[11].

What remained[12] of Ira Silverstein, her father, was housed[13] in a halfway house[14] ten miles[15] from the campus of Reston University. She drove, enjoying the time alone[16]. She listened to Tom Waits sing that he hoped he didn't fall in love, but of course, he does. She pulled into the lot[17]. The house, a converted mansion[18] on a large tract of land[19], was nicer than most[20]. Lucy's entire salary pretty much went here[21].

She parked near her father's old car, a rusted-out[22] yellow VW Beetle[23]. The Beetle was always in the exact same spot[24]. She doubted that it had moved from there in the past year. Her father had freedom here. He could leave anytime. He could check himself in and check out[25]. But the sad fact was, he almost never left his room. The leftist bumper stickers[26] that had adorned the vehicle had all faded away[27]. Lucy

1. Le fanfaron s'était envolé.
2. se le reprocha
3. pour cacher son passé
4. brun sale
5. n'avait pas trouvé ça si facile
6. processus lent
7. préservait le lien avec
8. avait disparu depuis longtemps
9. De même que
10. les biens
11. que lui-même, quasiment
12. Ce qu'il restait
13. demeurait
14. centre de réadaptation
15. à 16 km
16. moment solitaire
17. s'engagea dans le parking
18. manoir
19. vaste terrain
20. plus agréable que bien d'autres
21. y passait presque en totalité
22. toute rouillée
23. Coccinelle Volkswagen
24. place
25. entrer et sortir librement
26. autocollants gauchistes
27. étaient tout décolorés

had a copy of the VW key and every once in a while she started it up[1], just to keep the battery in operating order[2]. Doing that, just sitting in the car, brought flashbacks. She saw Ira driving it, the full beard[3], the windows open, the smile, the wave and honk[4] to everyone he passed.

She never had the heart to take it out for a spin[5].

Lucy signed in at the front desk[6]. This house was fairly specialized, catering to older residents[7] with lifelong drug and mental issues[8]. There seemed to be a tremendous range[9] in here, everything from those who appeared totally "normal" to people who could double as extras[10] in *One Flew Over the Cuckoo's Nest*[11].

Ira was a little of both.

She stopped in his doorway. Ira's back was to her.[12] He wore the familiar hemp[13] poncho. His gray hair was an every-direction shock[14]. "Let's Live for Today" by The Grass Roots, a classic from 1967, boomed[15] from what her father still called a "hi-fi." Lucy paused as Warren Entner did the big "1,2,3,4" countdown[16] before the group blasted in for another[17] "Sha-la-la-la-la, let's live for today." She closed her eyes and mouthed along with the words[18].

Great, great stuff.

There were beads[19] in the room and tie-dye[20] and a "Where Have All The Flowers Gone" poster. Lucy smiled, but there was little joy in it. Nostalgia was one thing – a deteriorating mind another.

Early[21] dementia had crept in[22] – from age or drug use, no one could say – and staked a claim[23]. Ira had always been spacey[24] and living in the past, so it was hard to say how gradual the slide[25] had been. That was what the doctors said. But Lucy knew that the initial break[26], the initial push down the slide[27], had occurred that summer. Ira took a lot of the blame for[28] what happened in those woods. It was his camp. He should have done more to protect his campers.

1. la faisait démarrer
2. en état de marche
3. barbe fournie
4. le salut et le coup de klaxon
5. pour faire un tour
6. réception
7. accueillant les personnes âgées
8. ayant toujours eu des problèmes de drogue ou des problèmes psychologiques
9. incroyable éventail
10. être des figurants
11. Vol au-dessus d'un nid de coucou
12. Ira lui tournait le dos.
13. en chanvre
14. masse ébouriffée
15. retentissait à plein volume
16. compte à rebours
17. ne crie encore
18. chanta les paroles en silence
19. des colliers de perles
20. des tissus à dégradés de couleurs
21. précoce
22. s'était déclarée
23. installée
24. avait toujours plané
25. dégringolade
26. détonateur
27. ce qui avait tout déclenché
28. C'est à Ira que l'on avait le plus reproché

The media went after him but not as hard as the families. Ira was too sweet a man to handle it. It broke him.

Ira barely left his room now. His mind bounced around decades[1], but this one – the sixties – was the only one he felt comfortable in. Half the time he actually thought it was still 1968[2]. Other times he knew the truth – you could see it in his expression – but he just didn't want to face it[3]. So as part of[4] the new "validation therapy[5]," his doctors let his room, for all intents and purposes, be[6] 1968.'

The doctor had explained that this sort of dementia did not improve with age, so you want the patient to be as happy and stress free as possible[7], even if that means living something of a lie[8]. In short[9], Ira wanted it to be 1968. That was where he was happiest. So why fight it?

"Hey, Ira."

Ira – he had never wanted her to call him "Dad" – did the slow "meds" turn[10] toward her voice. He raised his hand, as though underwater, and waved. "Hey, Luce."

She blinked away the tears[11]. He always recognized her, always knew who she was. If the fact that he was living in 1968 and his daughter hadn't even been born then seemed like a contradiction, well, it was. But that never shattered[12] Ira's illusion.

He smiled at her. Ira had always been too big-hearted[13], too generous, too childlike[14] and naive, for a world this cruel[15]. She would refer to him as an[16] "ex-hippie" but that implied that at some point Ira gave up being[17] a hippie. Long after everyone else had turned in[18] their tie-dyes and flower power[19] and peace beads[20], after the others had gotten haircuts[21] and shaved off their beards[22], Ira stayed true to[23] the cause.

During Lucy's wonderful childhood, Ira had never raised his voice to her. He had almost no filter,

1. était balloté d'une époque à l'autre
2. pensait vraiment être encore en 1968
3. l'affronter
4. dans le cadre de
5. thérapie de validation
6. rester, en somme, en
7. le moins stressé possible
8. vivre dans le mensonge
9. En fait
10. se tourna avec lenteur, comme le font ceux qui sont bourrés de médocs
11. ravala ses larmes
12. n'avait jamais brisé
13. été trop bon
14. puéril
15. aussi cruel
16. l'aurait bien qualifié de
17. cela aurait supposé qu'Ira ait arrêté d'être
18. eurent rangé
19. leurs symboles pacifistes
20. leurs colliers peace and love
21. eurent coupé leurs cheveux
22. et rasé leur barbe
23. fidèle à

no boundaries[1], wanting his daughter to see and experience everything, even what was probably inappropriate. Weirdly enough, that lack of censorship[2] had made his only child, Lucy Silverstein, somewhat prudish by the day's standards[3].

"I'm so happy you're here...," Ira said, half stumbling toward her.

She took a step in[4] and embraced him[5]. Her father smelled of age and body odor[6]. The hemp needed to be cleaned.

"How are you feeling, Ira?"

"Great. Never better.[7]"

He opened a bottle and took a vitamin. Ira did that a lot. Despite his noncapitalist ways[8], her father had made[9] a small fortune in vitamins during the early seventies. He cashed out[10] and bought that property[11] on the Pennsylvania/New Jersey border. For a while he ran it as a commune[12]. But that didn't last. So he turned it[13] into a summer camp.

"So how are you?" she asked.

"Never better, Luce."

And then he started crying. Lucy sat with him and held his hand. He cried, then he laughed, then he cried again. He kept telling her over and over[14] how much he loved her.

"You're the world[15], Luce," he said. "I see you... I see everything that should be. You know what I mean?"

"I love you too, Ira."

"See? That's what I mean. I'm the richest man in the world."

Then he cried again.

She couldn't stay long. She needed to get back to her office and see what Lonnie had learned. Ira's head was on her shoulder. The dandruff[16] and odor were getting to her[17]. When a nurse came in, Lucy used the interruption to extricate herself from him. She hated herself for it.[18]

"I'll be back next week, okay?"

1. limites
2. absence de censure
3. assez prude pour l'époque
4. entra dans la pièce
5. le prit dans ses bras
6. la transpiration
7. Comme jamais.
8. ses convictions non capitalistes
9. gagné
10. avait tout revendu
11. propriété
12. l'avait gérée comme une communauté
13. il l'avait transformée
14. encore et encore
15. Tu es tout pour moi
16. pellicules
17. l'incommodaient
18. Elle s'en voulut.

1. Comment va-t-il ?
2. de pure forme
3. allaient tous mal
4. ces derniers temps
5. ses changements d'humeur
6. désagréable
7. cela ne remonte pas aussi loin
8. Le cœur de Lucy fit un bond.
9. perd les pédales
10. Il se met à fulminer contre
11. des trucs comme ça
12. se mure dans son silence
13. Ça fait froid dans le dos.
14. et encore moins
15. bat parfois la campagne
16. Du bout du couloir
17. Il faut que je file.
18. regarda à nouveau

Ira nodded. He was smiling when she left.

In the corridor the nurse – Lucy forgot her name – was waiting for her. "How has he been?[1]" Lucy asked.

This was normally a rhetorical[2] question. These patients were all bad,[3] but their families didn't want to hear that. So the nurse would normally say, "Oh, he's doing just fine," but this time, she said, "Your father has been more agitated lately[4]."

"How so?"

"Ira is normally the sweetest, most gentle man in the universe. But his mood swings[5] – "

"He's always had mood swings."

"Not like these."

"Has he been nasty[6]?"

"No. It's not that...."

"Then what?"

She shrugged. "He's been talking about the past a lot."

"He always talks about the sixties."

"No, not that far in the past[7]."

"What then?"

"He talks about a summer camp."

Lucy felt a slow thud in her chest.[8] "What does he say?"

"He says he owned a summer camp. And then he loses it[9]. He starts ranting about[10] blood and the woods and the dark, stuff like that[11]. Then he clams up[12]. It's creepy.[13] And before last week, I never even heard him say a word about a camp, let alone[14] that he owned one. Unless, of course, well, Ira's mind does wander[15]. Maybe he's just imagining he did?"

It was said as a question, but Lucy didn't answer it. From down the hall[16] another nurse called, "Rebecca?"

The nurse, who she now realized was named Rebecca, said, "I have to run.[17]"

When Lucy was alone in the corridor, she looked back[18] in the room. Her father's back was to her. He was staring at[1] the wall. She wondered what was going on in his head. What he wasn't telling her.

What he really knew about that night.

She tore herself away[2] and headed toward the exit. She reached the receptionist, who asked her to sign out[3]. Each patient had his own page. The receptionist flipped to Ira's[4] and spun[5] the book for Lucy to sign. She had the pen in her hand and was about to do the same absent-minded scribble[6] she had done on the way in[7] when she stopped.

There was another name there.

Last week. Ira had another visitor. His first and only[8] visitor besides, well, her. Ever. She frowned and read the name. It was wholly unfamiliar.[9]

Who the hell was[10] Manolo Santiago?

1. regardait fixement

2. s'éloigna à contrecœur

3. signer le registre

4. tourna les pages jusqu'à celle d'Ira

5. retourna

6. gribouillis distrait

7. en arrivant

8. premier et unique

9. Il lui était totalement inconnu.

10. Qui diable était

Chapter 10

THE FIRST SKELETON

My father's photograph was still in my hand.

I needed now to make a detour on the way to my visit with Raya Singh. I looked at the index card. The First Skeleton. Implication[1]: There would be more than one.

But let's start with this one – my father.

There was only one person who could help me when it came to[2] my dad and his potential skeletons[3]. I took out my cell phone and held down the number six[4]. I rarely called this number, but it was still on my speed dial[5]. My guess is[6], it would always be.

He answered on the first ring in his low rumble of a voice[7]. "Paul."

Even the one word was thick with an accent.[8]

"Hi, Uncle Sosh."

Sosh wasn't really my uncle. He was a close[9] family friend from the old country. I hadn't seen him in[10] three months, not since my father's funeral, but as soon as I heard his voice, I instantly saw the big bear of a man[11]. My father said that Uncle Sosh had been the most powerful and feared[12] man in Pulko-

1. Sous-entendu
2. s'agissant de
3. éventuels squelettes dans le placard
4. appuyai sur le 6
5. encore dans mes numéros préenregistrés
6. À mon avis
7. de sa voix basse et rocailleuse
8. Rien qu'à ce seul mot on entendait son accent prononcé.
9. proche
10. depuis
11. sa carrure de grand ours
12. redouté

vo, the town on the outskirts[1] of Leningrad where they'd both been raised[2].

"It's been too long," he said.

"I know. I'm sorry about that."

"Acch," he said, as though disgusted[3] by my apology[4]. "But I thought that you would call today."

That surprised me. "Why?"

"Because, my young nephew, we need to talk."

"About what?"

"About why I never talk about anything over the phone."

Sosh's business[5] was, if not illegal, on the shadier side of the street[6].

"I'm at my place in the city." Sosh had an expansive[7] penthouse[8] on 36th Street in Manhattan. "When can you be here?"

"Half an hour if there's no traffic," I said.

"Splendid. I will see you then."

"Uncle Sosh?"

He waited. I looked at the photograph of my father on the passenger seat.

"Can you give me an idea what it's about[9]?"

"It's about your past, Pavel," he said through that thick accent, using my Russian name. "It's about what should stay in your past."

"What the hell does that mean?"

"We'll talk," he said again. And then he hung up.

There was no traffic, so the ride to[10] Uncle Sosh's was closer to[11] twenty-five minutes. The doorman[12] wore one of those ridiculous uniforms with rope tassels[13]. The look[14], interestingly enough with Sosh living here, reminded me of something Brezhnev[15] would have worn for the May Day parade[16]. The doorman knew my face[17] and had been told that I was arriving. If the doorman isn't told in advance, he doesn't ring up[18]. You just don't get in.

1. à la périphérie
2. où ils avaient grandi
3. comme s'il était écœuré
4. mes excuses
5. Les activités
6. sans être illégales, étaient un peu louches
7. vaste
8. [appartement de luxe avec terrasse]
9. de ce dont il s'agit
10. trajet jusque chez
11. ne prit que
12. portier
13. des passementeries
14. Ce style
15. Brejnev
16. défilé du 1er mai
17. me connaissait
18. il ne prévient pas

Sosh's old friend Alexei stood at the elevator door. Alexei Kokorov worked security for[1] Sosh, had[2] for as long as I could remember[3]. He was probably in his late sixties, a few years younger than Sosh, and as ugly a man as you'd ever see[4]. His nose was bulbous[5] and red, his face filled with spider veins[6] from, I assumed, too much drink. His jacket and pants didn't fit right[7], but his build[8] was not the kind made for haute couture.

Alexei didn't seem happy to see me, but he didn't look like lots of laughs[9] in general. He held the elevator door open for me. I stepped in without saying a word. He gave me a curt nod[10] and let the door close. I was alone.

The elevator opened into the[11] penthouse.

Uncle Sosh stood a few feet from the door. The room was huge. The furniture was cubist. The picture window[12] showed off an incredible view[13], but the walls had this thick wallpaper, tapestry-like, in a color that probably had some fancy[14] name like "Merlot" but looked to me like blood.

Sosh's face lit up[15] when he saw me. He spread his hands wide[16]. One of my most vivid[17] childhood memories was the size of those hands. They were still huge. He had grayed over the years[18], but even now, when I calculated that he was probably in his early seventies, I still felt the size and power and something approaching awe[19].

I stopped outside the elevator.

"What," he said to me, "you too old for a hug[20] now?"

We both stepped toward each other. The embrace[21] was, per his Russian background[22], a true bear hug[23]. Strength emanated from him. His forearms were still thick coils[24]. He pulled me close, and I felt as though he could simply tighten his grip[25] and snap my spine[26].

1. assurait la sécurité de
2. et ce
3. d'aussi longtemps que je me souvienne
4. c'était un homme d'une rare laideur
5. bulbeux
6. couperosé
7. ne tombaient pas bien
8. carrure
9. il n'avait jamais l'air de rigoler
10. me salua sèchement
11. L'ascenseur permettait d'accéder directement au
12. baie vitrée
13. offrait une vue incroyable
14. pompeux
15. s'illumina
16. ouvrit grand les bras
17. les plus marquants
18. Avec les années, ses cheveux grisonnaient
19. comme de l'admiration et du respect
20. pour que je te serre dans mes bras
21. embrassade
22. du fait de ses origines russes
23. une étreinte virile, en fait
24. encore très puissants
25. serrer son emprise
26. briser ma colonne

After a few seconds, Sosh grabbed my arms near the biceps and held me at arm's length[1] so he could take a good look.

"Your father," he said, his voice thick with more[2] than accent this time. "You look just like your father."

Sosh had arrived from the Soviet Union not long after we did. He worked for InTourist, the Soviet tour company[3], in their Manhattan office. His job was to help facilitate American tourists who wished to visit Moscow and what was then called Leningrad.

That was a long time ago. Since the fall[4] of the Soviet government, he dabbled in that murky enterprise[5] people labeled[6] "import-export." I never knew what that meant exactly, but it had paid for this penthouse.

Sosh looked at me another moment or two. He wore a white shirt unbuttoned low enough[7] to see the V-neck undershirt[8]. A huge tuft[9] of gray chest hair jutted out[10]. I waited. This would not take long. Uncle Sosh was not one for casual talk[11].

As if reading my mind[12], Sosh looked me hard in the eye[13] and said, "I have been getting calls.[14]"

"From?"

"Old friends."

I waited.

"From the old country," he said.

"I'm not sure I follow[15]."

"People have been asking questions."

"Sosh?"

"Yes?"

"On the phone you were worried about being overheard[16]. Are you worried about that here?"

"No. Here it is completely safe[17]. I have the room swept weekly.[18]"

"Great, then how about stopping with the cryptic[19] and telling me what you're talking about?"

He smiled. He liked that. "There are people. Americans. They are in Moscow and throwing money around[20] and asking questions."

1. à bout de bras
2. empreinte d'autre chose
3. tour-opérateur
4. la chute
5. trempait dans cette activité trouble
6. qu'on appelait
7. déboutonnée assez bas
8. col en V de son maillot de corps
9. touffe
10. dépassait
11. n'aimait pas trop échanger des banalités
12. s'il lisait dans mes pensées
13. droit dans les yeux
14. J'ai reçu des coups de fil.
15. de comprendre
16. craignais d'être sur écoute
17. totalement sûr
18. Je fais passer cette pièce au peigne fin toutes les semaines.
19. si tu arrêtais d'être énigmatique
20. distribuent de l'argent

I nodded to myself. “Questions about what?”

“About your father.”

“What kind of questions?”

“You remember the old rumors?”

“You’re kidding me.[1]”

But he wasn’t. And in a weird way, it made sense[2]. The First Skeleton. I should have guessed.

I remembered the rumors, of course. They had nearly destroyed my family.

My sister and I were born in what was then called the Soviet Union during what was then called the Cold War. My father had been a medical doctor but lost his license[3] on charges[4] of incompetence trumped up[5] because he was Jewish. That was how it was in those days.

At the same time, a reform[6] synagogue here in the United States – Skokie, Illinois, to be more specific – was working hard on behalf[7] of Soviet Jewry[8] . During the midseventies, Soviet Jewry was something of a cause célèbre in American temples[9] – getting Jews out of the Soviet Union.

We got lucky. They got us out[10].

For a long time we were heralded in our new land as heroes[11]. My father spoke passionately at Friday night services[12] about the plight[13] of the Soviet Jew. Kids wore buttons in support[14]. Money was donated.[15] But about a year into our stay[16], my father and the head rabbi[17] had a falling-out[18], and suddenly there were whispers[19] that my father had gotten out of the Soviet Union because he was actually KGB[20], that he wasn’t even Jewish, that it was all a ruse. The charges were pathetic and contradictory and false and now, well, more than twenty-five years old.

I shook my head. “So they’re trying to prove that my father was KGB?”

“Yes.”

Friggin[21]’ Jenrette. I got it, I guessed. I was something of a public figure[22] now. The charges, even

1. Tu plaisantes.
2. c’était cohérent
3. avait perdu le droit d’exercer
4. sur la base d’accusations
5. fabriquées de toutes pièces
6. du judaïsme réformé
7. en faveur
8. la communauté juive d’Union soviétique
9. lieux de culte
10. parvinrent à nous extraire de Russie
11. dans notre nouveau pays, on nous acclamait en héros
12. célébrations
13. situation désespérée
14. des badges en soutien
15. Il y eut des dons d’argent.
16. après notre installation
17. grand rabbin
18. se fâchèrent
19. le bruit se répandit
20. en réalité du KGB
21. Quelle enflure ce
22. pour ainsi dire un personnage public

if ultimately proven false[1], would be damaging[2]. I should know.[3] Twenty-five years ago, my family had lost pretty much everything due to those accusations. We left Skokie, moved east[4] to Newark. Our family was never the same.

I looked up.[5] "On the phone you said you'd thought I'd call."

"If you hadn't, I would have called you today."

"To warn me?[6]"

"Yes."

"So," I said, "they must have something."

The big man did not reply. I watched his face. And it was as if my entire world, everything I grew up believing[7], slowly shifted[8].

"Was he KGB, Sosh?" I asked.

"It was a long time ago," Sosh said.

"Does that mean yes?"

Sosh smiled slowly. "You don't understand how it was."

"And again I say: Does that mean yes?"

"No, Pavel. But your father... maybe he was supposed to be[9]."

"What's that supposed to mean?"

"Do you know how I came to this country?"

"You worked for a travel company[10]."

"It was the Soviet Union, Pavel. There were no companies. InTourist was run by[11] the government. Everything was run by the government. Do you understand?"

"I guess."

"So when the Soviet government had a chance[12] to send someone to live in New York City, do you think they sent the man who was most competent in booking vacations[13]? Or do you think they sent someone who might help them in other ways[14]?"

I thought about the size of his hands. I thought about his strength. "So you were KGB?"

1. même si elles se révélaient fausses au final
2. seraient compromettantes
3. J'en savais quelque chose.
4. avions déménagé sur la côte est
5. Je levai les yeux.
6. Pour me mettre en garde ?
7. tout ce en quoi j'avais cru en grandissant
8. basculait
9. censé en être
10. agence de voyages
11. sous contrôle du
12. eurent l'opportunité
13. le plus compétent pour s'occuper d'une agence de voyages
14. serait susceptible de les aider à d'autres niveaux

"I was a colonel in the military[1]. We didn't call it KGB. But yes, I guess you would call me" – he made quote marks with his fingers[2] – "'a spy[3]' I would meet with American officials[4]. I would try to bribe them[5]. People always think we learn important things – things that can change the balance of power[6]. That's such nonsense[7]. We learned nothing relevant[8]. Not ever. And the American spies? They never learned anything about us either. We passed nonsense from side to side.[9] It was a silly game."

"And my father?"

"The Soviet government let him out. Your Jewish friends think that they applied enough pressure[10]. But please. Did a bunch[11] of Jews in a synagogue really think they could pressure a government that answered to no one[12]? It's almost funny when you think about it."

"So you're saying... ?"

"I'm just telling you how it was. Did your father promise he would help the regime? Of course. But it was just to get out. It's complicated, Pavel. You can't imagine what it was like for him. Your father was a good doctor and a better man[13]. The government made up charges that he committed medical malpractice[14]. They took away his license. Then your grandmother and grandfather... my God, Natasha's wonderful parents... you're too young to remember – "

"I remember," I said.

"Do you?"

I wondered if I really did. I have that image of my grandfather, my Popi, and the shock of white hair[15] and maybe his boisterous[16] laugh, and my grandmother, my Noni, gently scolding him[17]. But I was three when they were taken away[18]. Did I really remember them, or has that old photo I still keep out come to life?[19] Was it a real memory[20] or something I'd created from my mother's stories?

1. l'armée
2. il forma des guillemets avec ses doigts
3. un espion
4. responsables
5. les soudoyer
6. rapport de forces
7. tellement absurde
8. de pertinent
9. Seules des informations sans importance passaient d'un camp à l'autre
10. que c'était grâce à la pression qu'ils avaient exercée
11. poignée
12. ne rendait de comptes à personne
13. quelqu'un de bien
14. d'avoir commis une erreur médicale
15. tignasse blanche
16. sonore
17. qui le grondait gentiment
18. ils furent arrêtés
19. cette vieille photo toujours exposée chez moi prenait-elle vie ?
20. souvenir

"Your grandparents were intellectuals – university professors. Your grandfather headed[1] the history department. Your grandmother was a brilliant mathematician. You know this, yes?"

I nodded. "My mother said she learned more from the debates[2] at the dinner table than at school."

Sosh smiled. "Probably true. The most brilliant academics[3] sought out[4] your grandparents. But, of course, that drew[5] the attention of the government. They were labeled radicals[6]. They were considered dangerous. Do you remember when they were arrested?"

"I remember," I said, "the aftermath[7]."

He closed his eyes for a long second. "What it did to your mother?"

"Yes."

"Natasha was never the same. You understand that?"

"I do."

"So here he was, your father. He had lost so much – his career, his reputation, his license and now your mother's parents. And suddenly, down like he was[8], the government gave your father a way out[9]. A chance for a fresh start[10]."

"A life in the USA."

"Yes."

"And all he had to do was spy?"

Sosh waved a dismissive hand[11] in my direction. "Don't you get it? It was a big game. What could a man like your father learn? Even if he tried – which he didn't. What could he tell them?"

"And my mother?"

"Natasha was just a woman to them[12]. The government cared nothing for the woman[13]. She was a problem for a while. Like I said, her parents, your grandparents, were radicals in their eyes. You say you remembered when they were taken?"

"I think I do."

1. dirigeait
2. lors des discussions
3. universitaires
4. faisaient appel à
5. éveilla
6. catalogués comme radicaux
7. les répercussions
8. alors qu'il était au plus bas
9. porte de sortie
10. de repartir à zéro
11. fit un geste dédaigneux
12. son épouse pour eux
13. se fichait éperdument d'elle

"Your grandparents formed[1] a group, trying to get the human rights abuses out to the public[2]. They were making headway[3] until a traitor turned them in[4]. The agents came at night."

He stopped.

"What?" I said.

"This isn't easy to talk about. What happened to them."

I shrugged. "You can't hurt them now."

He did not reply.

"What happened, Sosh?"

"They were sent to a gulag – a work camp. The conditions were terrible. Your grandparents were not young. You know how it ended?"

"They died," I said.

Sosh turned away from me then. He moved over to the window. He had a great view of the Hudson. There were two mega-cruise ships[5] in port. You could turn to the left and even see the Statue of Liberty. Manhattan is so small, eight miles[6] from end to end[7], and like with Sosh, you just always feel its power.

"Sosh?"

When he spoke again, his voice was soft. "Do you know how they died?"

"Like you said before. The conditions were terrible. My grandfather had a heart condition[8]."

He still hadn't turned toward me. "The government wouldn't treat him[9]. Wouldn't even give him his medicine.[10] He was dead within[11] three months."

I waited.

"So what aren't you telling me, Sosh?"

"Do you know what happened to your grandmother?"

"I know what my mother told me."

"Tell me," he said.

"Noni got sick too. With her husband gone, her heart sorta gave out[12]. You hear about it all the time in long-term[13] couples. One dies[14], then the other gives up[15]."

1. avaient constitué
2. dénoncer les atteintes aux droits de l'homme
3. Ils progressaient bien
4. les dénonce
5. énormes paquebots de croisière
6. 12,8 km
7. d'un bout à l'autre
8. des problèmes cardiaques
9. a refusé de le soigner
10. Il ne voulait même pas lui fournir ses médicaments.
11. en moins de
12. son cœur aurait lâché
13. ensemble depuis longtemps
14. Si l'un d'eux meurt
15. se laisse mourir à son tour

He said nothing.

"Sosh?"

"In a sense[1]," he said, "I guess that was true."

"In a sense?"

Sosh kept his eyes on whatever was out the window. "Your grandmother committed suicide."

My body stiffened[2]. I started shaking my head.

"She hung herself[3] with a sheet[4]."

I just sat there. I thought of that picture of my Noni. I thought of that knowing smile[5]. I thought of the stories my mother told me about her, about her sharp mind[6] and sharper tongue[7]. Suicide.

"Did my mother know?" I asked.

"Yes."

"She never told me."

"Maybe I shouldn't have either."

"Why did you?"

"I need you to see how it was. Your mother was a beautiful woman. So lovely and delicate. Your father adored her. But when her parents were taken and then, well, put to death really[8], she was never the same. You sensed it[9], yes? A melancholy there?[10] Even before your sister."

I said nothing, but I had indeed[11] sensed it. "I guess I wanted you to know how it was," he said. "For your mother. So maybe you'd understand more."

"Sosh?"

He waited. He still had not turned from the window.

"Do you know where my mother is?"

The big man didn't answer for a long time.

"Sosh?"

"I used to know," he said. "When she first ran away.[12]"

I swallowed. "Where did she go?"

"Natasha went home."

"I don't understand."

"She ran back[13] to Russia."

"Why?"

1. D'une certaine façon
2. se raidit
3. s'est pendue
4. drap
5. sourire complice
6. esprit vif
7. sa parole incisive
8. en quelque sorte exécutés
9. Tu l'as senti
10. Cette mélancolie en elle ?
11. effectivement
12. Lorsqu'elle s'est enfuie.
13. est repartie

"You can't blame her[1], Pavel."

"I don't. I want to know why."

"You can run away from your home like they did. You try to change. You hate your government but never your people[2]. Your homeland[3] is your homeland. Always."

He turned to me. Our eyes locked.[4]

"And that's why she ran?"

He just stood there.

"That was her reasoning?" I said, almost shouting. I felt something in my blood tick[5]. "Because her homeland was always her homeland?"

"You're not listening."

"No, Sosh, I'm listening. Your homeland is your homeland. That's a load of crap.[6] How about your family is your family? How about your husband is your husband – or more to the point[7], how about your son is your son?"

He did not reply.

"What about us[8], Sosh? What about me and Dad?"

"I don't have an answer for you, Pavel."

"Do you know where she is now?"

"No."

"Is that the truth?"

"It is."

"But you could find her, couldn't you?"

He didn't nod but he didn't shake his head either.

"You have a child," Sosh said to me. 'You have a good career[9]."

"So?"

"So this is all so long ago[10]. The past is for the dead[11], Pavel. You don't want to bring the dead back. You want to bury them[12] and move on[13]."

"My mother isn't dead," I said. "Is she?"

"I don't know."

"So why are you talking about the dead? And Sosh? While we're talking about the dead[14], here's one more thing to chew over[15]" – I couldn't stop myself,

1. le lui reprocher
2. ton peuple
3. pays natal
4. Nous nous regardâmes dans les yeux.
5. sentis mon sang battre dans mes veines
6. Ce ne sont que des conneries.
7. plus précisément
8. Et nous, alors
9. belle carrière
10. tout ça date tellement
11. appartient aux morts
12. dois les enterrer
13. avancer
14. Puisque l'on parle des morts
15. à méditer

so I just said it – "I'm not even sure my sister is dead anymore."

I expected to see shock[1] on his face. I didn't. He barely seemed surprised[2].

"To you[3]," he said.

"To me, what?"

"To you," he said, "they should both be dead[4]."

1. Je m'attendais à voir de la stupéfaction
2. eut à peine l'air surpris
3. Pour toi
4. il vaudrait mieux qu'elles soient mortes toutes les deux

Chapter 11

I shook off[1] Uncle Sosh's words and headed back through[2] the Lincoln Tunnel. I needed to focus[3] on two things and two things only: Focus One[4], convict[5] those two damned sons of bitches[6] who had raped Chamique Johnson. And Focus Two, find out where the hell Gil Perez had been[7] for the past twenty years.

I checked[8] the address Detective York had given me for the witness[9]/girlfriend. Raya Singh worked at an Indian restaurant called Curry Up[10] and Wait. I hate pun titles[11]. Or do I love them? Let's go with love.[12]

I was on my way.

I still had the picture of my father in the front seat. I didn't much worry about those KGB allegations. I had almost expected it after my conversation with Sosh. But now I read the index card again:

THE FIRST SKELETON

The First. That again implied that more would be coming.[13] Clearly Monsieur Jenrette, probably with financial help from Marantz, was sparing no expense[14]. If they found out about those old accusations against

1. mis de côté
2. rentrai par
3. Il fallait que je me concentre
4. Objectif numéro un
5. faire condamner
6. salopards
7. où diable était passé Gil Perez
8. vérifiai
9. témoin
10. [jeu de mots avec hurry up]
11. les noms qui jouent sur les mots
12. Disons que je les aime.
13. Cela signifiait qu'il y en aurait d'autres.
14. ne regardait pas à la dépense

my father – more than twenty-five years old now – they were clearly desperate[1] and hungry[2].

What would they find?

I was not a bad guy. But I wasn't perfect either. No one was. They would find something. They would blow it out of proportion[3]. It could seriously damage[4] JaneCare, my reputation, my political ambition – but then again Chamique had skeletons too. I had convinced her to take them all out and show them to the world. Could I ask less of myself?

When I arrived at the Indian restaurant, I threw the car into park[5] and turned off the ignition[6]. I was not in my jurisdiction[7], but I didn't think that would matter much. I took a look out the car window, thought again about that skeleton and called Loren Muse. When she answered I identified myself and said, "I may have a small problem."

"What's that?" Muse asked.

"Jenrette's father is coming after me[8]."

"How?"

"He's digging into my past[9]."

"Will he find anything?"

"You dig into anybody's past," I said, "you find something."

"Not mine[10]," she said.

"Really? How about those dead bodies[11] in Reno?"

"Cleared of all charges.[12]"

"Great, terrific."

"I'm just playing with you[13], Cope. Making a funny.[14]"

"You're hilarious[15], Muse. Your comic timing.[16] It's pro-like[17]."

"Okay, cut to the chase then[18]. What do you need from me?"

"You're friends with some of the local private eyes[19], right?"

"Right."

1. prêts à tout
2. sur les dents
3. le monteraient en épingle
4. gravement compromettre
5. je me garai
6. coupai le contact
7. secteur
8. me cherche des noises
9. fouille mon passé
10. Pas dans le mien
11. cadavres
12. Totalement blanchie.
13. Je me paie ta tête, c'est tout
14. Je plaisante.
15. tordante
16. Toujours la blague au bon moment.
17. très professionnel
18. alors dis-moi carrément
19. détectives privés

"Call around.[1] See if you can find out who's on me[2]."

"Okay, I'm on it[3]."

"Muse?"

"What?"

"This isn't a priority. If the manpower isn't there[4], don't worry about it."

"It's there, Cope. Like I said, I'm on it."

"How do you think we did[5] today?"

"It was a good day for the good guys[6]," she said.

"Yeah."

"But probably not good enough."

"Cal and Jim?"

"I'm in the mood to gun down[7] every man with those names."

"Get on it[8]," I said and hung up.

In terms of interior decorating, Indian restaurants seem to break down[9] into two categories – very dark and very bright. This one was bright and colorful[10] in the pseudostyle of a Hindu temple, albeit a really cheesy one[11]. There were faux-mosaic[12] and lit-up[13] statues of Ganesh and other deities[14] with which I am wholly unfamiliar[15]. The waitresses were costumed in belly-revealing aqua[16]; the outfits[17] reminded me of what the evil[18] sister wore on *I Dream of Jeannie*[19].

We all hold on to our stereotypes[20], but the whole scene looked as if a Bollywood musical number[21] were about to break out[22]. I try to have an appreciation for[23] various foreign cultures, but no matter how hard I try[24], I detest the music they play in Indian restaurants. Right now it sounded like a sitar was torturing a cat.

The hostess frowned when I entered. "How many?" she asked.

"I'm not here to eat," I said.

She just waited.

"Is Raya Singh here?"

"Who?"

1. Appelle-les.
2. qui colle à mes basques
3. je m'en occupe
4. Si tu n'as pas le temps
5. qu'on s'en est sortis
6. une bonne journée pour les gentils
7. J'ai envie de flinguer
8. Au travail
9. se diviser
10. bariolé
11. mais alors très kitsch
12. mosaïques en trompe-l'œil
13. lumineuses
14. divinités
15. auxquelles je ne connais rien
16. portaient du turquoise, le ventre à l'air
17. tenues
18. méchante
19. [Jinny de mes rêves, série où l'héroïne est un mauvais génie et une princesse des Mille et Une Nuits]
20. sommes tous prisonniers de nos clichés
21. une scène de comédie musicale
22. allait commencer
23. m'initier
24. malgré tous mes efforts

I repeated the name.

"I don't... oh, wait, she's the new girl." She folded her arms across her chest and said nothing.

"Is she here?" I said.

"Who wants to know?"

I did the eyebrow arch.[1] I wasn't good with it. I was going for rakish[2] but it always came out more like constipation[3]. "The President of the United States."

"Huh?"

I handed her a business card[4]. She read it and then surprised me by shouting out, "Raya! Raya Singh!"

Raya Singh stepped forward and I stepped back[5]. She was younger than I'd expected, early twenties[6], and absolutely stunning[7]. The first thing you noticed – couldn't help but notice in that aqua getup[8] – was that Raya Singh had more curves[9] than seemed anatomically possible. She stood still[10] but it looked as though she were moving. Her hair was tousled[11] and black and begged to be touched[12]. Her skin was more gold than brown and she had almond[13] eyes that a man could slip into and never find his way back out of[14].

"Raya Singh?" I said.

"Yes."

"My name is Paul Copeland. I'm the prosecutor for Essex County. Could we talk a moment?"

"Is this about the murder?"

"Yes."

"Then of course."

Her voice was polished[15] with a hint[16] of a New England-boarding-school[17] accent that shouted refinement over geographical locale[18]. I was trying not to stare[19]. She saw that and smiled a little. I don't want to sound like some kind of pervert because it wasn't like that. Female[20] beauty gets to me[21]. I don't think I'm alone in that[22]. It gets to me like a work of art gets to me. It gets to me like a Rembrandt or Michelangelo. It gets to me like night views of Par-

1. Je levai un sourcil.
2. Je voulais prendre un air canaille
3. au final, j'avais plutôt l'air constipé
4. carte de visite
5. s'avança dans la pièce tandis que je reculai
6. à peine vingt ans
7. ravissante
8. accoutrement
9. formes
10. se tenait immobile
11. ébouriffés
12. ne demandaient qu'à être caressés
13. en amande
14. à vous faire chavirer
15. distinguée
16. un soupçon
17. d'une pension
18. trop raffiné pour l'endroit où elle travaillait
19. de ne pas la dévisager
20. des femmes
21. me touche
22. être un cas isolé

is or when the sun rises on the Grand Canyon or sets[1] in the turquoise of an Arizona sky. My thoughts were not illicit[2]. They were, I self-rationalized[3], rather artistic.

She led me outside onto the street, where it was quieter. She wrapped her arms around herself[4] as though she were cold. The move[5], like pretty much every[6] move she made, was nearly a double entendre[7]. Probably couldn't help it. Everything about her[8] made you think about moonlit skies[9] and four-poster beds[10] – and that, I guess, shoots down[11] my "rather artistic" reasoning. I was tempted to offer her my coat or something, but it wasn't cold at all. Oh, and I wasn't wearing a coat.

"Do you know a man named Manolo Santiago?" I asked.

"He was murdered," she said.

Her voice had a strange lilt to it[12], as if she were reading for a part[13].

"But you knew him?"

"I did, yes."

"You were lovers[14]?"

"Not yet."

"Not yet?"

"Our relationship," she said, "was platonic."

My eyes moved to the pavement[15] and then across the street. Better. I didn't really care so much[16] about the murder or who had committed it. I cared about finding out about Manolo Santiago.

"Do you know where Mr. Santiago lived?"

"No, I'm sorry, I don't."

"How did you two meet?"

"He approached me[17] on the street."

"Just like that? He just walked up to you[18] on the street?"

"Yes," she said.

"And then?"

1. se couche
2. n'étaient pas coupables
3. me justifiai-je
4. mit ses bras autour de sa taille
5. Ce geste
6. à peu près tous les
7. suggestif
8. Tout chez elle
9. des ciels au clair de lune
10. des lits à baldaquin
11. démonte
12. une curieuse intonation
13. passait une audition
14. amants
15. trottoir
16. Je me souciais peu
17. m'a abordée
18. est juste venu vers vous

"He asked me if I would like to grab a cup of coffee[1]."

"And you did?"

"Yes."

I risked another look at her.[2] Beautiful. That aqua against the[3] dark skin... total killer[4]. "Do you always do that?" I asked.

"Do what?"

"Meet a stranger and accept his invitation to grab coffee with him?"

That seemed to amuse her. "Do I need to justify my behavior to you, Mr. Copeland?"

"No."

She said nothing.

I said, "We need to learn more about Mr. Santiago."

"May I ask why?"

"Manolo Santiago was an alias. I'm trying to find out his real name, for one thing[5]."

"I wouldn't know it."

"At the risk of overstepping my bounds[6]," I said, "I'm having trouble[7] understanding."

"Understanding what?"

"Men must hit on you[8] all the time," I said.

The smile was crooked and knowing.[9] "That's very flattering, Mr. Copeland, thank you."

I tried to stay on message[10]. "So why did you go with him?"

"Does it matter?"

"It might tell me[11] something about him."

"I can't imagine what. Suppose, for example, I told you that I found him handsome[12]. Would that help?"

"Did you?"

"Did I what – find him handsome?" Another smile. A tousled lock[13] dropped across her right eye. "You almost sound jealous."

"Ms. Singh?"

"Yes?"

1. prendre un café
2. Je la regardai à nouveau à la dérobée.
3. sur cette
4. vraiment irrésistible
5. d'abord
6. Sans vouloir dépasser les bornes
7. j'ai du mal à
8. vous draguer
9. Elle fit un sourire en coin, d'un air entendu.
10. de rester concentré
11. me révéler
12. bel homme
13. mèche rebelle

"I'm investigating a murder. So maybe we can stop now with the head games[1]."

"Do you think we can?" She tucked the hair back[2]. I held my ground.[3] "Well, okay then," she said. "Fair enough.[4]"

"Can you help me figure out[5] who he really was?"

She thought about it. "Maybe through his cell-phone records[6]?"

"We checked the one he had on him. Your call was the only one on it."

"He had another number," she said. "Before that."

"Do you remember it?"

She nodded and gave it to me. I took out a small pen and wrote it on the back of one of my cards.

"Anything else?"

"Not really."

I took out another card and wrote down my mobile phone number. "If you think of anything else, will you call me?"

"Of course."

I handed it to her. She just looked at me and smiled.

"What?"

"You're not wearing a wedding band[7], Mr. Copeland."

"I'm not married."

"Divorced or widowed[8]?"

"How do you know I'm not a lifelong bachelor[9]?"

Raya Singh did not bother replying.

"Widowed," I said.

"I'm sorry."

"Thank you."

"How long has it been?"

I was going to tell her none of her goddamn business[10], but I wanted to keep her in my good graces[11]. And damned if she wasn't beautiful.[12] "Nearly six years."

"I see," she said.

She looked at me with those eyes.[13]

"Thank you for your cooperation," I said.

1. ces petits jeux
2. bloqua la mèche derrière son oreille
3. Je tins bon.
4. Très bien.
5. à trouver
6. grâce aux relevés d'appels de son portable
7. d'alliance
8. veuf
9. célibataire endurci
10. que ce n'était pas ses oignons
11. qu'on reste en bons termes
12. Et Dieu qu'elle était belle.
13. Elle avait vraiment des yeux à se damner.

"Why don't you ask me out[1]?" she asked.

"Excuse me?"

"I know you think I'm pretty. I'm single[2], you're single. Why don't you ask me out?"

"I don't mix my work life with my personal[3]," I said.

"I came here from Calcutta. Have you been?"

The change in subjects threw me for a second[4]. The accent also didn't seem to match that locale[5], but that didn't mean much nowadays[6]. I told her I had never been, but I obviously knew of it.

"What you've heard," she said. "It's even worse."

Again I said nothing, wondering where she was going with this[7].

"I have a life plan[8]," she said. "The first part was getting here. To the United States."

"And the second part?"

"People here will do anything to get ahead[9]. Some play the lottery. Some have dreams of being, I don't know, professional athletes. Some turn to crime or strip or sell themselves. I know my assets[10]. I am beautiful. I am also a nice person and I have learned how to be" – she stopped and considered her words[11] – "good for a man. I will make a man incredibly happy. I will listen to him. I will be by his side. I will lift his spirits[12]. I will make his nights special.[13] I will give myself to him[14] whenever he wants and in whatever way he wants. And I will do it gladly[15]."

Oookay, I thought.

We were in the middle of a busy street[16] but I swear there was so much silence I could hear a cricket chirp[17]. My mouth felt very dry.

"Manolo Santiago," I said in a voice that sounded far away[18]. "Did you think he might be that man?"

"I thought he might be," she said. "But he wasn't. You seem nice. Like you would treat a woman well." Raya Singh might have moved toward me, I can't be sure. But she suddenly seemed closer[19]. "I can see

1. ne me donnez-vous pas rendez-vous
2. célibataire
3. le professionnel et le personnel
4. me désarçonna un instant
5. ne cadrait pas non plus avec cette région du monde
6. ne signifiait pas grand-chose de nos jours
7. où elle voulait en venir
8. un projet de vie
9. sont prêts à tout pour y arriver
10. ai conscience de mes atouts
11. choisit ses mots
12. lui remonterai le moral
13. Avec moi, ses nuits seront torrides.
14. m'offrirai à lui
15. avec plaisir
16. rue passante
17. que j'aurais pu entendre une mouche voler
18. semblait lointaine
19. très près

that you are troubled[1]. That you don't sleep well at night. So how do you know, Mr. Copeland?"

"How do I know what?"

"That I'm not the one[2]. That I'm not the one who will make you deliriously happy. That you wouldn't sleep soundly next to me[3]."

Whoa.

"I don't," I said.

She just looked at me. I felt the look in my toes.[4] Oh, I was being played[5]. I knew that. And yet this direct line[6], her lay-it-out-with-no-BS approach[7]... I found it oddly endearing[8].

Or maybe it was the blinded-by-beauty thing again[9].

"I have to go," I said. "You have my number."

"Mr. Copeland?" I waited.

"Why are you really here?"

"Excuse me?"

"What is your interest in Manolo's murder?"

"I thought I explained that. I'm the county prosecutor – "

"That's not why you're here."

I waited. She just stared at me. Finally I asked, "What makes you say that?"

Her reply landed like a left hook[10]. "Did you kill him?"

"What?"

"I said – "

"I heard you. Of course not. Why would you ask that?"

But Raya Singh shook it off[11]. "Good-bye, Mr. Copeland." She gave me one more[12] smile that made me feel like a fish dropped on a dock[13]. "I hope you find what you're looking for."

1. perturbé
2. celle qu'il vous faut
3. paisiblement à mes côtés
4. Ça me fit de l'effet de la tête aux pieds.
5. elle faisait tout pour me séduire
6. ses paroles franches
7. sa façon d'y aller sans détour [BS : abréviation de bullshit]
8. curieusement attachante
9. à nouveau cette beauté aveuglante
10. me fit l'effet d'un crochet du gauche
11. éluda la question
12. m'adressa un autre
13. qui me laissa pantois

Chapter 12

Lucy wanted to Google the name "Manolo Santiago" – he was probably a reporter doing a story[1] on that son of a bitch, Wayne Steubens, the Summer Slasher – but Lonnie was waiting for her in the office. He didn't look up when she entered. She stopped over him[2], aiming for mild intimidation[3].

"You know who sent the journals," she said.

"I can't be sure."

"But?"

Lonnie took a deep breath[4], readying himself[5], she hoped, to take the plunge[6]. "Do you know much about tracing[7] e-mail messages?"

"No," Lucy said, moving back to her desk.

"When you receive an e-mail, you know how there's all this gobbledygook[8] about paths[9] and ESMTP[10] and Message IDs[11]?"

"Pretend I do.[12]"

"Basically[13] it shows how the e-mail got to you[14]. Where it went, where it came from, what route via what Internet mail service to get from point A to point B. Like a bunch of postmarks[15]."

"Okay."

1. journaliste rédigeant un article
2. et se pencha au-dessus de lui
3. pour l'intimider un peu
4. respira un bon coup
5. prêt
6. à se jeter à l'eau
7. retrouver l'origine
8. charabia
9. sur les chemins d'accès
10. le transfert de mails vers les serveurs
11. les identifiants de messagerie
12. Fais comme si je savais.
13. En gros,
14. t'est parvenu
15. tout un tas de cachets de la poste

"Of course, there are ways of sending it out anonymously. But usually, even if you do that, there are some footprints[1]."

"Great, Lonnie, super." He was stalling[2]. "So can I assume[3] you found some of these footprints in the e-mail with[4] that journal attached[5]?"

"Yes," Lonnie said. He looked up now and managed a smile. "I'm not going to ask you why you want the name anymore."

"Good."

"Because I know you, Lucy. Like most hot chicks[6], you're a major pain in the ass[7]. But you're also frighteningly ethical[8]. If you need to betray the trust[9] of your class – betray your students and me and everything you believe – there must be a good reason. A life-or-death reason, I'm betting[10]."

Lucy said nothing.

"It is life or death, right?"

"Just tell me, Lonnie."

"The e-mail came from a bank of computers[11] at the Frost Library[12]."

"The library," she repeated. "There must be, what, fifty computers in there?"

"About that."

"So we'll never figure out who sent it."

Lonnie made a yes-and-no gesture with a head tilt[13]. "We know what time it was sent. Six forty-two p.m. the day before yesterday."

"And that helps us how?"

"The students who use the computer. They need to sign in[14]. They don't have to sign in to a particular computer – the staff did away with that[15] two years ago – but in order to get a computer, you reserve it for the hour[16]. So I went to the library and got the time sheets[17]. I compared a list of students in your class with students who had signed up for[18] a computer during the hour between six and seven p.m. the day before yesterday."

1. des traces
2. gagnait du temps
3. considérer
4. qui avait
5. en pièce jointe
6. nanas canon
7. sacrée emmerdeuse
8. as aussi un grand sens moral
9. trahir la confiance
10. je parie
11. groupe d'ordinateurs
12. bibliothèque
13. fit oui et non de la tête
14. s'inscrire
15. le personnel a arrêté cette procédure
16. pour un créneau d'une heure
17. feuilles de présence
18. avaient réservé

He stopped.

"And?"

"There was only one hit[1] with a student in this class."

"Who?"

Lonnie walked over to the window. He looked down at the quad. "I'll give you a hint[2]," he said.

"Lonnie, I'm not really in the mood – "

"Her nose," he said, "is brown.[3]"

Lucy froze[4]. "Sylvia Potter?"

His back was still to her.

"Lonnie, are you telling me that Sylvia Potter wrote that journal entry?"

"Yes," he said. "That's exactly what I'm telling you."

On the way back to the office, I called Loren Muse.

"I need another favor," I said.

"Shoot.[5]"

"I need you to find out all you can about a phone number. Who owned the phone. Who the guy called. Everything."

"What's the number?"

I gave her the number Raya Singh had told me.

"Give me ten minutes."

"That's it?[6]"

"Hey, I didn't become chief investigator because I have a hot ass[7]."

"Says who?[8]"

She laughed. "I like when you're a little fresh[9], Cope."

"Don't get used to it.[10]"

I hung up. My line[11] had been inappropriate – or was it a justifiable comeback[12] to her "hot ass" joke? It is simplistic to criticize political correctness[13]. The extremes make it an easy target for ridicule.[14] But I've also seen what it's like in an office workplace when that stuff is allowed to go on[15]. It can be intimidating and dark[16].

1. une seule concordance
2. un indice
3. C'est une lèche-bottes, dit-il.
4. se figea
5. Vas-y.
6. C'est tout ?
7. pour mon sex-appeal
8. C'est toi qui le dis.
9. J'aime bien quand t'es un peu effronté
10. Ne t'y habitue pas.
11. réplique
12. repartie excusable
13. le politiquement correct
14. Il y a de tels abus qu'il est facile de s'en moquer.
15. quand on laisse faire ce genre de choses
16. sinistre

1. en apparence
2. excessives
3. règles pour la sécurité des enfants
4. casque de cycliste
5. à tout prix
6. paillis
7. cage à poules
8. parcourir trois pâtés de maisons
9. au fait
10. protège-dents
11. de se moquer de tout ça
12. petit malin
13. à tout son répertoire
14. à cette époque
15. le mal était tapi
16. des camps de vacances
17. où l'on négligeait les règles de sécurité
18. avaient filé en douce
19. annuaire téléphonique
20. faire un saut à
21. littérature
22. passer quand j'aurai terminé

It's like those seemingly[1] overcautious[2] kid-safety rules[3] nowadays. Your child has to wear a bike helmet[4] no matter what[5]. You have to use a special mulch[6] in playgrounds and you can't have any jungle gym[7] where a kid could climb too high and oh yeah, your child shouldn't walk three blocks[8] without an escort and wait[9], where is your mouth guard[10] and eye protection? And it is so easy to poke fun at that stuff[11] and then some wiseass[12] sends out a random[13] e-mail saying, "Hey, we all did that and survived." But the truth is, a lot of kids didn't survive.

Kids did have a ton of freedom back then[14]. They did not know what evil lurked[15] in the darkness. Some of them went to sleepaway camp[16] in the days when security was lax[17] and you let kids be kids. Some of those kids sneaked[18] into the woods at night and were never seen again.

Lucy Gold called Sylvia Potter's room. There was no answer. Not surprising. She checked the school phone directory[19], but they didn't list mobile numbers. Lucy remembered seeing Sylvia using a BlackBerry, so she e-mailed a brief message asking Sylvia to call her as soon as possible.

It took less than ten minutes to get a response.

"You wanted me to call, Professor Gold?"

"I did, Sylvia, thank you. Do you think you could stop by[20] my office?"

"When?"

"Now, if that's possible."

Several seconds of silence.

"Sylvia?"

"My English lit[21] class is about to start," she said. "I'm presenting my final project today. Can I come by when I'm done[22]?"

"That would be fine," Lucy said.

"I should be there in about two hours."

"Great, I'll be here."

More silence.

"Can you tell me what this is about, Professor Gold?"

"It can keep[1], Sylvia. Don't worry about it. I'll see you after your class."

"Hey."

It was Loren Muse. I was back in the courthouse the next morning. Flair Hickory's cross[2] would start in a few minutes.

"Hey," I said.

"You look like hell.[3]"

"Wow, you are a trained[4] detective."

"You worried about this cross?"

"Of course."

"Chamique will be fine. You did a helluva job[5]."

I nodded, tried to get my head back into the game[6]. Muse walked next to me.

"Oh," she said, "that phone number you gave me? Bad news."

I waited.

"It's a throwaway."

Meaning[7] someone bought it with cash[8] with a preset number of minutes on it[9] and didn't leave a name. "I don't need to know who bought it," I said. "I just need to know what calls the phone made[10] or received."

"Tough to do[11]," she said. "And impossible through the normal[12] sources. Whoever it was[13], he bought it online[14] from some fly-by-night posing as another fly-by-night[15]. It'll take me a while to track it all down[16] and apply enough pressure to get records."

I shook my head. We entered the courtroom.

"Another thing," she said. "You heard of MVD?"

"Most Valuable Detection," I said.

"Right, biggest private-eye firm[17] in the state. Cingle Shaker, the woman I have on[18] the frat boys, used to work there. Rumor has it[19] they got a no-expense-

1. Cela peut attendre
2. contre-interrogatoire
3. Tu as une sale tête.
4. perspicace
5. un super boulot [helluva : hell of a]
6. j'essayai de fixer à nouveau mon attention sur le procès
7. C'est-à-dire que
8. l'avait payé en liquide
9. un forfait pour un certain nombre de minutes
10. a passés
11. Pas évident à faire
12. habituelles
13. Qui que soit l'individu
14. sur Internet
15. à un opérateur véreux se faisant passer pour un autre opérateur véreux
16. pour remonter à la source
17. agence de détectives privés
18. que j'ai mise sur
19. Il paraît

spared, seek-'n'-destroy investigation going on with you[1]."

I reached the front of the courtroom. "Super." I handed her an old picture of Gil Perez.

She looked at it. "What?"

"Do we still have Farrell Lynch doing the computer work[2]?"

"We do."

"Ask him to do an age progression on this[3]. Age him twenty years. Tell him to give him a shaved head too."

Loren Muse was about to follow up[4], but something in my face stopped her. She shrugged and peeled off[5]. I sat down. Judge Pierce came in. We all rose. And then Chamique Johnson took the stand[6].

Flair Hickory stood and carefully buttoned his jacket. I frowned. The last time I'd seen a powder blue[7] suit in that shade[8] was in a prom[9] picture from 1978. He smiled at Chamique.

"Good morning, Miss Johnson."

Chamique looked terrified. "Morning," she managed.

Flair introduced himself[10] as if they'd just stumbled across each other[11] at a cocktail party. He segued into[12] Chamique's criminal record. He was gentle but firm. She had been arrested for prostitution, correct? She had been arrested for drugs, correct? She had been accused of rolling a john[13] and taking eighty-four dollars, correct?

I didn't object.

This was all part of my warts-and-all[14] strategy. I had raised much of this[15] during my own examination, but Flair's cross was effective[16]. He didn't ask her yet to explain any of her testimony. He simply warmed up[17] by sticking to facts[18] and police records[19].

After twenty minutes, Flair began his cross in earnest[20]. "You have smoked marijuana, have you not?"

1. qu'une enquête qui coûtera les yeux de la tête a été lancée pour te couler
2. à l'informatique
3. d'en faire un vieillissement
4. d'enchaîner
5. s'en alla
6. prit place à la barre
7. bleu pastel
8. de cette couleur
9. de bal de fin d'année
10. se présenta
11. s'ils se rencontraient par hasard
12. passa méthodiquement en revue
13. avoir fait les poches à un client
14. visant à ne rien cacher
15. J'en avais dévoilé une bonne partie
16. efficace
17. s'échauffait
18. collant aux faits
19. au casier judiciaire
20. démarra réellement le contre-interrogatoire

Chamique said, "Yeah."

"Did you smoke any the night of your alleged attack[1]?"

"No."

"No?" Flair put his hand on his chest as though this answer shocked him to the core[2]. "Hmm. Did you imbibe[3] any alcohol?"

"Im-what?"

"Did you drink anything alcoholic[4]? A beer or wine maybe?"

"No."

"Nothing?"

"Nothing."

"Hmm. How about a regular drink[5]? Maybe a soda?"

I was going to object, but again my strategy was to let her handle this[6] as much as she could.

"I had some punch," Chamique said.

"Punch, I see. And it was nonalcoholic[7]?"

"That's what they said."

"Who?"

"The guys."

"Which guys?"

She hesitated. "Jerry."

"Jerry Flynn?"

"Yeah."

"And who else?"

"Huh?[8]"

"You said guys. With an *s* at the end. As in more than one?[9] Jerry Flynn would constitute[10] one guy. So who else told you that the punch you consumed – by the way[11], how many glasses did you have[12]?"

"I don't know."

"More than one."

"I guess."

"Please don't guess[13], Miss Johnson. Would you say more than one?"

"Probably, yeah."

"More than two?"

1. agression présumée
2. le choquait profondément
3. absorbé
4. d'alcoolisé
5. boisson normale
6. gérer ça
7. sans alcool
8. Quoi ?
9. Comme s'il y en avait plus d'un ?
10. représente
11. au fait
12. avez-vous bus
13. n'imaginez pas

"I don't know."

"But it's possible?"

"Yeah, maybe."

"So maybe more than two. More than three?"

"I don't think so."

"But you can't be sure[1]."

Chamique shrugged.

"You'll need to speak up[2]."

"I don't think I had three. Probably two. Maybe not even that much[3]."

"And the only person who told you that the punch was nonalcoholic was Jerry Flynn. Is that correct?"

"I think."

"Before you said 'guys' as in more than one. But now you're saying just one person. Are you changing your testimony?"

I stood. "Objection."

Flair waved me off[4]. "He's right, small matter[5], let's move on[6]." He cleared his throat and put a hand on his right hip[7]. "Did you take any drugs that night?"

"No."

"Not even a puff[8] from, say, a marijuana cigarette?"

Chamique shook her head, and then, remembering that she needed to speak, she leaned into[9] the microphone and said, "No, I did not."

"Hmm, okay. So when did you last do any sort of drugs[10]?"

I stood again. "Objection. The word *drugs* could be anything – aspirin, Tylenol..."

Flair looked amused. "You don't think everyone here knows what I'm talking about?"

"I would prefer clarification[11]."

"Ms. Johnson, I am talking about illegal drugs here[12]. Like marijuana. Or cocaine. Or LSD or heroin. Something like that. Do you understand?"

"Yeah, I think so."

"So when did you last take any illegal drug?"

"I don't remember."

1. vous n'en êtes pas sûre
2. devez parler plus fort
3. même pas autant
4. repoussa d'un geste mon objection
5. broutille
6. poursuivons
7. sur sa hanche droite
8. une bouffée
9. se pencha sur
10. avez-vous pris de la drogue, sous toute forme, pour la dernière fois
11. que vous précisiez
12. dans le cas présent

"You said that you didn't take any the night of the party."

"That's right."

"How about the night before the party?"

"No."

"The night before that?"

Chamique squirmed just a little bit[1] and when she said, "No," I wasn't sure that I believed her.

"Let me see if I can help nail down the timetable[2]. Your son is fifteen months old, is that correct?"

"Yeah."

"Have you done any illegal drugs since he's been born[3]?"

Her voice was very quiet. "Yeah."

"Can you tell us what kind[4]?"

I stood yet again[5]. "I object. We get the point.[6] Ms. Johnson has done drugs in the past. No one denies that.[7] That doesn't make what Mr. Hickory's clients did any less horrible. What's the difference when?[8]"

The judge looked at Flair. "Mr. Hickory?"

"We believe that Ms. Johnson is a habitual drug user[9]. We believe that she was high[10] that night and the jury should understand that when assessing the integrity[11] of her testimony."

"Ms. Johnson has already stated[12] that she had not taken any drugs that night or *imbibed*" – I put the sarcastic emphasis[13] this time – "any alcohol."

"And I," Flair said, "have the right to cast doubt on her recollections[14]. The punch was indeed spiked[15]. I will produce Mr. Flynn, who will testify that the defendant[16] knew that when she drank it. I also want to establish that this is a woman who did not hesitate to do drugs, even when she was mothering a young child[17] – "

"Your Honor!" I shouted.

"Okay, enough." The judge cracked the gavel[18]. "Can we move along, Mr. Hickory?"

1. se tortilla un tout petit peu
2. aider à vous rafraîchir la mémoire pour que nous soyons sûrs des dates
3. depuis qu'il est né
4. de quel type
5. encore une fois
6. Nous avons bien compris.
7. Personne ne le réfute.
8. En quoi le moment fait-il une différence ?
9. consomme régulièrement de la drogue
10. qu'elle était sous son emprise
11. lorsqu'ils jugeront de la validité
12. déclaré
13. j'insistai avec sarcasme
14. le droit de mettre en doute ses souvenirs
15. alcoolisé
16. victime présumée
17. lorsqu'elle s'occupait d'un jeune enfant
18. actionna son marteau

"We can, Your Honor."

I sat back down. My objection had been stupid. It looked as if I was trying to get in the way[1] and worse, I had given Flair the chance to offer more narrative[2]. My strategy had been to stay silent. I had lost my discipline, and it had cost us[3].

"Ms. Johnson, you are accusing these boys of raping you, is that correct?"

I was on my feet.[4] "Objection. She's not a lawyer or familiar with legal definitions[5]. She told you what they did to her. It is the court's job to find the correct terminology."

Flair looked amused again. "I'm not asking her for a legal definition. I'm curious about her own vernacular[6]."

"Why? Are you going to give her a vocabulary test?"

"Your Honor," Flair said, "may I please question this witness?"

"Why don't you explain what you're after[7], Mr. Hickory?"

"Fine, I'll rephrase.[8] Miss Johnson, when you are talking to your friends, do you tell them that you were raped?"

She hesitated. "Yeah."

"Uh-huh. And tell me, Ms. Johnson, do you know anyone else who has claimed to be raped[9]?"

Me again. "Objection. Relevance?"

"I'll allow it."

Flair was standing near Chamique. "You can answer," he said, like he was helping her out[10].

"Yeah."

"Who?"

"Coupla[11] the girls I work with."

"How many?"

She looked up as if trying to remember. "I can think of two.[12]"

"Would these be[13] strippers or prostitutes?"

"Both.[14]"

1. d'interférer
2. l'opportunité d'en dire plus
3. on l'avait payé
4. Je me levai d'un coup.
5. rompue aux définitions juridiques
6. de connaître ses propres termes
7. votre intention
8. Fort bien, je vais reformuler.
9. qui affirme avoir été violée
10. comme s'il lui venait en aide
11. Deux ou trois [A couple of]
12. J'en ai deux en tête.
13. Seraient-elles
14. Les deux.

"One of each or – "

"No, they both do both[1]."

"I see. Did these crimes occur while they were working or while they were on their leisure time?"

I was up again. "Your Honor, I mean, enough[2]. What's the relevance?[3]"

"My distinguished colleague[4] is right," Flair said, gesturing with a full arm swing[5] in my direction. "When he's right, he's right. I withdraw[6] the question."

He smiled at me. I sat down slowly, hating every moment of it[7].

"Ms. Johnson, do you know any rapists?"

Me again. "You mean, besides[8] your clients?"

Flair just gave me a look and then turned to the jury as if to say, *My*[9], *wasn't that the lowest cheap shot ever*[10]*?* And truth: It was[11].

For her part[12], Chamique said, "I don't understand what you mean."

"No matter, my dear," Flair said, as if her answer would bore him[13]. "I'll get back to that later.[14]"

I hate when Flair says that.

"During this purported[15] attack, did my clients, Mr. Jenrette and Mr. Marantz, did they wear masks?"

"No."

"Did they wear disguises of any sort[16]?"

"No."

"Did they try to hide their faces?"

"No."

Flair Hickory shook his head as if this was the most puzzling thing[17] he had ever heard.

"And according to your testimony, you were grabbed against your will[18] and dragged into the room. Is that correct?"

"Yes."

"The room where Mr. Jenrette and Mr. Marantz resided?"

"Yes."

1. toutes les deux font les deux
2. vraiment, cela suffit
3. En quoi est-ce pertinent ?
4. éminent confrère
5. en agitant amplement son bras
6. retire
7. totalement écœuré
8. en dehors de
9. Eh bien
10. si ça, ce n'est pas un coup bas
11. honnêtement, c'était le cas
12. De son côté
13. allait le barber
14. J'y reviendrai plus tard.
15. prétendue
16. de quelconques déguisements
17. la chose la plus curieuse
18. avez été empoignée contre votre gré

"They didn't attack you outside, in the dark, or some place that couldn't be traced back to them[1]. Isn't that correct?"

"Yes."

"Odd, don't you think?"

I was about to object again, but I let it go[2].

"So it is your testimony[3] that two men raped you, that they didn't wear masks or do anything to disguise themselves, that they in fact showed you their faces, that they did this in their room with at least one witness watching you being forced to enter[4]. Is that correct?"

I begged[5] Chamique not to sound wishy-washy[6]. She didn't. "That sounds right, yeah."

"And yet[7], for some reason" – again Flair looked like the most perplexed man imaginable[8] – "they used aliases[9]?"

No reply. Good.

Flair Hickory continued to shake his head as though someone had demanded he make[10] two plus two equal[11] five. "Your attackers used the names Cal and Jim instead of their own. That's your testimony, is it not, Miss Johnson?"

"It is."

"Does that make any sense to you?[12]"

"Objection," I said. "Nothing about[13] this brutal crime makes sense to her."

"Oh, I understand that," Flair Hickory said. "I was just hoping, being that she was there[14], that Ms. Johnson might have a theory on why they would let their faces be seen and attack her in their own room – and yet use aliases." He smiled sweetly[15]. "Do you have one, Miss Johnson?"

"One what?"

"A theory on why[16] two boys named Edward and Barry would call themselves Jim and Cal?"

"No."

1. ne permettant pas de remonter jusqu'à eux
2. je le laissai faire
3. vous témoignez bien
4. être entraînée de force à l'intérieur
5. Je priais pour que
6. n'ait pas l'air trop gnangnan
7. pourtant
8. prit un air extrêmement perplexe
9. des faux noms
10. comme si on exigeait de lui qu'il démontre que
11. font
12. Cela vous paraît-il cohérent ?
13. Rien de ce qui touche à
14. étant donné qu'elle y était
15. gentiment
16. expliquant pourquoi

Flair Hickory walked back to his desk. "Before, I asked you if you knew any rapists. Do you remember that?"

"Yeah."

"Good. Do you?"

"I don't think so."

Flair nodded and picked up[1] a sheet of paper. "How about a man currently being incarcerated[2] in Rahway on charges of sexual battery[3] named – and please pay attention, Ms. Johnson – *Jim* Broodway?"

Chamique's eyes grew wide[4]. "You mean James?"

"I mean, Jim – or James, if you want the formal[5] name – Broodway who used to reside[6] at 1189 Central Avenue in the city of Newark, New Jersey. Do you know him?"

"Yeah." Her voice was soft. "I used to know him.[7]"

"Did you know that he is now in prison?"

She shrugged. "I know a lot of guys who are now in prison."

"I'm certain you do" – for the first time, there was bite[8] in Flair's voice – "but that wasn't my question. I asked you if you knew that Jim Broodway was in prison."

"He's not Jim. He's James – "

"I will ask one more time, Miss Johnson, and then I will ask the court to demand an answer[9] – "

I was up. "Objection. He's badgering[10] the witness."

"Overruled.[11] Answer the question."

"I heard something about it," Chamique said, and her tone was meek[12].

Flair did the dramatic sigh[13]. "Yes or no, Miss Johnson, did you know that Jim Broodway is currently serving time[14] in a state penitentiary[15]?"

"Yes."

"There.[16] Was that so hard?"

Me again. "Your Honor..."

"No need for the dramatics[17], Mr. Hickory. Get on with it."

1. saisit
2. actuellement incarcéré
3. pour agression sexuelle
4. écarquilla les yeux
5. officiel
6. demeurait
7. Je l'ai connu.
8. un ton incisif
9. d'exiger que vous répondiez
10. harcèle
11. Rejeté.
12. docile
13. soupira exagérément
14. purge actuellement sa peine
15. prison d'état
16. Bon.
17. Inutile de faire toute cette comédie

Flair Hickory walked back to his chair. "Have you ever had sex with Jim Broodway?"

"His name is James!" Chamique said again.

"Let's call him 'Mr. Broodway' for the sake[1] of this discussion, shall we? Have you ever had sex with Mr. Broodway?"

I couldn't just let this go. "Objection. Her sex life is irrelevant to this case[2]. The law is clear here[3]."

Judge Pierce looked at Flair. "Mr. Hickory?"

"I am not trying to besmirch[4] Miss Johnson's reputation or imply[5] that she was a woman of loose morals[6]," Flair said. "Opposing counsel[7] already explained very clearly that Miss Johnson has worked as a prostitute and has engaged in[8] a variety of sexual activities with a wide variety of men."

When will I learn to keep my mouth shut?

"The point I am trying to raise[9] is a different one and will not at all embarrass the defendant. She has admitted having sex with men. The fact that Mr. Broodway might be one of them is hardly stapling[10] a scarlet letter[11] to her chest."

"It's prejudicial[12]," I countered.

Flair looked at me as if I'd just dropped out of the backside of a horse[13]. "I just explained to you why it is very much not[14]. But the truth is, Chamique Johnson has accused two youths[15] of a very serious crime. She has testified that a man named Jim raped her. What I am asking, plain and simple[16], is this: Did she ever have sex with Mr. Jim Broodway – or James, if she prefers – who is currently serving time in a state penitentiary for sexual battery?"

I saw now where this was going. And it wasn't good.

"I'll allow it," the judge said.

I sat back down.

"Miss Johnson, have you ever had sexual relations with Mr. Broodway?"

A tear rolled down her cheek. "Yeah."

1. dans l'intérêt
2. n'a rien à voir avec cette affaire
3. limpide à ce propos
4. souiller
5. de sous-entendre
6. mœurs légères
7. La partie adverse
8. se livre à
9. soulever
10. ne veut pas dire qu'on lui colle
11. [La Lettre écarlate, de N. Hawthorne : l'héroïne accusée d'adultère est condamnée à porter la lettre A sur sa poitrine]
12. C'est préjudiciable
13. je débarquais
14. ce n'est pas du tout le cas
15. jeunes gens
16. purement et simplement

"More than once?[1]"

"Yeah."

It looked like Flair was going to try to be more specific[2], but he knew better than to pile on[3]. He changed directions a little[4]. "Were you ever drunk or high while having sex[5] with Mr. Broodway?"

"Might have been.[6]"

"Yes or no?"

His voice was soft but firm[7]. There was a hint of outrage[8] now too.

"Yes."

She was crying harder[9] now.

I stood. "Quick recess[10], Your Honor."

Flair dropped the hammer[11] before the judge could reply. "Was there ever another man involved in[12] your sexual encounters[13] with Jim Broodway?"

The courtroom exploded.

"Your Honor!" I shouted.

"Order![14]" The judge used the gavel. "Order!"

The room quieted[15] quickly. Judge Pierce looked down at me[16]. "I know how hard[17] this is to listen to, but I'm going to allow this question." He turned to Chamique. "Please answer."

The court stenographer read the question again. Chamique sat there and let the tears spill down[18] her face. When the stenographer finished, Chamique said, "No."

"Mr. Broodway will testify that – "

"He let some friend of his watch[19]!" Chamique cried out[20]. "That's all. I never let him touch me! You hear me? Not ever![21]"

The room was silent. I tried to keep my head up[22], tried not to close my eyes.

"So," Flair Hickory said, "you had sex with a man named Jim – "

"James! His name is James!"

1. Plus d'une fois ?
2. tenter d'être plus précis
3. savait qu'il valait mieux ne pas en rajouter
4. changea un peu de cap
5. quand vous aviez des relations sexuelles
6. C'est peut-être arrivé.
7. douce mais ferme
8. touche d'indignation
9. plus fort
10. [Je demande] une brève suspension
11. enfonça le clou
12. Un autre homme a-t-il déjà participé à
13. rapports
14. Silence !
15. se tut
16. baissa les yeux vers moi
17. pénible
18. sur son siège, laissa les larmes ruisseler sur
19. a laissé un de ses amis regarder
20. s'écria
21. Pas une seule fois !
22. la tête haute

" – and another man was in the room and yet you don't know how you came up with[1] the names Jim and Cal?"

"I don't know no Cal.[2] And his name is James."

Flair Hickory moved closer to her. His face showed concern now[3], as if he were reaching out to her[4]. "Are you sure you didn't imagine this, Miss Johnson?"

His voice sounded like one of those TV help doctors.

She wiped[5] her face. "Yeah, Mr. Hickory. I'm sure. Damned sure.[6]"

But Flair did not back down[7].

"I don't necessarily say you're lying," he went on, and I bit back my objection[8], "but isn't there a chance that maybe you had too much punch – not your fault, of course, you thought it was nonalcoholic – and then you engaged in[9] a consensual[10] act and just flashed back to[11] some other time period? Wouldn't that explain your insisting[12] that the two men who raped you were named Jim and Cal?"

I was up on my feet to say that was two questions, but Flair again knew what he was doing.

"Withdrawn[13]," Flair Hickory said, as if this whole thing[14] was just the saddest thing for all parties involved[15]. "I have no further[16] questions."

1. d'où vous sortez
2. Je connais pas de Cal.
3. exprimait de l'inquiétude
4. voulait l'aider
5. essuya
6. Sacrément sûre.
7. ne fléchit pas
8. me retins d'objecter
9. vous avez participé
10. consenti
11. vous vous êtes simplement rappelée
12. le fait que vous souteniez
13. Je retire cette question
14. tout cet épisode
15. bien malheureux pour toutes les parties en présence
16. n'ai pas d'autres

Chapter 13

While Lucy waited for Sylvia Potter, she tried to Google the name from Ira's visitor's log[1]: Manolo Santiago. There were lots of hits[2], but nothing that helped[3]. He wasn't a reporter[4] – or no hits showed that to be the case[5] anyhow. So who was he? And why would he visit her father?

She could ask Ira, of course. If he remembered.

Two hours passed. Then three and four. She called Sylvia's room. No answer. She tried e-mailing the Black-Berry again. No response.[6]

This wasn't good.

How the hell would Sylvia Potter know about her past?

Lucy checked the student directory. Sylvia Potter lived in Stone House down in the social quad[7]. She decided to walk over and see what she could find.

There was an obvious magic to a college campus.[8] There is no entity more protected, more shielded[9], and while[10] it was easy to complain about that, it was also how it should be. Some things grow better in a vacuum[11]. It was a place to feel safe when you're young – but when you're older, like her and Lonnie, it started becoming a place to hide.

1. registre des visites

2. beaucoup de résultats

3. rien de concluant

4. journaliste

5. ne démontrait que ce soit le cas

6. Aucune réaction.

7. dans la résidence universitaire

8. Un campus est indéniablement un lieu magique.

9. plus préservée

10. même si

11. poussent mieux en vase clos

Stone House used to be Psi U's fraternity house. Ten years ago, the college did away with[1] fraternities, calling them "anti-intellectual." Lucy didn't disagree[2] that fraternities had plenty of negative qualities and connotations, but the idea of outlawing them[3] seemed heavy-handed[4] and a tad[5] too fascist for her taste. There was a case going on[6] at a nearby college involving a fraternity and a rape. But if it isn't a fraternity, then it would be a lacrosse[7] team or a group of hard hats[8] in a strip club or rowdy rockers[9] at a nightclub. She wasn't sure of the answer, but she knew that it wasn't to rid yourself of every institution you didn't like.

Punish the crime, she thought, not the freedom.

The outside of the house was still a gorgeous Georgian brick[10]. The inside had been stripped[11] of all personality. Gone were the tapestries and wood paneling[12] and rich mahogany[13] of its storied[14] past, replaced with off-whites[15] and beiges and all things neutral. Seemed a shame.

Students meandered about[16]. Her entrance drew a few stares[17] but not too many. Stereos – or more likely, those iPod speaker systems – blared[18]. Doors were open. She saw posters of Che[19] on the wall. Maybe she was more like her father than she realized. University campuses were also caught in the[20] sixties. Styles and music might change, but[21] that sentiment was always there.

She took the center stairwell[22], also scrubbed of its originality[23]. Sylvia Potter lived in a single[24] on the second floor. Lucy found her door. There was one of those erasable boards[25], the kind where you write notes with a marker, but there wasn't a blemish on it[26]. The board had been put on straight[27] and perfectly centered. On the top, the name "Sylvia" was written in a script[28] that almost looked like professional calligraphy. There was a pink flower next to

1. s'était débarrassée des
2. ne contestait pas
3. de les proscrire
4. lui semblait excessive
5. un tantinet
6. une affaire en cours
7. la crosse [sport collectif, buts marqués avec une crosse]
8. réactionnaires
9. rockeurs bagarreurs
10. somptueux, en brique de style georgien
11. dépouillé
12. tapisseries et les boiseries
13. l'acajou opulent
14. légendaire
15. blancs cassés
16. flânaient
17. attira quelques regards
18. beuglaient
19. [Che Guevara]
20. sous l'influence des
21. avaient beau changer
22. escalier central
23. dont toute originalité avait été effacée
24. chambre individuelle
25. tableaux effaçables
26. n'y avait pas une trace dessus
27. accroché bien droit
28. d'une écriture

her name. It seemed so out of place, this whole door[1], separate and apart[2] and from another era[3].

Lucy knocked on the door. There was no reply. She tried the knob[4]. It was locked. She thought about leaving a note on the door – that was what those erasable boards were there for – but she didn't want to mar it up[5]. Plus it seemed a little desperate.[6] She had called already. She had e-mailed. Stopping by like this was going a step too far[7].

She started back down[8] the stairs when the front door of Stone House opened. Sylvia Potter entered. She saw Lucy and stiffened[9]. Lucy took the rest of the steps[10] and stopped in front of Sylvia. She said nothing, trying to meet the girl's eyes. Sylvia looked everywhere but[11] directly at Lucy.

"Oh hi, Professor Gold."

Lucy kept silent.

"Class ran late[12], I'm so sorry. And then I had this other project due[13] tomorrow. And I figured it was late and you'd be gone and it could just wait till tomorrow."

She was babbling[14]. Lucy let her.

"Do you want me to stop by tomorrow?" Sylvia asked.

"Do you have time now?"

Sylvia looked at her watch without really looking at it. "I'm really so crazy with this project. Can it wait until tomorrow?"

"Who is the project for?"

"What?"

"What professor assigned you[15] the project, Sylvia? If I take up too much of your time[16], I can write them a note[17]."

Silence.

"We can go to your room," Lucy said. "Talk there."

Sylvia finally met her eye. "Professor Gold?"

Lucy waited.

"I don't think I want to talk to you."

1. si déplacée, cette porte
2. différente et à part
3. d'une autre époque
4. poignée
5. le salir
6. Et puis cela faisait un peu désespéré.
7. aller un peu trop loin
8. commençait à descendre
9. se raidit
10. descendit les marches restantes
11. sauf
12. a duré plus longtemps
13. cet autre devoir à rendre pour
14. bredouillait
15. t'a donné
16. te fais perdre trop de temps
17. lui écrire un mot

1. *Comment pouvez-vous savoir*

"It's about your journal."

"My... ?" She shook her head. "But I sent it in anonymously. How would you know[1] which is mine?"

"Sylvia – "

"You said! You promised! They were anonymous. You said that."

"I know what I said."

"How did you... ?" She straightened up. "I don't want to talk to you."

2. *prit un ton ferme*
3. *tenait bon*
4. *me forcer*

Lucy made her voice firm[2]. "You have to."

But Sylvia wasn't backing down[3]. "No, I don't. You can't make me[4]. And... my God, how could you do that? Tell us it's anonymous and confidential and then..."

"This is really important."

5. *au doyen*
6. *serez renvoyée*
7. *les dévisageaient à présent*

"No, it's not. I don't have to talk to you. And if you say anything about it, I will tell the dean[5] what you did. You'll get fired[6]."

Other students were staring now[7]. Lucy was losing control of the situation. "Please, Sylvia, I need to know – "

"Nothing!"

"Sylvia – "

8. *tranquille*

"I don't have to tell you a thing! Leave me alone[8]!"

Sylvia Potter turned, opened the door, and ran away.

Chapter 14

After Flair Hickory finished with Chamique, I met with Loren Muse in my office.

"Wow," Loren said. "That sucked.[1]"

"Get on that name thing[2]," I said.

"What name thing?"

"Find out if anyone called Broodway 'Jim,' or if, as Chamique insists, he went by[3] James."

Muse frowned.

"What?"

"You think that's going to help?"

"It can't hurt.[4]"

"You still believe her?"

"Come on, Muse. This is a smoke screen[5]."

"It's a good one."

"Your friend Cingle learn anything?"

"Not yet."

The judge called the court day over[6], thank God. Flair had handed me my head[7]. I know that it is supposed to be about justice[8] and that it's not a competition or anything like that, but let's get real[9].

Cal and Jim were back and stronger than ever[10].

My cell phone rang. I looked at the caller ID[11]. I didn't recognize the number. I put the phone to my ear and said, "Hello?"

1. Ça craint.
2. Mets-toi sur cette histoire de noms
3. il se faisait appeler
4. Ça peut pas faire de mal.
5. écran de fumée
6. avait mis fin à cette journée d'audience
7. m'avait offert ma propre tête sur un plateau
8. qu'il s'agit normalement de justice
9. soyons réalistes
10. plus virulents que jamais
11. le numéro affiché

"It is Raya."

Raya Singh. The comely[1] Indian waitress. I felt my throat go dry[2].

"How are you?"

"Fine."

"Did you think of something?"

Muse looked at me. I tried to look at her as if to say, This is private[3]. For an investigator, Muse could be slow on the pickup[4]. Or maybe that was intentional[5].

"I probably should have said something earlier," Raya Singh said.

I waited.

"But you showing up like that[6]. It surprised me. I'm still not sure what the right thing to do is."

"Ms. Singh?"

"Please call me Raya."

"Raya," I said, "I have no idea what you're talking about."

"It was why I asked why you were really there. Do you remember?"

"Yes."

"Do you know why I asked that – about what you really wanted?"

I thought about it and went with honest[7]: "Because of the unprofessional way I was ogling you[8]?"

"No," she said.

"Okay, I'm game[9]. Why did you ask? And come to think of it[10], why did you ask if I killed him?"

Muse arched[11] an eyebrow. I didn't much care.

Raya Singh didn't reply.

"Miss Singh?" Then: "Raya?"

"Because," she said, "he mentioned[12] your name."

I thought that maybe I'd heard wrong[13], so I asked something stupid. "Who mentioned my name?"

Her voice had a hint of impatience. "Who are we talking about?"

"Manolo Santiago mentioned my name?"

"Yes, of course."

1. très avenante
2. gorge se dessécher
3. c'est personnel
4. longue à la détente
5. voulu
6. le fait que vous débarquiez comme ça
7. optai pour la franchise
8. la façon très peu professionnelle dont je vous reluquais
9. je donne ma langue au chat
10. tant que j'y pense
11. haussa
12. a cité
13. mal entendu

"And you didn't think you should tell me this before?"

"I didn't know if I could trust you."

"And what changed your mind?"

"I looked you up[1] on the Internet. You really are the county prosecutor."

"What did Santiago say about me?"

"He said you lied about something."

"About what?"

"I don't know."

I pushed ahead.[2] "Who did he say it to?"

"A man. I don't know his name. He also had clippings[3] about you in his apartment."

"His apartment? I thought you said you didn't know where he lived."

"That's when I didn't trust you."

"And you do now?"

She did not reply to that one[4] directly. "Pick me up[5] at the restaurant in one hour," Raya Singh said, "and I'll show you where Manolo lived."

1. J'ai cherché votre nom

2. J'insistai.

3. des coupures de presse

4. ne répondit pas à ça

5. Passez me prendre

Chapter 15

When Lucy came back to her office, Lonnie was there, holding up sheets of paper[1].

"What's that?" she asked.

"More of that journal."

She tried hard not to snap the pages from his hand[2].

"Did you find Sylvia?" he asked.

"Yes."

"And?"

"And she went crazy on me[3] and won't talk[4]."

Lonnie sat in the chair and threw his feet up on her desk. "You want me to try?"

"I don't think that's a good idea."

Lonnie gave her the winning smile. "I can be pretty persuasive[5]."

"You're willing to put out[6] just to help me?"

"If I must.[7]"

"I would worry so about your reputation." She sat back, gripping the pages. "Did you read this already?"

"Yep."

She just nodded and started in for herself[8]:

P broke our embrace and darted[9] toward the scream.

1. tenant des feuilles de papier
2. s'efforça de ne pas lui arracher les feuilles des mains
3. m'a fait une scène
4. refuse de parler
5. convaincant
6. prêt à passer à la casserole
7. S'il le faut.
8. se plongea dedans silencieusement
9. se précipita

I called after him[1]*, but he didn't stop. Two seconds later, it was like the night had swallowed him whole*[2]*. I tried to follow. But it was dark. I should have known these woods better than P. This was his first year here.*
The screaming voice had been a girl's[3]*. That much I could tell.*[4] *I trekked*[5] *through the woods. I didn't call out anymore. For some reason I was scared to*[6]*. I wanted to find P, but I didn't want anyone to know where I was. I know that doesn't make much sense, but that was how I felt.*
I was scared.
There was moonlight. Moonlight in the woods changes the color of everything. It is like one of those poster lights[7] *my dad used to have. They called them black lights, even though they were more like purple. They changed the color of everything around them. So did the moon.*
So when I finally found P and I saw the strange color on his shirt, I didn't recognize what it was at first. I couldn't tell the shade of crimson[8]*. It looked more like liquid blue*[9]*. He looked at me. His eyes were wide*[10]*.*
"We have to go," he said. "And we can't tell anyone we were ever out here[11]*...."*

That was it.[12] Lucy read it two more times. Then she put the story down[13]. Lonnie was watching her.

"So," he said, dragging out the word[14], "I assume[15] that you are the narrator of this little tale[16]?"

"What?"

"I've been trying to figure this out[17], Lucy, and I've only come up with one possible explanation. You're the girl in the story. Someone is writing about you."

"That's ridiculous," she said.

"Come on, Luce. We have tales of incest in that pile, for crying out loud[18]. We aren't even searching those

1. Je criai son nom
2. l'avait totalement englouti
3. était celle d'une fille
4. Ça, c'était clair.
5. J'avançais péniblement
6. j'avais peur de le faire
7. tubes lumineux [fluorescents]
8. discerner la couleur pourpre
9. un bleu limpide
10. écarquillés
11. qu'on a mis les pieds ici
12. C'était tout.
13. elle posa les feuilles de papier
14. en s'éternisant sur ce mot
15. je suppose
16. la narratrice de cette petite histoire
17. d'y comprendre quelque chose
18. bon sang de bonsoir

kids out.[1] Yet you're all uptight[2] about this scream-in-the-woods[3] story?"

"Let it go[4], Lonnie."

He shook his head. "Sorry, sweetie, not my nature[5]. Even if you weren't superfine[6] and I didn't want to get in your pants[7]."

She didn't bother with a retort[8].

"I'd like to help if I can."

"You can't."

"I know more than you think."

Lucy looked up at him.

"What are you talking about?"

"You, uh, you won't get mad at me[9]?"

She waited.

"I did a little research on you." Her stomach dropped[10], but she kept it off her face[11].

"Lucy Gold isn't your real name. You changed it."

"How do you know that?"

"Come on, Luce. You know how easy it is with a computer?"

She said nothing.

"Something about this journal kept bugging me[12]," he went on. "This stuff about a camp[13]. I was young, but I remember hearing about the[14] Summer Slasher. So I did a little more research." He tried to give her the cocky smile[15]. "You should go back to blond[16]."

"It was a tough time[17] in my life."

"I can imagine."

"That's why I changed my name."

"Oh, I get that. Your family took a big hit[18]. You wanted to get out from under that[19]."

"Yes."

"And now, for some weird reason, it's coming back."

She nodded.

"Why?" Lonnie asked.

"I don't know."

"I'd like to help."

"Like I said, I'm not sure how[20]."

1. On n'essaie même pas de savoir qui en sont les victimes.
2. tu es totalement crispée
3. de hurlement dans les bois
4. Laisse tomber
5. c'est pas mon genre
6. super belle
7. coucher avec toi
8. ne prit pas la peine de rétorquer
9. te mettre en colère
10. Son estomac se noua
11. ne le montra pas
12. m'obsédait
13. histoire de colonie
14. avoir entendu parler du
15. lui décocher son sourire narquois
16. redevenir blonde
17. période éprouvante
18. a énormément souffert
19. te libérer de tout ça
20. je ne vois pas comment

"Can I ask you something?"

She shrugged.

"I did a little digging.[1] You know that the Discovery Channel did a special[2] on the murders a few years ago?"

"I know," she said.

"They don't talk about you being there. In the woods that night, I mean."

She said nothing.

"So what gives?[3]"

"I can't talk about it."

"Who is P? It's Paul Copeland, right? You know he's a DA or something[4] now."

She shook her head.

"You're not making this easy[5]," he said.

She kept her mouth closed.

"Okay," he said, standing. "I'll help anyway."

"How?"

"Sylvia Potter."

"What about her?"

"I'll get her to talk[6]."

"How?"

Lonnie headed for the door. "I got my ways.[7]"

On the way back[8] to the Indian restaurant, I took a detour and visited Jane's grave[9].

I was not sure why. I did not do it that often[10] – maybe three times a year. I don't really feel my wife's presence here. Her parents picked out the burial site[11] with Jane. "It means a lot to them[12]," she'd explained on her deathbed. And it did. It distracted her parents, especially her mother, and made them feel as though they were doing something useful.

I didn't much care. I was in denial about Jane ever dying[13] – even when it got bad[14], *really* bad, I still thought she'd somehow pull through[15]. And to me death is death – final[16], the end, nothing coming after[17], the finish line[18], no more. Fancy caskets[19] and

1. J'ai fait quelques recherches.
2. émission spéciale
3. Alors qu'est-ce qu'il s'y est passé ?
4. un truc comme ça
5. ne facilites pas les choses
6. la ferai parler
7. J'ai mes méthodes.
8. En retournant
9. je me rendis sur la tombe de Jane
10. si souvent que ça
11. avaient choisi l'emplacement
12. C'est très important pour eux
13. Je niais le fait que Jane puisse mourir
14. son état s'était aggravé
15. s'en sortirait d'une façon ou d'une autre
16. définitive
17. il n'y a rien après
18. ligne d'arrivée
19. Les cercueils sophistiqués

well-tended graveyards[1], even ones as well tended as Jane's, don't change that.

I parked in the lot and walked the path[2]. Her grave had fresh flowers on it. We of the Hebrew faith[3] do not do that. We put stones on the marker[4]. I liked that, though I am not sure why. Flowers, something so alive and bright, seemed obscene against the gray[5] of her tomb. My wife, my beautiful Jane, was rotting[6] six feet below those freshly cut lilies[7]. That seemed like an outrage to me.

I sat on a concrete bench[8]. I didn't talk to her. It was so bad in the end. Jane suffered. I watched. For a while anyway. We got hospice[9] – Jane wanted to die at home – but then there was her weight loss[10] and the smell and the decay[11] and the groans[12]. The sound that I remembered most, the one that still invaded my sleep, was the awful coughing noise[13], more a choke[14] really, when Jane couldn't get the phlegm up[15] and it would hurt so much and she would be so uncomfortable and it went on for months and months and I tried to be strong but I wasn't as strong as Jane and she knew that.

There was a time early in[16] our relationship when she knew that I was having doubts. I had lost a sister. My mother had run off on me[17]. And now, for the first time in a long time, I was letting a woman into my life. I remember late one night when I couldn't sleep and I was staring at the ceiling and Jane was sleeping next to me. I remember that I heard her deep breath, then so sweet and perfect and so different from what it would be in the end. Her breathing shortened[18] as she slowly came awake[19]. She put her arms around me and moved close.

"I'm not her," she said softly, as if she could read my thoughts. "I will never abandon you."

But in the end, she did.

I had dated[20] since her death. I have even had some fairly intense emotional commitments[21]. One day I

1. les cimetières bien entretenus
2. pris le sentier
3. Nous, dans la religion judaïque,
4. des cailloux sur la stèle
5. par rapport au gris
6. pourrissait
7. lis fraîchement coupés
8. banc en béton
9. [hôpital pour patients en phase terminale]
10. perte de poids
11. déchéance
12. gémissements
13. bruit de toux
14. plutôt un cri de suffocation
15. faire remonter les mucosités
16. À un moment, au début de
17. m'avait abandonné
18. sa respiration se fit plus courte
19. s'éveillait lentement
20. J'avais eu des aventures
21. des coups de cœur assez intenses

hope to find someone and remarry. But right now, as I thought about that night in our bed, I realized that it would probably not happen.

I'm not her, my wife had said.

And of course, she meant my mother.

I looked at the tombstone[1]. I read my wife's name. Loving Mother, Daughter and Wife. There were some kind of angel wings on the sides[2]. I pictured[3] my in-laws picking those out[4], just the right size[5] angel wings, just the right design, all that. They had bought the plot[6] next to Jane's without telling me. If I didn't remarry, I guess, it would be mine. If I did, well, I don't know what my in-laws would do with it.

I wanted to ask my Jane for help. I wanted to ask her to search around up wherever she was[7] and see if she could find my sister and let me know if Camille was alive or dead. I smiled like a dope.[8] Then I stopped.

I'm sure cell phones in graveyards are no-nos[9]. But I didn't think Jane would mind. I took the phone out of my pocket and pressed down on that six button[10] again.

Sosh answered on the first ring.

"I have a favor to ask," I said.

"I told you before. Not on the phone."

"Find my mother, Sosh."

Silence.

"You can do it. I'm asking.[11] In the memory[12] of my father and sister. Find my mother for me."

"And if I can't?"

"You can."

"Your mother has been gone a long time[13]."

"I know."

"Have you considered the fact[14] that maybe she doesn't want to be found?"

"I have," I said.

"And?"

"And tough[15]," I said. "We don't always get what we want.[16] So find her for me, Sosh. Please."

1. pierre tombale
2. comme des ailes d'ange, sur les côtés
3. J'imaginais
4. en train de les choisir
5. de dimensions idéales
6. l'emplacement
7. chercher un peu partout, là-haut, où qu'elle soit
8. Je souris bêtement.
9. ça ne se fait pas
10. j'appuyai sur cette touche six
11. Je te le demande.
12. En souvenir
13. est partie depuis longtemps
14. songé à l'éventualité
15. Eh bien tant pis
16. On n'obtient pas toujours ce qu'on veut.

1. Tu nous manques
2. à voix haute

I hung up the phone. I looked at my wife's stone again.

"We miss you[1]," I said out loud[2] to my dead wife. "Cara and I. We miss you very, very much."

Then I stood up and walked back to my car.

Chapter 16

Raya Singh was waiting for me in the restaurant parking lot. She had turned in[1] the aqua waitress uniform for[2] jeans and a dark blue blouse. Her hair was pulled back in a ponytail[3]. The effect was no less dazzling[4]. I shook my head. I had just visited my wife's grave. Now I was inappropriately admiring[5] the beauty of a young woman.

It was an interesting world.

She slipped[6] into the passenger seat. She smelled great[7].

"Where to?[8]" I asked.

"Do you know where Route 17 is?"

"Yes."

"Take it north[9]."

I pulled out[10] of the lot. "Do you want to start telling me the truth?" I asked.

"I have never lied to you," she said. "I decided not to tell you certain things."

"Are you still claiming[11] you just met Santiago on the street?"

"I am."

I didn't believe her.

"Have you ever heard him mention the name Perez?"

She did not reply.

1. avait troqué
2. contre
3. étaient tirés en queue de cheval
4. n'en était pas moins éblouissant
5. Et là, j'admirais de façon déplacée
6. se glissa
7. sentait très bon
8. Où allons-nous ?
9. en direction du nord
10. Je sortis
11. Vous prétendez toujours

I pressed.[1] "Gil Perez?"

"The exit[2] for 17 is on the right."

"I know where the exit is, Raya."

I glanced at her in perfect profile.[3] She stared out the window, looking achingly beautiful[4].

"Tell me about hearing him say my name[5]," I said.

"I told you already."

"Tell me again."

She took a deep, silent breath. Her eyes closed for a moment.

"Manolo said you lied."

"Lied about what?"

"Lied about something involving[6]" – she hesitated – "involving woods or a forest or something like that."

I felt my heart lurch across[7] my chest. "He said that? About woods or a forest?"

"Yes."

"What were his exact words?"

"I don't remember."

"Try."

"'Paul Copeland lied about what happened in those woods.'" Then she tilted her head. "Oh, wait."

I did.

Then she said something that almost made me turn off the road[8]. She said, "Lucy."

"What?"

"That was the other name. He said, 'Paul Copeland lied about what happened in those woods. So did Lucy.[9]'"

Now it was my turn to be struck silent[10].

"Paul," Raya said, "who is this Lucy?"

We took the rest of the ride[11] in silence.

I was lost in thoughts of Lucy. I tried to remember the feel of her flaxen hair[12], the wondrous smell of it[13]. But I couldn't. That was the thing.[14] The memories

1. J'insistai.
2. sortie
3. J'observai son profil parfait.
4. belle à en pleurer
5. Racontez-moi comment vous l'avez entendu citer mon nom
6. concernant
7. bondir dans
8. me fit presque quitter la route
9. Et Lucy aussi.
10. d'être frappé de mutisme
11. Le reste du trajet se déroula
12. de ce que je ressentais en touchant ses cheveux blond pâle
13. de leur parfum extraordinaire
14. C'était le problème.

seemed so clouded[1]. I couldn't remember what was real and what my imagination had conjured up[2]. I just remembered the wonder[3]. I remembered the lust[4]. We were both new[5], both clumsy[6], both inexperienced, but it was like something in a Bob Seger[7] song or maybe Meat Loaf's[8] "Bat Out of Hell[9]." God, that lust. How had it started? And when did that lust seemingly segue into[10] something approaching love?

Summer romances come to an end. That was part of the deal.[11] They are built like certain plants or insects, not able to survive more than one season. I thought Luce and I would be different. We were, I guess, but not in the way that I thought. I truly believed that we would never let each other go[12].

The young are so dumb[13].

The AmeriSuites efficiency unit[14] was in Ramsey, New Jersey. Raya had a key. She opened the door to a room on the third floor. I would describe the decor to you except that the only word to describe it would be *nondescript*[15]. The furnishing had all the personality of, well, an efficiency unit on a road called Route 17 in northern New Jersey.

When we stepped into the room, Raya let out a little gasp[16].

"What?" I said.

Her eyes took in[17] the whole room. "There were tons of[18] papers on that table," she said. "Files[19], magazines, pens, pencils."

"It's empty now."

Raya opened a drawer[20]. "His clothes are gone."

We did a pretty thorough search.[21] Everything was gone – there were no papers, no files, no magazine articles, no toothbrush, no personal items, nothing. Raya sat on the couch. "Someone came back and cleared this place out[22]."

"When were you here last?"

"Three days ago."

I started for[23] the door. "Come on."

1. confus
2. avait produit
3. de l'émerveillement
4. du désir
5. novices
6. maladroits
7. [chanteur de rock américain]
8. [acteur et chanteur de rock américain]
9. Comme un dérаté [chanson et premier album]
10. s'était-il apparemment mué en
11. Cela allait avec.
12. qu'on ne se séparerait jamais
13. stupides
14. [hôtel de type « appart hôtel »]
15. quelconque
16. poussa un petit cri de surprise
17. Elle balaya d'un regard
18. des tas de
19. Des dossiers
20. tiroir
21. On fouilla partout.
22. a vidé cet endroit
23. Je me dirigeai vers

"Where are you going?"

"I'm going to talk to someone at the front desk."

But there was a kid working there. He gave us pretty much nothing[1]. The occupant had signed in as[2] Manolo Santiago. He had paid in cash, leaving a cash deposit.[3] The room was paid for[4] until the end of the month. And no, the kid didn't remember what[5] Mr. Santiago looked like[6] or anything about him. That was one of the problems with these kinds of units[7]. You don't have to go in through the lobby[8]. It was easy to be anonymous.

Raya and I headed back to Santiago's room.

"You said there were papers?"

"Yes."

"What did they say?"

"I didn't pry.[9]"

"Raya," I said.

"What?"

"I have to be honest here. I'm not fully buying the ignorant act.[10]"

She just looked at me[11] with those damn[12] eyes.

"What?"

"You want me to trust you."

"Yes."

"Why should I?"

I thought about that.

"You lied to me when we met," she said.

"About what?"

"You said you were just investigating his murder. Like a regular[13] detective or something. But that wasn't true, was it?"

I said nothing.

"Manolo," she went on[14]. "He didn't trust you. I read those articles. I know something happened to all of you in those woods twenty years ago. He thought you lied about it[15]."

I still said nothing.

1. ne nous apprit presque rien
2. s'était enregistré sous le nom de
3. Il avait payé en espèces, même la caution.
4. réglée
5. à quoi
6. ressemblait
7. ce type d'hébergement
8. passer par la réception pour entrer
9. Je n'ai pas farfouillé.
10. J'ai du mal à vous croire quand vous jouez les idiotes.
11. se contenta de me regarder
12. satanés
13. normal
14. poursuivit-elle
15. à ce propos

"And now you expect me to tell you everything. Would you? If you were in my position[1], would you tell everything you knew[2]?"

I took a second, gathered my thoughts[3]. She had a point.[4] "So you saw those articles?"

"Yes."

"Then you know that I was at that camp that summer."

"I do."

"And you know that my sister disappeared that night too."

She nodded.

I turned to her. "That's why I'm here."

"You're here to avenge[5] your sister?"

"No," I said. "I'm here to find her."

"But I thought she was dead. Wayne Steubens murdered her."

"That was what I used to think."

Raya turned away for a moment. Then she looked right through me[6]. "So what did you lie about?"

"Nothing."

The eyes again. "You can trust me," she said.

"I do."

She waited. I waited too. "Who is Lucy?"

"She's a girl who was at the camp."

"What else? What's her connection to this?[7]"

"Her father owned the camp[8]," I said. Then I added, "She was also my girlfriend at the time[9]."

"And how did you both lie?"

"We didn't lie."

"So what was Manolo talking about?"

"Damned if I know.[10] That's what I'm trying to find out."

"I don't understand. What makes you so sure[11] your sister is alive?"

"I'm not sure," I said. "But I think there's a decent enough chance[12]."

"Why?"

1. à ma place
2. tout ce que vous savez
3. rassemblant mes esprits
4. Elle n'avait pas tort.
5. pour venger
6. me regarda comme si je n'étais pas là
7. Qu'est-ce qu'elle a à voir avec ça ?
8. était le propriétaire du camp
9. à cette époque
10. Je n'en sais rien du tout.
11. Pourquoi êtes-vous si sûr
12. qu'il existe une bonne probabilité

"Because of Manolo."

"What about him?"

I studied her face and wondered if I was getting played[1] here. "You clammed up[2] before when I mentioned the name Gil Perez," I said.

"His name was in those articles. He was killed that night too."

"No," I said.

"I don't understand."

"Do you know why Manolo was looking into[3] what happened that night?"

"He never said."

"Weren't you curious?"

She shrugged. "He said it was business[4]."

"Raya," I said. "Manolo Santiago wasn't his real name."

I hesitated, seeing if she would jump in[5], volunteer something[6]. She didn't.

"His real name," I went on, "was Gil Perez."

She took a second to process this.[7] "The boy from the woods?"

"Yes."

"Are you sure?"

Good question. But I said, "Yes," without any hesitation.

She thought about it. "And what you're telling me now – if it's true – was that he was alive this whole time[8]."

I nodded.

"And if he was alive..." Raya Singh stopped. So I finished it for her[9].

"Maybe my sister is too."

"Or maybe," she said, "Manolo – Gil, whatever you call him[10] – killed them all[11]."

Strange. I hadn't thought of that. It actually made some sense. Gil kills them all, leaves evidence[12] he was a victim too. But was Gil clever enough to pull

1. si elle se moquait de moi
2. n'avez pas répondu
3. faisait des recherches sur
4. professionnel
5. pour voir si elle allait intervenir
6. dire spontanément quelque chose
7. Elle réfléchit un instant, digérant cette information.
8. pendant tout ce temps
9. j'achevai la phrase à sa place
10. quel que soit son nom
11. les a tous tués
12. laisse des preuves indiquant

something like that off[1]? And how do you explain Wayne Steubens?

Unless[2] Wayne was telling the truth...

"If that's the case," I said, "then I'll find that out."

Raya frowned. "Manolo said you and Lucy were lying. If he killed them, why would he say something like that? Why would he have all this paperwork[3] and be looking into what happened? If he did it, he would know the answers, wouldn't he?"

She crossed the room and stood directly in front of[4] me. So damn young and beautiful. I actually wanted[5] to kiss her.

"What aren't you telling me?" she asked.

My cell phone rang. I glanced at the caller ID. It was Loren Muse. I hit[6] the ON button and said, "What's up?"

"We got a problem," Muse said.

I closed my eyes and waited.

"It's Chamique. She wants to recant[7]."

My office is in the center of Newark. I keep hearing[8] that there is a revitalization going on[9] in this city. I don't see it. The city has been decaying[10] for as long as I can remember. But I have gotten to[11] know this city well. The history is still there, beneath[12] the surface. The people are wonderful. We as a society are big on stereotyping cities[13] the way we do[14] ethnic groups or minorities. It is easy to hate them from a distance[15]. I remember Jane's conservative parents and their disdain for all things gay[16]. Her college roommate[17], Helen, unbeknownst to them[18], was gay. When they met her, both her mother and father simply loved Helen. When they learned Helen was a lesbian, they still loved her. Then they loved her partner[19].

That was how it often was.[20] It was easy to hate gays or blacks or Jews or Arabs. It was more difficult to hate individuals[21].

1. pour réussir un tel coup
2. À moins que
3. tous ces documents
4. se plaça juste devant
5. J'avais vraiment envie
6. J'appuyai sur
7. se rétracter
8. Je n'arrête pas d'entendre
9. un nouvel essor, actuellement
10. se délabre
11. je suis parvenu à
12. au-dessous de
13. Notre société a le chic pour cataloguer les villes
14. comme nous le faisons avec
15. de loin
16. mépris envers tout ce qui concernait l'homosexualité
17. camarade de chambre
18. sans qu'ils le sachent
19. sa compagne
20. Ça se passait souvent comme ça.
21. des individus

Newark was like that. You could hate it as a mass[1], but so many neighborhoods[2] and shopkeepers[3] and citizens had a charm and strength that you couldn't help but be drawn in[4] and care about[5] and want to make it better.

Chamique sat in my office. She was so damned young, but you could see the hard written[6] on her face. Life had not been easy for this girl. It would probably not get any easier[7]. Her attorney, Horace Foley, wore too much cologne[8] and had eyes spaced too widely apart[9]. I am an attorney, so I don't like the prejudices that are made against[10] my profession, but I was fairly confident[11] that if an ambulance drove by, this guy would jump through my third-floor window to slow it down[12].

"We would like to see you drop[13] the charges on Mr. Jenrette and Mr. Marantz," Foley said.

"Can't do that," I said. I looked at Chamique. She did not have her head down, but she wasn't exactly clamoring for eye contact[14]. "Did you lie on the stand yesterday?" I asked her.

"My client would never lie," Foley said.

I ignored him, met Chamique's eyes. She said, "You're never going to convict them[15] anyway."

"You don't know that."

"You serious?"

"I am."

Chamique smiled at me, as if I were the most naive creature that God had ever created. "You don't understand, do you?"

"Oh, I understand. They're offering money if you recant. The sum has now reached a level where your attorney here, Mr. Who-Needs-A-Shower-When-There's-Cologne[16], thinks it makes sense to do it."

"What did you call me?"

I looked at Muse. "Open a window, will you[17]?"

"Got it, Cope."

"Hey! What did you call me?"

1. dans sa globalité
2. de quartiers
3. de commerçants
4. on ne pouvait s'empêcher d'être séduit
5. de s'en préoccuper
6. on lisait de la dureté
7. s'améliorer
8. se parfumait trop
9. beaucoup trop écartés
10. préjugés qui s'exercent à l'encontre de
11. assez convaincu
12. que ce type était si rapace qu'il fondrait sur n'importe quelle victime
13. que vous abandonniez
14. fuyait un peu mon regard
15. Ils ne seront jamais reconnus coupables
16. Pourquoi se laver quand on peut se parfumer
17. tu veux bien

"The window is open. Feel free to jump out.[1]" I looked back at Chamique. "If you recant now, that means your testimony today and yesterday was a lie. It means you committed perjury[2]. It means you had this office spend[3] millions of tax dollars[4] on your lie – your perjury. That's a crime. You'll go to jail."

Foley said, "Talk to me, Mr. Copeland, not my client."

"Talk to you? I can't even breathe around you."

"I won't stand for this – [5]"

"Shh[6]," I said. Then I cupped my ear with my hand[7]. "Listen to the crinkling sound[8].'"

"To what?"

"I think your cologne is peeling my wallpaper[9]. If you listen closely, you can hear it. Shh, listen."

Even Chamique smiled a little.

"Don't recant," I said to her.

"I have to."

"Then I'll charge you[10]."

Her attorney was ready to do battle[11] again, but Chamique put her hand on his arm. "You won't do that, Mr. Copeland."

"I will."

But she knew better[12]. I was bluffing.[13] She was a poor, scared rape victim who had a chance of cashing in[14] – making more money than she would probably see again in her lifetime[15]. Who the hell was I to lecture her[16] on values[17] and justice?

She and her attorney stood. Horace Foley said, "We sign the agreement[18] in the morning."

I didn't say anything. Part of me felt relief[19], and that shamed me[20]. JaneCare would survive now. My father's memory – okay, my political career – wouldn't take an unnecessary hit[21]. Best off, I was off the hook.[22] It wasn't my doing.[23] It was Chamique's.

Chamique offered me her hand. I took it. "Thank you," she said.

1. N'hésitez pas à sauter.
2. vous êtes rendue coupable de parjure
3. vous avez fait dépenser à ce bureau
4. d'argent public
5. Je ne tolérerai pas ce...
6. Chut
7. plaçai ma main derrière mon oreille
8. ce léger bruit de froissement
9. est en train de décoller mon papier peint
10. je vous inculperai
11. prêt à batailler
12. m'avait bien cerné
13. Je bluffais.
14. de ramasser le paquet
15. de toute son existence
16. Qui étais-je, bon sang, pour lui faire la leçon
17. les valeurs
18. l'accord
19. J'étais en partie soulagé
20. j'en ressentis de la honte
21. ne serait pas compromise inutilement
22. La meilleure, c'est que je m'en tirais bien.
23. Cela ne venait pas de moi.

"Don't do this," I said, but there was nothing left in my try[1]. She could see that. She smiled. Then they left my office. First Chamique, then her attorney. His cologne stayed behind as a memento[2].

Muse shrugged and said, "What can you do?"

I was wondering that myself.

I got home and had dinner with Cara. She had a "homework" assignment[3] that consisted of finding things that were red in magazines and cutting them out[4]. This would seem like a very easy task, but of course, nothing we found together would work for her[5]. She didn't like the red wagon[6] or the model[7]'s red dress or even the red fire engine[8]. The problem, I soon realized, was that I was showing enthusiasm[9] for what she'd find. I would say, "That dress *is* red, sweetie! You're right! I think that would be perfect!"

After about twenty minutes of this, I saw the error of my ways[10]. When she stumbled across[11] a picture of a bottle of a ketchup, I made my voice flat[12] and shrugged my shoulders and said, "I don't really like ketchup."

She grabbed the scissors with the safety handles[13] and went to work.

Kids.

Cara started singing a song as she cut. The song was from a cartoon TV show[14] called *Dora the Explorer*[15] and basically[16] consisted of singing the word *backpack*[17] over and over again[18] until the head of a nearby[19] parent exploded into a million pieces. I had made the mistake about two months ago of buying her a Dora the Explorer Talking[20] Backpack ("backpack, backpack," repeat) with matching talking Map[21] (song: "I'm the map, I'm the map, I'm the map," repeat). When her cousin, Madison, came over[22], they would often play Dora the Explorer. One of them would play the role of Dora. The other would be a monkey with the rather interesting moniker[23]

1. cette tentative pour la faire changer d'avis sonnait creux
2. en souvenir
3. un « devoir » à faire
4. à les découper
5. ne lui convenait
6. chariot
7. mannequin
8. camion de pompiers rouge
9. je m'enthousiasmais
10. que mon approche n'était pas la bonne
11. tomba sur
12. pris un ton neutre
13. à poignées sécurisées pour les enfants
14. dessin animé
15. Dora l'exploratrice
16. essentiellement
17. sac à dos
18. indéfiniment
19. se trouvant non loin de là
20. parlant
21. carte parlante assortie
22. venait à la maison
23. doté d'un surnom assez curieux

"Boots[1]." You don't often meet monkeys named for footwear[2].

I was thinking about that, about Boots, about the way Cara and her cousin would argue over[3] who would be Dora and who would be Boots, when it struck me like the proverbial thunderbolt[4].

I froze. I actually stopped and just sat there[5]. Even Cara saw it.

"Daddy?"

"One second, kitten[6]."

I ran upstairs, my footsteps shaking[7] the house. Where the hell were those bills[8] from the frat house? I started tearing apart[9] the room. It took me a few minutes to find them – I had been ready to throw them all away after my meeting this morning.

Bang[10], there they were.

I riffled through them.[11] I found the online charges[12], the monthly ones[13], and then I grabbed the phone and called Muse's number. She answered on the first ring.

"What's up?"

"When you were in college," I asked, "how often did you pull all-nighters[14]?"

"Twice a week[15] minimum."

"How did you keep yourself awake?"

"M&Ms. Lots of them. The oranges[16] are amphetamines, I swear."

"Buy as many as you need. You can even expense them[17]."

"I like the tone of your voice, Cope."

"I have an idea, but I don't know if we have the time."

"Don't worry about the time. What's the idea concerning?"

"It concerns," I said, "our old buddies[18] Cal and Jim."

1. [Babouche]
2. portant le nom d'une chaussure
3. se disputait pour savoir
4. lorsqu'une idée jaillit en un éclair
5. restai immobile
6. chaton
7. ébranlant
8. factures
9. à tout retourner dans
10. Bingo
11. Je les passai en revue.
12. les factures des commandes en ligne
13. celles qui étaient mensuelles
14. quelle était la fréquence de tes nuits blanches
15. Deux fois par semaine
16. Ceux qui sont orange
17. les passer en notes de frais
18. vieux potes

Chapter 17

I got Cologne Lawyer Foley's home number and woke him up[1].

"Don't sign those papers until the afternoon," I said.

"Why?"

"Because if you do, I will make sure[2] my office comes down on you and your client as hard as they can[3]. I will let it be known[4] that we don't cut deals[5] with Horace Foley, that we always make sure the client serves the maximum time[6]."

"You can't do that."

I said nothing.

"I have an obligation to my client."

"Tell her I asked for the extra time[7]. Tell her it's in her best interest[8]."

"And what do I say to the other side?"

"I don't know, Foley, find something wrong[9] with the paperwork maybe, whatever[10]. Just stall[11] until the afternoon."

"And how is that in my client's best interest?"

"If I get lucky and hurt them, you can renegotiate. More moola[12] in your pockets."

He paused. Then: "Hey, Cope?"

"What?"

"She's a strange kid. Chamique, I mean."

1. le réveillai
2. je veillerai à ce que
3. tombe à bras raccourcis sur vous et votre cliente
4. passerai le mot
5. qu'on ne négocie rien
6. purge la peine la plus longue
7. délai supplémentaire
8. c'est dans son intérêt
9. trouvez quelque chose qui ne va pas
10. n'importe quoi
11. Gagnez simplement du temps
12. Plus de fric

"How so?[1]"

"Most of them would have taken the money right away. I've had to push her because, frankly, taking the money early is her best move[2]. We both know that. But she wouldn't hear of it[3] until they sandbagged her[4] with that Jim/James thing yesterday. See, before that, despite what she said in court, she was more interested in them going to jail than the financial payoff[5]. She really wanted justice."

"And that surprises you?"

"You're new on this job[6]. Me, I've been doing this for twenty-seven years. You grow[7] cynical. So yeah, she surprised the hell out of me[8]."

"Is there a point to your telling me all this?[9]"

"Yeah, there is. Me, you know what I'm all about[10]. Getting my one-third of the settlement[11]. But Chamique is different. This is life-changing[12] money for her. So whatever you're up to[13], Mr. Prosecutor, don't screw it up for her[14]."

Lucy drank alone.

It was night. Lucy lived on campus in faculty housing[15]. The place was beyond[16] depressing. Most professors worked hard and long and saved money in the hopes[17] that they could move the hell out[18] of faculty housing. Lucy had lived here for a year now. Before her, an English-lit professor named Amanda Simon had spent three decades of spinsterhood[19] in this very unit. Lung[20] cancer cut her down[21] at the age of fifty-eight. Her remnants remained[22] in the smoky smell left behind[23]. Despite ripping up the wall-to-wall carpeting[24] and repainting the entire place, the cigarette stench[25] remained. It was a little like living in an ashtray[26].

Lucy was a vodka girl. She looked out the window. In the distance, she heard music. This was a college campus. There was always music playing. She checked her watch. Midnight.

1. Comment ça ?
2. c'est la meilleure tactique, pour elle
3. elle ne voulait pas en entendre parler
4. qu'ils s'acharnent sur elle
5. indemnité financière
6. dans le métier
7. On devient
8. elle m'a vachement surpris
9. Dans quel but me dites-vous tout ça ?
10. ce qui m'intéresse
11. mon tiers de la transaction
12. qui va changer sa vie
13. quel que soit votre plan
14. ne lui gâchez pas tout ça en vous plantant
15. un logement universitaire
16. plus que
17. en espérant
18. pouvoir dégager
19. trente ans de célibat
20. du poumon
21. l'avait fauchée
22. Il restait des traces d'elle
23. l'odeur de cigarette qu'elle avait laissée derrière elle
24. Même après avoir arraché la moquette
25. puanteur
26. cendrier

She flipped on[1] her own tinny-speaker[2] iPod stereo and set it[3] on a playlist she called "Mellow[4]." Each song was not only slow but a total heart ripper[5]. So she would drink her vodka and sit in her depressing apartment and smell the smoke from a dead woman and listen to aching[6] songs of[7] loss and want[8] and devastation. Pitiful, but sometimes it was enough to feel. It didn't matter if it hurt or not. Just to feel.

Right now, Joseph Arthur[9] was singing "Honey and the Moon." He sang to his true love[10] that if she weren't real, he would make her up[11]. Wow, what a thing. Lucy tried to imagine a man, a worthy man[12], saying that to her. It made her shake her head in wonder[13].

She closed her eyes and tried to put the pieces together. Nothing fit[14]. The past was rising up again. Lucy had spent her entire adult life running away from those dam woods at her father's camp. She had fled across the country, all the way to California, and she had fled all the way back again. She had changed her name and hair color. But the past always followed. Sometimes it would let her gain a comfortable lead[15] – lulled her into thinking[16] that she had put enough distance between that night and the present day – but the dead always closed the gap[17].

In the end that awful night always found her.

But this time... how? Those journal entries... how could they exist? Sylvia Potter had barely been born[18] when the Summer Slasher struck Camp PLUS (Peace Love Understanding Summer). What could she know about it? Of course, like Lonnie, she might have gone online, done some research, figured out[19] that Lucy had a past. Or maybe someone, someone older and wiser[20], had told her something.

But still. How would she know? For that matter[21], how would anyone know? Only one person knew that Lucy had lied about what happened that night.

And, of course, Paul wouldn't say anything.

1. alluma
2. dont le haut-parleur égrenait un son métallique
3. le régla
4. Mélo
5. elle vous déchirait le cœur
6. douloureuses
7. parlant de
8. de désir
9. [chanteur pop/rock]
10. à l'amour de sa vie
11. il l'inventerait
12. un homme bien
13. l'air songeur
14. ne collait
15. lui laissait une confortable avance
16. lui faisant croire
17. la rattrapaient toujours
18. venait à peine de naître
19. avoir découvert
20. de plus habile
21. D'ailleurs

She stared through the clear[1] liquid in her glass. Paul. Paul Copeland. She could still see him with those gangly[2] arms and legs, that lean torso[3], that long hair, that knock-a-girl-back[4] smile. Interestingly enough, they had met through their fathers. Paul's old man, an ob-gyn[5] in his old country[6], had escaped[7] repression in the Soviet Union only to find plenty of it[8] here in the good ol'[9] USA. Ira, Lucy's bleeding-heart[10] father, could never resist a tale of woe like that[11]. So Ira hired Vladimir Copeland to be camp doctor. Gave his family a chance to escape Newark in the summer.

Lucy could still see it – their car, a broken-down[12] Oldsmobile Ciera, kicking up the dirt road[13], coming to a stop, the four doors opening seemingly at the same time, the family of four stepping out as one. At that moment, when Lucy first saw Paul and their eyes met, it was boom, crack, thunderbolt[14]. And she could see that he felt the same. There are those rare moments in life – when you feel that jolt and it feels great[15] and it hurts like hell[16], but you're feeling, really feeling, and suddenly colors seem brighter and sounds have more clarity and foods taste better[17] and you never, not even for a minute, stop thinking about him and you know, just know, that he is feeling exactly the same way about you.

"Like that," Lucy said out loud and took another swig[18] of her vodka and tonic. Like with these pathetic songs she played over and over. A feeling. A rush of emotion.[19] A high or a low, didn't matter. But it wasn't the same anymore. What had Elton John sung, via those Bernie Taupin[20] lyrics[21], about vodka and tonic? Something about taking a couple of vodka and tonics to set you on your feet again[22].

That hadn't worked for Lucy. But hey, why give up[23] now?

The little voice in her head said, *Stop drinking.*

The much bigger voice told the little voice to shut up or get its ass kicked[24].

1. limpide
2. dégingandés
3. torse mince
4. séducteur
5. gynécologue obstétricien
6. pays d'origine
7. avait fui
8. pour mieux la subir
9. nos bons vieux
10. sentimental
11. une histoire aussi poignante
12. en piteux état
13. faisant voler la poussière du chemin de terre
14. ce fut le coup de foudre
15. ressentez ce choc, que c'est grandiose
16. fait affreusement mal
17. les aliments ont meilleur goût
18. avala une autre lampée
19. Une bouffée d'émotion.
20. [chanteur et parolier d'Elton John]
21. paroles des chansons
22. pour se remettre sur pied
23. renoncer
24. de la fermer sinon ça allait barder

Lucy made a fist[1] and put it in the air[2]. “Go, Big Voice!”

She laughed, and that sound, the sound of her own laugh alone in this still room, frightened her. Rob Thomas[3] came on her “Mellow” list, asking if he could just hold her while she falls apart[4], if he could just hold her while they both fall down. She nodded. Yes, he could. Rob reminded her that she was cold and scared and broken[5], and damn her[6], she wanted to listen to this song with Paul.

Paul.

He would want to know about these journals.

It had been twenty years since she’d seen him, but six years ago, Lucy had looked him up[7] on the Internet. She had not wanted to. She knew that Paul was a door best left closed[8]. But she had gotten drunk – big surprise – and while some people “drunk dialed[9],” Lucy had “drunk Googled.”

What she’d found was both sobering and unsurprising[10]. Paul was married. He worked as an attorney. He had a young daughter. Lucy had even managed to find a picture of his gorgeous[11] wife from a well-to-do[12] family at some charity function[13]. Jane – that was his wife’s name – was tall and lean and wore pearls. She looked good in pearls. She had that whole meant-for-pearls thing going on[14].

Another swig.

Things might have changed in six years, but back then Paul was living in Ridgewood, New Jersey, a scant[15] twenty miles from where Lucy now was. She looked across the room[16] at her computer.

Paul should be told, shouldn’t he?

And it would be no problem to do another quick Google search. Just get a phone number for him – home or, better, office. She could contact him. Warn him, really. Totally on the up-and-up.[17] No agenda[18], no hidden meanings[19], nothing like that.

1. serra le poing
2. le brandit en l'air
3. [chanteur du groupe Matchbox 20 et artiste solo]
4. la soutenir pendant qu'elle craquait
5. en miettes
6. bon sang
7. l'avait cherché
8. qui devait rester fermée
9. [appeler d'anciennes connaissances en étant ivre]
10. sans surprise et avait agi comme une douche froide
11. splendide
12. aisée
13. soirée de bienfaisance
14. l'air d'être née pour porter des perles
15. à peine à
16. à l'autre bout de la pièce
17. Tout ce qu'il y a de plus honnête.
18. Sans idée préconçue
19. sous-entendus

She put down the vodka and tonic. Rain fell outside the window. Her computer was already on[1]. Her screen saver[2] was, yep, the Windows default[3] one. No family vacation picture. No slideshow[4] of the kids or even that spinster staple[5]: photograph of a pet[6]. Just that Windows logo bopping around, like the monitor was sticking its tongue out at her[7].

Beyond pathetic.[8]

She brought up her home page[9] and was about to type when she heard the knock on the door. She stopped, waited.

Another knock. Lucy checked the small clock in the bottom right-hand[10] corner of her computer.

Twelve-seventeen a.m.[11]

Awfully late for a visitor.

"Who is it?"

No reply. "Who – "

"It's Sylvia Potter."

There were tears in that voice. Lucy stood and stumbled[12] to the kitchen. She dumped[13] the rest of her drink into the sink and put the bottle back in its cabinet[14]. Vodka didn't smell, at least not much, so she was okay on that count[15]. She took a quick look in the mirror. The image in it looked like hell[16], but there wasn't much she could do about that now.

"Coming."

She opened the door and Sylvia tumbled in[17] as if she'd been leaning[18] against it. The girl was soaked[19]. The air-conditioning was set on high[20]. Lucy almost made some comment about her catching her death[21], but it sounded like something a mother would say. She closed the door.

Sylvia said, "I'm sorry it's so late."

"Don't worry about it. I was up.[22]"

She stopped in the center of the room. "I'm sorry about before."

"That's okay."

1. allumé
2. économiseur d'écran
3. par défaut
4. diaporama
5. ni même cet incontournable de toute vieille fille
6. animal de compagnie
7. dansant sur l'écran comme si ce dernier lui tirait la langue
8. C'était plus que pathétique.
9. afficha sa page d'accueil
10. en bas à droite
11. Minuit dix-sept.
12. tituba
13. jeta
14. placard
15. de ce point de vue
16. L'image renvoyée était affreuse
17. tomba presque à l'intérieur
18. s'était appuyée
19. trempée
20. réglé à fond
21. faillit lui dire qu'elle allait attraper froid
22. Je n'étais pas couchée.

"No, it's just..." Sylvia looked around. She wrapped her arms around her body.

"Do you want a towel[1] or something?"

"No."

"Can I get you something to drink?"

"I'm okay."

Lucy gestured for[2] Sylvia to have a seat. Sylvia collapsed[3] on the Ikea couch. Lucy hated Ikea and their graphics-only instruction manuals[4], seemingly designed[5] by NASA engineers. Lucy sat next to her and waited.

"How did you find out I wrote that journal?" Sylvia asked.

"It's not important."

"I sent it anonymously."

"I know."

"And you said they would be confidential."

"I know. I'm sorry about that."

Sylvia wiped her nose[6] and looked off[7]. Her hair was still dripping.[8]

"I even lied to you," Sylvia said.

"How's that?[9]"

"About what I wrote. When I visited your office the other day. Do you remember?"

"Yes."

"Do you remember what I said my paper was about?"

Lucy thought for a second. "Your first time.[10]"

Sylvia smiled but there was nothing behind it[11]. "I guess, in a sick way[12], that was true."

Lucy thought about that too. Then she said, "I'm not sure I follow, Sylvia."

Sylvia did not say anything for a long time. Lucy remembered that Lonnie said he would help get her to talk. But he was supposed to wait until the morning[13].

"Did Lonnie visit you tonight?"

"Lonnie Berger? From class?"

"Yes."

1. serviette
2. d'un geste, invita
3. s'écroula
4. notices de montage rien qu'avec des schémas
5. apparemment conçues
6. essuya son nez
7. regarda au loin
8. L'eau gouttait encore de ses cheveux.
9. Comment ça ?
10. Ton premier rapport sexuel.
11. mais sans expression
12. d'une façon assez odieuse
13. censé attendre le lendemain

"No. Why would Lonnie visit me?"

"It's not important. So you just came here on your own?"

Sylvia swallowed and looked unsure of herself[1]. "Was I wrong to?[2]"

"No, not at all. I'm glad you're here."

"I'm really scared," Sylvia said.

Lucy nodded, tried to appear reassuring, encouraging. Forcing this issue would only backfire.[3] So she waited. She waited for a full two[4] minutes before breaking[5].

"There's no reason to be scared," Lucy said.

"What do you think I should do?"

"Tell me everything, okay?"

"I have. I mean, the majority of it."

Lucy wondered how to play this[6]. "Who is P?"

Sylvia frowned. "What?"

"In your journal. You talk about a boy named P. Who is P?"

"What are you talking about?"

Lucy stopped. Tried again.

"Tell me exactly why you're here, Sylvia."

But now Sylvia was being cagey[7]. "Why did you come to my room today?"

"Because I wanted to talk about your journal."

"Then why are you asking me about a guy named P? I didn't call anyone P. I said straight out[8] that it was..." The words stuck in her throat[9]. She closed her eyes and whispered, "... my father."

The dam broke.[10] The tears came down[11] like the rain, in sheets[12].

Lucy closed her eyes. The incest story. The one that had struck her and Lonnie with such horror[13]. Damn. Lonnie had gotten it wrong[14]. Sylvia hadn't written the journal about that night in the woods.

"Your father molested you[15] when you were twelve," Lucy said.

1. perplexe
2. J'ai eu tort ?
3. Insister lourdement serait contre-productif.
4. deux bonnes
5. avant de reprendre la conversation
6. se demanda comment aborder le sujet
7. devenait méfiante
8. J'ai dit ouvertement
9. restèrent bloqués dans sa gorge
10. La digue se rompit.
11. ruisselèrent
12. à torrents
13. les avaient tant horrifiés, Lonnie et elle
14. s'était planté
15. t'a agressée sexuellement

Sylvia's face was in her hands. Her sobs sounded as if they were being ripped out of her chest[1]. Her entire body quaked[2] as she nodded her head. Lucy looked at this poor girl, so anxious to please, and pictured[3] the father. She reached out her hand[4] and put it on Sylvia's. Then she moved closer and put her arms around the girl. Sylvia leaned into[5] her chest and cried. Lucy shushed her and rocked her and held her[6].

1. résonnaient comme s'ils lui déchiraient le cœur
2. tremblait
3. imagina
4. tendit la main
5. se blottit contre
6. la calma et la berça dans ses bras

Chapter 18

I hadn't slept. Neither had Muse. I managed a quick electric shave.[1] I smelled so bad I debated asking[2] Horace Foley if I could borrow[3] his cologne.

"Get me that paperwork[4]," I told Muse.

"As soon as I can."

When the judge called us to order[5], I called a – gasp[6] – surprise witness.

"The People call Gerald Flynn."

Flynn had been the "nice" boy[7] who'd invited Chamique Johnson to the party. He looked the part, too[8], what with his too-smooth skin, nicely parted blond locks[9], wide[10] blue eyes that seemed to gaze at everything with naïveté. Because there was a chance I would end my side of the case at any time[11], the defense had made sure Flynn was waiting[12]. He was, after all, supposed to be their key witness.

Flynn had steadfastly backed[13] his fraternity brothers[14]. But it was one thing to lie to the police and even in depositions. It was another to do it during "the show.[15]" I looked back at Muse. She sat in the last row[16] and tried to keep a straight[17] face. The results were mixed[18]. Muse would not be my first choice as a poker buddy[19].

I asked him to say his name for the record[20].

1. J'eus juste le temps de me passer un rapide coup de rasoir électrique.
2. que j'envisageai de demander à
3. lui emprunter
4. Récupère-moi ces documents
5. déclara l'audience ouverte
6. tenez-vous bien !
7. gentil garçon
8. C'était bien l'impression qu'il donnait
9. avec sa peau trop lisse, ses boucles blondes, sa raie soignée
10. de grands
11. que je jette l'éponge à tout moment
12. s'était assurée d'avoir Flynn sous la main
13. constamment soutenu
14. ses camarades de la résidence
15. Le faire pendant le procès, c'était autre chose.
16. au dernier rang
17. impassible
18. résultat était mitigé
19. partenaire de poker
20. pour le procès-verbal

"Gerald Flynn."

"But you go by[1] Jerry, isn't that correct?"

"Yes."

"Fine, let's start from the beginning, shall we? When did you first[2] meet the defendant, Ms. Chamique Johnson?"

Chamique had come today. She was sitting near the center in the second-to-last[3] row with Horace Foley. Interesting spot to sit[4]. Like she didn't want to commit[5]. I had heard some screaming[6] in the corridors earlier in the morning. The Jenrette and Marantz families were not pleased with the last-minute snafu[7] in their Chamique retraction[8]. They had tried to nail it down[9], but it hadn't worked out[10]. So we were starting late. Still they were ready. Their court faces[11], concerned[12], serious, engaged[13], were back in place[14].

It was a temporary delay, they figured[15]. Just a few more hours.

"When she came to the fraternity house on October twelfth," he replied.

"You remember the date?"

"Yes."

I made a face like, *My, my*[16]*, isn't that interesting*, even though it wasn't. Sure, he would know[17] the date. This was a part of his life now too.

"Why was Ms. Johnson at your fraternity house?"

"She was hired[18] as an exotic dancer."

"Did you hire her?"

"No. Well, I mean, the whole fraternity did[19]. But I wasn't the one who made the booking[20] or anything."

"I see. So she came to your fraternity house and performed[21] an exotic dance?"

"Yes."

"And you watched this dance?"

"I did."

"What did you think of it?"

Mort Pubin was up. "Objection!"

1. on vous appelle
2. pour la première fois
3. avant-dernier
4. qu'elle soit assise là
5. s'impliquer
6. des vociférations
7. le pataquès de dernière minute
8. dans la rétractation de Chamique
9. tenté d'obtenir celle-ci
10. n'avait pas marché
11. Leurs masques de circonstance
12. inquiets
13. impliqués
14. étaient à nouveau de mise
15. s'imaginaient-ils
16. Dis donc
17. Bien sûr qu'il connaissait
18. avait été engagée
19. c'était toute la résidence
20. ce n'est pas moi qui ai fait la réservation
21. a exécuté

The judge was already scowling in my direction[1]. "Mr. Copeland?"

"According to[2] Ms. Johnson, Mr. Flynn here invited her to the party where the rape took place. I am trying to understand why he would do that."

"So ask him that," Pubin said.

"Your Honor, may I please do this in my own way?"

Judge Pierce said, "Try to rephrase."

I turned back to Flynn. "Did you think Ms. Johnson was a good exotic dancer?" I asked.

"I guess."

"Yes or no?"

"Not great. But yeah, I thought she was pretty good[3]."

"Did you think she was attractive?"

"Yeah, I mean, I guess so."

"Yes or no?"

"Objection!" Pubin again. "He doesn't have to answer a question like that yes or no[4]. Maybe he thought she was mildly attractive[5]. It isn't always yes or no."

"I agree, Mort," I said, surprising him. "Let me rephrase, Mr. Flynn – how would you describe her attractiveness[6]?"

"Like on a one-to-ten scale[7]?"

"That would be splendid, Mr. Flynn. On a one-to-ten scale."

He thought about it. "Seven, maybe an eight."

"Fine, thank you. And at some point[8] in the evening, did you talk to Ms. Johnson?"

"Yes."

"What did you talk about?"

"I don't know."

"Try to remember."

"I asked her where she lived. She said Irvington. I asked her if she went to school or if she had a boyfriend. That kinda thing.[9] She told me about having[10] a kid. She asked me what I was studying. I said I wanted to go to medical school[11]."

1. me faisait déjà les gros yeux
2. Selon
3. assez bonne
4. par oui ou non
5. modérément séduisante
6. son charme
7. sur une échelle de un à dix
8. à un moment donné
9. Ce genre de trucs.
10. qu'elle avait
11. en fac de médecine

"Anything else?"

"It was like that."

"I see. How long would you say you talked with her?"

"I don't know."

"Let me see if I can help you then. Was it more than five minutes?"

"Yes."

"More than an hour?"

"No, I don't think so."

"More than a half an hour?"

"I'm not sure."

"More than ten minutes?"

"I think so."

Judge Pierce interrupted, telling me that we got the point[1] and that I should move it along[2].

"How did Ms. Johnson depart[3] that particular event[4], if you know?"

"A car came and picked her up[5]."

"Oh, was she the only exotic dancer there that evening?"

"No."

"How many others were there?"

"There were three altogether[6]."

"Thank you. Did the other two leave with Ms. Johnson?"

"Yes."

"Did you talk with either of them[7]?"

"Not really. Maybe a hello."

"Would it be fair to say[8] that Chamique Johnson was the only one of the three exotic dancers you had a conversation with?"

Pubin looked as though he wanted to object but then he decided to let it go.

"Yes," Flynn said. "That would be fair."

Enough prelims.[9] "Chamique Johnson testified that she made extra money by performing a sexual

1. nous avions bien compris
2. qu'il fallait que j'avance
3. Mlle Johnson est-elle partie de
4. cette soirée-là
5. est venue la chercher
6. en tout
7. l'une ou l'autre
8. exact de déclarer
9. Assez de préliminaires.

act on[1] several of the young men at the party. Do you know if that's true?"

"I don't know."

"Really? So you didn't engage[2] her services?"

"I did not."

"And you never heard a word mentioned by any of your fraternity brothers about Ms. Johnson performing acts of a sexual nature on them?"

Flynn was trapped[3]. He was either going to lie[4] or admit an illegal activity was going on. He did the dumbest thing of all[5] – he took the middle road[6]. "I may have heard some whispers[7]."

Nice and wishy-washy, making him look like a total liar.[8]

I put on my best incredulous tone[9]. "May have heard some whispers?"

"Yes."

"So you're not sure if you heard some whispers," I said, as if this was the most ridiculous thing I had ever heard in my life, "but you may have. You simply cannot remember if you heard whispers or not. Is that your testimony?"

Flair stood this time. "Your Honor?"

The judge looked at him.

"Is this a rape case or is Mr. Copeland now working vice[10]?" He spread his hands. "Is his rape case so weak[11] now, so far-fetched[12], that he is now fishing to indict[13] these boys on soliciting[14] a prostitute?"

I said, "That's not what I'm after[15]."

Flair smiled at me. "Then please ask this witness questions that concern this alleged assault. Don't ask him to recite every misbehavior[16] he's ever seen a friend commit."

The judge said, "Let's move on, Mr. Copeland."

Friggin[17]' Flair.

"Did you ask Ms. Johnson for her phone number?"

"Yes."

"Why?"

1. en se livrant à des actes sexuels avec
2. n'avez pas eu recours à
3. pris au piège
4. allait soit mentir
5. la chose la plus idiote
6. choisit un entre-deux
7. des rumeurs
8. C'était tellement charmant et cucul que cela donnait vraiment l'impression qu'il mentait.
9. ton le plus incrédule
10. M. Copeland travaille-t-il à présent à la brigade des mœurs
11. fragile
12. tiré par les cheveux
13. cherche la petite bête pour inculper
14. d'avoir sollicité
15. ce que je cherche à prouver
16. raconter tous les écarts de conduite
17. Satané

"I thought I might call her."

"You liked her?"

"I was attracted to her[1], yes."

"Because she was a seven, maybe an eight?" I waved[2] before Pubin could move. "Withdrawn. Did there come a time when you[3] called Ms. Johnson?"

"Yes."

"Can you tell us when, and as best as you can, please tell us what was said in that conversation?"

"Ten days later I called and asked her if she wanted to come to a party at the fraternity."

"Did you want her to dance exotically again?"

"No," Flynn said. I saw him swallow[4] and his eyes were a little wet[5] now. "I asked her as a guest.[6]"

I let that sit.[7] I looked at Jerry Flynn. I let the jury look at him. There was something in his face. Had he liked Chamique Johnson? I let the moment linger[8]. Because I was confused[9]. I had thought that Jerry Flynn was part of it – that he had called Chamique and set her up[10]. I tried to work it through[11] in my head.

The judge said, "Mr. Copeland."

"Did Ms. Johnson accept your invitation?"

"Yes."

"When you say you invited her as your" – I made quote marks[12] with my fingers – "'guest,' do you really mean 'date[13]'?"

"Yes."

I followed him through meeting her[14] and getting her punch.

"Did you tell her it was spiked with alcohol?" I asked.

"Yes."

It was a lie. And it looked like a lie, but I wanted to emphasize the ridiculousness of that claim[15].

"Tell me how that conversation went[16]," I said.

"I don't understand the question."

1. Elle m'attirait
2. Je fis un geste de la main
3. Avez-vous, à moment donné
4. avaler sa salive
5. humides
6. C'était mon invitée.
7. Je me tus et attendis un peu.
8. ce moment se prolonger
9. perplexe
10. pour la piéger
11. de comprendre la situation
12. des guillemets
13. voulez-vous dire, en fait, que vous vouliez sortir avec elle
14. Je lui fis raconter comment il était allé la chercher
15. rendre cette affirmation encore plus ridicule
16. s'est déroulée

"Did you ask Ms. Johnson if she wanted something to drink?"

"Yes."

"And did she say yes?"

"Yes."

"And then what did you say?"

"I asked her if she wanted some punch."

"And what did she say?"

"She said yes."

"And then what?"

He shifted in his chair. "I said it was spiked."

I arched the eyebrow. "Just like that?"

"Objection!" Pubin rose. "Just like what? He said it was spiked. Asked and answered."

He was right. Leave them with the obvious lie.[1] I waved to the judge that I would let it go. I started walking him through[2] the night. Flynn stuck to[3] the story he'd already told, about how Chamique got drunk[4], how she started flirting with Edward Jenrette.

"How did you react when that happened?"

He shrugged. "Edward is a senior[5], I'm a freshman[6]. It happens."

"So you think Chamique was impressed because Mr. Jenrette was older?"

Again Pubin decided to not object.

"I don't know," Flynn said. "Maybe."

"Oh, by the way[7], have you ever been in Mr. Marantz and Mr. Jenrette's room?"

"Sure."

"How many times?"

"I don't know. A lot."

"Really? But you're just a freshman."

"They're still[8] my friends."

I made my skeptical face.[9] "Have you been in there more than once[10]?"

"Yes."

"More than ten times?"

"Yes."

1. Qu'ils restent sur ce mensonge éhonté.
2. Je lui fis décrire le déroulement de
3. s'en tint à
4. s'était soûlée
5. en licence
6. en première année
7. au fait
8. tout de même
9. Je pris un air sceptique.
10. plus d'une fois

I made my face even more skeptical. "Okay then, tell me: What sort of stereo or music system do they have in the room?"

Flynn answered it immediately. "They have a Bose speakers[1] iPod system."

I knew that already. We had searched[2] the room. We had pictures.

"How about the television in their room? How big is it?"

He smiled as if he'd seen my trap[3]. "They don't have one."

"No television at all?"

"None."

"Okay then, back to[4] the night in question..."

Flynn continued to weave his tale[5]. He started partying[6] with his friends. He saw Chamique start up[7] the stairs holding hands[8] with Jenrette. He didn't know what happened after that, of course. Then later that night, he met up with Chamique again[9] and walked her[10] to the bus stop.

"Did she seem upset?" I asked.

Flynn said no, just the opposite[11]. Chamique was "smiling" and "happy" and light as air[12]. His Pollyanna[13] description was overkill[14].

"So when Chamique Johnson talked about going out to the keg[15] with you and then walking upstairs and being grabbed in the corridor." I said, "that was all a lie?"

Flynn was smart enough not to bite[16]. "I'm telling you what I saw."

"Do you know anyone named Cal or Jim?"

He thought about it. "I know a couple of guys named Jim. I don't think I know any Cals."

"Are you aware[17] that Ms. Johnson claimed[18] the men who raped her were named" – I didn't want Flair objecting with his semantics game[19] but I did roll my eyes a little when I said the word *named* – "Cal and Jim?"

1. avec des baffles Bose
2. perquisitionné
3. piège
4. retournons à
5. débiter son histoire
6. à faire la fête
7. monter
8. main dans la main
9. avait revu Chamique
10. l'avait raccompagnée
11. bien au contraire
12. l'esprit léger
13. digne de Pollyana [héroïne résolument optimiste d'un roman des années 1920]
14. excessive
15. fût de bière
16. fut assez malin pour ne pas mordre à l'hameçon
17. Êtes-vous au courant
18. a affirmé
19. petit jeu sémantique

He was wondering how to handle that one[1]. He went with the truth.[2] "I heard that."

"Was there anyone named Cal or Jim at the party?"

"Not that I'm aware of.[3]"

"I see. And would you know any reason why Mr. Jenrette and Mr. Marantz would call themselves that?"

"No."

"Ever heard[4] those two names together[5]? I mean, before the alleged rape?"

"Not that I can recall.[6]"

"So you can't shine a light on[7] why Ms. Johnson would testify that her attackers were named Cal and Jim?"

Pubin shouted his objection. "How could he possibly know why this deranged, intoxicated[8] woman would lie?"

I kept my eyes on the witness. "Nothing comes to mind[9], Mr. Flynn?"

"Nothing," he said firmly.

I looked back at Loren Muse. Her head was down, fiddling with[10] her BlackBerry. She glanced up[11], met my eye, nodded once[12].

"Your Honor," I said, "I have more questions for this witness but this might make a good place to break for lunch[13]."

Judge Pierce agreed.

I tried not to sprint over to[14] Loren Muse.

"We got it," she said with a grin[15]. "The fax is in your office."

1. comment répondre à cette question sans embûches
2. Il opta pour la vérité.
3. Pas à ma connaissance.
4. Vous avez déjà entendu
5. associés
6. Non, pas que je me souvienne.
7. ne pouvez pas expliquer
8. perturbée et ivre
9. qui ne vous vienne à l'esprit
10. tandis qu'elle pianotait sur
11. leva les yeux
12. hocha la tête une fois
13. c'est peut-être le bon moment pour une pause-déjeuner
14. de ne pas courir vers
15. en souriant

Chapter 19

Lucy was lucky that she had no morning class[1]. Between the amount she drank[2] and the late night[3] with Sylvia Potter, she had stayed in bed until noon[4]. When she rose she placed a call to[5] one of the school counselors[6], Katherine Lucas, a therapist[7] Lucy had always thought was really good. She explained the situation with Sylvia. Lucas would have a better idea what to do.

She thought about the journal entry that had started this all[8]. The woods. The screams. The blood. Sylvia Potter hadn't sent it. So who had?

No clue.[9]

Last night, she had decided to call Paul. He needed to know about this, she'd concluded. But had that been the booze talking[10]? Now that it was sobering daylight[11], did that still seem to be a good idea?

An hour later, she found Paul's work number[12] on the computer. He was the Essex County prosecutor – and, alas[13], a widower. Jane had died of cancer. Paul had set up a charity[14] in her name. Lucy wondered how she felt about all that, but there was no way she could sort through that[15] right now.

With a shaking hand[16] she dialed[17] the number. When she reached the switchboard operator[18], she

1. de ne pas avoir de cours ce matin
2. tout ce qu'elle avait bu
3. le fait d'avoir veillé tard
4. midi
5. passa un coup de fil à
6. psychologues scolaires
7. thérapeute
8. tout déclenché
9. Aucune idée.
10. était-ce l'alcool qui l'avait poussée à cette décision
11. Maintenant qu'il faisait jour et que l'effet de l'alcool s'estompait
12. numéro professionnel
13. hélas
14. fondé une œuvre de bienfaisance
15. il n'était pas question de réfléchir à tout ça
16. D'une main tremblante
17. composa
18. standardiste

asked to speak to Paul Copeland. It hurt when she said that. She realized[1] that she hadn't said his name out loud[2] in twenty years.

Paul Copeland.

A woman answered and said, "County prosecutor."

"I would like to speak to Paul Copeland, please."

"May I ask who's calling?"

"I'm an old friend," she said.

Nothing.

"My name is Lucy. Tell him it's Lucy. From twenty years ago."

"Do you have a last name[3], Lucy?"

"Just tell him that, okay?"

"Prosecutor Copeland isn't in the office at the moment. Would you like to leave a number so he can return your call[4]?"

Lucy gave her the numbers for her home, her office, her mobile.

"May I tell him what this is in reference to[5]?"

"Just tell him that it's Lucy. And that it's important."

Muse and I were in my office. The door was closed. We had ordered in[6] deli[7] sandwiches for lunch. I was having chicken salad on whole wheat[8]. Muse was downing[9] a meatball sub[10] that was the approximate size of a surfboard[11].

I had the fax in my hands. "Where is your private eye? Cingle whatever[12]?"

"Shaker. Cingle Shaker. She'll be here."

I sat and looked over[13] my notes.

"Do you want to talk it out[14]?" she asked.

"No."

She had a big grin on her face.

"What?" I said.

"I hate to say this[15], Cope, you being my boss and all[16], but you're a doggone genius[17]."

"Yeah," I said. "I guess I am."

I went back to my notes.

1. se rendit compte
2. prononcé son nom à voix haute
3. nom de famille
4. pour qu'il vous rappelle
5. de quoi il s'agit
6. On s'était fait livrer
7. de chez un traiteur
8. dans du pain complet
9. engloutissait
10. [sandwich allongé]
11. planche de surf
12. je-sais-pas-quoi
13. examinai
14. qu'on passe tout en revue
15. Ça m'embête de le dire
16. car t'es mon patron et tout et tout
17. sacré génie

Muse said, "You want me to leave you alone?"

"No. I may think of something I need you to do."

She lifted the sandwich. I was surprised that she could do it without the use of an industrial crane[1]. "Your predecessor," Muse said, teeth-diving[2] into the sandwich. "With big cases, sometimes he would sit there and stare[3] and say he was getting into a zone[4]. Like he was Michael Jordan. You do that?"

"No."

"So" – more chewing, some swallowing[5] – "would it distract you if I raised another issue[6]?"

"You mean something that doesn't involve[7] this case?"

"That's what I mean."

I looked up. "Actually, I could use the distraction[8]. What's on your mind?"

She looked off to the right, took a moment or two[9]. Then she said, "I have friends in Manhattan homicide[10]."

I had an idea where this was going. I took a delicate bite[11] of my chicken-salad sandwich. "Dry," I said.

"What?"

"The chicken salad. It's dry." I put it down and wiped my finger with the napkin[12]. "Let me guess. One of your homicide friends told you about the murder of Manolo Santiago?"

"Yeah."

"Did they tell you what my theory was?"

"About him being one of the boys[13] who the Summer Slasher murdered at that camp, even though his parents say it's not him?"

"That would be the one.[14]"

"Yeah, they told me."

"And?"

"And they think you're crackers[15]."

I smiled. "What about you?"

1. grue industrielle
2. en mordant à pleines dents
3. avec le regard fixe
4. qu'il se préparait au combat
5. elle mâcha encore puis avala
6. je soulevais une autre question
7. n'a rien à voir avec
8. passer à autre chose me ferait du bien
9. regarda au loin vers la droite, s'accorda un instant
10. brigade criminelle
11. bouchée
12. serviette
13. Que c'est l'un des adolescents
14. C'est bien ça.
15. taré

"I would have thought you were crackers. Except now" – she pointed to the fax – "I see what you're capable of. So I guess what I'm saying is, I want in[1]."

"In on what?[2]"

"You know what. You're going to investigate[3], right? You're going to see if you can figure out what really happened in those woods?"

"I am," I said.

She spread her hands.[4] "I want in."

"I can't have you taking up county business with[5] my personal affairs."

"First off[6]," Muse said, "while everyone is sure that Wayne Steubens killed them all, the homicide file is technically still open. In fact, a quadruple homicide, when you think about it, remains unsolved[7]."

"That did not take place in our county."

"We don't know that. We only know where the bodies were found. And one victim, your sister, lived in this very city."

"That's stretching it.[8]"

"Second, I am hired[9] to work forty hours a week. I do closer to[10] eighty. You know that. It is why you promoted me[11]. So what I do outside of those forty hours is up to me[12]. Or I'll up it to[13] one hundred, I don't care. And before you ask, no, this isn't just a favor for my boss. Let's face it[14], I'm an investigator. Solving it would be a heck of a feather in my cap[15]. So what do you say?"

I shrugged. "What the hell.[16]"

"I'm in?"

"You're in."

She looked very pleased. "So what's step one[17]?"

I thought about it. There was something I had to do. I had avoided it. I couldn't avoid it any longer.

"Wayne Steubens," I said.

"The Summer Slasher."

"I need to see him."

"You knew him, right?"

1. que je veux participer
2. À quoi ?
3. mener une enquête
4. Elle tendit les mains avec emphase.
5. Je ne peux pas te demander de consacrer une partie de ton temps de travail à
6. D'abord
7. n'est toujours pas résolu
8. Tu tires un peu sur la corde.
9. on m'a engagée
10. J'en fais plutôt
11. m'as accordé une promotion
12. ne regarde que moi
13. j'en ferai jusqu'à
14. Soyons honnêtes
15. ce serait un sacré bon point pour moi
16. Et puis zut.
17. on commence par quoi

I nodded. "We were both counselors[1] at that camp."

"I think I read that he doesn't allow visitors[2]."

"We need to change his mind[3]," I said.

"He's in a maximum security facility[4] in Virginia," Muse said. "I can make some calls."

Muse already knew where Steubens was being held[5]. Incredible.

"Do that," I said.

There was a knock on my door and my secretary, Jocelyn Durels, stuck her head[6] in the door. "Messages," she said. "You want me to stick them on your desk?"

I waved my fingers for her to hand them to me[7]. "Anything important?"

"Not really. A fair amount[8] from media. You'd think they'd know you're in court, but they still call."

I took the messages and started sorting through them[9]. I looked up at Muse. She was glancing around. There was almost nothing personal in this office. When I first moved in, I put a picture of Cara on my credenza[10]. Two days later we arrested a child molester[11] who had done unspeakable[12] things to a girl around Cara's age[13]. We talked about it in this office and I kept looking over at my daughter and finally I had to turn the picture around so it faced the wall[14]. That night, I brought the picture back home.

This was no place[15] for Cara. This was not even a place for her picture.

I was pawing through[16] the messages when something caught my eye[17].

My secretary uses the old-fashioned pink note sheets[18], the ones where she can keep a yellow copy in her book[19], and writes the messages by hand[20]. Her handwriting is impeccable.

The caller, according to my pink message, was:

Lucy ??

1. tous les deux moniteurs
2. qu'il refuse toutes les visites
3. le faire changer d'avis
4. quartier de haute sécurité
5. était emprisonné
6. passa la tête
7. pour qu'elle me les remette
8. Un bon nombre
9. à les trier
10. table de travail
11. un violeur d'enfants
12. innommables
13. d'à peu près l'âge de Cara
14. pour qu'elle soit face au mur
15. Ce bureau n'était pas un endroit
16. Je passai rapidement en revue
17. m'interpella
18. ces anciennes fiches roses pour noter les messages
19. registre
20. à la main

I stared at the name for a moment. Lucy. It couldn't be.[1]

There was a work number, a home number and a mobile[2]. All three had area codes[3] that indicated Lucy Double-Question-Mark[4] lived, worked and, uh, mobilized[5] in New Jersey.

I grabbed the phone and hit the intercom[6]. "Jocelyn?"

"Yes?"

"I'm seeing a message here from someone named Lucy," I said.

"Yes. She called about an hour ago."

"You didn't write a last name."

"She wouldn't give one[7]. That's why I put the question marks."

"I don't understand. You asked her for a last name and she wouldn't give one?"

"That's right."

"What else did she say?"

"On the bottom of[8] the page."

"What?"

"Did you read my notes on the bottom of the page?"

"No."

She just waited, not saying the obvious[9]. I scanned down[10] the sheet and read:

Says she's an old friend from twenty years ago.

I read the words again. And again.

"Ground control[11] to Major Cope."

It was Muse. She hadn't said the words – she sang them, using[12] the old David Bowie tune[13]. I startled up.[14] "You sing," I said, "like you pick out[15] shoes."

"Very funny." She gestured at my message and arched one eyebrow. "So who is this Lucy, big guy[16]? An old lover[17]?"

I said nothing.

1. Ce n'était pas possible.
2. téléphone portable
3. des indicatifs régionaux
4. double point d'interrogation
5. téléphonait avec son portable [jeu de mots basé sur « mobile »]
6. actionnai la touche Interphone
7. n'a pas voulu le communiquer
8. En bas de
9. sans dire ce qui allait de soi
10. Je scrutai le bas de
11. Contrôle au sol
12. en reprenant
13. l'air de cette vieille chanson de David Bowie [Space Oddity]
14. Je levai la tête en sursautant.
15. aussi bien que tu choisis
16. mon grand
17. ancienne petite amie

"Oh, damn." Her arched eyebrow dropped.[1] "I was just messing around[2]. I didn't mean to..."

"Don't worry about it, Muse."

"Don't you worry about it either, Cope. At least not until later."

Her gaze turned to[3] the clock behind me. I looked too. She was right. Lunch was over. This would have to wait. I didn't know what Lucy wanted. Or maybe I did. The past was coming back. All of it. The dead, it seemed, were digging their way out of the ground now.[4]

But that was all for later[5]. I grabbed the fax and stood.

Muse rose too. "Showtime," she said.

I nodded. More than showtime. I was going to destroy those sons of bitches. And I was going to try like hell not to enjoy it too much[6].

On the stand[7] after lunch, Jerry Flynn looked fairly composed[8]. I had done little damage[9] in the morning. There was no reason to think the afternoon would be any different[10].

"Mr. Flynn," I began, "do you like pornography?"

I didn't even wait for the obvious.[11] I turned to Mort Pubin and made a sarcastic hand gesture, as though I had just introduced him[12] and was ushering him onstage[13].

"Objection!"

Pubin didn't even need to elaborate[14]. The judge gave me a disapproving[15] look. I shrugged and said, "Exhibit[16] eighteen." I picked up the sheet of paper. "This is a bill sent to the fraternity house for online expenses. Do you recognize it?"

He looked at it. "I don't pay the bills. The treasurer does[17]."

"Yes, Mr. Rich Devin, who testified that this is indeed[18] the fraternity bill."

1. Elle laissa retomber son sourcil.
2. faisais juste l'andouille
3. Elle jeta un coup d'œil à
4. Apparemment, les morts sortaient de leurs tombes.
5. tout ça devrait attendre
6. vraiment me retenir d'y prendre trop de plaisir
7. À la barre
8. avait l'air plutôt calme
9. n'avais pas fait trop de dégâts
10. que cet après-midi, ce serait différent
11. Je pris les devants.
12. venais de le présenter
13. que je l'invitais à monter sur scène
14. d'entrer dans les détails
15. réprobateur
16. Pièce à conviction
17. trésorier s'en charge
18. c'est bien

The judge looked over to Flair and Mort. "Any objection?"

"We will stipulate that it is a bill from the fraternity house," Flair said.

"Do you see this entry[1] here?" I pointed to a line[2] near the top.

"Yes."

"Can you read what it says?"

"Netflix."

"That's with one *x* at the end." I spelled "Netflix" out loud.[3] "What's Netflix, if you know?"

"It's a DVD rental[4] service. You do it through the mail.[5] You get to keep[6] three DVDs at all times[7]. When you mail one back[8], you get another sent to you[9]."

"Good, thank you." I nodded and moved[10] my fingers down a few rows[11]. "Could you read this line to me?"

He hesitated.

"Mr. Flynn?" I said.

He cleared his throat. "HotFlixxx," he said.

"With three *x*'s at the end, correct?" Again I spelled it out loud.

"Yes."

He looked as though he was about to be sick[12].

"Can you tell me what HotFlixxx is?"

"It's like Netflix," he said.

"It's a DVD movie rental service?"

"Yes."

"How is it different from[13] Netflix, if you know?"

He turned red[14]. "They rent, uh, different kinds of movies."

"What kind?"

"Um, well, adult movies[15]."

"I see. So before I asked if you liked pornography – perhaps a better question would have been, Do you ever watch[16] pornographic movies?"

He squirmed. "Sometimes," he said.

1. ce qui est écrit
2. J'indiquai une ligne
3. J'épelai « Netflix » à voix haute.
4. de location de DVD
5. Cela se fait par la poste.
6. Vous pouvez avoir
7. en permanence
8. en renvoyez un
9. un autre vous est expédié
10. déplaçai
11. de quelques lignes vers le bas
12. sur le point de vomir
13. Quelle est la différence avec
14. devint écarlate
15. des films pour adultes
16. Vous arrive-t-il de regarder

"Nothing wrong with that, son.[1]" Without looking behind me, knowing he was up[2], I pointed at opposing counsel's chair[3]. "And I bet[4] Mr. Pubin is standing to tell us he enjoys them too, especially the plots[5]."

"Objection!" Pubin said.

"Withdrawn," I said. I turned back to Flynn. "Is there any pornographic movie in particular that you like?"

The color drained from his face.[6] It was as if the question had turned a spigot[7]. His head swiveled[8] toward the defense table. I moved just enough to block his view[9]. Flynn coughed into his fist[10] and said, "Can I plead the Fifth[11]?"

"For what?" I asked.

Flair Hickory stood. "The witness has asked for counsel[12]."

"Your Honor," I said, "when I went to law school[13], we learned that the Fifth Amendment was to be used to prevent self-incrimination[14] and – correct me if I'm wrong here[15] – but, well, is there a law on the books[16] against having a favorite pornographic movie?"

Flair said, "Can we have a ten-minute recess[17]?"

"No way[18], Your Honor."

"The witness," Flair went on, "has asked for counsel."

"No, he didn't. He asked to plead the Fifth. And tell you what[19], Mr. Flynn – I will give you immunity[20]."

"Immunity for what?" Flair asked.

"For whatever he wants. I don't want this witness off[21] the stand."

Judge Pierce looked back at Flair Hickory. He took his time. If Flair got ahold of him[22], I would be in trouble. They would come up with something. I glanced behind me at Jenrette and Marantz. They hadn't moved, hadn't warned counsel[23].

"No recess," the judge said.

Flair Hickory wilted back into his seat[24].

1. Il n'y a pas de mal à ça, fiston.
2. sachant qu'il était debout
3. le banc de la partie adverse
4. je parie
5. surtout les intrigues
6. Son visage devint livide.
7. j'avais ouvert une vanne avec cette question
8. pivota
9. pour lui bloquer la vue
10. toussota dans son poing
11. invoquer le Cinquième Amendement
12. a demandé l'avis de l'avocat
13. j'ai fait mes études de droit
14. l'auto-accusation
15. sauf erreur de ma part
16. existe-t-il une loi
17. suspension
18. Pas question
19. vous savez quoi
20. vous accorderai l'immunité
21. que ce témoin quitte
22. parvenait à le convaincre
23. mis en garde leurs avocats
24. se recroquevilla sur son siège

I went back to Jerry Flynn. "Do you have a favorite pornographic movie?"

"No," he said.

"Have you ever heard of a pornographic movie called" – I pretended[1] now to be checking[2] a piece of paper but I knew the name by heart – "a movie called *Romancing His Bone*[3]?"

He must have seen it coming, but the question still zapped him[4] like a cattle prod[5]. "Uh, can you repeat that title?"

I repeated it. "Have you seen or heard of it?"

"I don't think so."

"Don't think so," I repeated. "So you may have?"

"I'm not sure. I'm not good with movie titles."

"Well, let's see if I can refresh your recollection[6]."

I had the fax Muse had just given me. I passed a copy[7] to opposing counsel and made it an exhibit[8]. Then I started back in[9]: "According to[10] HotFlixxx, a copy of that DVD had been in the possession of the fraternity house for the past six months[11]. And again according to Hot-Flixxx's records[12], the movie was mailed back to them the day after Ms. Johnson reported the assault[13] to the police."

Silence.

Pubin looked as though he'd swallowed his tongue[14]. Flair was too good to show anything. He read the fax as though it were an amusing ditty[15] from *The Family Circus*[16].

I moved closer to Flynn. "Does that refresh your memory?"

"I don't know."

"You don't know? Then let's try something else." I looked toward the back of the room. Loren Muse was standing by the door[17]. She was grinning[18]. I nodded. She opened the door and a woman who looked like a gorgeous Amazon in a B movie stepped forward[19].

1. je fis semblant
2. de consulter
3. [expression signifiant se masturber]
4. le désarçonna
5. comme s'il avait reçu un coup d'aiguillon
6. vous rafraîchir la mémoire
7. exemplaire
8. en fis une pièce à conviction
9. je poursuivis
10. Selon
11. pendant ces six derniers mois
12. registres
13. a signalé son agression
14. avalé sa langue
15. chansonnette
16. [célèbre bande dessinée publiée dans les journaux dans les années 1960, mettant en scène la vie de famille]
17. se tenait près de la porte
18. souriait
19. d'un film de série B s'avança

1. entra dans la salle en se pavanant
2. son bistro préféré
3. retenir son souffle en la voyant
4. ancienne actrice de porno
5. avait réussi
6. à rapidement faire parler
7. silhouette si sexy
8. que ça méritait bien une décoration
9. On l'a peut-être évoqué.
10. Vous parlez bien du
11. fait nouveau
12. là-bas, qui sert de catalyseur
13. baisser
14. s'effondrèrent
15. Ravi d'avoir pu vous aider
16. lui fit signe
17. film

Muse's private eye, Cingle Shaker, strutted into the room[1] as if it were her favorite watering hole[2]. The room itself seemed to gasp at the sight[3].

I said, "Do you recognize the woman who just walked into the room?"

He did not reply. The judge said, "Mr. Flynn?"

"Yes." Flynn cleared his throat to gain time. "I recognize her."

"How do you know her?"

"I met her at a bar last night."

"I see. And did you two talk about the movie *Romancing His Bone?*

Cingle had pretended to be an ex-porno actress[4]. She had gotten[5] several frat boys to open up in a hurry[6]. Like Muse had said – it must have been *really* difficult, a woman with a figure so shapely[7] it could draw a citation[8], getting frat boys to talk.

Flynn said, "We might have said something about it.[9]"

"'It' being the[10] movie?"

"Yes."

"Hmm," I said, again as if this were a curious development[11]. "So now, with Ms. Shaker out there as a catalyst[12], do you remember the film *Romancing His Bone?*"

He tried not to drop[13] his head, but the shoulders went[14]. "Yeah," Flynn said, "I guess I remember it."

"Glad I could help[15]," I said.

Pubin rose to object, but the judge waved him[16] to sit.

"In fact," I went on, "you told Ms. Shaker that *Romancing His Bone* was the entire fraternity's favorite porno flick[17], didn't you?"

He hesitated.

"It's okay, Jerry. Three of your brothers told Ms. Shaker the same thing."

Mort Pubin: "Objection!"

I looked back at Cingle Shaker. So did everyone else. Cingle smiled and waved[1] as though she were a celebrity in the audience and had just been introduced. I wheeled out the TV[2] with a DVD player attached[3]. The offending[4] DVD was already in it. Muse had cued it up to the relevant scene[5].

"Your Honor, last night one of my investigators visited King David's Smut Palace in New York City." I looked at the jury and said, "See, it's open twenty-four hours, though why someone might need to go there at, say, three in the morning is beyond me[6] – "

"Mr. Copeland."

The judge correctly[7] stopped me with a disapproving gaze, but the jury had smiled. That was good. I wanted the mood loose[8]. And then, when the contrast came[9], when they saw what was on that DVD, I wanted to wallop them[10].

"Anyway, my investigator purchased all of the X-rated[11] movies ordered on HotFlixxx by the frat house in the past six months, including[12] *Romancing His Bone.* I would now like to show a scene I believe is relevant[13]."

Everything stopped.[14] All eyes turned toward the judge's bench[15]. Arnold Pierce took his time. He stroked his chin[16]. I held my breath. There wasn't a sound. Everyone leaned forward[17]. Pierce stroked his chin some more. I wanted to wring the answer out of him.[18]

Then he simply nodded and said, "Go ahead.[19] I'll allow it."

"Wait!" Mort Pubin objected, did everything he could, wanted voir dire[20] and all that. Flair Hickory joined in. But it was a waste of energy[21]. Eventually[22] the courtroom curtains were closed so that there would be no glare[23]. And then, without explaining what they were about to see, I hit the Play button[24].

The setting[25] was a run-of-the-mill[26] bedroom. Looked like a king-size[27] bed. Three participants.

1. salua
2. Je sortis le téléviseur
3. intégré
4. incriminé
5. l'avait calé sur la scène à visionner
6. ça me dépasse
7. à juste raison
8. détendre l'atmosphère
9. par effet de contraste
10. je voulais que cela leur flanque un coup
11. classés X
12. y compris
13. qui, je le crois, est pertinente
14. L'atmosphère se figea.
15. la chaire du juge
16. se caressa le menton
17. se pencha en avant
18. J'aurais voulu lui extorquer sa réponse.
19. Allez-y.
20. [droit anglo-saxon, procédure permettant au juge d'interroger un témoin]
21. peine perdue
22. Au bout du compte
23. pour qu'il n'y ait pas de reflet
24. la touche Lecture
25. décor
26. ordinaire
27. très grand

The scene opened with very little foreplay[1]. A rough[2] ménage à trois started up[3]. There were two men. There was one girl.

The two men were white. The girl was black.

The white men tossed her about[4] like a plaything[5]. They sneered[6] and laughed and talked to each other throughout[7]:

"Turn her over[8], Cal.... Yeah, Jim, like that... Flip her[9], Cal...."

I watched the jury's reaction rather than the screen. Children playact.[10] My daughter and niece acted out[11] Dora the Explorer. Jenrette and Marantz, as sick as it was[12], had acted out[13] a scene from a pornographic movie. The courtroom was tomb still[14]. I watched the faces in the gallery collapse[15], even those behind Jenrette and Marantz, as the black girl in the movie screamed, as the two white men used their names and laughed cruelly.

"Bend her over[16], Jim.... Whoa, Cal, the bitch[17] is loving it.... Do her[18], Jim, yeah, harder...."

Like that. Cal and Jim. On and on.[19] Their voices were cruel, awful, hell spawned[20]. I looked toward the back of the room and found Chamique Johnson. Her spine was straight.[21] Her head was high.

"Woo hoo, Jim... Yeah, my turn..."

Chamique met my eye and nodded[22]. I nodded back. There were tears on her cheeks.

I couldn't be sure, but I think there were tears on mine too.

1. débutait quasiment sans préliminaires
2. brutal
3. s'engageait
4. se la passaient
5. jouet
6. ricanaient
7. tout le long
8. Tourne-la
9. Retourne-la
10. Des enfants qui jouent à faire semblant.
11. avaient joué à
12. aussi répugnant que ce soit
13. reproduit
14. muette comme une tombe
15. l'expression effondrée de l'auditoire
16. Penche-la en avant
17. cette salope
18. Baise-la
19. Encore et encore.
20. démoniaques
21. Elle se tenait droite.
22. croisa mon regard et hocha la tête

Chapter 20

Flair Hickory and Mort Pubin got[1] a half-hour recess. When the judge rose to leave[2], the courtroom exploded. I no-commented my way back[3] to my office. Muse followed me. She was this tiny[4] thing but she played like she was my Secret Service agent.

When we closed the office door, she put up her palm[5]. "High five![6]"

I just looked at her. She put down[7] her hand.

"It's over, Cope."

"Not quite yet[8]," I said.

"But in a half hour?"

I nodded. "It will be over. But in the meantime[9], there's still work to do."

I moved back around[10] to the conference table. The message from Lucy was sitting there[11]. I had managed to do my brain-partition thing[12] during my Flynn questioning[13]. I had kept Lucy out[14]. But now, as much as I wanted[15] to spend a few minutes basking in the glory of the moment[16], the message was calling out to me[17] again.

Muse saw me looking down at[18] the note.

"A friend from twenty years ago," Muse said. "That's when the Camp PLUS incident occurred[19]."

I looked at her.

1. obtinrent
2. se leva pour partir
3. En refusant tout commentaire, je retournai
4. fluette
5. me présenta la paume de sa main
6. Tope-là !
7. rabaissa
8. Pas encore tout à fait
9. entre-temps
10. fis le tour
11. était posé là
12. à compartimenter mon esprit
13. interrogatoire
14. n'avais pas pensé à Lucy
15. alors que j'aurais bien aimé
16. à savourer cet instant de gloire
17. m'interpellait
18. que je regardais
19. a eu lieu

"It's connected[1], isn't it?"

"I don't know," I said. "But probably."

"What's her last name?"

"Silverstein. Lucy Silverstein."

"Right," Muse said, sitting back[2] and crossing her arms[3]. "That's what I figured[4]."

"How did you figure that?"

"Come on, Cope. You know me."

"That you're too nosy for your own good?[5]"

"Part of what makes me so attractive.[6]"

"Nosiness[7] and maybe your footwear[8]. So when did you read up on me[9]?"

"Soon as I heard you were taking over as[10] county prosecutor."

I wasn't surprised.

"Oh, and I brushed up on the case[11] before I told you I wanted in."

I looked at the message again.

"She was your girlfriend," Muse said.

"Summer romance," I said. "We were kids."

"When was the last time you heard from her[12]?"

"It's been a long time."

We just sat there for a moment. I could hear the commotion outside[13] the door. I ignored it. So did Muse. Neither one of us spoke. We just sat there with that message on the table.

Finally Muse stood. "I got some work to do."

"Go," I said.

"You'll be able to make it back[14] to court without me?"

"I'll muddle through[15]," I said.

When Muse reached the door, she turned back to me. "Are you going to call her?"

"Later."

"You want me to run her name[16]? See what I come up with?"

I thought about it. "Not yet."

"Why not?"

1. Il y a un lien
2. en se calant sur son siège
3. en croisant les bras
4. ce que je pensais
5. Que tu ne peux pas t'empêcher de fouiner ?
6. C'est ce qui fait mon charme.
7. Ta curiosité
8. chaussures
9. as-tu fait des recherches sur moi
10. reprenais le poste de
11. j'ai passé en revue le dossier de cette affaire
12. que tu as eu de ses nouvelles
13. J'entendais l'agitation, de l'autre côté de
14. retourner
15. Je me débrouillerai
16. que je fasse une recherche sur son nom

"Because she used to mean something to me[1], Muse. I don't feel like having you poke around in her life[2]."

Muse put her hands up. "Okay, okay, sheesh, don't bite my head off[3]. I wasn't talking about dragging her[4] in here with cuffs[5]. I was talking about running a routine background check[6]."

"Don't, okay? At least, not yet."

"I'll get to work on your prison visit to Wayne Steubens then."

"Thank you."

"This Cal and Jim thing. You're not going to let it slip away[7], are you?"

"Not a chance.[8]"

My one worry[9] was that the defense would claim[10] that Chamique Johnson had watched the movie too and made up[11] her story based on it[12] or had deluded herself into thinking[13] the movie was real. I was helped by several factors, however. One, it was easy to establish that the movie had not been playing[14] on the fraternity's big-screen TV in the public room. Enough witnesses would back that up[15]. Second, I had established via Jerry Flynn and photographs taken by the police that Marantz and Jenrette did not have a television set in their room, so she couldn't have seen it there.

Still, it was the only direction I could see them going in[16]. A DVD could be played on a computer. Flimsy[17], true, but I really didn't want to leave much of an out[18]. Jerry Flynn was what I refer to as a "bullfight[19]" witness. In a bullfight, the bull comes out and a bunch of guys – not the matador – wave capes around[20]. The bull charges until exhausted[21]. Then picadors on horseback come out with long lances and jam them[22] into a gland behind the bull's neck muscle, drawing blood[23] and swelling[24] the neck so that the bull can't turn his head much. Then some other

1. c'est quelqu'un qui a compté pour moi
2. n'ai pas envie que tu fouines dans sa vie
3. inutile de me rembarrer, bon sang
4. la traîner
5. menottée
6. simplement vérifier ses antécédents
7. la laisser te filer entre les doigts
8. Aucun risque.
9. Ma seule inquiétude
10. affirme
11. fabriqué
12. en s'en inspirant
13. qu'elle s'était persuadée
14. n'avait pas été diffusé
15. le confirmeraient
16. la seule ligne de défense qu'ils pouvaient adopter, à mon avis
17. C'était léger
18. rien laisser au hasard
19. de corrida
20. agitent leur cape tout autour
21. jusqu'à épuisement
22. les enfoncent
23. ce qui fait saigner
24. et enfler

guys run up and throw banderillas[1] – gaily decorated daggers[2] – into the bull's flanks[3], near his shoulders[4]. More blood. The bull is half-dead already.

After all that, the matador – from the Spanish *matar* or "to kill" – comes in and finishes the job with a sword[5].

That was my job now. I had made my witness run into exhaustion[6] and jammed a lance into his neck and stuck some colorful darts[7] into him. So now it was time to bring out the sword.

Flair Hickory did everything in his considerable power to prevent this. He called for a recess, claiming that we had never produced this film before and that it was unfair and that it should have been given to them during discovery[8], blah, blah, blah. I fought back.[9] The film had been in the possession of his clients, after all. We only found a copy ourselves last night. The witness had confirmed that it had been watched in the fraternity house. If Mr. Hickory wanted to claim his clients never saw it, he could put them on the stand.

Flair took his time arguing[10]. He stalled, asked and got some sidebars[11] with the judge, tried with some success to give Jerry Flynn a chance to catch his breath[12].

But it didn't work.

I could see that the moment Flynn sat in that chair. He had been too seriously wounded by those darts and that lance. The movie had been the final blow[13]. He had shut his eyes while it played, shut them so tightly that I think he was trying to close his ears[14].

I could tell you that Flynn probably wasn't a bad kid. The truth was, as he now testified, he had liked Chamique. He had asked her out legitimately on a date. But when the upperclassmen[15] got wind of it[16], they teased and bullied him into[17] going along with[18] their sick "movie reenactment[19]" plan. And Flynn the Freshman folded[20].

1. se précipitent et plantent des banderilles
2. des piques décorées de couleurs vives
3. flancs
4. son encolure
5. à l'épée
6. poussé mon témoin à l'épuisement
7. flèches
8. [phase avant le procès où chaque partie peut obtenir la divulgation de pièces de la partie adverse]
9. Je ripostai.
10. prit son temps pour argumenter
11. demanda et obtint des apartés
12. reprendre son souffle
13. le coup de grâce
14. se boucher les oreilles
15. [étudiants de 3ᵉ ou 4ᵉ année]
16. l'avaient appris
17. s'étaient moqués et l'avaient forcé à
18. se soumettre à
19. reconstitution
20. s'était plié à leur volonté

"I hated myself for doing it," he said. "But you have to understand."

No, I don't, I wanted to say. But I didn't. Instead I just looked at him until he lowered his eyes. Then I looked at the jury with a slight challenge[1] in my eyes. Seconds passed.

Finally I turned to Flair Hickory and said, "Your witness.[2]"

It took me a while to get alone[3].

After my ridiculous act of indignation at Muse, I decided to do some amateur sleuthing[4]. I Googled Lucy's phone numbers. Two gave me nothing, but the third, her work number, showed me that it was the direct line to a professor at Reston University named Lucy Gold.

Gold. *Silver*-stein. Cute.[5]

I had already known it was "my" Lucy, but this pretty much confirmed it. The question was, What do I do about it? The answer was fairly simple. Call her back. See what she wants.

I was not big on coincidence.[6] I hadn't heard a word[7] from this woman in twenty years. Now suddenly she had called and wouldn't leave a last name. It had to be connected to[8] Gil Perez's death. It had to be connected to the Camp PLUS incident.

That was obvious.

Partitioning your life.[9] It should have been easy to leave her behind[10]. A summer fling[11], even an intense one, is just that – a fling. I might have loved her, probably did, but I was just a kid. Kid love[12] doesn't survive blood and dead bodies. There are doors. I closed that one. Lucy was gone. It took me a long time to accept that. But I did and I kept that damn door shut[13].

Now I would have to open it.

Muse had wanted to run a background check. I should have said yes. I let emotion dictate my decision. I should have waited. Seeing her name was a

1. un léger air de défi
2. Le témoin est à vous.
3. avant de me retrouver seul
4. de jouer les détectives amateurs
5. C'était malin.
6. Je ne croyais pas beaucoup aux coïncidences.
7. pas eu la moindre nouvelle
8. Il devait forcément y avoir un rapport avec
9. Compartimenter sa vie.
10. de l'oublier
11. amourette
12. Les amours de jeunesse
13. je m'étais astreint à garder cette fichue porte bien fermée

blow[1]. I should have taken my time, dealt with the[2] blow, seen things more clearly. But I didn't.

Maybe I shouldn't call yet.

No, I told myself. Enough with the stalling.[3]

I picked up the phone and dialed her home. On the fourth ring, the phone was picked up. A woman's voice said, "I'm not home, but at the beep please leave a message."

The beep came too fast. I wasn't ready for it. So I hung up.

Very mature.[4]

My head swam.[5] Twenty years. It had been twenty years. Lucy would be thirty-seven now. I wondered if she was still as beautiful. When I think back on it[6], she had the kind of looks that would do well with maturity[7]. Some women are like that.

Get your head in the game[8]*, Cope.*

I was trying. But hearing her voice, sounding exactly the same[9]... it was the aural equivalent of hooking up with your old college roommate[10]: After ten seconds, the years melt away[11] and it's like you're back in the dorm room[12] and nothing has changed. That was how this was. She sounded the same.[13] I was eighteen again.

I took a few deep breaths. There was a knock on the door.

"Come in."

Muse stuck her head in the room. "Did you call her yet?[14]"

"I tried her home number. No answer."

"You probably won't get her now," Muse said. "She's in class."

"And you know this because?"

"Because I'm chief investigator. I don't have to listen to everything you say."

She sat and threw her practical-shoed feet up on[15] the table. She studied my face and didn't speak. I

1. m'avait fait un choc
2. encaisser ce
3. Fini les atermoiements.
4. Quelle maturité !
5. La tête me tournait.
6. En y repensant
7. physique qui vieillissait bien
8. Reste concentré
9. qui n'avait pas changé
10. c'était un peu comme reprendre contact avec un ancien camarade de chambre
11. s'effacent
12. chambre d'étudiant
13. À sa voix, elle était la même.
14. Ça y est, tu l'as appelée ?
15. balança ses pieds chaussés de confortables chaussures sur

kept quiet too. Finally she said, "Do you want me to leave?"

"Tell me what you got first."

She tried hard not to smile. "She changed her name seventeen years ago. It's Lucy Gold now."

I nodded. "That would have been right after the settlement.[1]"

"What settlement? Oh, wait, you guys sued[2] the camp, right?"

"The victims' families."

"And Lucy's father owned the camp."

"Right."

"Nasty?[3]"

"I don't know. I wasn't that involved."

"But you guys won?"

"Sure. It was a summer camp with practically no security." I squirmed[4] when I said that. "The families got Silverstein's biggest asset[5]."

"The camp itself."

"Yep.[6] We sold the land to a developer[7]."

"All of it?"

"There was a provision involving[8] the woods. It's fairly unusable land[9], so it's held in some kind of public trust[10]. You can't build on it."

"Is the camp still there?"

I shook my head. "The developer tore down[11] the old cabins[12] and built some gated community[13]."

"How much did you guys get?"

"After lawyer fees[14], each family ended up with more than eight hundred grand[15]."

Her eyes widened. "Wow."

"Yeah. Losing a child is a great moneymaker[16]."

"I didn't mean – "

I waved her off. "I know. I'm just being an ass.[17]"

She didn't argue. "It must have changed things," Muse said.

I didn't answer right away. The money had been held in a joint account[18]. My mother took off with a

1. Elle a dû le faire tout de suite après la transaction.
2. vous avez intenté une action contre
3. Ça a été violent ?
4. J'étais mal à l'aise
5. le bien le plus important
6. Ouais.
7. promoteur
8. une disposition concernant
9. un terrain quasiment inexploitable
10. il est géré par une sorte de fondation
11. a démoli
12. cabanes
13. une résidence sécurisée
14. paiement des honoraires d'avocat
15. 800 000 dollars
16. rapporte beaucoup d'argent
17. Je fais l'idiot.
18. déposé sur un compte commun

hundred grand[1]. She left the rest for us. Generous of her, I guess. Dad and I moved out of Newark, moved to a decent[2] place in Montclair. I had already gotten a scholarship[3] to Rutgers[4], but now I set my sights on[5] Columbia Law[6] in New York. I met Jane there.

"Yeah," I said. "It changed things."

"Do you want to know more about your old flame[7]?"

I nodded.

"She went to UCLA[8]. Majored in[9] psychology. She got a graduate degree[10] from USC[11] in the same[12], another in English from Stanford. I don't have her entire work history yet, but she's currently down the road[13] at Reston U. Started last year. She, uh, she got two DUIs[14] when she lived in California. One in 2001. Another in 2003. Pleaded out[15] both times. Other than that, her record is clean[16]."

I sat there. DUI. That didn't sound like Lucy. Her father, Ira, the head counselor, had been a major stoner[17] – so much so that she'd had no interest in anything that would provide a high[18]. Now she had two DUIs. It was hard to fathom[19]. But of course, the girl I knew was not even of legal drinking age. She had been happy and a little naive and well-adjusted[20], and her family had money and her father was a seemingly harmless[21] free spirit.

All that had died that night in the woods too.

"Another thing," Muse said. She shifted in the seat, aiming for nonchalance[22]. "Lucy Silverstein, aka Gold, isn't married. I haven't done all the checking yet, but from what I see, she's never been married either."

I didn't know what to make of that. It certainly had no bearing[23] on what was going on now. But it still pierced me[24]. She was such a lively[25] thing, so bright and energetic and so damn easy to love. How could she have remained single[26] all these years? And then there were those DUIs.

"What time does her class end?" I asked.

"Twenty minutes."

1. 100 000 dollars
2. respectable
3. bourse d'études
4. [université du New Jersey]
5. je visais
6. [faculté de droit de l'université Columbia]
7. ton ex
8. [université de Californie]
9. Elle a fait des études de
10. doctorat
11. [University of Southern California]
12. dans cette même discipline
13. juste à côté
14. a été arrêtée deux fois pour conduite en état d'ivresse
15. Elle a plaidé coupable [accord passé entre avocat et procureur]
16. vierge
17. grand camé
18. qui puisse faire planer
19. difficile à comprendre
20. équilibrée
21. inoffensif
22. en prenant un air détaché
23. incidence
24. m'affligea quand même
25. gaie
26. rester célibataire

"Okay. I'll call her then. Anything else?"

"Wayne Steubens doesn't allow visitors, except for his immediate family[1] and lawyer. But I'm working on it. I got some other irons in the fire[2], but that's about it for now[3]."

"Don't spend too much time on it."

"I'm not."

I looked at the clock. Twenty minutes.

"I should probably go," Muse said.

"Yeah."

She stood. "Oh, one more thing."

"What?"

"Do you want to see a picture of her?"

I looked up.

"Reston University has faculty pages. There are pictures of all the professors." She held up[4] a small piece of paper. "I got the URL right here."

She didn't wait for my reply. She dropped the address[5] on the table and left me alone.

I had twenty minutes. Why not?

I brought up my default page. I use one with Yahoo where you can choose a lot of your content[6]. I had news[7], my sports teams, my two favorite comic strips[8] – *Doonesbury* and *FoxTrot* – stuff like that[9]. I typed in[10] the Reston University Web site page Muse had given me.

And there she was.

It wasn't Lucy's most flattering[11] photograph. Her smile was tight[12], her expression grim[13]. She had posed for the picture, but you could see that she really didn't want to. The blond hair was gone. That happens with age, I know, but I had a feeling[14] that it was intentional[15]. The color didn't look right on her. She was older – duh[16] – but as I had predicted[17], it worked on her[18]. Her face was thinner. The high cheekbones[19] were more pronounced.

And damn if she didn't still look beautiful.[20]

1. famille proche
2. plusieurs fers au feu
3. à peu près tout, pour l'instant
4. brandit
5. déposa la feuille sur laquelle figurait le lien
6. une grande partie de votre contenu
7. les informations
8. bandes dessinées
9. des trucs comme ça
10. Je saisis le lien de
11. la plus avantageuse
12. crispé
13. sombre
14. j'eus le sentiment
15. voulu
16. non, sans blague !
17. prévu
18. cela lui allait bien
19. Ses pommettes saillantes
20. Et bon Dieu, elle était toujours aussi belle.

Looking at her face, something long dormant came alive[1] and started twisting in my gut[2]. I didn't need that now. There were enough complications in my life. I didn't need those old feelings resurfacing[3]. I read her short bio[4], learned nothing. Nowadays students rank classes[5] and professors. You could often find that information online. I did. Lucy was clearly beloved by her students. Her rankings[6] were incredible. I read a few of the student comments. They made the class sound life-altering.[7] I smiled and felt a strange sense of pride.

Twenty minutes passed.

I gave it another five[8], pictured her saying goodbye to students, talking to a few who loitered behind[9], packing her lessons and sundries[10] in some beat-up[11] faux leather[12] bag.

I picked up my office phone. I buzzed out to[13] Jocelyn.

"Yes?"

"No calls," I said. "No interruptions."

"Okay."

I pressed for an outside line. I dialed Lucy's cell phone. On the third ring I heard her voice say, "Hello?"

My heart leapt into my throat[14] but I managed to say, "It's me, Luce."

And then, a few seconds later, I heard her start to cry.

1. qui sommeillait depuis longtemps se raviva
2. s'agita au creux de mon estomac
3. resurgissent
4. biographie
5. notent leurs cours
6. Son palmarès
7. On aurait dit que ses cours changeaient leur vie.
8. Je laissai passer cinq minutes de plus
9. s'attardaient
10. ses affaires
11. tout usé
12. en similicuir
13. J'appelai
14. Mon cœur tressaillit et ma gorge se noua

Chapter 21

"Luce?" I said into the phone. "You okay?"

"I'm fine. It's just..."

"Yeah, I know."

"I can't believe I did that."

"You always were an easy cry[1]," I said, regretting it the moment it came out. But she snorted a laugh[2].

"Not anymore," she said.

Silence.

Then I said, "Where are you?"

"I work at Reston University. I'm walking across the commons[3]."

"Oh," I said, because I didn't know what else to say.

"I'm sorry about leaving such a cryptic[4] message. I don't go by Silverstein anymore[5]."

I didn't want her to know I already knew this. But I didn't want to lie either. So again I gave a noncommittal[6] "Oh."

More silence. She broke it this time.

"Man, this is awkward.[7]"

I smiled. "I know."

"I feel like a big dope[8]," she said. "Like I'm sixteen again and worried about a new zit[9]."

"Same here," I said.

1. as toujours pleuré pour un rien

2. pouffa de rire

3. traverse le campus

4. énigmatique

5. ne m'appelle plus Silverstein

6. évasif

7. Bon sang, c'est gênant, tout ça.

8. me sens idiote

9. que je stressais à cause d'un bouton [d'acné]

"We never really change, do we? I mean, inside, we're always a scared kid, wondering what we're going to be when we grow up[1]."

I was still smiling, but I thought about her never being married and the DUIs. We don't change, I guess, but our path certainly does[2].

"It's good to hear your voice, Luce."

"Yours too."

Silence.

"I was calling because..." Lucy stopped. Then: "I don't even know how to say this, so let me ask a question. Has anything strange happened to you lately?"

"Strange how?[3]"

"Strange as in about-that-night strange[4]."

I should have expected her to say something like that – knew it was coming[5] – but the smile still fled[6] as if I'd been punched[7]. "Yes."

Silence.

"What the hell is going on, Paul?"

"I don't know."

"I think we need to figure it out[8]."

"I agree."

"Do you want to meet?[9]"

"Yes."

"It's going to be weird," she said.

"I know."

"I mean, I don't want it to be. And that's not why I called. To see you. But I think we should meet up[10] and discuss this, don't you?"

"I do," I said.

"I'm babbling. I babble when I get nervous."

"I remember," I said. And then, again, I regretted saying that, so I quickly added, "Where should we meet?"

"Do you know where Reston University is?"

"Yes."

"I have another class and then student appointments until seven-thirty," Lucy said. "Do you want to

1. on sera grand
2. contrairement à nos trajectoires, cependant
3. Comment ça, étrange ?
4. par rapport à cette fameuse nuit
5. je l'avais vu arriver
6. s'effaça quand même
7. on m'avait mis K.-O.
8. devons le découvrir
9. Tu veux qu'on se voie ?
10. nous rencontrer

meet me at my office? It's in the Armstrong Building. Say, eight o'clock?"

"I'll be there."

When I arrived home I was surprised to find the press camped out[1] in front of my house. You often hear about that – about the press doing stuff like that[2] – but this was my first experience with it. The local cops were on hand[3], clearly excited to be doing something that seemed quasi-big time[4]. They stood on either side of the driveway so that I could pull in[5]. The press didn't try to stop them. In fact, when I pulled in, the press barely seemed to notice.

Greta gave me the conquering-hero welcome[6]. She was full[7] of kisses and quick hugs and congratulations. I love Greta. There are some people you know are pure good, who are always on your side. There aren't many of them. But there are some. Greta would jump in the way of a bullet for me[8]. And she made me want to protect her.

In that way she reminded me of my sister.

"Where's Cara?" I asked.

"Bob took Cara and Madison to Baumgart's for dinner."

Estelle was in the kitchen, doing laundry[9]. "I need to go out tonight," I said to her.

"No problem."

Greta said, "Cara can sleep over[10] at our house."

"I think I'd rather[11] she slept at home tonight, thanks."

She followed me into the den. The front door opened and Bob came in with the two girls. Again I envisioned[12] my daughter sprinting into my arms[13] while screaming, "Daddy! You're home! "That didn't happen. But she did smile and she did come over to me. I swept her up in my arms[14] and kissed her hard. She held the smile[15] but wiped her cheek[16]. Hey, I'll take it[17].

1. que les médias s'étaient installés

2. ce genre de trucs

3. flics du coin étaient là

4. sortait un peu de l'ordinaire

5. pour que je puisse me garer

6. m'accueillit en vainqueur

7. Elle me couvrit

8. se ferait tuer pour me protéger

9. en train de faire une lessive

10. passer la nuit

11. que je préférerais qu'

12. j'imaginai

13. se précipitant dans mes bras

14. la soulevai dans mes bras

15. continua à sourire

16. s'essuya la joue

17. je m'en contente

Bob slapped my back. "Congrats on[1] the trial," he said.

"It's not over yet."

"That's not what the media is saying. Either way it should get that Jenrette off our back[2]."

"Or more desperate.[3]"

His face paled a little. If you were to cast[4] Bob in a movie, he'd be the bad-guy rich[5] Republican. His complexion was ruddy, his jowls thick[6], his fingers short and stubby[7]. Here was another example[8] of where appearances could be deceiving[9]. Bob's background was totally blue collar[10]. He studied and worked hard. Nothing had ever been given to him or made easy.

Cara came back into the room carrying a DVD. She held it up as though it were an offering[11]. I closed my eyes, and remembering what day of the week it was, I cursed to myself[12]. Then I said to my little girl, "It's movie night.'"

She still held up the DVD. Her eyes were wide. She was smiling. On the cover was something animated or computer-generated[13] with talking cars or maybe farm animals or zoo animals, something from Pixar or Disney, something I had seen a hundred times already.

"That's right. Will you make popcorn?"

I took a knee[14] so I was at her eye level. I put a hand on either shoulder. "Honey," I said, "Daddy has to go out tonight."

No reaction.

"I'm sorry, sweetie."

I waited for the tears. "Can Estelle watch it with me?"

"Sure, honey."

"And she can make popcorn?"

"Of course."

"Cool."

I'd been hoping for a little crestfallen[15]. No go.[16]

1. Félicitations pour
2. Quoi qu'il en soit, Jenrette ne devrait plus être sur notre dos
3. Ou encore plus, au contraire.
4. deviez attribuer un rôle à
5. méchant et riche
6. Il avait le teint rougeaud, de grosses bajoues
7. boudinés
8. Cela prouvait encore une fois
9. qu'il ne faut pas se fier aux apparences
10. venait du monde ouvrier
11. offrande
12. jurai en silence
13. La jaquette indiquait qu'il s'agissait d'un film d'animation ou de synthèse
14. m'agenouillai
15. une mine un peu déconfite
16. Mais rien.

Cara skipped away[1]. I looked at Bob. He looked at me as if to say, *Kids – what can you do?*

"Inside[2]," I said, gesturing toward my daughter. "On the inside, she's really crushed[3]."

Bob laughed as my cell phone buzzed. The readout simply said[4], NEW JERSEY, but I recognized the number and felt a little jolt[5]. I picked it up and said, "Hello?"

"Nice job today, All-Star.[6]"

"Mr. Governor," I said.

"That's not correct."

"Excuse me?"

"'Mr. Governor.' You would properly address[7] the President of the United States as Mr.[8] President, but governors are addressed as either Governor or by their last name, for example, Governor Stallion[9] or Governor Chick Magnet[10]."

"Or," I said, "how about Governor Anal Compulsive[11]."

"There's that.[12]"

I smiled. During my freshman year at Rutgers, I first met (now Governor) Dave Markie at a party. He intimidated me. I was the immigrant's son[13]. His father was a United States senator. But that was the beauty of college. It is made for strange bedfellows.[14] We ended up becoming close friends.

Dave's critics could not help but notice this friendship[15] when he appointed me[16] to my current post as Essex County prosecutor. The guv[17] shrugged and pushed me through[18]. I had gotten very good press already[19], and at the risk of caring about[20] what I shouldn't care about, today[21] should have helped my possible bid for a congressional seat[22].

"So, big day, no? You da man.[23] Woo hoo. Go, Cope, go, Cope, it's your birthday[24]."

"Trying to appeal to[25] your hip-hop constituency[26]?"

"Trying to understand my teenage daughter. Anyway, congrats."

"Thanks."

1. partit en sautillant
2. Au fond d'elle-même
3. anéantie
4. Sur l'écran s'affichait simplement
5. ressentis un léger choc
6. quelle vedette !
7. Tu peux appeler
8. Monsieur le
9. Étalon
10. Piège à filles
11. Obsédé sexuel
12. Ça aussi.
13. fils d'immigré
14. Ça fait de drôles de tandems.
15. Cette amitié n'avait pu échapper aux détracteurs de Dave
16. m'avait nommé
17. gouverneur
18. ne s'en était pas soucié et m'avait fait passer
19. J'avais déjà bonne presse
20. sans vouloir donner de l'importance à
21. l'événement d'aujourd'hui
22. ma probable candidature au Congrès
23. T'es le meilleur [You the man]
24. c'est ta journée [forme de rap]
25. J'essaies de plaire à
26. électorat

"I'm still no-commenting this case to death.[1]"

"I've never heard you say 'no comment' in your life."

"Sure you have[2], just in creative ways: I believe in our judicial system, all citizens are innocent until proven guilty[3], the wheels of justice will turn[4], I am not judge and jury, we should wait for all the facts to come in[5]."

"Cliché as no comment.[6]"

"Cliché as no comment and every comment[7]," he corrected. "So how is everything, Cope?"

"Fine."

"You dating?[8]"

"Some."

"Dude[9], you're single. You're good-looking. You got some money in the bank. Do you see where I'm going with this?"

"You're subtle[10], Dave, but I think I can follow."

Dave Markie had always been a lady slayer[11]. He was okay-looking[12], but the man had a gift for pick-up[13] that could be conservatively called dazzling[14]. He had that sort of charisma where he made every woman feel as though she was the most beautiful and fascinating person in the world. It was all an act.[15] He just wanted to nail them[16]. Nothing but.[17] Still, I had never seen anybody better at picking up women.

Dave was married now, of course, had two polished[18] children, but I had little doubt that there was some side action[19]. Some men can't help it. It is instinctive and primitive. The idea of Dave Markie not hitting on[20] a woman was simply anathema[21].

"Good news," he said. "I'm coming up to Newark."

"What for?"

"Newark is the largest city in my state, that's why, and I value all my constituents[22]."

"Uh-huh."

"And I want to see you. It's been too long."

"I'm kinda busy[23] with this case."

"You can't make time for[24] your governor?"

1. Pour l'instant, je me garderai bien de faire le moindre commentaire sur cette affaire.
2. Bien sûr que si
3. jusqu'à preuve du contraire
4. la justice fera son travail
5. d'avoir connaissance de tous les faits
6. Aussi banal que « sans commentaire ».
7. que tout commentaire
8. Tu vois quelqu'un ?
9. Mec
10. subtil
11. un vrai tombeur
12. pas mal physiquement
13. avait un don pour draguer
14. qualifié, au bas mot, d'éblouissant
15. Tout ça, c'était de la comédie.
16. les mettre dans son lit
17. Seulement ça.
18. bien élevés
19. sur le fait qu'il ait des aventures
20. ne draguant pas
21. totalement insensée
22. j'apprécie tous mes électeurs
23. assez débordé
24. ne peut pas accorder du temps à

"What's up, Dave?"

"It involves[1] what we talked about before."

My possible congressional run[2]. "Good news?" I said.

"No."

Silence.

"I think there's a problem," he said.

"What kind of problem?"

His voice switched back to jovial. "Could be nothing[3], Cope. We'll talk. Let's make it your office.[4] Say, lunchtime?"

"Okay."

"Get those sandwiches. From that place on Brandford."

"Hobby's."

"Exactly. The fully dressed turkey breast[5] on homemade rye[6]. Get yourself one too. See you then."

Lucy Gold's office building was the otherwise-lovely quad's resident eyesore[7], a seventies "mod" structure[8] that was supposed to look futuristic[9] but somehow looked dated[10] three years after completion[11]. The rest of the quad edifices were handsome brick that begged for more ivy[12]. I parked in the lot in the southwest corner. I tilted[13] the rearview mirror and then, to paraphrase Springsteen, I checked my look[14] in that mirror and wanted to change my clothes, my hair, my face.

I parked and walked across the commons. I passed[15] a dozen students. The girls were much prettier than I remembered, but that was probably my aging. I nodded at them as I walked by. They didn't nod back. When I went to college there was a guy in my class who was thirty-eight years old. He'd gone to the military and skipped getting his BA[16]. I remembered how he stuck out[17] on campus because he looked so goddamn old. That was my age now. Hard to fathom. I was the same age as that seemingly old geezer[18].

1. Ça concerne
2. éventuelle participation aux élections législatives
3. C'est peut-être rien de sérieux
4. Disons qu'on se voit à ton bureau.
5. filet de dinde garni
6. pain de seigle fait maison
7. une horreur qui gâchait la belle cour de la résidence universitaire
8. bâtiment à la mode dans les années 1970
9. censé paraître futuriste
10. avait déjà l'air ringard
11. après sa construction
12. où la vigne vierge ne demandait qu'à pousser
13. J'inclinai
14. m'inspectai
15. croisai
16. avant de passer sa licence
17. dénotait
18. celui que je prenais pour un vioc

I continued to think such inane thoughts[1] because they helped me ignore where I was going. I wore an untucked[2] white dress shirt[3], blue jeans, blue blazer, Ferragamo loafers[4] without socks. Mr. Casual Chic[5].

When I approached the building, I could actually feel my body shaking. I scolded myself.[6] I was a grown man[7]. I had been married. I was a father and a widower. I had last seen this woman more than half my life ago.

When do we grow out of[8] this?

I checked the directory, even though Lucy had told me that her office was on the third floor, door B. There it was. Professor Lucille Gold. Three-B. I managed to press the right button in the elevator. I turned left when I got out on the third floor, even though the sign with the[9] "A-E" had an arrow pointing[10] right.

I found her door. There was a sign-up sheet[11] with her office hours. Most of the time slots[12] were taken. There was also a class schedule[13] and something about when assignments were due[14]. I almost breathed into my hand and smelled it[15], but I was already working[16] a peppermint Altoid.

I knocked, two sharp raps with the knuckles[17]. Confident[18], I thought. Manly.[19]

God, I'm pathetic.

"Come in."

Her voice made my stomach drop. I opened the door and stepped into the room. She stood near the window. The sun was still out[20], and a shadow cut across her[21]. She was still damn beautiful. I took the hit[22] and stayed where I was. For a moment we just stood there, fifteen feet apart, neither moving.

"How's the lighting?[23]" she said.

"Excuse me?"

"I was trying to figure out where to be[24]. You know, when you knocked. Do I answer the door? Nah, too much of an early close-up[25]. Do I stay at my desk with a pencil in my hand? Should I look up

1. ce genre d'idioties
2. au-dessus du pantalon
3. chemise à manches longues
4. mocassins
5. chic décontracté
6. Je râlai contre moi-même.
7. adulte
8. arrive-t-on à dépasser
9. l'écriteau indiquant
10. flèche pointant vers la
11. feuille de présence
12. créneaux horaires
13. emploi du temps
14. devaient être rendus
15. faillis vérifier mon haleine
16. mâchais déjà
17. coups secs avec le poing
18. Aie de l'assurance
19. Sois viril.
20. brillait encore
21. se projetait sur elle
22. J'encaissai le choc
23. Ça va, la lumière ?
24. calculer où me placer
25. trop tôt pour un gros plan

at you over[1] my half-moon reading glasses? Anyway, I had a friend of mine help me[2] test out all the angles. He thought I looked best with this one – across the room, the shade half drawn[3]."

I smiled. "You look terrific.[4]"

"So do you. How many outfits[5] did you try on?"

"Only this one," I said. "But I've been told in the past it's my A-game look[6]. You?"

"I tried on three blouses."

"I like this one," I said. "You always looked good in green."

"I had blond hair back then."

"Yeah, but you still have the green eyes," I said. "Can I come in?"

She nodded. "Close the door."

"Should we, I don't know, hug or something?"

"Not yet."

Lucy sat at her desk chair. I sat in the chair in front of the desk.

"This is so messed up[7]," she said.

"I know."

"I have a million things I want to ask you."

"Me too."

"I saw online about your wife[8]," she said. "I'm sorry."

I nodded. "How's your father?"

"Not well."

"I'm sorry to hear that."

"All that free love and drugs – eventually they take a toll[9]. Ira also... he never got over[10] what happened, you know?"

I guessed that I did.

"How about your parents?" Lucy asked.

"My father died a few months ago."

"I'm sorry to hear that. I remember him so well from that summer[11]."

"It was the last time he was happy," I said.

"Because of your sister?"

1. te regarder par-dessus
2. un ami m'a aidée à
3. le store à moitié tiré
4. Tu es superbe.
5. tenues
6. meilleur look
7. C'est déboussolant, tout ça
8. J'ai appris, pour ta femme, sur Internet
9. ça finit par laisser des traces
10. ne s'est jamais remis de
11. cet été-là

"Because of a lot of things. Your father gave him the chance to be a doctor again. He loved that – practicing[1] medicine. He never got to do it again[2]."

"I'm sorry."

"My father really didn't want to be part of the lawsuit[3] – he adored Ira – but he needed to blame someone and my mom pushed him. All the other families were on board[4]."

"You don't need to explain."

I stopped. She was right.

"And your mother?" she asked.

"Their marriage didn't survive."

The answer did not seem to surprise her.

"Do you mind if I put on my professional hat[5]?" she asked.

"Not at all."

"Losing a child is a ridiculous strain on[6] a marriage," Lucy said. "Most people think that only the strongest[7] marriages survive that sort of blow[8]. That's not true. I've studied it. I've seen marriages one might describe as 'crappy[9]' endure and even improve[10]. I've seen ones that seemed destined to last forever crack apart like cheap plaster[11]. Do you two have a good relationship?"

"My mother and I?"

"Yes."

"I haven't seen her in[12] eighteen years."

We sat there.

"You've lost a lot of people, Paul."

"You're not going to psychoanalyze me[13], are you?"

"No, nothing like that." She sat back and looked up and away[14]. It was a look that sent me right back[15]. We would sit out[16] in the camp's old baseball field, where the grass was overgrown[17], and I would hold her and she would look up and away like that.

"When I was in college," Lucy began, "I had this friend. She was a twin[18]. Fraternal[19], not identical. I guess that doesn't make much of a difference, but

1. exercer
2. n'a jamais pu le refaire
3. participer au procès
4. en faisaient partie
5. ma casquette de psy
6. peut peser vraiment lourd sur
7. les plus solides
8. à ce genre d'épreuve
9. merdiques
10. le supporter et même se renforcer
11. se fissurer comme du mauvais plâtre
12. depuis
13. me psychanalyser
14. leva les yeux puis les détourna
15. m'expédia des années en arrière
16. On allait s'asseoir
17. était haute
18. Elle avait une jumelle
19. C'étaient des fausses jumelles

with the identical, there seems to be a stronger bond[1]. Anyway, when we were sophomores[2] her sister died in a car crash. My friend had the strangest reaction. She was devastated, of course, but part of her was almost relieved[3]. She thought, Well, that's it. God got me.[4] That was my turn. I'm okay for now. I gave at the office.[5] You lose a twin sister like that, you're sorta safe[6] the rest of your life. One heartbreaking[7] tragedy per person. You know what I mean?"

"I do."

"But life isn't like that. Some get a lifetime pass[8]. Others, like you, get more than your share[9]. Much more. And the worst part is, it doesn't make you immune to[10] even more."

"Life ain't[11] fair," I said.

"Amen." Then she smiled at me. "This is so weird, isn't it?"

"Yes."

"I know we were together for, what, six weeks?"

"Something like that."

"And it was just a summer fling, when you think about it. You've probably had dozens of girls since then."

"Dozens?" I repeated.

"What, more like hundreds?"

"At the very least[12]," I said.

Silence. I felt something well up in my chest[13].

"But you were special, Lucy. You were..."

I stopped.

"Yeah, I know," she said. "So were you. That's why this is awkward. I want to know everything about you. But I'm not sure now is the time[14]."

It was as if a surgeon was at work[15], a time-warping[16] plastic[17] surgeon maybe. He had snipped off[18] the last twenty years, pulled my eighteen-year-old self up[19] to meet my thirty-eight-year-old one, done it almost seamlessly[20].

"So what made you call me?" I asked.

1. lien plus fort
2. étions en deuxième année
3. soulagée
4. C'est la volonté divine.
5. J'ai déjà donné.
6. c'est comme si tu étais tranquille pour [sort of]
7. déchirante
8. sont épargnés toute leur vie
9. subissent plus que leur part
10. cela ne t'immunise pas contre
11. [is not]
12. Au minimum
13. monter en moi
14. que ce soit le bon moment
15. un chirurgien était à l'œuvre
16. qui arrêterait le temps
17. esthétique
18. avait supprimé d'un coup de scalpel
19. fait réapparaître celui que j'étais à 18 ans
20. et ce, presque sans transition

"The strange thing?"

"Yeah."

"You said you had one too."

I nodded.

"Would you mind going first?[1]" she asked. "You know, like when we messed around[2]?"

"Ouch.[3]"

"Sorry." She stopped, crossed her arms over her chest as if cold. "I'm babbling like a ditz[4]. Can't help it."

"You haven't changed, Luce."

"Yeah, Cope. I've changed. You wouldn't believe how much I've changed."

Our eyes met, really met, for the first time since I entered the room. I'm not big on reading people's eyes[5]. I have seen too many good liars to believe much of what I see. But she was telling me something there, a tale[6], and the tale had a lot of pain in it[7].

I didn't want any lies between the two of us.

"Do you know what I do now?" I asked.

"You're the county prosecutor. I saw that online too."

"Right. That gives me access to information. One of my investigators did a quick background check on you[8]."

"I see. So you know about my drinking and driving[9]."

I said nothing.

"I drank too much, Cope. Still do. But I don't drive anymore."

"Not my business."

"No, it's not. But I'm glad you told me." She leaned back, folded her hands[10], placed them in her lap. "So tell me what happened, Cope."

"A few days ago, a couple of Manhattan homicide detectives showed me an unidentified male victim," I said. "I think the man – a man they said was in his mid to late thirties[11] – was Gil Perez."

1. Ça t'embête pas de commencer ?
2. quand on a couché ensemble
3. Aïe.
4. comme une cruche
5. Lire dans le regard des autres, ce n'est pas mon fort
6. une histoire
7. renfermait beaucoup de souffrance
8. une petite vérification de tes antécédents
9. ma conduite en état d'ivresse
10. joignit les mains
11. qui, d'après eux, avait entre 35 et 40 ans

Her jaw dropped.[1] "Our Gil?"

"Yes."

"How the hell is that possible?"

"I don't know."

"He's been alive all this time?"

"Apparently."

She stopped and shook her head. "Wait, did you tell his parents?"

"The police brought them in[2] to ID him."

"What did they say?"

"They said it wasn't Gil. That Gil died twenty years ago."

She collapsed back[3] in the chair. "Wow." I watched her tap her lower lip as she mulled it over[4]. Another gesture straight back from our camp days[5]. "So what has Gil been doing all this time?"

"Wait. You're not going to ask me if I'm sure it's him?"

"Of course you're sure. You wouldn't have said it if you weren't. So his parents are either lying or, more likely, in denial[6]."

"Yes."

"Which one?"

"I'm not sure. But I'm leaning toward lying[7]."

"We should confront them."

"We?"

"Yes. What else have you learned[8] about Gil?"

"Not much." I shifted in my seat. "How about you?[9] What happened?"

"My students write anonymous journals. I got one that pretty much described[10] what happened to us that night."

I thought I was hearing wrong[11]. "A student journal?"

"Yep. They had a lot of it right.[12] How we went into the woods. How we were messing around. How we heard the scream."

1. Elle en resta bouche bée.
2. les a fait venir
3. se laissa retomber
4. en réfléchissant à tout ça
5. remontant tout droit à l'époque du camp
6. dans le déni
7. je penche pour le mensonge
8. Qu'as-tu appris d'autre
9. Et de ton côté ?
10. qui décrivait plutôt bien
11. que j'avais mal entendu
12. Beaucoup de choses correspondaient à la réalité.

I was still having trouble understanding. "A journal written by one of your students?"

"Yeah."

"And you have no idea who wrote it?"

"Nope."

I thought about it. "Who knows your real identity?"

"I don't know. I didn't change identities[1], just my name. It wouldn't be that hard to find."

"And when did you get this journal?"

"Monday."

"Pretty much the day after Gil was murdered."

We sat and let that settle.[2]

I asked, "Do you have the journal here?"

"I made you a copy."

She handed the pages across the desk. I read them. It brought it back.[3] It hurt, reading it. I wondered about[4] the heart stuff[5], about never getting over[6] the mysterious "P." But when I put it down, the first thing I said to her was, "This isn't what happened."

"I know."

"But it's close[7]."

She nodded.

"I met this young woman who knew Gil. She said she overheard him[8] talking about us. He said that we lied."

Lucy kept still[9] for a moment. She spun the chair[10] so that now I saw her profile. "We did."

"Not about anything that mattered," I said.

"We were making love," she said, "while they were being murdered."

I said nothing. I partitioned again[11]. That was how I got through my day[12]. Because if I didn't partition, I would remember that I was the counselor on guard duty[13] that night. That I shouldn't have sneaked off with my girlfriend. That I should have watched them better[14]. That if I had been a responsible kid, if I had done what I was supposed to, I wouldn't have said I had done head counts when I hadn't[15]. I wouldn't

1. changé d'identité
2. On digéra cette information en silence.
3. Tout refit surface.
4. Je m'interrogeai sur
5. les trucs sentimentaux
6. sur le fait de n'avoir jamais réussi à oublier
7. proche
8. qu'elle l'avait entendu
9. silencieuse
10. fit pivoter sa chaise
11. compartimentai à nouveau mes pensées
12. comme ça que j'avais tenu toute la journée
13. de garde
14. mieux les surveiller
15. que j'avais fait l'appel alors que c'était faux

have lied about it the next morning. We would have known that they were gone since the night before, not just that morning. So maybe, while I put check marks next to cabin inspections[1] that I had never done, my sister was having her throat slashed.

Lucy said, "We were just kids, Cope."

Still nothing.

"They sneaked out. They would have sneaked out if we were there or not."

Probably not, I thought. I would have been there. I would have spotted them[2]. Or I would have noticed empty beds when I did my rounds[3]. I did none of that. I went off and had a good time[4] with my girlfriend. And the next morning, when they weren't there, I figured that they were just having fun. Gil had been dating[5] Margot, though I thought they'd broken up[6]. My sister was seeing Doug Billingham, though they weren't[7] too serious. They had run off, were having fun[8].

So I lied. I said I'd checked the cabins and that they'd been safely tucked away[9]. Because I didn't realize the danger. I said I was alone that night – I stuck to that lie[10] for too long – because I wanted to protect Lucy. Isn't that strange? I didn't know all the damage[11]. So yeah, I lied. Once Margot Green was found, I admitted most of the truth – that I'd been negligent on guard duty. But I left off[12] Lucy's role. And once I stuck with that lie, I was afraid to go back and tell the whole truth. They were suspicious of me[13] already – I still remember Sheriff Lowell's skeptical[14] face – and if I admitted it later, the police would wonder why I lied in the first place. It was irrelevant anyway.

What difference did it make if I was alone or with somebody? Either way, I didn't watch out for them.

During the lawsuit, Ira Silverstein's office[15] tried to lay some of the blame on me[16]. But I was only a kid. There were twelve cabins on the boys' side of the

1. alors que je cochais les cases pour l'inspection des cabanes

2. les aurais repérés

3. mes rondes

4. J'étais parti m'amuser

5. sortait avec

6. rompu

7. même si ce n'était pas

8. s'étaient enfuis pour aller s'amuser

9. étaient dans leurs lits, en sécurité

10. j'avais persévéré dans ce mensonge

11. n'avais pas conscience de tous les dégâts

12. n'avais rien dit du

13. me soupçonnaient

14. sceptique

15. les avocats

16. rejeter une partie des responsabilités sur moi

camp alone[1]. Even if I had been in position[2], it would have been easy enough to sneak out. The security was inadequate[3]. That was true. Legally, it wasn't my fault.

Legally.

"My father used to go back to those woods," I said.

She turned toward me.

"He would go digging."

"For what?"

"For my sister. He told us he was going fishing. But I knew. He did it for two years."

"What made him stop?"

"My mother left us. I think he figured that his obsession had cost him too much already. He hired private eyes instead. Called some old friends. But I don't think he dug anymore."

I looked at her desk. It was a mess.[4] Papers were scattered[5], some half-tumbling off[6] like a frozen waterfall[7]. There were open textbooks sprawled out[8] like wounded[9] soldiers.

"That's the problem when you don't have a body[10]," I said. "I assume you've studied the stages of grief[11]?"

"I have." She nodded, seeing it. "The first step is denial."

"Exactly. In a sense, we never got past that[12]."

"No body, ergo[13], denial. You needed proof to move on[14]."

"My father did. I mean, I was sure Wayne had killed her. But then I would see my father going out like that."

"It made you doubt."

"Let's just say it kept the possibility alive[15] in my mind."

"And what about your mother?"

"She grew more and more distant[16]. My parents never had the greatest marriage. There were cracks[17] already. When my sister died – or whatever the hell happened – she totally withdrew from him[18]."

1. rien que dans la partie du camp réservée aux garçons
2. à mon poste
3. n'était pas suffisante
4. Il était en désordre.
5. éparpillés
6. prêts à tomber par terre
7. cascade gelée
8. Des manuels ouverts étaient éparpillés çà et là
9. blessés
10. il n'y a pas de corps
11. les étapes du deuil
12. on ne l'a jamais dépassé
13. donc
14. passer à autre chose
15. que cela maintenait cette éventualité
16. s'est montrée de plus en plus distante
17. des fêlures
18. s'est totalement détachée de lui

We both went quiet. The last remnants of sunlight were fading away.[1] The sky was turning into a purple swirl.[2] I looked out the window to my left. She looked out too. We sat there, the closest we had been to each other[3] in twenty years.

I said before that the years had been surgically removed[4]. They seemed to return now. The sadness was back. I could see it on her. The long-lasting destruction to my family from that night[5] was obvious. I had hoped that Lucy had been able to get past it[6]. But she hadn't. There hadn't been closure[7] for her either. I don't know what else had happened to her over the last twenty years. To blame that one incident for the sadness I saw in her eyes would be too pat[8]. But I could see it now. I could see myself pulling away from her[9] that very night.

The student journal had talked about how she had never gotten over me. I don't natter myself to that degree.[10] But she had never gotten over[11] that night. What it did to her father. What it did to her childhood.

"Paul?"

She was still looking out the window.

"Yes?"

"What do we do now?"

"We find out what really happened in those woods."

1. Les derniers rayons de soleil disparaissaient.

2. Le ciel prenait des teintes violettes.

3. plus proches l'un de l'autre que nous ne l'avions été

4. ôtées par la chirurgie

5. L'effet destructeur que cette nuit avait exercé sur ma famille depuis longtemps

6. avait pu y échapper

7. La page n'avait pas pu se tourner

8. trop simpliste

9. prendre mes distances vis-à-vis d'elle

10. Je ne me la raconte pas à ce point.

11. ne s'était jamais remise de

Chapter 22

I remember on a trip[1] to Italy seeing tapestries[2] that seem to change perspective depending on where you stand[3]. If you move to the right, the table appears to be facing the right[4]. If you move to the left, the table follows you.

Governor Dave Markie was the human embodiment of that[5]. When he walked into the room he had the ability to make every person feel as though[6] he were facing and looking at them. In his youth I had seen him score with[7] so many women, again not because of his looks[8], but because he seemed so interested in them. There was a hypnotic intensity in his gaze.[9] I remember a lesbian friend at Rutgers who said, "When Dave Markie looks at you like that, heck, I'd switch teams for the night[10]."

He brought that into my office.[11] Jocelyn Durels, my secretary, tittered[12]. Loren Muse's face flushed[13]. Even the U.S. Attorney[14], Joan Thurston, had a smile on her face that showed me what she must have looked like[15] when she had[16] her first kiss in the seventh grade[17].

Most would say that it was the power of the office[18]. But I'd known him before the office. The office was a power enhancer, not creator[19].

1. lors d'un voyage
2. avoir vu des tapisseries
3. selon l'endroit où l'on se trouve
4. a l'air d'être face à la droite
5. incarnait cela
6. ce talent de donner à tout le monde l'impression
7. avoir un tel succès avec
8. là encore, non pas grâce à son physique
9. Son regard avait une intensité hypnotique.
10. changerais bien de bord juste pour une nuit
11. C'est ce qui se passa dans mon bureau.
12. rit sottement
13. s'empourpra
14. procureur fédéral
15. me révéla quelle avait dû être son expression
16. avait reçu
17. en cinquième
18. le pouvoir de la fonction
19. n'était pas à l'origine du pouvoir, elle l'amplifiait

We greeted each other[1] with a hug. I noticed that guys did that now – hugged as a greeting. I liked it, the true human contact. I don't have a lot of real friends, so the ones I do have are hugely[2] important to me. They were specially picked[3], and I love every one of them.

"You don't want all these people here[4]," Dave whispered to me.

We pulled back from the embrace.[5] He had a smile on his face, but I got the message. I cleared everyone out[6] of my office. Joan Thurston stayed behind[7]. I knew her pretty well. The U.S. Attorney's office was right down the street. We tried to cooperate, help each other out. We had similar jurisdiction – Essex County had plenty of crime in it – but she was only interested in the big stuff[8]. Right now that mostly meant terrorism and political corruption. When her office stumbled across[9] other crimes, they let us handle them[10].

As soon as the door closed, leaving the three of us alone, the smile slipped off[11] Dave's face. We sat at my conference table. I was on one side. They took the other.

"Bad?" I said.

"Very."

I put my hands out and gestured with my fingers for them to bring it on[12]. Dave looked at Joan Thurston. She cleared her throat.

"As we speak[13], my detectives are entering[14] the offices of the charitable institution known as JaneCare. They have a warrant[15]. We'll be taking records and files[16]. I had hoped to keep it quiet, but the media already has a hold of it[17]."

I felt my pulse do a two-step[18]. "This is crap."

Neither one of them spoke.

"It's Jenrette. He's pressuring me[19] to go easy on[20] his son."

"We know," Dave said.

1. On se salua
2. énormément
3. triés sur le volet
4. Il y a un peu trop de monde ici
5. On s'écarta l'un de l'autre.
6. fis sortir tout le monde
7. resta
8. les affaires importantes
9. tombait sur
10. nous laissaient nous en occuper
11. disparut du
12. d'un signe de la main, les invitai à parler
13. En ce moment même
14. pénètrent dans
15. mandat [de perquisition]
16. allons saisir les registres et les dossiers
17. s'en sont déjà emparé
18. s'emballer
19. fait pression sur moi
20. pour que j'y aille mollo avec

"So?"

He looked over at Thurston.

"So that doesn't make the charges untrue[1]."

"What the hell are you talking about?"

"Jenrette's investigators went places where we never would[2]. They found improprieties[3]. They brought them to the attention of one of my best people. My guy did more digging[4]. We tried to keep it quiet. We know what charges can do to a charity."

I didn't like where this was going. "You found something?"

"Your brother-in-law has been skimming[5]."

"Bob? No way.[6]"

"He's diverted[7] at least a hundred grand[8]."

"To what?[9]"

She handed me two sheets of paper. I scanned down them.

"Your brother-in-law is putting in[10] a pool, right?"

I said nothing.

"Fifty grand was given to Marston Pools in various payments and listed[11] here as a building expansion[12]. Did JaneCare have a building expansion?"

I said nothing.

"Another almost thirty grand was given to Barry's Landscaping. The expense is listed as beautifying the surrounding areas[13]."

Our office was half a converted two-house dwelling[14] in downtown Newark. There were no plans to expand or beautify. We didn't need more space. We were concentrating on raising money[15] for treatments and cures. That had been our focus[16]. I saw too much abuse in the charity system, what with fund-raising expenses[17] far outpacing[18] the amount that went into the good works[19]. Bob and I had talked about that. We had the same vision.

I felt sick.[20]

Dave said, "We can't play favorites[21]. You know that."

1. ne veut pas dire que les accusations sont fausses
2. ont poussé leurs recherches plus que nous ne l'aurions fait
3. des irrégularités
4. a creusé un peu plus
5. a fraudé
6. Impossible.
7. a détourné
8. 100 000 dollars
9. Dans quel but ?
10. se fait construire
11. sont comptabilisés
12. en tant qu'agrandissement des locaux
13. embellissement des espaces verts
14. se trouvait dans une maison mitoyenne réaménagée
15. Notre but était de trouver de l'argent
16. objectif
17. notamment les frais de levée de fonds
18. qui dépassaient largement
19. la somme allouée aux œuvres charitables
20. J'eus la nausée.
21. faire du favoritisme

"I do," I said.

"And even if we wanted to keep it quiet for friendship's sake[1], we couldn't. The media has been tipped off[2]. Joan here is about to hold a press conference."

"Are you going to arrest him?"

"Yes."

"When?"

She looked at Dave. "He's in custody now[3]. We picked him up an hour ago."

I thought about Greta. I thought about Madison. A pool. Bob had stolen from my wife's charity to build a goddamn[4] pool.

"You spared him[5] the perp walk[6]?"

"No. They're going to run him through the gauntlet[7] in about ten minutes. I'm here as a friend, but we both agreed we would go after cases like this[8]. I can't play favorites."

I nodded. We had agreed. I didn't know what to think.

Dave rose. Joan Thurston followed. "Get him somebody good[9], Cope. It's going to be ugly, I think."

I flicked on[10] the TV and watched Bob's perp walk. No, it wasn't carried live[11] on CNN or Fox, but News 12 New Jersey, our local twenty-four-hour news station[12], carried it. There would be pictures in all the big Jersey papers[13] like the *Star-Ledger* and the *Bergen Record*. Some of the local major network affiliates[14] might run something[15], though I doubted it.

The perp walk lasted seconds. Bob was cuffed[16]. He didn't duck his head[17]. He looked, as so many do, dazed and childlike[18]. I felt nauseous. I called Greta at home and on her cell. No answer. I left messages on both.

Muse sat with me throughout[19]. When they moved on to another story, she said, "That sucked."

"It did."

"You should ask Flair to rep him[20]."

1. au nom de l'amitié
2. ont été prévenus
3. déjà en garde à vue
4. une foutue
5. lui avez épargné
6. [« exhibition » du prévenu, menotté et escorté de policiers]
7. le présenter à la foule
8. traiterions ce genre d'affaire
9. un bon avocat
10. J'allumai
11. retransmis en direct
12. chaîne d'information continue
13. les principaux journaux du New Jersey
14. les principales antennes régionales
15. en parleraient peut-être
16. menotté
17. ne baissait pas la tête
18. sidéré et puéril
19. tout le long
20. de le défendre

"Conflict of interest."

"Why? Because of this case?"

"Yes."

"I don't see how. They're unconnected."

"His client's father, EJ Jenrette, started the investigation."

"Oh, right." She sat back. "Damn."

I said nothing.

"You in the mood to[1] talk about Gil Perez and your sister?".

"I am."

"As you know, twenty years ago they found their ripped clothes[2] and blood in the woods."

I nodded.

"All the blood was O positive[3]. So were both of the missing.[4] Four out of ten people are[5], so it's not that surprising. They didn't have DNA[6] tests back then, so there was no way to know for certain. I checked. Even if we rush it[7], the DNA tests will take a minimum of three weeks. Probably longer."

I was only half listening[8]. I kept flashing to[9] Bob, to his face during that perp walk. I thought about Greta, sweet, kind Greta, and how this was going to destroy her. I thought about my wife, my Jane, how this namesake charity[10] was about to be leveled[11]. I had set it up as a memorial to the wife I'd failed in life[12]. Now, again, I had failed her.

"Plus with DNA tests, we need something to compare it to[13]. We could use your blood for your sister, but we'd need a member of the Perez family to cooperate too."

"What else?"

"You don't really need the DNA on Perez."

"Why's that?"

"Farrell Lynch finished the age progression."

She handed me two photographs. The first was the morgue shot[14] of Manolo Santiago. The second was

1. J'es d'humeur à
2. vêtements déchirés
3. du groupe 0 +
4. Comme les deux personnes disparues.
5. 4 personnes sur 10 le sont
6. ADN
7. en faisant vite
8. n'écoutais qu'à moitié
9. revoyais sans cesse
10. fondation portant son nom
11. allait être anéantie
12. que je n'avais pas su protéger de son vivant
13. avec quoi les comparer
14. photo à la morgue

the age-progression shot derived from[1] the photograph I'd given her of Gil Perez.

A total match.[2]

"Wow," I said.

"I got you the address for Perez's parents." She handed me a slip[3] of paper. I looked at it. They lived in Park Ridge. Less than an hour from here.

"Are you going to confront them?" Muse asked me.

"Yes."

"You want me to go?"

I shook my head. Lucy had already insisted on joining me[4]. That would be enough.

"I also have a thought[5]," she said.

"What's that?"

"The technology in finding buried bodies[6] is much better now than it was twenty years ago. Do you remember Andrew Barrett?"

"Lab guy[7] at John Jay[8]? Talkative[9] and strange."

"And a genius. Right, that's him. Anyway, he's probably the country's top expert[10] with this new ground-penetrating radar machine[11]. He pretty much invented it and claims he can cover a lot of ground[12] quickly."

"The area is too large."

"But we can try some of it, right? Look, Barrett is dying[13] to try this new baby out[14]. He says he needs the fieldwork[15]."

"You already talked to him?"

"Sure, why not?"

I shrugged. "You're the investigator."

I glanced back at the TV. They were already replaying[16] Bob's perp walk. He looked even more pathetic this time. My hands tightened into fists.[17]

"Cope?"

I looked at her.

"We gotta go[18] to court," she said.

I nodded, rose without speaking. She opened the door. A few minutes later, I spotted EJ Jenrette in the

1. simulation de vieillissement à partir de
2. Cela correspondait parfaitement.
3. bout
4. pour se joindre à moi
5. une idée
6. utilisée pour trouver des corps enterrés
7. Le type du labo
8. [John Jay College of Criminal Justice, New York]
9. Bavard
10. meilleur expert
11. géoradar
12. il affirme qu'il peut inspecter beaucoup de terrain
13. meurt d'envie
14. d'expérimenter son nouvel engin
15. de ce travail sur le terrain
16. rediffusaient déjà
17. Je serrai les poings.
18. Faut qu'on aille

lobby. He was purposely standing in my path[1]. He was also grinning at me[2].

Muse stopped and tried to steer me[3]. "Let's move to the left. We can go in through – "

"No."

I kept walking straight[4]. Rage consumed me. Muse rushed to catch up with my steps[5]. EJ Jenrette stayed still, watching my approach.

Muse put a hand on my shoulder. "Cope..."

I didn't break stride[6]. "I'm fine."

EJ kept grinning. I met his eye. He stayed in my path. I walked up[7] and stopped so that our faces were inches apart[8]. The idiot was still grinning at me.

"I warned you," EJ said.

I matched his grin[9] and leaned in very close.

"The word has been passed around[10]," I said.

"What?"

"Any inmate who gets Little Edward to service him[11] receives preferential treatment[12]. Your boy is going to be the bitch of his block[13]."

I walked away without waiting for a reaction. Muse stumbled after me[14].

"That was classy," she said.

I kept moving. It was a false threat[15], of course – the sins of the father should never fall to the son[16] – but if that image stuck when EJ laid his head on his goose-down pillow[17], so be it[18].

Muse jumped in front of me. "You gotta calm down, Cope."

"I forget, Muse – are you my investigator or my shrink[19]?"

She put her hands up in a surrender gesture[20] and let me pass. I sat at my seat and waited for the judge.

What the hell had Bob been thinking?

Some days, court is about sound and fury signifying nothing[21]. This was one of them. Flair and Mort knew that they were in deep trouble. They wanted to exclude the pornographic DVD because we hadn't

1. se tenait volontairement sur mon chemin
2. me souriait, ostensiblement
3. me faire changer de direction
4. droit devant moi
5. accéléra pour me rattraper
6. ne ralentis pas
7. avançai jusqu'à lui
8. ne furent plus qu'à quelques centimètres
9. souris à mon tour
10. On a fait passer le message
11. Tout prisonnier qui se tapera le petit Edward
12. un traitement de faveur
13. la pute de son quartier
14. me rattrapa péniblement
15. menace en l'air
16. les enfants ne doivent pas payer pour les péchés de leur père
17. hantait EJ quand il poserait sa tête sur son oreiller en duvet d'oie
18. tant mieux
19. psy
20. pour indiquer qu'elle laissait tomber
21. le tribunal, c'est beaucoup de bruit pour rien [Macbeth, acte V, scène 5]

produced it earlier. They tried for a mistrial[1]. They made motions[2] and handed in findings[3] and research and papers. Their interns and paralegals[4] must have been up all night.

Judge Pierce listened, the bushy eyebrows low[5]. He had his hand on his chin and looked very, well, judicial[6]. He did not comment. He used terms like "under advisement[7]." I wasn't worried. They had nothing. But a thought began to worm its way in and gnaw[8]. They had gone after me. They had gone after me hard[9].

Might they not do the same[10] with the judge?

I watched his face. It gave away nothing.[11] I looked at his eyes, looked for some sort of telltale sign[12] that he wasn't sleeping. There was nothing there, but that didn't mean anything.

We finished up by three p.m. I went back to my office and checked my messages. Nothing from Greta. I called her again. Still no answer. I tried Bob's cell too. More nothing.[13] I left a message.

I looked at those two photographs – the aged Gil Perez, the dead Manolo Santiago. Then I called Lucy. She picked up on the first ring.

"Hey," Lucy answered. And unlike[14] last night, there was a lilt[15] in her voice. I was thrown back again.[16]

"Hey."

There was a weird, almost happy pause.

"I got the address for Mr. and Mrs. Perez," I said. "I want to take another run at them[17]."

"When?"

"Now. They don't live far from you. I can pick you up on the way."

"I'll be ready."

1. tentèrent le vice de procédure

2. firent des requêtes

3. déposèrent des conclusions

4. Leurs stagiaires et assistants

5. en fronçant ses sourcils broussailleux

6. et faisait vraiment, disons, très juge

7. en délibéré

8. faire son chemin et à me miner

9. violemment

10. Et s'ils faisaient de même

11. Rien ne transparaissait.

12. signe révélateur

13. Rien non plus.

14. contrairement à

15. note mélodieuse

16. Cela me renvoya à nouveau dans le passé.

17. retenter ma chance avec eux

Chapter 23

Lucy looked fabulous.

She wore a snug[1] green pullover that clung exactly as it should[2]. Her hair was tied back in a ponytail[3]. She tucked a strand[4] behind her ear. She wore glasses tonight, and I liked the way they looked.

As soon as she got into the car, Lucy checked out[5] the CDs. "Counting Crows[6]," she said. "*August and Everything After.*"

"You like it?"

"Best debut[7] of the past two decades."

I nodded.

She slid it into the slot[8]. "Round Here" came on. We drove and listened. When Adam Duritz sang about a woman saying you should take a shot[9], that her walls were crumbling[10], I risked a glance[11]. Lucy's eyes were wet.

"You okay?"

"What other CDs you got?"

"What do you want?"

"Something hot and sexy[12]."

"Meat Loaf." I lifted the CD case into view. "A little *Bat Out of Hell?*"

"Oh my[13]," she said. "You remember?"

"I rarely travel without it."

1. moulant
2. lui allait parfaitement
3. queue de cheval
4. ramena une mèche
5. passa en revue
6. [groupe de rock alternatif des années 1990]
7. premier album
8. le glissa dans le lecteur
9. « tu devrais tenter ta chance »
10. et que tout s'écroule autour d'elle
11. jetai un regard furtif
12. de sexy et sensuel
13. Oh là là

"God, you always were a hopeless[1] romantic," she said.

"How about a little 'Paradise by the Dashboard Light[2]'?"

"Yes, but skip to the part[3] where she makes him promise to love her forever before she gives it up[4]."

"Gives it up," I repeated. "Love that phrase[5]."

She turned so her body faced me. "What line did you use on me?[6]"

"Probably my patented seducer[7]."

"Which is?"

I put a whine in my voice.[8] "Please? Come on, *pretty* please?"

She laughed.

"Hey, it worked on you[9]."

"But I'm easy[10]."

"Right, forgot that."

She playfully slapped[11] my arm. I smiled. She turned away. We listened to Meat Loaf in silence for a little while.

"Cope?"

"What?"

"You were my first.[12]"

I almost slammed on the brakes[13].

"I know I pretended otherwise[14]. My father and I and that whole crazy free-love lifestyle[15]. But I never.[16] You were my first. You were the first man I ever loved."

The silence was heavy[17].

"Of course, after you, I boinked[18] everybody."

I shook my head, looked to my right. She was smiling again.

I made the right turn per the perky voice[19] of my navigation system[20].

The Perezes lived in a condo development[21] in Park Ridge.

"Are they expecting us?" Lucy asked.

"No."

1. incorrigible
2. à la lueur du tableau de bord
3. va directement au passage
4. avant de céder
5. expression
6. Et avec moi, tu as utilisé quelle réplique ?
7. celle du séducteur invétéré que je suis
8. Je pris un ton plaintif.
9. ça a marché avec toi
10. c'est facile avec moi
11. tapota malicieusement
12. Tu as été le premier.
13. faillis piler net
14. que je faisais croire le contraire
15. tout ce mode de vie délirant basé sur l'amour libre
16. Mais ce n'était pas moi.
17. pesant
18. me suis fait
19. tournai à droite, comme le dictait la voix enjouée
20. GPS
21. zone résidentielle

"How do you know they're home?" she asked.

"I called right before I picked you up. My number comes up private on caller ID[1]. When I heard Mrs. Perez answer, I disguised my voice and asked for Harold. She said I had the wrong number[2]. I said I was sorry and hung up."

"Wow, you're good at this."

"I try to remain humble."

We headed out of the car. The property was neatly landscaped[3]. The air was syrupy with some kind of blossom.[4] I couldn't place it. Lilacs[5] maybe. The smell was too strong, cloying[6], like someone had spilled cheap shampoo[7].

Before I knocked, the door opened. It was Mrs. Perez. She did not say hi or offer up much of a greeting[8]. She looked at me with hooded eyes[9] and waited.

"We need to talk," I said.

Her eyes moved toward Lucy. "Who are you?"

"Lucy Silverstein," she said.

Mrs. Perez closed her eyes. "Ira's daughter."

"Yes."

Her shoulders seemed to sag[10].

"May we come in?" I said.

"If I say no?"

I met her eye. "I'm not letting this go.[11]"

"What go?[12] That man was not my son."

"Please," I said. "Five minutes."

Mrs. Perez sighed and stepped back[13]. We entered. The shampoo smell was even stronger in here. Too strong. She closed the door and led us to a couch[14].

"Is Mr. Perez home?"

"No."

There were noises coming from one of the bedrooms. In the corner were some cardboard boxes[15]. The inscription on the side indicated that they were medical supplies[16]. I looked around the room. Everything, other than[17] those boxes, was so in place, so

1. s'affiche en mode privé
2. que c'était une erreur
3. était entourée d'un joli jardin
4. Un lourd parfum de fleurs imprégnait l'atmosphère.
5. Du lilas
6. écœurante
7. répandu du shampoing bon marché
8. nous accueillit froidement et sans dire « bonjour »
9. derrière ses paupières tombantes
10. s'affaisser
11. Je ne laisserai pas tomber.
12. Laisser tomber quoi ?
13. soupira et fit un pas en arrière
14. canapé
15. boîtes en carton
16. qu'il s'agissait de matériel médical
17. à part

coordinated, you would swear[1] they bought the model unit[2].

The unit had a fireplace[3]. I stood and walked over to the mantel[4]. There were family photographs. I looked at them. There were no pictures of the Perez parents. There were no pictures of Gil. The mantel was full of images of people I assumed to be[5] Gil's two brothers and one sister.

One brother was in a wheelchair[6].

"That's Tomás," she said, pointing to a picture of the smiling boy in the wheelchair graduating[7] from Kean University. "He has CP. Do you know what that is?"

"Cerebral palsy.[8]"

"Yes."

"How old is he?"

"Tomás is thirty-three now."

"And who's that?"

"Eduardo," she said. Her expression said not to press it[9]. Eduardo looked like a hard case[10]. I remembered Gil telling me that his brother was a gang member or something, but I hadn't believed it.

I pointed to the girl. "I remember Gil talking about her," I said. "She was, what, two years older? I remember he said that she was trying to get into college or something."

"Glenda is a lawyer," Mrs. Perez said, and her chest puffed out[11]. "She went to Columbia Law School."

"Really? So did I," I said.

Mrs. Perez smiled. She moved back to the couch. "Tomás lives in the unit next door[12]. We knocked down a common wall.[13]"

"He can live on his own[14]?"

"I take care of him. We also have nursing[15]."

"Is he home now?"

"Yes."

I nodded, sat back down. I didn't know why I cared about that. I wondered though. Did he know about

1. que l'on aurait juré
2. maison témoin
3. cheminée
4. dessus de celle-ci
5. qui, j'imaginais, étaient
6. en fauteuil roulant
7. le jour de sa remise de diplôme
8. Paralysie cérébrale.
9. nous incita à ne pas insister
10. cas difficile
11. se gonfla d'orgueil
12. la maison d'à côté
13. On a abattu un mur mitoyen.
14. seul
15. un service de soins à domicile

his brother, about what had happened to him, about where he'd been the past twenty years?

Lucy had not left her seat. She remained quiet letting me take the lead[1]. She was soaking in everything[2], studying the house, probably putting on her psychology suit[3].

Mrs. Perez looked at me. "Why are you here?"

"The body we found belonged to Gil."

"I already explained to you – "

I held up the manila envelope.

"What's that?"

I reached in and slipped out the top[4] photograph. It was the old one, from camp. I put it on the coffee table[5]. She stared down at the image of her son. I watched[6] her face to see the reaction. Nothing seemed to move or change, or maybe it was just happening so subtly that I couldn't see the transformation. One moment[7] she looked okay. Then, seamlessly[8], everything collapsed[9]. The mask cracked, laying the devastation bare[10].

She closed her eyes. "Why are you showing me this?"

"The scar."

Her eyes stayed closed.

"You said Gil's scar was on the right arm. But look at this photograph. It was on the left."

She didn't speak.

"Mrs. Perez?"

"That man was not my son. My son was murdered by Wayne Steubens twenty years ago."

"No."

I reached into the envelope. Lucy leaned in[11]. She hadn't seen this picture yet. I took out the photograph. "This is Manolo Santiago, the man from the morgue."

Lucy startled up[12]. "What was his name?"

"Manolo Santiago."

Lucy looked stunned[13].

1. me laissant mener l'entretien
2. s'imprégnait de tout
3. probablement avec sa casquette de psy
4. sortis la première
5. table basse
6. J'épiai
7. Pendant un instant
8. sans crier gare
9. s'écroula
10. révélant l'étendue de son chagrin
11. se pencha pour voir
12. tressaillit
13. abasourdie

"What?" I said.

She shook me off.[1] I continued.

"And this" – I plucked out[2] the final photograph – "is a computer rendering[3] using age-progression software[4]. In other words, my lab guy took the old photograph of Gil and aged him twenty years. Then he matched[5] the shaved head and facial hair[6] of Manolo Santiago."

I put the pictures next to one another.

"Take a look, Mrs. Perez."

She did. She looked for a long time. "He looks like him maybe. That's all. Or maybe you just think all Latinos look alike[7]."

"Mrs. Perez?" It was Lucy, speaking directly to Gil's mother for the first time since we entered. "Why don't you keep any[8] pictures of Gil up there?" Lucy pointed to the fireplace mantel.

Mrs. Perez did not follow the finger. She stared at Lucy. "Do you have any children, Ms. Silverstein?"

"No."

"Then you wouldn't understand[9]."

'With all due respect[10], Mrs. Perez, that's a load of crap."

Mrs. Perez looked like she'd just been slapped.[11]

"You have pictures up there from when the children were young, when Gil was still alive. But not one[12] photograph of your son? I've counseled parents who are grieving[13]. All of them kept a picture out. All of them. Then you lied about which arm was scarred. You didn't forget. A mother doesn't make that mistake. You can see the pictures here. They don't lie. And lastly[14], Paul hasn't hit you with[15] the coup de grace."

I had no idea what the coup de grace was. So I stayed silent.

"The DNA test, Mrs. Perez. We got the results on the way over here. They're just preliminary, but it's a match[16]. It's your son."

1. Elle me fit signe de ne pas faire attention à elle.
2. j'extirpai
3. une simulation informatique
4. un logiciel de vieillissement
5. lui a mis
6. la barbe
7. que tous les latinos se ressemblent
8. n'avez-vous aucune
9. ne pouvez pas comprendre
10. Avec tout le respect que je vous dois
11. On aurait dit que Mme Perez venait de recevoir une gifle
12. pas une seule
13. suivi des parents en deuil
14. pour finir
15. ne vous a pas encore donné
16. cela correspond

Man[1], I thought, she's good.

"DNA?" Mrs. Perez shouted. "I didn't give anyone permission to run[2] a DNA test."

"The police don't need your permission," Lucy said. "After all, according to you, Manolo Santiago is not your son."

"But... but how did they get my DNA?"

I took that one.[3] "We're not at liberty to say[4]."

"You... you can do that?"

"We can, yes."

Mrs. Perez sat back. For a long time she didn't speak. We waited her out.

"You're lying."

"What?"

"The DNA test is wrong," she said, "or you are lying. That man is not my son. My son was murdered twenty years ago. So was your sister. They died at your father's summer camp because no one watched them. You are both chasing ghosts[5], that's all."

I looked over at Lucy, hoping she would have a clue here[6].

Mrs. Perez rose.

"I want you to leave now."

"Please," I said. "My sister disappeared that night too."

"I can't help you."

I was going to say more, but Lucy shook me off[7]. I decided that it might be better to regroup[8], see what she thought and had to say before I pressed.

When we were outside the door, Mrs. Perez said, "Don't come back. Let me grieve in peace[9]."

"I thought your son died twenty years ago."

"You never get over it," Mrs. Perez said.

"No," Lucy went on. "But at some point[10], you don't want to be left to grieve in peace anymore."

Lucy didn't follow up[11] after that. I headed back to her. The door closed. After we slipped into my car, I said, "Well?"

1. Ça alors
2. n'ai autorisé personne à pratiquer
3. J'intervins
4. n'avons pas le droit de le dire
5. Vous poursuivez des fantômes, vous deux
6. qu'elle aurait une idée
7. m'en dissuada d'un geste
8. qu'il valait mieux qu'on échange nos impressions
9. pleurer en paix
10. à un moment donné
11. n'enchaîna pas

"Mrs. Perez is definitely lying[1]."

"Nice bluff," I said.

"The DNA test?"

"Yeah."

Lucy let that go[2]. "In there. You mentioned the name Manolo Santiago."

"That was Gil's alias."

She was processing.[3] I waited another moment or two and then said, "What?"

"I visited my father yesterday. At his, uh, home. I checked the logbook[4]. He's had only one visitor other than me in the past month. A man named Manolo Santiago."

"Whoa," I said.

"Yes."

I tried to let it settle. It wouldn't.[5] "So why would Gil Perez visit your father?"

"Good question."

I thought about what Raya Singh had said, about Lucy and me lying. "Can you ask Ira?"

"I'll try. He's not well. His mind has a habit of wandering.[6]"

"Worth a try.[7]"

She nodded. I made a right turn, decided to change subjects.

"What makes you so sure Mrs. Perez is lying?" I asked.

"She's grieving, for one thing[8]. That smell? It's candles. She was wearing black. You could see the red in the eyes[9], the slump of the shoulders[10]. All that. Second[11], the pictures."

"What about them?"

"I wasn't lying in there. It is very unusual[12] to have pictures dating back to[13] childhood and leaving out[14] a dead child. On its own[15], it wouldn't mean much[16], but did you notice the funny spacing[17]? There weren't enough pictures for that mantel. My guess is, she

1. ment, assurément

2. ne releva pas

3. Elle réfléchissait.

4. registre

5. Pas moyen.

6. Son esprit divague maintenant.

7. Ça vaut le coup d'essayer.

8. premièrement

9. ses yeux rougis

10. ses épaules affaissées

11. Deuxièmement

12. très peu courant

13. remontant à

14. de laisser de côté

15. En soi

16. ça ne signifie pas grand-chose

17. curieux espacement

took away the pictures with Gil in them. Just in case something like this happened."

"You mean if someone came by?"

"I don't know exactly. But I think Mrs. Perez was getting rid of evidence[1]. She figured that she was the only one with pictures to use for identification. She couldn't have thought that you'd still have one from that summer."

I thought about it.

"Her reactions were all wrong[2], Cope. Like she was playing a role. She's lying."

"So the question is, what was she lying about?"

"When in doubt, go with the most obvious."

"Which is?"

Lucy shrugged. "Gil helped Wayne kill them. That would explain everything. People always assumed[3] that Steubens had an accomplice[4] – how else did he bury those bodies so fast? But maybe it was only one[5] body."

"My sister's."

"Right. Then Wayne and Gil staged it to look like[6] Gil died too. Maybe Gil has always been helping Wayne. Who knows?"

I said nothing.

"If that's the case," I said, "then my sister is dead."

"I know."

I said nothing.

"Cope?"

"What?"

"It's not your fault."

I said nothing.

"If anything," she said, "it's mine.[7]"

I stopped the car. "How do you figure that?[8]"

"You wanted to stay there that night. You wanted to work guard duty. I'm the one who lured you into[9] the woods."

"Lured?"

She said nothing.

1. se débarrassait des preuves
2. complètement faussées
3. ont toujours pensé
4. complice
5. qu'il n'y avait qu'un
6. ont tout mis en scène pour faire croire que
7. Ce serait plutôt la mienne, dit-elle.
8. Pourquoi penses-tu ça ?
9. C'est moi qui t'ai attiré dans

"You're kidding, right?"

"No," she said.

"I had a mind of my own[1], Lucy. You didn't make me do anything."

She stayed quiet. Then she said, "You still blame yourself[2]."

I felt my grip tighten on the wheel[3]. "No, I don't."

"Yeah, Cope, you do. Come on. Despite[4] this recent revelation, you knew that your sister had to be dead. You were hoping for a second chance. You were hoping to still find redemption."

"That psychology degree of yours," I said. "It's really paying off[5], huh?"

"I don't mean to – "

"How about you[6], Luce?" My voice had more bite than I intended[7]. "Do you blame yourself? Is that why you drink so damn much?"

Silence.

"I shouldn't have said that," I said.

Her voice was soft. "You don't know anything about my life."

"I know. I'm sorry. It's none of my business."

"Those DUIs were a long time ago."

I said nothing. She turned away from me and looked out the window. We drove in silence.

"You may be right," I said.

Her eyes stayed on the window.

"Here is something I've never told anyone," I said. I felt my face flush[8] and the tears push against my eyes[9]. "After the night in the woods, my father never looked at me the same[10]."

She turned toward me.

"I could have been projecting.[11] I mean, you're right. I did blame myself to some degree[12]. What if we hadn't gone off? What if I had just stayed where I was supposed to? And maybe the look[13] on his face was just the pure devastation of a parent losing

1. étais assez grand pour prendre mes décisions tout seul

2. t'en veux toujours

3. mes mains serrer le volant

4. Malgré

5. Il se révèle drôlement utile

6. Et toi alors

7. devint plus mordante que je ne l'aurais voulu

8. mon visage s'empourprer

9. me monter aux yeux

10. ne m'a plus jamais regardé de la même façon

11. Peut-être n'était-ce que mon interprétation.

12. dans une certaine mesure

13. cette expression

a child. But I always thought there was something more in it. Something almost accusatory.[1]"

She put a hand on my arm. "Oh, Cope."

I kept driving. "So maybe you're on to something[2]. Maybe I do need to make amends for the past[3]. But what about you?"

"What about me?"

"Why are you delving into this[4]? What do you hope to gain after all these years?"

"Are you kidding?"

"No. What are you after exactly?[5]"

"The life I knew ended[6] that night. Don't you get that?"

I said nothing.

"The families – including yours[7] – dragged[8] my father into court. You took away everything we had. Ira wasn't built for that kind of hit[9]. He couldn't take the stress[10]."

I waited for her to say more. She didn't.

"I understand that," I said. "But what are you after now? I mean, like you said, I'm trying to rescue my sister. Short of that[11], I'm trying to find out what really happened to her. What are you after?"

She didn't reply. I drove some more. The skies were starting to darken.[12]

"You don't know how[13] vulnerable I feel being here," she said.

I wasn't sure how to answer that. So I said, "I would never hurt you." Silence.

"Part of it is[14]," she said, "it feels like I lived[15] two lives. The one before that night, where things were going pretty well[16], and the one after, where things aren't[17]. And yeah, I know how pathetic that sounds. But sometimes it feels like I was pushed down a hill that night and I've been stumbling down ever since[18]. That sometimes I sort of get my bearings[19] but the hill is so steep[20] that I can never really get balanced again[21] and then I start tumbling again[22]. So perhaps

1. Comme une pointe d'accusation.
2. peut-être as-tu mis le doigt sur quelque chose
3. me racheter par rapport au passé
4. t'impliques-tu là-dedans
5. Que cherches-tu précisément ?
6. Ma vie d'alors s'est achevée
7. y compris la tienne
8. ont traîné
9. n'était pas armé pour ce genre d'épreuve
10. supporter la pression
11. À part ça
12. Le ciel commençait à s'assombrir.
13. Tu ne peux pas savoir à quel point
14. D'une certaine façon
15. j'ai l'impression d'avoir vécu
16. se passaient plutôt bien
17. où elles se passent mal
18. que depuis, je n'arrête pas de dévaler la pente
19. j'arrive à me stabiliser
20. abrupte
21. jamais vraiment retrouver mon équilibre
22. recommence à dégringoler

– I don't know – but perhaps if I figure out what really happened that night, if I can make some good[1] out of all that bad, I'll stop tumbling."

She had been so magnificent when I knew her. I wanted to remind her of that. I wanted to tell her that she was being overly[2] melodramatic, that she was still beautiful and successful and that she still had so much going for her[3]. But I knew that it would sound too patronizing[4].

So instead I said, "It's so damn good[5] to see you again, Lucy."

She squeezed her eyes shut[6] as though I had struck her[7]. I thought about what she said, about not wanting to be too vulnerable. I thought about that journal, all that talk about not finding another love like that, not ever. I wanted to reach out and take her hand[8], but I knew for both of us right now, it was too raw[9], that even a move[10] like that would be too much and not enough.

1. faire quelque chose de bien
2. démesurément
3. tellement d'atouts
4. paternaliste
5. Cela fait un bien fou
6. ferma les yeux très fort
7. l'avais frappée
8. lui prendre la main
9. tout était trop à fleur de peau
10. geste

Chapter 24

I dropped off Lucy back at[1] her office.

"In the morning," she said, "I'll visit Ira and see what he can tell me about Manolo Santiago."

"Okay."

Lucy reached for the door handle[2]. "I have a bunch of papers[3] to correct."

"I'll walk you in.[4]"

"Don't."

Lucy slipped out of the car. I watched her walk toward the door. My stomach tightened[5]. I tried to sort through what I was feeling right now, but it just felt like a rush of emotion[6]. Hard to distinguish what was what.[7]

My cell phone rang. I looked at the caller ID and saw it was Muse.

"How did it go with Perez's mother?" Muse asked.

"I think she's lying."

"I got something you might find interesting."

"I'm listening."

"Mr. Perez hangs at a local bar[8] called Smith Brothers. He likes hanging out with the boys[9], plays some darts[10], that kind of thing. Moderate drinker from what I hear.[11] But the last two nights, he got really lit up[12]. Started crying and picking fights[13]."

1. déposai Lucy à
2. tendit la main pour ouvrir sa portière
3. un tas de devoirs
4. Je te raccompagne.
5. estomac se noua
6. j'étais trop submergé par l'émotion
7. Difficile d'y voir clair.
8. fréquente un bar du coin
9. y passer du temps avec des copains
10. il y joue aux fléchettes
11. Ce n'est pas un gros buveur, d'après ce qu'on dit.
12. il était complètement bourré
13. à chercher la bagarre

"Grieving[1]," I said.

At the morgue, Mrs. Perez had been the strong one. He had leaned on her.[2] I remember that I could see the cracks there.

"And either way, liquor loosens the tongue[3]," Muse said.

"True enough."

"Perez is there now, by the way. At the bar. Might be a good place to take a run at him[4]."

"On my way.[5]"

"There is one more thing."

"I'm listening."

"Wayne Steubens will see you[6]."

I think I stopped breathing. "When?"

"Tomorrow. He's serving his time[7] at Red Onion State Prison in Virginia. I also hooked you up to meet with[8] Geoff Bedford at the FBI office afterward. He was the special agent in charge of Steubens's case."

"Can't.[9] We have court."

"Can. One of your associates can handle it[10] for a day. I have you booked[11] on the morning flight."

I don't know what I expected the bar to be[12]. Something tougher[13], I guessed. The place could have been a chain restaurant like T.G.I. Friday's or Bennigan's, something like that. The bar was bigger[14] than in most of those places, the dining area obviously smaller[15]. They had wood paneling[16] and free-popcorn machines[17] and loud music from the eighties. Right now Tears for Fears was singing "Head Over Heels."

In my day, they would have called this a yuppie[18] bar. There were young men in loosened ties[19] and women trying hard to look business-y[20]. The men drank beer out of bottles[21], trying hard to look like they were having a good time with their buddies[22] while checking out the ladies[23]. The ladies drank wine or faux martinis and eyed the guys more sur-

1. Il est en deuil
2. Elle avait été, en quelque sorte, sa béquille.
3. l'alcool délie les langues
4. pour lui rendre une petite visite
5. J'y vais.
6. accepte de te voir
7. effectue sa peine
8. t'ai aussi décroché un rendez-vous avec
9. Impossible.
10. collaborateurs peut s'en charger
11. t'ai réservé une place
12. quel style de bar je m'attendais à trouver
13. de plus mal-famé
14. occupait plus de place
15. et l'espace restaurant était donc plus réduit
16. Il y avait des boiseries
17. distributeurs gratuits de pop-corn
18. [jeunes cadres dynamiques]
19. à la cravate à moitié défaite
20. faisant tout pour avoir l'air de femmes d'affaires
21. à la bouteille
22. potes
23. tout en matant les nanas

reptitiously[1]. I shook my head. The Discovery Channel[2] should film a mating special[3] in here.

This didn't look like a hangout for a guy[4] like Jorge Perez, but I found him toward the back[5]. He sat at the bar with four or five comrades in arms[6], men who knew how to drink, men who hulked over[7] their alcohol as though it were a baby chick[8] in need of protection. They watched the twenty-first-century yuppies milling about them[9] with hooded eyes.

I came up behind Mr. Perez and put a hand on his shoulder. He turned toward me slowly. So did his comrades. His eyes were red and runny[10]. I decided to try a direct route[11].

"My condolences," I said.

He seemed puzzled. The other guys with him, all Latino men in their late fifties[12], looked at me as though I'd been ogling[13] their daughters. They wore work clothes. Mr. Perez had on a Polo shirt and khaki pants[14]. I wondered if that meant anything, but I couldn't imagine what.

"What do you want?" he asked me.

"To talk."

"How did you find me?"

I ignored the question. "I saw your face[15] at the morgue. Why are you lying about Gil?"

His eyes narrowed.[16] "Who you calling a liar?"

The other men stared at me a little harder[17].

"Maybe we could talk in private."

He shook his head. "No."

"You know that my sister disappeared that night, right?"

He turned away from me and grabbed[18] his beer. His back was to me when he said, "Yeah, I know."

"That was your son in the morgue."

He still kept his back to me.

"Mr. Perez?"

"Get out of here."

"I'm not going anywhere."

1. jetaient aux gars des regards plus furtifs
2. [chaîne TV dédiée à la nature et aux sciences]
3. émission spéciale consacrée à la parade nuptiale
4. l'endroit idéal pour un type comme
5. vers le fond
6. compagnons d'armes
7. des hommes imposants, couvant
8. poussin
9. qui grouillaient autour d'eux
10. larmoyants
11. d'y aller franco
12. frôlant la soixantaine
13. j'avais lorgné
14. un pantalon de treillis
15. la tête que vous faisiez
16. Il plissa les yeux.
17. me dévisagèrent un peu plus
18. saisit

The other men, tough[1] men, men who had spent their lives working outdoors and with their hands, glared at me[2]. One slid off[3] his bar stool[4].

"Sit down," I said to him.

He didn't move. I met his eyes and held it.[5] Another man stood and folded his arms at me[6].

"Do you know who I am?" I said.

I reached into my pocket and pulled out my prosecutor badge[7]. Yes, I have one. The truth is, I am the top law-enforcement officer[8] for Essex County. I didn't like being threatened. Bullies piss me off.[9] You know the old yarn[10] about standing up to a bully[11]? It was only true if you could back it up[12]. I could.

"You all better be legal[13]," I said. "Your family better be legal, your friends better be legal. People you accidentally bump into[14] on the streets – they all better be legal."

The narrow eyes opened a little wider[15].

"Let me see some ID[16]," I said. "All of you."

The one who had stood first put up his hands. "Hey, we don't want no trouble."

"Then get lost[17]."

They threw down some bills[18] and left. They didn't run, didn't hurry, but they didn't want to stick around either[19]. I would normally feel bad about making idle threats, quasi-abusing[20] my power like that, but they had more or less asked for it.

Perez turned to me, clearly unhappy[21].

"Hey," I said, "what's the point of carrying a badge if I don't use it?"

"Haven't you done enough?" he asked me.

The bar stool next to him was open[22]. I took it. I signaled for the bartender[23] and ordered a draft[24] of "whatever he's having[25]," pointing to Jorge Perez's mug.

"That was your son in the morgue," I said. "I could show you the proof, but we both know it."

1. robustes
2. me jetèrent des regards noirs
3. descendit de
4. tabouret
5. Nos yeux se croisèrent et je soutins son regard.
6. me toisa, les bras croisés
7. insigne
8. représentant de la loi au sommet de la hiérarchie
9. Les brutes me mettent en rogne.
10. ce vieil adage
11. qui dit qu'il faut toujours tenir tête à une brute
12. vous en avez les moyens
13. d'être en règle
14. que vous rencontrez par hasard
15. s'écarquillèrent un peu
16. Faites-moi voir vos papiers
17. fichez le camp
18. jetèrent quelques billets sur le bar
19. traîner non plus
20. abusant presque de
21. mécontent
22. libre
23. fis signe au barman
24. pression
25. la même chose que lui

He drained[1] his beer and signaled for another[2]. It arrived with mine. I picked up my mug as though to offer a toast[3]. He just looked at me and kept his beer on the bar. I took a deep sip[4]. The first sip of beer on a hot day is like that first finger-dip when you open a new jar of peanut butter[5]. I enjoyed[6] what could only be called God's nectar[7].

"There are two ways to play it[8]," I went on. "You keep pretending it's not him. I've already ordered a DNA test. You know about those, don't you, Mr. Perez?"

He looked out over the crowd[9]. "Who doesn't anymore?"

"Right, I know. *CSI*[10], all those cop shows[11] on TV. So you know it won't be a problem for us to prove that Manolo Santiago was Gil."

Perez took another sip. His hand shook. His face had fault lines[12] now. I pressed on.

"So the question is, once we prove it's your son, what happens? My guess is[13], you and your wife will try to peddle some 'gasp! – we had no idea' crap[14]. But that won't hold[15]. You start off looking like[16] liars. Then my people start investigating for real. We check all the phone records, all the bank records, we knock on doors, we ask your friends and neighbors about you, we ask about your children – "

"Leave my children out of it."

"No way," I said.

"That's not right."

"What's not right is you lying about your son."

He shook his head. "You don't understand."

"Like hell I don't.[17] My sister was in those woods that night too."

Tears filled his eyes.[18]

"I'll go after you[19], your wife, your children. I will dig and dig and trust me[20], I will find something."

1. avala d'un trait
2. en demanda une autre
3. comme si j'allais trinquer
4. longue gorgée
5. entamer, avec son doigt, un pot de beurre de cacahouètes
6. savourais
7. le nectar des dieux
8. deux façons de la jouer
9. tourna son regard par-delà la foule
10. [Les Experts]
11. séries policières
12. Son visage montrait qu'il accusait le coup
13. À mon avis
14. de nous débiter des conneries, du genre « Oh ! On ne savait pas »
15. ça ne prendra pas
16. commencez à passer pour
17. Évidemment que non, bon Dieu.
18. Ses yeux se remplirent de larmes.
19. ne vous lâcherai pas, ni vous
20. vous pouvez me croire

He stared at his beer. The tears escaped and trickled down[1] his face. He didn't wipe them away[2]. "Damn," he said.

"What happened, Mr. Perez?"

"Nothing."

He lowered his head. I moved so that my face was close to his.

"Did your son kill my sister?"

He looked up. His eyes searched my face as if desperately seeking some kind of solace[3] that would never be there. I held my ground.

"I'm not talking to you anymore," Perez said.

"Did he? Is that what you're trying to cover up[4]?"

"We're not covering up anything."

"I'm not making idle threats here[5], Mr. Perez. I'll go after you. I'll go after your children."

His hands moved so fast I didn't have time to react. He grabbed my lapels[6] with both hands and pulled me close. He had a good twenty years on me, but I could feel his strength. I got my bearings quickly enough[7] and, remembering one of the few martial arts moves[8] I learned when I was a kid, slashed down on his forearms[9].

He released me[10]. I don't know if my blow did it[11] or it was just a decision on his part. But he let go. He stood. I stood too. The bartender was watching us now.

"You need help, Mr. Perez?" he asked.

I had the badge out again. "You reporting all your tips to the IRS[12]?"

He backed off. Everyone lies. Everyone has stuff they keep buried[13]. Everyone breaks laws[14] and keeps secrets.

Perez and I stared at each other. Then Perez said to me, "I'm going to make this simple for you.[15]"

I waited.

"If you go after my children, I'll go after yours."

1. glissèrent le long
2. ne les essuya pas
3. comme pour chercher désespérément une source de réconfort
4. cacher
5. Je ne plaisante pas
6. m'empoigna par le revers de ma veste
7. me ressaisis assez vite
8. prises
9. je frappai violemment ses avant-bras
10. me lâcha
11. si c'était grâce à mon coup
12. déclares tous tes pourboires aux impôts
13. a quelque chose à cacher
14. enfreint la loi
15. Je vais être très clair.

1. mon sang se figer dans mes veines
2. Je me fous que vous portiez un insigne.
3. Trouve tout ce que tu peux

I felt my blood tick[1]. "What the hell does that mean?"

"It means," he said, "I don't care what sort of badge you carry.[2] You don't threaten to go after a man's children."

He walked out the door. I thought about his words. I didn't like them. Then I picked up my cell phone and called Muse.

"Dig up everything you can[3] on the Perezes," I said.

Chapter 25

Greta finally returned my call[1].

I was on my way home, still in the car, and I struggled to find[2] that damn "hands-free[3]" so that the Essex County prosecutor would not be caught breaking the law.

"Where are you?" Greta asked.

I could hear the tears in her voice.

"I'm on my way home."

"Do you mind if I meet you there?"

"Of course not. I called before – "

"I was down at the courthouse."

"Did Bob make bail?[4]"

"Yes. He's upstairs getting Madison to bed."

"Did he tell you – "

"What time will you be home?"

"Fifteen, twenty minutes tops[5]."

"I'll see you in an hour, okay?"

Greta hung up before I could answer.

Cara was still awake when I got home. I was glad for that. I put her to bed and we played her new favorite game, called "ghost." Ghost is basically hide-and-seek and tag combined[6]. One person hides. When that person is found[7], he tries to tag the finder[8] before the finder gets back to home base[9]. What

1. finit par me rappeler
2. j'essayai de trouver
3. kit mains libres
4. Est-ce que Bob a obtenu la liberté sous caution ?
5. maxi
6. un mélange de cache-cache et de chat perché
7. découverte
8. elle essaie d'attraper celui qui l'a trouvée
9. ne regagne son camp

made our version of the game extra-silly[1] was that we played it in her bed. This severely limited your hiding spots[2] and chances to reach[3] home base. Cara would duck under the covers[4] and I would pretend[5] I couldn't find her. Then she would close her eyes and I would put my head under the pillow[6]. She was as good at pretending as I was. Sometimes I would hide by putting my face right in front of her eyes, so she would see me the second she opened them. We both laughed, well, like children. It was dumb and silly[7] and Cara would outgrow it very soon[8] and I didn't ever want her to.

By the time Greta arrived, using the key I had given her years ago, I was so lost in the bliss of[9] my daughter that I'd almost forgotten everything – young men who rape, young girls who vanish in the woods, serial killers who slit throats, brothers-in-law who betray your trust[10], grieving fathers who threaten little girls. But the jangle[11] in the door brought it all back to me.

"I have to go," I told Cara.

"One more turn[12]," she pleaded[13].

"Your aunt Greta is here. I need to talk to her, okay?"

"One more? Please?"

Children will always beg for one more[14]. And if you give in[15], they will do it again and again. Once[16] you give in, they will never stop. They will always ask for one more. So I said, "Okay, one more."

Cara smiled and hid and I found her and she tagged me and then I said I had to go and she begged for one more, but I'm nothing if not consistent[17] so I kissed her cheek and left her begging, nearly in tears[18].

Greta stood at the bottom of the steps. She wasn't pale. Her eyes were dry. Her mouth was a straight line that[19] accentuated her already too-prominent jowls[20].

"Isn't Bob coming?" I asked.

1. super idiote
2. les endroits où se cacher
3. la possibilité d'atteindre
4. se cachait sous les couvertures
5. faisais comme si
6. sous l'oreiller
7. vraiment bébête
8. bientôt, Cara serait trop grande pour ça
9. nageais dans un tel bonheur avec
10. trahissent votre confiance
11. bruit des clés
12. Encore une fois
13. réclama-t-elle
14. vous supplient toujours pour avoir « encore une fois »
15. cédez
16. Une fois que
17. je suis tout ce qu'il y a de plus cohérent
18. en train de supplier, au bord des larmes
19. pincée, ce qui
20. mâchoire déjà trop saillante

"He's watching[1] Madison. And his lawyer is coming over."

"Who does he have?"

"Hester Crimstein."

I knew her. She was very good.

I came down the stairs. I usually kissed her cheek. I didn't today. I wasn't sure what to do exactly. I also didn't know what to say. Greta moved toward the den. I followed. We sat on the couch. I took her hands in mine. I looked at that face, that plain face, and, as always, saw angels[2]. I adored Greta. I really did. My heart broke for her.

"What's going on?" I asked.

"You need to help Bob," she said. Then: "Help us."

"I will do whatever I can. You know that."

Her hands felt ice cold[3]. She lowered her head and then looked straight at me[4].

"You have to say you loaned us[5] the money," Greta said in pure monotone[6]. "That you knew about it. That we agreed to pay you back with interest[7]."

I just sat there.

"Paul?"

"You want me to lie?"

"You just said you would do whatever you could."

"Are you saying" – I had to stop – "are you saying Bob took the money? That he stole from the charity?[8]"

Her voice was firm. "He borrowed[9] the money, Paul."

"You're kidding, right?"

Greta took her hands away from mine. "You don't understand."

"Then explain it to me."

"He'll go to jail," she said. "My husband. Madison's father. Bob will go to jail. Do you get that? It will ruin[10] all our lives."

"Bob should have thought of that before he stole from a charity."

1. garde

2. visage banal, qui, à mes yeux, comme toujours, était celui d'un ange

3. étaient glacées

4. droit dans les yeux

5. que tu nous as prêté

6. d'un ton totalement monocorde

7. te rembourser avec intérêts

8. Qu'il a volé de l'argent à la fondation ?

9. a emprunté

10. va détruire

"He didn't steal. He borrowed. It's been tough[1] for him at work. Did you know he lost his two biggest accounts[2]?"

"No. Why didn't he tell me?"

"What was he going to say?"

"So he thought the answer[3] was to steal?"

"He didn't..." She stopped mid-denial[4], shook her head. "It's not that simple. We had signed the papers and committed to[5] the pool. We made a mistake. We overextended.[6]"

"What about your family money?"

"After Jane died, my parents thought it best to keep everything in trust[7]. I can't touch it."

I shook my head. "So he stole?"

"Will you stop saying that? Look." She handed me photocopied sheets. "Bob was keeping tabs[8] on every cent he took. He was using[9] six percent interest. He would pay it all back once he got on his feet[10]. It was just a way of tiding us over[11]."

I scanned through the papers, tried to see something that would help them, show me that he hadn't truly done what they said. But there was nothing. There were handwritten[12] notes that could have been put there at any time. My heart sank.[13]

"Did you know about this?" I asked her.

"That's not relevant.[14]"

"Like hell it isn't. Did you know?"

"No," she said. "He didn't tell me where the money came from. But listen, do you know how many hours Bob put into[15] JaneCare? He was director. A man in that position should have had a full-time salary. Six figures[16] at least."

"Please tell me you're not going to justify it that way."

"I will justify it any way I can. I love my husband. You know him. Bob's a good man. He borrowed the money and would have returned it before anybody noticed. This type of thing is done[17] all the time.

1. difficile
2. principaux donateurs
3. solution
4. au milieu de son démenti
5. on s'était engagés pour
6. C'était au-dessus de nos moyens.
7. que tout soit entre les mains d'un administrateur
8. gardait une trace
9. appliquait
10. dès qu'il se serait remis à flot
11. pour nous dépanner
12. manuscrites
13. Cela me désespéra.
14. Cela n'a pas d'importance.
15. combien d'heures Bob a consacrées à
16. un salaire à plein temps de plus de 100 000 dollars
17. se pratique

You know that. But because of who you are and this damn rape case, the police stumbled across it[1]. And because of who you are, they will make an example of him. They'll destroy the man I love. And if they destroy him, they destroy me and my family. Do you get that, Paul?"

I did get it. I had seen it done before. She was right. They would put[2] the entire family through the wringer[3]. I tried to push past[4] my anger. I tried to see it Greta's way, tried to accept her excuses.

"I don't know what you want me to do," I said.

"This is my life we're talking about."

I flinched[5] when she said that.

"Save us. Please."

"By lying?"

"It was a loan[6]. He just didn't have time to tell you."

I closed my eyes and shook my head. "He stole from a charity. He stole from your sister's charity."

"Not my sister's," she said. "Yours."

I let that one go. "I wish I could help, Greta."

"You're turning your back on us?"

"I'm not turning my back. But I can't lie for you."

She just stared at me. The angel was gone.[7] "I would do it for you. You know that."

I said nothing.

"You've failed everyone in your life," Greta said. "You didn't look out for[8] your sister at that camp. And in the end, when my sister was suffering the most[9]..." She stopped.

The room temperature dialed down ten degrees[10]. That sleeping snake in my belly[11] woke up and started to slither[12].

I met her eye. "Say it. Go ahead[13], say it."

"JaneCare wasn't about[14] Jane. It was about you. It was about your guilt. My sister was dying. She was in pain. I was there[15], at her deathbed[16]. And you weren't."

1. est tombée dessus
2. passeraient
3. à la moulinette
4. dépasser
5. tressaillis
6. prêt
7. Elle n'avait plus rien d'angélique.
8. n'as pas fait attention à
9. souffrait le plus
10. devint glaciale
11. vieille douleur dans mon ventre
12. s'intensifia
13. Vas-y
14. n'a rien à voir avec
15. Moi j'y étais
16. à son chevet

The unending[1] suffering. Days turned to[2] weeks, weeks to months. I was there. I watched it all. Most of it anyway. I watched the woman I adored, my tower of strength[3], wither away[4]. I watched the light dim from her eyes[5]. I smelled death on her, on the woman who smelled of lilacs when I had made love to her outside on a rainy afternoon. And toward the end, I couldn't take it[6]. I couldn't watch the final light go out[7]. I cracked.[8] The worst moment of my life. I cracked and ran[9] and my Jane died without me. Greta was right. I had failed to stay on watch.[10] Again. I will never get over it – and the guilt did indeed drive me to[11] start up JaneCare.

Greta knew what I'd done, of course. As she just pointed out, she alone was there in the end. But we'd never talked about it. Not once had she thrown my greatest shame in my face[12]. I always wanted to know if Jane asked for me[13] in the end. If she knew that I wasn't there. But I never have. I thought about asking now, but what difference would it make? What answer would satisfy me? What answer did I deserve to hear?

Greta stood. "You won't help us?[14]"

"I'll help. I won't lie."

"If it could save Jane, would you lie?"

I said nothing.

"If lying would have saved Jane's life – if lying would bring back your sister – would you do it?"

"That's a hell of a hypothetical.[15]"

"No, it's not. Because this is my life we're talking about. You won't lie to save it. And that's pretty typical of you[16], Cope. You're willing to do anything[17] for the dead. It's the living you're not so good with.[18]"

1. interminable
2. se transformaient en
3. mon pilier
4. dépérir
5. faiblir dans son regard
6. ne pouvais plus le supporter
7. s'éteindre
8. J'avais craqué.
9. j'avais fui
10. J'avais déserté mon poste à ses côtés.
11. c'était bien la culpabilité qui m'avait poussé à
12. jeté au visage la pire honte de ma vie
13. m'avait réclamé
14. Tu ne veux pas nous aider ?
15. C'est sacrément hypothètique.
16. ça te ressemble bien
17. Tu ferais n'importe quoi
18. Mais avec les vivants, tu es nul.

Chapter 26

Muse had faxed me a three-page summary[1] on Wayne Steubens.

Count on Muse. She didn't send me the entire file[2]. She had read it herself and given me the main points[3]. Most of it I knew. I remember that when Wayne was arrested, many wondered why he decided to kill campers. Did he have a bad experience at a summer camp? One psychiatrist explained that while Steubens hadn't talked[4], he believed that he had been sexually molested[5] at a summer camp during his childhood. Another psychiatrist, however, surmised[6] that it was just the ease of the kill[7]: Steubens had slaughtered[8] his first four victims at Camp PLUS and gotten away with it[9]. He associated that rush, that thrill[10], with summer camps and thus continued the pattern[11].

Wayne hadn't worked at the other camps. That would have been too obvious, of course. But circumstances had been his undoing[12]. A top FBI profiler named Geoff Bedford had nailed him that way. Wayne had been under moderate suspicion[13] for those first four murders. By the time the boy was slaughtered in Indiana, Bedford started to look at[14] anyone who could have been in all those spots[15] at the same time.

1. une synthèse de trois pages

2. dossier complet

3. principaux éléments

4. bien que Steubens n'ait rien dit

5. victime d'abus sexuels

6. présumait

7. dû à la facilité de ce type de meurtre

8. massacré

9. il n'avait pas été arrêté

10. cette pulsion, cette excitation

11. donc, avait continué sur le même schéma

12. avaient causé sa perte

13. vaguement soupçonné

14. s'intéresser à

15. aurait pu se trouver dans tous ces endroits

The most obvious place to start was[1] with the counselors at the camp.

Including, I knew, me.

Originally[2] Bedford found nothing in Indiana, the site of the second murder, but there had been an ATM withdrawal[3] in Wayne Steubens's name two towns away from the murder[4] of the boy in Virginia. That was the big break.[5] So Bedford did more serious digging. Wayne Steubens hadn't made any ATM withdrawals in Indiana, but there was one in Everett, Pennsylvania, and another in Columbus, Ohio, in a pattern that suggested[6] that he had driven his car from his home in New York out that way. He had no alibi and eventually they found a small motel owner near Muncie who positively[7] identified him. Bedford dug some more and got a warrant.

They found souvenirs buried in Steubens's yard[8].

There were no souvenirs from that first group of murders. But those, the theory went[9], were probably his first killings[10] and he either had no time for souvenirs or didn't think to collect them[11].

Wayne refused to talk. He claimed innocence. He said that he'd been set up[12].

They convicted him[13] of the Virginia and Indiana murders. That was where the most evidence was[14]. They didn't have enough for the camp. And there were problems with that case. He had only used a knife. How had he managed to kill four of them? How had he gotten them into[15] the woods? How had he disposed[16] of two of the bodies? They could all be explained – he only had time to get rid of two bodies, he chased them[17] deep in the woods – but the case wasn't neat[18]. With the murders in Indiana and Virginia, it was open and shut[19].

Lucy called near midnight.

"How did it go with Jorge Perez?" she asked.

"You're right. They're lying. But he wouldn't talk either."

1. Le plus logique, c'était de commencer
2. Au début
3. retrait d'argent à un distributeur
4. dans une ville voisine du lieu du meurtre
5. Cela avait marqué un tournant.
6. ce qui semblait indiquer
7. formellement
8. jardin
9. selon les théories
10. meurtres
11. à en récupérer
12. qu'il avait été piégé
13. Il fut déclaré coupable
14. là que les preuves étaient accablantes
15. les avait-il attirés dans
16. s'était-il débarrassé
17. les avait poursuivis
18. l'affaire n'était pas claire
19. il n'y avait pas l'ombre d'un doute

"So what's the next step?"

"I meet with Wayne Steubens."

"For real?[1]"

"Yep."

"When?"

"Tomorrow morning."

Silence.

"Lucy?"

"Yeah."

"When he was first arrested[2], what did you think?"

"What do you mean?"

"Wayne was, what, twenty years old that summer?"

"Yes."

"I was a counselor in the red cabin," I said. "He was two down[3] at the yellow. I saw him every day. We worked[4] that basketball court for a week straight[5], just the two of us. And, yeah, I thought he was off[6]. But a killer?"

"It's not like there's a tattoo or something.[7] You work with criminals. You know that."

"I guess. You knew him too, right?"

"I did."

"What did you think?"

"I thought he was a dickhead[8]."

I smiled in spite of myself[9]. "Did you think he was capable of this?"

"Of what, slitting throats and burying people alive? No, Cope. I didn't think that."

"He didn't kill Gil Perez."

"But he killed those other people. You know that."

"I guess."

"And come on, you know he had to be the one[10] who killed Margot and Doug. I mean, what other theory is there – he happened to be[11] a counselor at a camp where murders took place and then took up killing himself[12]?"

"It's not impossible," I said.

"Huh?"

1. Vraiment ?

2. Lorsqu'on l'a arrêté

3. deux cabanes plus loin

4. avons travaillé sur

5. pendant toute une semaine

6. bizarre

7. Ce n'est pas non plus écrit sur leur front.

8. un con

9. malgré moi

10. que c'est forcément lui

11. il se trouve qu'il était

12. il est lui-même devenu un meurtrier

"Maybe those murders set Wayne off somehow[1]. Maybe he had that potential and that summer, being a counselor at a camp where throats were slit, maybe that was the catalyst."

"You really buy that?[2]"

"Guess not, but who knows?"

"One other thing I remember about him," she said.

"What?"

"Wayne was a pathological liar[3]. I mean, now that I have that big-time psychology degree[4] I know the technical term for it. But even then. Do you remember that at all? He would lie about anything[5]. Just to lie. It was his natural reaction. He'd lie about what he had for breakfast."

I thought about it. "Yeah, I do remember. Part of it was[6] normal camp boasting[7]. He was this rich kid and he'd try to fit in with us wrong-siders[8]. He was a drug dealer, he said. He was in a gang. He had this girlfriend from home who posed in *Playboy*. Everything he said was crap."

"Remember that[9]," she said, "when you talk to him."

"I will."

Silence. The sleeping snake[10] was gone. Now I felt other dormant feelings stir[11]. There was still something there, with Lucy. I don't know if it was real or nostalgia or a result[12] of all this stress, but I felt it and I didn't want to ignore it and I knew I'd have to.

"You still there?" she said.

"I am."

"This is still weird[13], isn't it? Us, I mean.[14]"

"Yes, it is."

"Just so you know[15]," Lucy said, "you're not alone. I'm there too, okay?"

"Okay."

"Does that help?"

"Yes. Does it help you?"

"It does. It would suck[16] if I was the only one feeling this way."

1. ont déclenché les pulsions de Wayne, en quelque sorte
2. Tu y crois vraiment ?
3. menteur pathologique
4. super diplôme de psychologie
5. mentait à propos de tout
6. C'était en partie
7. des vantardises de colo
8. s'intégrer avec nous, les défavorisés
9. Il faudra t'en souvenir
10. vieille douleur
11. d'autres sensations latentes se manifestaient
12. la conséquence
13. C'est quand même bizarre
14. Nous, je veux dire.
15. Je veux juste que tu saches
16. Ce serait nul

I smiled.

"Good night, Cope."

"Good night, Luce."

Serial killing[1] – or at least, having a severely compromised conscience[2] – must be pretty stress free[3], because Wayne Steubens had barely aged[4] in twenty years. He had been a good-looking guy back when I knew him. He still was. He had a buzz cut[5] now as opposed to those wavy, out-sailing-with-Mummy locks[6], but it looked good on him[7]. I knew that he only got out of his cell an hour a day, but he must have spent it in the sun because he had none of that typical prison pallor[8].

Wayne Steubens gave me a winning[9], near-perfect smile. "Are you here to invite me to a camp reunion[10]?"

"We're having it in the Rainbow Room[11] in Manhattan. Gosh[12], I hope you can attend[13]."

He howled with laughter[14] as if I had just cracked the gem of gems[15]. It wasn't, of course, but this interrogation was going to be a dance[16]. He had been questioned by the best federal officers in the land. He had been probed[17] by psychiatrists who knew every trick in The Psychopath's Handbook[18]. Normal venues[19] wouldn't work here. We had a past. We had even been somewhat friendly. I needed to use that.

His laughter segued into a chuckle[20] and then the smile slipped away[21]. "They still call you Cope?"

"Yes."

"So how are you, Cope?"

"Groovy[22]," I said.

"Groovy," Wayne repeated. "You sound like Uncle Ira."

At camp we used to call the elders[23] Uncle and Aunt.

"Ira was one crazy dude[24], wasn't he, Cope?"

"He was out there[25]."

1. Le meurtre en série
2. le fait d'en avoir lourd sur la conscience
3. ne devait pas être si stressant
4. à peine vieilli
5. les cheveux coupés ras
6. au lieu de ses cheveux ondulés de petit garçon à sa maman
7. lui allait bien
8. pâleur
9. charmant
10. à une réunion d'anciens de la colo
11. [restaurant panoramique sélect au Rockefeller Center]
12. Oh dis donc !
13. pourras venir
14. hurla de rire
15. j'avais fait la blague de l'année
16. n'allait pas être une partie de plaisir
17. expertisé
18. toutes les astuces du Guide du psychopathe
19. Un interrogatoire classique
20. devint un gloussement
21. s'envola
22. Super
23. personnes plus âgées
24. bien taré
25. un peu barré

"That he was.[1]" Wayne looked off. I tried to focus in on[2] his powder blue[3] eyes, but they kept darting around[4]. He seemed a bit manic[5]. I wondered if he was medicated[6] – probably – and then I wondered why I hadn't checked on that.

"So," Wayne said, "are you going to tell me why you're really here?" And then, before I could answer, he held up his palm. "Wait, no, don't tell me. Not yet."

I had expected something different. I don't know what exactly. I expected him to be more outwardly crazy or obvious[7]. By crazy, I meant like the raving lunatics you conjure up[8] when you think of serial killers – the piercing gaze[9], the scenery chewing[10], the intensity, the lip smacking[11], the hands clenching and unclenching[12], the rage right under the surface. But I didn't feel any of that with Wayne. By obvious, I meant the type of sociopaths we stumble across[13] every day, the smooth guys[14] you know are lying and capable of horrible things. I wasn't getting that vibe either.[15]

What I got from Wayne was something far more frightening[16]. Sitting here and talking to him – the man who in all likelihood had[17] murdered my sister and at least seven others – felt normal. Okay, even.

"It's been twenty years, Wayne. I need to know what happened in those woods."

"Why?"

"Because my sister was there."

"No, Cope, that's not what I meant." He leaned in a little. "Why now? As you pointed out, it's been twenty years. So why, old friend, do you need to know now?"

"I'm not sure," I said.

His eyes settled[18] and met mine. I tried to stay steady[19]. Role reversal.[20] The psychotic was trying to read me for a lie[21].

"The timing[22]," he said, "is very interesting."

"Why's that?"

"Because you're not my only recent surprise visitor."

1. Ça, c'est sûr.
2. fixer
3. bleu pastel
4. il regardait de tous côtés
5. surexcité
6. sous médicaments
7. plus ouvertement fou ou prévisible
8. ces fous à lier que vous imaginez
9. regard perçant
10. l'exagération
11. claquement de langue
12. qui se crispent et se décrispent
13. que l'on croise
14. types sans histoires
15. Je ne le percevais pas non plus comme ça.
16. de bien plus terrifiant
17. avait selon toute vraisemblance
18. Son regard se stabilisa
19. impassible
20. Inversion des rôles.
21. essayait de voir si je mentais
22. moment choisi

I nodded slowly, trying not to seem too anxious[1]. "Who else came?"

"Why should I tell you?"

"Why not?"

Wayne Steubens sat back. "You're still a good-looking guy, Cope."

"So are you," I said. "But I think us dating is out of the question[2]."

"I should be angry with you, really."

"Oh?"

"You spoiled that summer for me[3]."

Partitioning. I talked about that before. I know that my face showed nothing, but it was like razors were slicing through my gut[4]. I was making small talk with[5] a mass murderer[6]. I looked at his hands. I imagined the blood. I imagined the blade up against[7] the exposed[8] throat. Those hands. Those seemingly innocuous[9] hands that now sat folded[10] on the steel tabletop[11]. What had they done?

I kept my breath steady.

"How did I do that?" I asked.

"She would have been mine."

"Who would have been yours?"

"Lucy. She was bound to hook up with[12] somebody that summer. If you weren't there, I had more than an inside track[13], if you know what I mean."

I wasn't sure what to say to that, but I waded in[14]. "I thought you were interested in Margot Green."

He smiled. "She had some bod[15], huh?"

"Indeed.[16]"

"Such a major tease.[17] You remember that time when we were on the basketball court?"

I did remember. Instantly. Funny how that worked. Margot was the camp va-va-voom[18], and man, did she know it[19]. She always wore these excruciating halter tops[20] whose sole purpose[21] was to be more obscene than actual nudity[22]. On that day, some girl had gotten hurt[23] on the volleyball court. I don't remember

1. impatient
2. qu'il n'est pas question qu'on sorte ensemble
3. as gâché mon été
4. on aurait dit que des rasoirs me lacéraient les tripes
5. la conversation à
6. tueur en série
7. lame contre
8. nue
9. en apparence inoffensives
10. étaient croisées
11. plateau en acier de la table
12. allait forcément sortir avec
13. j'aurais été en position de force
14. je fonçai
15. était super bien foutue
16. Effectivement.
17. Une belle allumeuse.
18. canon
19. elle le savait bien
20. hauts bain de soleil irrésistibles
21. le seul but
22. que la véritable nudité
23. s'était blessée

the girl's name. I think she ended up with a broken leg, but who remembers anymore? What we all remember – the image I was sharing with this sicko[1] – was a panicked Margot Green sprinting past[2] the basketball court in that damn halter top, everything jiggling[3], screaming for help, and all of us, maybe thirty, forty boys on the basketball court, just stopping and staring slack-jawed[4].

Men are pigs, yes. But so are adolescents. It is an odd world. Nature demands that males[5] between the ages of, say, fourteen and seventeen become walking hormonal erections[6]. You can't help it. Yet, according to society, you are too young to do anything about it other than suffer. And that suffering increased tenfold[7] around a Margot Green.

God has some sense of humor, don't you think?

"I remember," I said.

"Such a tease," Wayne said. "You do know that she dumped[8] Gil?"

"Margot?"

"Yep. Right before the murder." He arched an eyebrow. "Makes you wonder[9], doesn't it?"

I didn't move, let him talk, hoped he'd say more. He did.

"I had her[10], you know. Margot. But she wasn't as good as Lucy." He put his hand to his mouth as though he had said too much. Quite a performance.[11] I stayed very still.

"You do know that we had a fling[12] before you arrived that summer, right? Lucy and me."

"Uh-huh.[13]"

"You look a little green[14], Cope. You aren't jealous, are you?"

"It was twenty years ago."

"It was, yes. And to be honest, I only got to second base[15]. Bet you got farther[16], Cope. Bet you popped that cherry[17], didn't you?"

1. taré
2. courant devant
3. avec tout qui ballotait
4. la dévorant des yeux
5. impose aux garçons
6. de se transformer en érections ambulantes
7. cette souffrance était multipliée par dix
8. avait largué
9. Il y a de quoi se poser des questions
10. me la suis tapée
11. Une belle comédie.
12. aventure
13. Mmh mmh.
14. Tu as le teint blême
15. l'ai seulement pelotée
16. Je parie que t'es allé plus loin
17. l'as dépucelée

He was trying to get a rise out of me[1]. I wouldn't play that game.

"A gentleman never kisses and tells[2]," I said.

"Right, sure. And don't get me wrong[3]. You two were something. A blind man could see it. You and Lucy were the real deal[4]. It was very special, wasn't it?"

He smiled at me and blinked rapidly.

"It was," I said, "a long time ago."

"You don't really believe that, do you? We get older, sure, but in most ways[5], we still feel exactly the same as we did back then. Don't you think?"

"Not really, Wayne."

"Well, life does march on[6], I guess. They give us Internet access, you know. No porno sites or anything like that, and they check all our communications. But I did a Web search on you. I know you're a widower with a six-year-old girl. I couldn't find her name online though. What is it?"

Couldn't help it this time – the effect was visceral. Hearing this psycho mention my daughter was worse than having her photograph in my office. I bit back[7] and got to the point[8].

"What happened in those woods, Wayne?"

"People died."

"Don't play games with me."

"Only one of us is playing games, Cope. If you want the truth, let's start with you. Why are you here now? Today. Because the timing is not coincidental[9]. We both know that."

I looked behind me. I knew that we were being watched[10]. I had requested no eavesdropping[11]. I signaled for[12] someone to come in. A guard opened the door.

"Sir?" he said to me.

"Has Mr. Steubens had any visitors over the past, say, two[13] weeks?"

"Yes, sir. One."

1. me cherchait
2. doit savoir rester discret
3. comprends-moi bien
4. c'était du sérieux
5. à bien des égards
6. continue
7. me maîtrisai
8. allai droit au but
9. n'a rien d'une coïncidence
10. observés
11. demandé à ne pas être sur écoute
12. fis signe à
13. au cours de ces, disons, deux dernières

"Who?"

"I can get that name for you, if you'd like."

"Please do.[1]"

The guard left. I looked back at Wayne. Wayne did not appear upset[2]. "Touché," he said. "But there's no need. I will tell you. A man named Curt Smith."

"I don't know that name."

"Ah, but he knows you. You see, he works for a company called MVD."

"A private detective?"

"Yes."

"And he came because he wanted" – I saw it now, those damn sons of bitches – "he wanted dirt on me[3]."

Wayne Steubens touched his nose and then pointed at me.

"What did he offer you?" I asked.

"His boss used to be a big fed[4]. He said that he could get me better treatment."

"Did you tell him anything?"

"No. For two reasons. One, his offer was total nonsense[5]. An ex-fed can't do anything for me."

"And two?"

Wayne Steubens leaned forward. He made sure I was looking him square in the eye[6]. "I want you to listen to me, Cope. I want you to listen to me very carefully[7]."

I held his gaze.[8]

"I have done a lot of bad things in my life. I won't go into details. There is no need. I have made mistakes. I have spent the past eighteen years in this hellhole[9] paying for them. I don't belong here.[10] I really don't. I won't talk about Indiana or Virginia or any of that. The people who died there – I didn't know them. They were strangers."

He stopped, closed his eyes, rubbed his face[11]. He had a wide face. The complexion was shiny, waxy even.[12] He opened his eyes again, made sure that I

1. S'il vous plaît.
2. n'avait pas l'air contrarié
3. apprendre des choses compromettantes sur moi
4. agent fédéral haut placé
5. totalement absurde
6. droit dans les yeux
7. attentivement
8. Je soutins son regard.
9. trou à rats
10. Je ne suis pas à ma place, ici.
11. se frotta le visage
12. Sa peau était luisante, cireuse même.

was still looking at him. I was. I couldn't have moved[1] if I wanted to.

"But – and here's your number-two reason. Cope – I have no idea what happened in those woods twenty years ago. Because I wasn't there. I don't know what happened to my friends – not *strangers*, Cope, friends – Margot Green or Doug Billingham or Gil Perez or your sister."

Silence.

"Did you kill those boys in Indiana and Virginia?" I asked.

"Would you believe me if I said no?"

"There was a lot of evidence."

"Yes, there was."

"But you're still proclaiming[2] your innocence."

"I am."

"Are you innocent, Wayne?"

"Let's focus on one thing at a time[3], shall we? I am talking to you about that summer. I am talking to you about that camp. I didn't kill anyone there. I don't know what happened in those woods."

I said nothing.

"You are a prosecutor now, right?"

I nodded.

"People are digging into your past[4]. I understand that. I wouldn't really pay too much attention. Except now[5] you're here too. Which means something happened. Something new. Something involving[6] that night."

"What's your point[7], Wayne?"

"You always thought I killed them," he said. "But now, for the first time, you're not so sure, are you?"

I said nothing.

"Something has changed. I can see it in your face. For the first time you seriously wonder if I had something to do with that night. And if you have learned something new, you have an obligation to tell me about it."

1. J'étais incapable de faire un mouvement, même

2. clames toujours

3. Concentrons-nous sur une seule chose à la fois

4. fouillent dans ton passé

5. Sauf que maintenant

6. qui concerne

7. Où veux-tu en venir

"I have no obligations, Wayne. You weren't tried[1] for those murders. You were tried and convicted[2] for murders in Indiana and Virginia."

He spread his arms[3]. "Then where's the harm in[4] telling me what you learned?"

I thought about that. He had a point.[5] If I told him that Gil Perez was still alive, it would do nothing to overturn his convictions[6] – because he wasn't convicted of killing Gil. But it would cast a long shadow[7]. A serial killer case is a bit like the proverbial and literal house of corpses[8]: If you learn that a victim wasn't murdered – at least, not then[9] and not by your serial killer – then that house of corpses could easily implode[10].

I chose discretion for now[11]. Until we had a positive ID on Gil Perez, there was no reason to say anything anyway. I looked at him. Was he a lunatic? I thought so. But how the hell could I be sure? Either way[12] I had learned all I could today. So I stood.

"Good-bye, Wayne."

"Good-bye, Cope."

I started for[13] the door.

"Cope?"

I turned.

"You know I didn't kill them, don't you?"

I did not reply.

"And if I didn't kill them," he went on, "you have to wonder about[14] everything that happened that night – not only to Margot, Doug, Gil and Camille. But what happened to me. And to you."

1. jugé
2. reconnu coupable
3. écarta les bras
4. quel mal y a-t-il à
5. Il n'avait pas tort.
6. ne casserait pas ses condamnations
7. cela sèmerait forcément un doute
8. comme cette fameuse histoire [allusion au film d'horreur, la Maison des 1 000 morts]
9. pas à ce moment-là
10. cela pourrait avoir un effet domino
11. pour l'instant
12. Dans les deux cas
13. me dirigeai
14. te poser des questions sur

Chapter 27

"Ira, look at me a second."

Lucy had waited until her father seemed his most lucid[1]. She sat across from him[2] in his room. Ira had broken out[3] his old vinyls[4] today. There were covers[5] with a longhaired James Taylor on *Sweet Baby James* and another of the Beatles crossing[6] Abbey Road (with a barefoot and therefore "dead" Paul[7]). Marvin Gaye wore a scarf for *What's Going On* and Jim Morrison moped sexuality on[8] the cover of the original[9] Doors album.

"Ira?"

He was smiling at[10] an old picture from their camp days. The yellow VW Beetle had been decorated by the oldest-girl bunk[11]. They put flowers and peace signs[12] all over it. Ira was standing in the middle with his arms crossed. The girls surrounded the car. Everyone wore shorts and T-shirts and sun-kissed smiles[13]. Lucy remembered that day. It had been a good one, one of those you stick in a box and put in a bottom drawer[14] and take out and look at when you're feeling particularly blue[15].

"Ira?"

He turned toward her. "I'm listening."

1. soit le plus lucide possible
2. face à lui
3. ressorti
4. vinyles
5. pochettes
6. traversant
7. Paul [McCartney] pieds nus et donc « mort » [selon la rumeur, remplacé par un sosie sur la pochette de l'album Abbey Road]
8. affichait avec indolence son sex-appeal sur
9. premier
10. en regardant
11. le groupe des filles les plus âgées
12. symboles de paix
13. et souriait, le teint hâlé
14. au fond d'un tiroir
15. déprimé

Barry McGuire's classic 1965 antiwar anthem[1], "Eve of Destruction," was playing. Troubling as this song was[2], it had always comforted[3] Lucy. The song paints a devastatingly bleak picture[4] of the world. He sings about the world exploding, about bodies in the Jordan River[5], about the fear of a nuclear button being pushed, about hate in Red China and Selma, Alabama (a forced rhyme[6], but it worked), about all the hypocrisy and hate in the world – and in the chorus[7] he almost mockingly asks how the listener can be naive enough to think that we aren't on the eve[8] of destruction.

So why did it comfort her?

Because it was true. The world was this terrible, awful place. The planet was on the brink back then[9]. But it had survived – some might even say thrived[10]. The world seems pretty horrible today too. You can't believe that we will get through it. McGuire's world had been just as scary[11]. Maybe scarier. Go back twenty years earlier[12] – World War II, Nazism. That must have made the sixties look like Disneyland. We got through that too.

We always seem to be on the eve of destruction. And we always seem to get through it[13].

Maybe we all survive the destruction we have wrought[14].

She shook her head. How naive. How Pollyanna-ish.[15] She should know better.[16]

Ira's beard was trimmed[17] today. His hair was still unruly[18]. The gray was taking on an almost blue tinge[19]. His hands shook and Lucy wondered if maybe Parkinson's was on the horizon[20]. His last years, she knew, would not be good. But then again, there really hadn't been many good ones in the past twenty.

"What is it, honey?"

His concern was so apparent. It had been one of Ira's great and honest charms – he so genuinely cared about[21] people. He was a terrific listener.[22] He saw

1. hymne pacifiste
2. Même si cette chanson était perturbante
3. réconforté
4. brosse un portrait terriblement sombre
5. le Jourdain
6. rime forcée
7. refrain
8. à la veille
9. au bord du gouffre, à l'époque
10. on pouvait même dire qu'elle avait prospéré
11. aussi effrayant
12. Vingt ans auparavant, il y avait eu
13. il semblerait qu'on s'en sorte toujours
14. engendrée
15. Quel optimisme béat.
16. Ce n'était pas raisonnable.
17. taillée
18. ébouriffés
19. avait des reflets presque bleus
20. s'il n'avait pas un début de Parkinson
21. se souciait réellement des
22. Il avait une grande capacité d'écoute.

pain and wanted to find a way to ease it[1]. Everyone felt that empathy with Ira – every camper, every parent, every friend. But when you were his only child[2], the person he loved above all else[3], it was like the warmest blanket[4] on the coldest day.

God, he'd been such a magnificent father. She missed that man so much.

"In the logbook, it says that a man named Manolo Santiago visited you." She tilted[5] her head. "Do you remember that, Ira?"

His smile slid away[6].

"Ira?"

"Yeah," he said. "I remember."

"What did he want?"

"To talk."

"To talk about what?"

He wrapped his lips over his teeth[7], as if forcing them to stay closed.

"Ira?"

He shook his head.

"Please tell me," she said.

Ira's mouth opened but nothing came out. When he finally spoke his voice was a hush[8]. "You know what he wanted to talk about."

Lucy looked over her shoulder. They were alone in the room. "Eve of Destruction" was over. The Mamas and the Papas came on[9] to tell them that all the leaves[10] were brown.

"The camp?" she said.

He nodded.

"What did he want to know?"

He started to cry.

"Ira?"

"I didn't want to go back there," he said.

"I know you didn't."

"He kept asking me.[11]"

"About what, Ira? What did he ask you about?"

He put his face in his hands. "Please..."

1. de la soulager
2. fille unique
3. par-dessus tout
4. couverture
5. pencha
6. disparut
7. serra les lèvres
8. il chuchota
9. enchaînèrent
10. feuilles des arbres
11. Il n'arrêtait pas de me le demander.

"Please what?"

"I can't go back there anymore. Do you understand? I can't go back there."

"It can't hurt you anymore."

He kept his face in his hands. His shoulders shook. "Those poor kids."

"Ira?" He looked so damn terrified. She said, "Daddy?"

"I let everyone down.[1]"

"No, you didn't."

His sobs were uncontrollable[2] now. Lucy got on her knees[3] in front of him. She felt the tears push against her eyes too.[4] "Please, Dad, look at me."

He wouldn't.[5] The nurse, Rebecca, stuck her head in the doorway[6].

"I'll go get[7] something," the nurse said.

Lucy held a hand up. "No."

Ira let out another cry.

"I think he needs something to calm him down."

"Not yet," Lucy said. "We're just... please leave us alone."

"I have a responsibility."

"He's fine. This is a private conversation. It's getting emotional[8], that's all."

"I'll get the doctor."

Lucy was about to tell her not to, but she was gone.

"Ira, please listen to me."

"No..."

"What did you say to him?"

"I could only protect so many.[9] Do you understand?"

She didn't. She put her hands on his cheeks and tried to lift his head[10]. His scream almost knocked her backward[11]. She let go. He backed up[12], knocking the chair to the ground[13]. He huddled[14] in the corner. "No...!"

"It's okay, Dad. It's – "

"No!"

1. J'ai déçu tout le monde.
2. Il sanglotait sans retenue
3. s'agenouilla
4. Elle aussi sentait les larmes lui monter aux yeux.
5. Il refusait.
6. passa la tête par la porte
7. Je vais chercher
8. C'est l'émotion
9. Je n'ai pu en protéger que quelques-uns.
10. lui faire lever la tête
11. la renversa presque en arrière
12. Il se leva en reculant
13. faisant tomber la chaise
14. se blottit

Nurse Rebecca came back with two other women. One Lucy recognized as the doctor. The other, another nurse, Lucy figured, had a hypodermic needle[1].

Rebecca said, "It's okay, Ira."

They started to approach him. Lucy stepped in the way[2]. "Get out," she said.

The doctor – her name tag read[3] JULIE CONTRUCCI – cleared her throat. "He's very agitated."

"So am I," Lucy said.

"Excuse me?"

"You said he's agitated. Big deal.[4] Being agitated is a part of life. I feel agitated sometimes. You feel agitated sometimes, right? Why can't he?"

"Because he's not well."

"He's fine. I need him lucid[5] for a few more minutes."

Ira let out another sob.

"You call this lucid?"

"I need time with him."

Dr. Contrucci folded her arms across her chest. "It's not up to you.[6]"

"I'm his daughter."

"Your father is here voluntarily. He can come and go as he pleases[7]. No court has ever declared him incompetent.[8] It's up to him."

Contrucci looked to Ira. "Do you want a sedative[9], Mr. Silverstein?"

Ira's eyes darted back and forth[10] like the cornered animal[11] he suddenly was.

"Mr. Silverstein?"

He stared at his daughter. He started crying again. "I didn't say anything, Lucy. What could I tell him?"

He started sobbing again. The doctor looked at Lucy. Lucy looked at her father. "It's okay, Ira."

"I love you, Luce."

"I love you too."

The nurses went over[12]. Ira stuck out[13] his arm. Ira smiled dreamily[14] when the needle went in[15]. It reminded Lucy of her childhood. He had smoked

1. seringue hypodermique
2. s'interposa
3. son badge mentionnait
4. Et alors.
5. J'ai besoin qu'il reste lucide
6. Ce n'est pas vous qui décidez.
7. comme bon lui semble
8. Aucun tribunal ne l'a déclaré irresponsable.
9. calmant
10. Ira lançait des regards à droite et à gauche
11. animal pris au piège
12. allèrent vers lui
13. tendit
14. d'un air rêveur
15. s'enfonça

grass[1] in front of her without worry[2]. She could remember him inhaling deeply[3], his smile like that, and now she wondered why he'd needed it. She remembered how it had picked up[4] after the camp. During her childhood years the drugs were just a part of him – a part of the "movement." But now she wondered. Like with her drinking. Was there some kind of addiction gene working[5]? Or was Ira, like Lucy, using outside[6] agents – drugs, booze[7] – to escape, to numb[8], to not face[9] the truth?

1. fumé de l'herbe
2. sans problème
3. le revoyait inhalant longuement la fumée
4. cela avait empiré
5. gène de l'addiction à l'œuvre
6. extérieurs
7. l'alcool
8. pour s'anesthésier
9. et ne pas faire face à

Chapter 28

"Please tell me you're joking."

FBI Special Agent Geoff Bedford and I were sitting at a regulation-size diner[1], the kind with the aluminum on the outside and signed[2] photographs of local anchors[3] on the inside. Bedford was trim[4] and sported a handlebar mustache[5] with waxed tips[6]. I'm sure that I had seen one of those in real life before, but I couldn't recall where. I kept expecting three other guys to join him for[7] a little barbershop[8] quartet work[9].

"I'm not," I said.

The waitress came by. She didn't call us hon. I hate that. Bedford had been reading the menu for food[10], but he just ordered coffee. I got the meaning[11] and ordered the same. We handed her the menus. Bedford waited until she was gone.

"Steubens did it, no question. He killed all those people. There was never any doubt in the past. There is no doubt now. And I'm not just talking about reasonable doubt here. There is absolutely no doubt at all."

"The first killings. The four in the woods."

"What about them?"

1. café-restaurant typique

2. dédicacées

3. des animateurs télé du coin

4. soigné

5. arborait une moustache en guidon de vélo

6. aux extrémités gominées

7. pour interpréter

8. [style de chanson, a cappella, issu des boutiques de barbier aux États-Unis, au début du XXe s.]

9. morceau pour quatuor

10. des plats

11. compris le message

"There was no evidence linking him[1] to those," I said.

"No physical evidence[2], no."

"Four victims," I said. "Two were young women. Margot Green and my sister?"

"That's right."

"But none of Steubens's other victims were female."

"Correct."

"All were males between the ages of sixteen and eighteen. Don't you find that odd?"

He looked at me as if I had suddenly grown a second head[3]. "Look, Mr. Copeland, I agreed to see you because, one, you're a county prosecutor, and two, your own sister died at the hands of this monster. But this line of questioning[4]..."

"I just visited Wayne Steubens," I said.

"I am aware of that.[5] And let me tell you, he is one damn good psychopath and pathological liar."

I thought about how Lucy had said the same thing. I also thought about how Wayne had said that he and Lucy had a little fling before I got to camp.

"I know that," I said.

"I'm not sure you do. Let me explain something to you. Wayne Steubens has been a part[6] of my life for nearly twenty years. Think about that. I've seen how convincing a liar he can be[7]."

I wasn't sure what tack to take here[8], so I just started tramping around[9]. "New evidence has come to light[10]," I said.

Bedford frowned. The tips of the mustache downturned with his lips[11]. "What are you talking about?"

"You know who Gil Perez is?"

"Of course I do. I know everything and everyone involved in this case."

"You never found his body."

"That's right. We didn't find your sister's either."

"How do you explain that?"

"You went to that camp. You know that area."

1. le reliant
2. Pas de preuve matérielle
3. comme si j'étais un extra-terrestre
4. ce genre d'interrogatoire
5. Je sais bien.
6. fait partie
7. qu'il pouvait mentir de façon très convaincante
8. n'étais pas certain de l'approche à adopter
9. je commençai en tournant autour du pot
10. sont apparues
11. s'abaissèrent lorsqu'il fit la moue

"I do."

"Do you know how many square miles[1] of woods there are out there?"

"I do."

He lifted his right hand and looked at it. "Hello, Mr. Needle[2]?" Then he did the same with his left. "Meet my friend Mr. Haystack.[3]"

"Wayne Steubens is a relatively small man."

"So?"

"So Doug was over six feet tall[4]. Gil was a tough kid[5]. How do you think Wayne surprised or overpowered all four of them[6]?"

"He had a knife, that's how[7]. Margot Green was tied up. He simply sliced her throat. We aren't sure of the order of the others[8]. They may have been tied up too – in different places in the woods. We just don't know. He ran down[9] Doug Billingham. Billingham's body was in a shallow grave[10] half a mile from Margot's. He had several stab wounds[11], some defensive wounds on the hands too[12]. We found blood and clothes belonging to your sister and Gil Perez. You know all this."

"I do."

Bedford tilted his chair way back[13] so that his feet went up on the toes[14]. "So tell me, Mr. Copeland. What is the new evidence that has suddenly come to light?"

"Gil Perez."

"What about him?"

"He didn't die that night. He died this week."

The chair dropped forward[15]. "Pardon me?"

I told him about Manolo Santiago being Gil Perez. I would say that he looked skeptical, but that makes it sound more in my favor than the reality[16]. In reality, Agent Bedford stared at me as if I were trying to convince him that the Easter Bunny was real[17].

"So let me get this straight[18]," he said when I finished. The waitress came back with our coffees. Bed-

1. milles carrés
2. Mme l'aiguille
3. Je vous présente mon amie la botte de foin.
4. plus de 1,80 m
5. gamin coriace
6. ait réussi à les prendre par surprise et à les maîtriser tous les quatre
7. voilà comment
8. dans quel ordre il s'y est pris, pour les autres
9. a capturé
10. une fosse peu profonde
11. avait reçu plusieurs coups de couteau
12. et présentait également des lésions aux mains, indiquant qu'il s'était défendu
13. se balança en arrière sur sa chaise
14. si bien que seule la pointe de ses pieds touchait le sol
15. retomba en avant
16. ce serait déformer la réalité à mon avantage
17. existait
18. Mettons bien les choses au point

ford added nothing to it[1]. He lifted the cup carefully and managed to keep the rim off his mustache[2]. "Perez's parents deny it's him. Manhattan homicide doesn't believe it's him. And you're telling me – "

"It's him."

Bedford chuckled[3]. "I think you've taken up enough of my[4] time, Mr. Copeland."

He put down his coffee and started to slide out of the booth[5].

"I know it's him. It's just a question of time before I prove it."

Bedford stopped. "Tell you what," he said. "Let's play your game.[6] Let's say it is indeed Gil Perez. That he survived that night."

"Okay."

"That doesn't let Wayne Steubens off the hook.[7] Not at all. There are many" – he looked at me hard[8] now – "who believed that maybe Steubens had an accomplice for the first murders. You yourself asked how he could have taken out so many[9]. Well, if there were two of them and only three victims, it makes it all a lot easier[10], don't you think?"

"So now you think maybe Perez was an accomplice?"

"No. Hell, I don't even believe he survived that night. I'm just playing hypotheticals.[11] If that body in the Manhattan morgue did end up being Gil Perez."

I added a packet of Splenda[12] and some milk to my coffee. "Are you familiar with[13] Sir Arthur Conan Doyle?" I asked.

"The guy who wrote Sherlock Holmes."

"Exactly. One of Sherlock's axioms goes something like this: 'It is a big mistake to theorize[14] before one has data[15] – because one begins to twist facts to suit[16] theories, instead of theories to suit facts[17].'"

"You're starting to try my patience[18], Mr. Copeland."

"I gave you a new fact. Rather than trying to rethink[19] what happened, you just immediately found a way to twist that fact to suit your theory."

1. ne mit rien dedans
2. prit soin que sa moustache ne touche pas le bord
3. émit un petit rire
4. que vous m'avez fait perdre assez de
5. se glisser hors du box
6. Entrons dans votre jeu.
7. Cela n'exonère en rien Wayne Steuben.
8. avec insistance
9. en supprimer autant
10. cela simplifie tout
11. J'émets simplement des hypothèses.
12. [succédané de sucre]
13. Vous connaissez
14. erreur capitale de bâtir des théories
15. données
16. déformer les faits pour qu'ils coïncident avec
17. faire coïncider les théories avec les faits
18. abuser de ma patience
19. Au lieu de reconsidérer

He just stared at me. I didn't blame him. I was coming on hard[1], but I needed to push[2].

"Do you know anything about Wayne Steubens's past?" he asked.

"Some."

"He fits the profile to a tee[3]."

"Profiles aren't evidence," I said.

"But they help. For instance, do you know that neighborhood animals went missing[4] when Steubens was a teen?"

"Really? Well, that's all the proof I need."

"May I give you an example to illustrate?"

"Please."

"We have an eyewitness to this[5]. A boy named Charlie Kadison. He didn't say anything back then because he was too scared. When Wayne Steubens was sixteen, he buried a small white dog – what's the breed[6], something French..."

"Bichon Frise?"

"That's it. He buried the dog up to its neck. So only its head was sticking out[7]. The thing couldn't move."

"Pretty sick.[8]"

"No, it gets worse."

He took another dainty sip[9]. I waited. He put the coffee back down and dabbed[10] his mouth with a napkin.

"So after he buries the body, your old camp buddy[11] goes to this Kadison kid's house. You see his family had one of those riding lawn mowers[12]. He asks to borrow it...."

He stopped, looked at me, and nodded.

"Eeuw[13]," I said.

"I have other cases like that. Maybe a dozen."

"And yet Wayne Steubens managed to land[14] a job working at that camp – "

"Big surprise. I mean, that Ira Silverstein seemed like such a stickler for[15] background checks."

1. J'y allais fort
2. devais insister
3. colle parfaitement au profil
4. dans le voisinage, des animaux ont disparu
5. un témoin qui a tout vu
6. race
7. dépassait
8. C'est dégoûtant.
9. but délicatement une autre gorgée
10. tamponna
11. vieux copain de colo
12. tracteurs-tondeuses à gazon
13. Pouah !
14. a réussi à décrocher
15. Vous pensez vraiment que Ira Silverstein était à cheval sur

"And no one thought of Wayne when those murders first occurred[1]?"

"We didn't know any of this. First off[2], the locals[3] were on the Camp PLUS case, not us. It wasn't federal. Not at first. On top of that, people were too scared to come forward[4] during Steubens's formative years[5]. Like Charlie Kadison. You have to also remember that Steubens came from a rich family. His father died when he was young, but his mother shielded him[6], paid people off, whatever. She was overprotective, by the way. Very conservative. Very strict."

"Another check mark[7] in your little serial killer profile kit?"

"It isn't just about[8] his profile, Mr. Copeland. You know the facts. He lived in New York yet somehow managed to be in all three areas – Virginia, Indiana, Pennsylvania – when the murders occurred. What are the odds of that?[9] And the kicker[10], of course: After we got a search warrant[11], we found items – classic trophies[12] – belonging to[13] all the victims on his property."

"Not all the victims," I said.

"Enough of them."

"But none from[14] those first four campers."

"That's correct."

"Why not?"

"My guess?[15] He probably was in a rush[16]. Steubens was still disposing of the bodies. He ran out of time."

"Again," I said, "it sounds a bit like fact twisting[17]."

He sat back and studied me. "So what is your theory, Mr. Copeland? Because I am dying to hear it[18]."

I said nothing.

He spread his arms. "That a serial killer who slit campers' throats in Indiana and Virginia happened to be[19] a counselor at a summer camp where at least two other victims had their throats slit?"

He had a point. I had been thinking about that from the get-go[20], and I couldn't get around it[21].

1. ont eu lieu
2. Pour commencer
3. flics du coin
4. pour aller trouver la police
5. la période où Steuben se faisait la main
6. l'a protégé
7. Une case de plus à cocher
8. Il ne s'agit pas que de
9. Quelles sont les probabilités que ce ne soit que le hasard ?
10. pour enfoncer le clou
11. Après avoir obtenu un mandat de perquisition
12. des trophées typiques
13. appartenant à
14. aucun qui appartienne à
15. Vous voulez mon avis ?
16. pressé
17. à de la déformation de faits
18. je meurs d'envie de l'entendre
19. était, comme par hasard
20. dès le début
21. je devais en tenir compte

"You know the facts, twisted or not. You're a prosecutor. Tell me what you think happened."

I thought about it. He waited. I thought about it some more.

"I don't know yet," I said. "Maybe it's too early to theorize. Maybe we need to gather more facts."

"And while you do that," he said, "a guy like Wayne Steubens kills a few more campers."

He had another point. I thought about the rape evidence against[1] Jenrette and Marantz. If you looked at it objectively, there was just as much[2] – probably more – against Wayne Steubens.

Or at least there had been.

"He didn't kill Gil Perez," I said.

"I hear you.[3] So take that out of the equation, for the sake of[4] this discussion. Say he didn't kill the Perez kid."

He held up both palms to the ceiling[5]. "What does that leave you with?[6]"

I mulled that over.[7] It leaves me, I thought, wondering what the hell really happened to my sister.

1. aux preuves de viol incriminant
2. En toute objectivité, il y en avait autant
3. J'ai bien compris.
4. dans le cadre de
5. leva les mains, paumes vers le haut
6. Qu'est-ce que ça vous suggère ?
7. Je méditai là-dessus.

Chapter 29

1. La porte n'était pas fermée que
2. Des requêtes et du vent
3. ce doit être d'un chiant
4. Comment tu fais pour pas te faire sauter la cervelle
5. Ça demande des efforts.
6. demain tu es libre
7. toutes les parties dans son bureau
8. à la première heure
9. Ils ont balancé ce truc de la décision en instance
10. je-sais-plus-qui
11. ce n'était probablement pas grand-chose
12. J'ai demandé à notre meilleur geek d'éplucher
13. corres-pondent à

An hour later I was sitting on a plane. The door had not yet closed when[1] Muse called me.

"How did it go with Steubens?" she asked.

"I'll tell you about it later. How was court?"

"Motions and nothingness[2] from what I hear. They used the phrase 'under advisement' a lot. Being a lawyer must be so friggin' boring[3]. How do you not blow your brains out[4] on days like that?"

"It takes work.[5] So nothing happened?"

"Nothing, but you have tomorrow off[6]. The judge wants to see all counsel in chambers[7] first thing[8] Thursday morning."

"Why?"

"That under-advisement stuff was tossed around[9], but your assistant whatshisname[10] said it probably wasn't a big deal[11]. Listen, I have something else for you."

"What?"

"I had our best computer weenie comb through[12] those journals sent to your friend Lucy."

"And?"

"And they matched[13] what you already knew. At first anyway."

"What do you mean, at first?"

"I took the information he gleaned[1] and then I made some calls, did some digging. And I found something interesting."

"What?"

"I think I know who sent her those journals."

"Who?"

"Do you have your BlackBerry with you?"

"Yes."

"There's a ton here.[2] Might be easier if I e-mail you all the details."

"Okay."

"I don't want to say any more. I'd rather see if you come up with[3] the same answer I do."

I thought about that and heard the echo of[4] my conversation with Geoff Bedford. "Don't want me twisting facts[5] to suit theories, eh?"

"Huh?[6]"

"Never mind[7], Muse. Just send me the e-mail."

Four hours after I left Geoff Bedford, I sat in the office adjacent to Lucy's, one normally used by an English professor, who was on sabbatical[8]. Lucy had the key.

She was looking out the window when her TA, a guy named Lonnie Berger, came in without knocking. Funny. Lonnie reminded me a bit of Lucy's father, Ira. He had that Peter Pan quality, an outcast wannabe.[9] I am not knocking[10] hippies or far-leftists[11] or whatever you want to call them. We need them. I am a firm believer[12] that you need those on both political ends[13], even (or maybe more so[14]) the ones you disagree with[15] and want to hate[16]. It would be boring without them. Your arguments wouldn't be as well honed[17]. Think about it at its core[18]: You can't have a left without a right. And you can't have a center without both[19].

1. qu'il a récupérées
2. Il y a énormément d'éléments.
3. Je préfère voir si tu parviens à
4. cela me fit penser à
5. Tu veux pas que je déforme les faits
6. Hein ?
7. T'inquiète
8. avait pris un congé sabbatique
9. Il tenait de Peter Pan, avec ce désir de marginalité.
10. Je ne critique pas
11. les gens d'extrême-gauche
12. Je suis convaincu
13. de ces gens qui sont aux deux extrêmes du monde politique
14. à plus forte raison
15. avec qui on n'est pas d'accord
16. que l'on a envie de haïr
17. aussi bien affûtés
18. du point de vue fondamental
19. ces deux-là

1. serveuse sexy
2. m'aperçut
3. se fit moins forte
4. lui tendis la
5. la serra
6. m'a informé
7. détectives
8. Tu n'as rien à nous dire ?
9. Toi, si
10. esquissa un sourire en coin
11. Il gagnait du temps.
12. s'effaça
13. et il fit semblant d'être choqué et offusqué
14. se mette à flancher
15. finit par s'écrouler sur
16. baissa la tête

"What's up, Luce? I got a big date with my hot waitress[1]...." Lonnie spotted me[2] and his voice sort of faded away[3]. "Who's this?"

Lucy was still looking out the window.

"And why are we in Professor Mitnick's office?"

"I'm Paul Copeland," I said.

I stuck out my[4] hand. He shook it[5].

"Whoa," Lonnie said. "You're the guy in the story, right? Mr. P or whatever. I mean, I read about the case online and..."

"Yes, Lucy filled me in[6] on your amateur sleuthing. As you probably know, I have some pretty good sleuths[7] – professional investigators, actually – who work for me."

He let go of my hand.

"Anything you want to share with us?[8]" I said.

"What are you talking about?"

"You were right, by the way. The e-mail did come from the Frost Library bank of computers at six forty-two p.m. But Sylvia Potter wasn't there between six and seven p.m."

He started backing away.

"You were[9], Lonnie."

He put on the crooked smile[10] and shook his head. Buying time.[11] "That's a bunch of crap. Hey, wait a second here...." The smile fled[12] as he faked shock and offense[13]. "C'mon, Luce, you can't believe that I..."

Lucy finally turned toward him. She didn't say anything.

Lonnie pointed at me. "You don't believe this guy, do you? He's..."

"I'm what?"

No reply. Lucy just stared at him. She didn't say a word. She just stared until he started to wither[14]. Lonnie eventually collapsed into[15] the chair.

"Damn," he said.

We waited. He hung his head[16].

"You don't understand."

"Tell us," I said.

He looked up at Lucy. "You really trust this guy?"

"A lot more than I trust you," she said.

"I wouldn't. He's bad news[1], Luce."

"Thanks for the glowing recommendation[2]," I said. "Now why did you send Lucy those journals?"

He started fiddling with an earring[3]. "I don't have to tell you a thing."

"Sure you do," I said. "I'm the county prosecutor."

"So?"

"So, Lonnie, I can have you arrested for harassment[4]."

"No, you can't. First off, you can't prove I sent anything."

"Sure I can. You think you're knowledgeable[5] with computers and you probably are in some two-bit, impress-the-coeds kind of way[6]. But the experts in my office – now, they're what you call trained[7] professionals. We already know you sent it. We already have the proof."

He considered that, debating if[8] he should continue to deny it or ride a fresh stream[9]. He chose the fresh. "So what? Even if I did send it, how is that harassment? Since when is it illegal to send a fictional story[10] to a college professor?"

He had a point.

Lucy said, "I can have you fired."

"Maybe, maybe not. But for the record[11], Luce, you'd have a lot more to explain than I do. You're the one lying about your background.[12] You're the one who changed your name to hide your past."

Lonnie liked[13] that argument. He sat up now[14] and crossed his arms and looked very smug[15]. I wanted very badly to punch him in the face.[16] Lucy kept staring at him. He couldn't face her straight on[17]. I moved back a little[18], gave her room[19].

"I thought we were friends," she said.

"We are."

"So?"

1. n'attire que des ennuis
2. ce brillant éloge
3. à tripoter l'une de ses boucles d'oreilles
4. pour harcèlement
5. tu t'y connais
6. mais juste assez pour impressionner les filles, avec ta technique à deux balles
7. très compétents
8. réfléchit à ça, se demandant si
9. partir sur de nouvelles bases
10. un récit de fiction
11. dois-je te rappeler
12. Toi, tu mens à propos de ton passé.
13. savoura
14. s'était redressé, à présent
15. avait l'air très satisfait
16. J'avais une énorme envie de lui envoyer mon poing dans la figure.
17. avait du mal à la regarder en face
18. me mis un peu en retrait
19. lui laissai de la place

He shook his head. "You don't understand."

"Then tell me."

Lonnie started fiddling with the earring again. "Not in front of him."

"Yeah, in front of me, Lonnie."

So much for backing off.[1]

I slapped him[2] on the shoulder. "I'm your new best pal[3]. You know why?"

"No."

"Because I'm a powerful and angry law-enforcement official[4]. And my guess is, if my investigators shake your tree[5], something will fall out."

"No way.[6]"

"Way[7]," I said. "Do you want examples?"

He kept quiet.

I held up my BlackBerry. "I have your arrest records[8] here. You want me to start listing them for you[9]?"

That made the smug go bye-bye.[10]

"I have them all, my friend. Even the sealed stuff[11]. That's what I mean when I say I'm a powerful and angry cop. I can screw with you five ways to Sunday.[12] So cut the crap[13] and tell me why you sent those journals."

I met Lucy's eye. She gave me the smallest of nods[14]. Maybe she understood. We had talked strategy before Lonnie got here. If she was alone with him, Lonnie would fall back on being Lonnie[15] – he would lie and tell stories and tap-dance and skate[16] and try to use their close relationship[17] against her. I knew the type. He would put on the cool, yeah-dude exterior[18], try to use that crooked-smile charm, but if you put enough pressure on him, a guy like Lonnie caves every time[19]. More than that, fear produces[20] a quicker and more honest response[21] with a Lonnie than playing on his supposed sympathies does[22].

He looked at Lucy now. "I didn't have a choice," he said.

1. Terminé, le retrait.
2. lui donnai une tape
3. meilleur pote
4. représentant des forces de l'ordre
5. viennent te secouer le cocotier
6. Certainement pas.
7. Mais si
8. la liste de tes arrestations
9. que je te les énumère
10. Exit le petit air satisfait.
11. les trucs non divulgués
12. Je te tiens, mais alors jusqu'au trognon.
13. arrête les conneries
14. hocha la tête imperceptiblement
15. se raccrocherait à son personnage
16. noierait le poisson
17. liens très forts
18. son air de mec trop cool
19. se dégonfle toujours
20. Surtout, la peur génère
21. réaction
22. qu'en essayant de l'attendrir

Starting to spout[1] excuses. Good.

"Truth is, I did it for you, Luce. To protect you. And, okay, myself. See, I didn't list those arrests on my Reston application[2]. If the school found out, I'd be out[3]. Just like that. That's what he told me."

"Who told you?" I said.

"I don't know the names."

"Lonnie..."

"I'm serious. They didn't say."

"So what did they say?"

"They promised me that this wouldn't hurt Lucy. They had no interest in her. They said what I was doing would be for her good[4], too, that" – Lonnie made a production of turning around toward me[5] – "that they were trying to catch a killer."

He looked at me as hard as he could[6], which wasn't very hard[7]. I waited for him to yell[8], "*J'accuse!*" When he didn't, I said, "Just so you know: On the inside I'm quaking.[9]"

"They think maybe you had something to do with those murders."

"Wonderful, thank you. So what happened next, Lonnie? They tell you to plant[10] these journals, right?"

"Yes."

"Who wrote them?"

"I don't know. I guess they did."

"You keep saying[11] they. How many of them were there?"

"Two."

"And what were their names, Lonnie?"

"I don't know. Look, they were private eyes, okay? Like that. They said they'd been hired by one of the victim's families."

One of the victim's families. A lie. A bald-faced[12] lie. It was MVD, the private investigation firm in Newark. It was suddenly starting to make a lot of sense.[13] All of this was.

"They mentioned the name of this client?"

1. Voilà qu'il débitait
2. dossier d'inscription
3. je serais viré
4. dans son intérêt
5. se retourna vers moi de manière théâtrale
6. me lança le regard le plus méchant qu'il pouvait
7. mais ça n'allait pas bien loin
8. qu'il se mette à crier
9. Au fond de moi, je frémis.
10. faire passer
11. Tu n'arrêtes pas de dire
12. flagrant
13. Tout d'un coup, cela devenait cohérent.

"No. They said it was confidential."

"I bet.[1] What else did they say?"

"They told me that their firm was looking into[2] these old murders. That they didn't believe the official version, blaming them on[3] the Summer Slasher."

I looked at Lucy. I had filled her in on my visits with Wayne Steubens and Geoff Bedford. We talked about that night, our own role, the mistakes we made, the past certainty[4] that all four were dead and that Wayne Steubens had killed them.

We had no idea what to think anymore.

"Anything else?"

"That's it."

"Oh, come on now[5], Lonnie."

"That's all I know, I swear."

"No, I don't think so. I mean, these guys sent Lucy those journals to get her to react[6], right?"

He said nothing.

"You were supposed to watch her. You were supposed to tell them what she said and did. That's why you came in here the other day and told her how you found out all that stuff online about her past. You hoped that she'd confide in you[7]. That was part of your assignment[8], wasn't it? You were supposed to exploit her trust[9] and worm your way even deeper into her good graces[10]."

"It wasn't like that."

"Sure it was. Did they offer you a bonus if you got that dirt[11]?"

"A bonus?"

"Yes, Lonnie, a bonus. As in more money."

"I didn't do this for money."

I shook my head. "That would be a lie.[12]"

"What?"

"Let's not pretend[13] it was all about fear of being exposed[14] or altruism in[15] finding a killer. They paid you, didn't they?"

1. Tu m'étonnes.
2. s'intéressait à
3. qui les attribue à
4. cette conviction ancienne
5. Allez, à d'autres
6. pour la faire réagir
7. qu'elle te ferait des confidences
8. mission
9. profiter de la confiance qu'elle avait en toi
10. faire en sorte qu'elle t'apprécie encore plus
11. une prime, si tu dégotais ces informations
12. Ça, c'est un mensonge.
13. Ne faisons pas comme si
14. tout tournait autour de la peur d'être démasqué
15. de la volonté désintéressée de

He opened his mouth to deny it. I closed it before he bothered.[1]

"The same investigators who dig up[2] old arrests," I said. "They have access to bank accounts. They can find, for example, five-thousand-dollar cash deposits[3]. Like the one you made five days ago at the Chase[4] in West Orange."

The mouth closed. I had to hand it to[5] Muse's investigating skills[6]. She really was incredible.

"I didn't do anything illegal," he said.

"That's debatable[7], but I'm not in the mood right now. Who wrote the journal?"

"I don't know. They gave me the pages, told me to feed it to her[8] slowly."

"And did they tell you how they got that information?"

"No."

"No idea?"

"They said they had sources. Look, they knew everything about me. They knew everything about Lucy. But they wanted *you*, pal[9]. That's all they cared about. Anything I could get her to say about[10] Paul Copeland – that was their main concern[11]. They think maybe you're a killer."

"No, they don't, Lonnie. They think maybe you're an idiot who can muddy up[12] my name."

Perplexed. Lonnie worked very hard on looking perplexed. He looked at Lucy. "I'm really sorry. I would never do anything to hurt you. You know that."

"Do me a favor[13], Lonnie," she said. "Just get the hell out of my face.[14]"

1. Je lui clouai le bec avant qu'il ne se fatigue à répondre.

2. Ces mêmes enquêteurs, ceux qui dénichent

3. des dépôts d'argent liquide

4. [nom d'une banque]

5. Tout le mérite revenait aux

6. talents

7. discutable

8. les lui communiquer

9. c'est toi qu'ils voulaient, mec

10. Tout ce que je pouvais lui faire dire sur

11. ce qui les intéressait le plus

12. salir

13. Fais-moi plaisir

14. Dégage de là.

Chapter 30

Alexander "Sosh" Siekierky stood alone in his penthouse.

Man gets used to[1] his environment. That was how it was. He was getting comfortable[2]. Too comfortable for a man with his beginnings[3]. This lifestyle was now the expected[4]. He wondered if he was still as tough as he once was, if he could still walk into those dens, those lairs[5], and lay waste[6] without fear. The answer, he was certain, was no. It wasn't age that had weakened him[7]. It was comfort.

As a young child, Sosh's family had gotten ensnared[8] in the horrible siege of Leningrad. The Nazis surrounded the city and caused unspeakable suffering. Sosh had turned five[9] on October 21, 1941, a month after the blockade began[10]. He would turn six and seven with the siege still on[11]. In January of 1942, with rations set at a quarter pound[12] of bread a day, Sosh's brother, Gavrel, age twelve, and his sister, Aline, age eight, died of starvation[13]. Sosh survived eating stray animals[14]. Cats mostly. People hear the stories, but they can't fathom the terror, the agony[15]. You are powerless. You just take it.[16]

But even that, even that horror – you get used to it. Like comfort, suffering can become the norm[17].

1. s'habitue à
2. commençait à s'encroûter
3. ayant débuté comme lui
4. considéré comme acquis, désormais
5. tanières, ces repaires
6. tout ravager
7. l'avait ramolli
8. avait été prise au piège
9. avait eu cinq ans
10. après le début du blocus
11. alors que l'état de siège perdurait
12. [environ 100 g]
13. étaient morts de faim
14. des animaux errants
15. imaginer la terreur, le supplice
16. Vous subissez, c'est tout.
17. devenir une habitude

Sosh remembered when he first came to the USA. You could buy food anywhere. There were no long lines[1]. There were no shortages[2]. He remembered buying a chicken. He kept it in his freezer. He couldn't believe it. A chicken. He would wake up late at night in a cold sweat[3]. He would run to the freezer and open it up and just stare at the chicken and feel safe.

He still did that.

Most of his old Soviet colleagues missed the old days[4]. They missed the power. A few had returned to the old country, but most had stayed. They were bitter[5] men. Sosh hired some of his old colleagues because he trusted them and wanted to help. They had history[6]. And when times were hard and his old KGB friends were feeling particularly sorry for themselves[7], Sosh knew that they too opened their refrigerators and marveled at how far they'd come[8].

You don't worry about happiness and fulfillment[9] when you're starving.

It is good to remember that.

You live among this ridiculous wealth[10] and you get lost. You worry about nonsense like spirituality and inner health[11] and satisfaction and relationships. You have no idea how lucky you are. You have no idea what it is like to starve[12], to watch yourself turn to bones[13], to sit by hopelessly while[14] someone you love, someone otherwise[15] young and healthy slowly dies, and a part of you, some horrible instinctive[16] part of you, is almost happy because now you will get a bite-and-a-half-size sliver of bread[17] today instead of just a bite size.

Those who believe that we are anything other than animals are blind[18]. All humans are savages. The ones who are well fed are just lazier[19]. They don't need to kill to get their food. So they dress up[20] and find so-called loftier pursuits[21] that make them believe that they are somehow above it all. Such nonsense. Savages are just hungrier. That was all.

1. files d'attente
2. de pénuries
3. saisi de sueurs froides
4. avaient la nostalgie du bon vieux temps
5. pleins d'amertume
6. une histoire en commun
7. s'apitoyaient sur eux-mêmes
8. n'en revenaient pas du chemin parcouru
9. de l'épanouissement
10. opulence
11. l'équilibre intérieur
12. d'être affamé
13. de se voir maigrir à vue d'œil
14. d'être là, impuissant, alors que
15. qui était
16. atrocement instinctive
17. une bouchée et demie de pain
18. aveugles
19. bien nourris sont simplement plus paresseux
20. s'habillent bien
21. des occupations soi-disant plus nobles

You do horrible things to survive. Anyone who believes that they are above that is delusional[1].

The message had come in on his computer.

That was how it worked nowadays[2]. Not by phone, not in person. Computers. E-mails. It was so easy to communicate that way and not be traced[3]. He wondered how the old Soviet regime[4] would have handled[5] the Internet. Controlling information had been such a large part of what they did. But how do you control it with something like the Internet? Or maybe it wasn't that big of a difference. In the end, the way you rounded up your enemies was through leaks[6]. People talked. People sold one another out[7]. People betrayed[8] their neighbors and loved ones[9]. Sometimes for a hunk[10] of bread. Sometimes for a ticket to freedom[11]. It all depended on how hungry you were.

Sosh read the message again. It was short and simple and Sosh wasn't sure what to do about it. They had a phone number. They had an address. But it was the first line of the e-mail that he kept coming back to[12]. So simply stated.[13]

He read it again:

WE FOUND HER.

And now he wondered what he should do about it.

I put a call in to[14] Muse. "Can you find Cingle Shaker for me?"

"I guess. Why, what's up?"

"I want to ask her some questions about how MVD works[15]."

"I'm on it.[16]"

I hung up and turned back to Lucy. She was still looking out the window.

"You okay?"

1. se font des illusions
2. de nos jours
3. sans se faire repérer
4. l'ancien régime soviétique
5. géré
6. c'était grâce aux fuites qu'on cernait l'ennemi
7. se vendaient les uns les autres
8. trahissaient
9. leurs êtres chers
10. gros morceau
11. en échange de la liberté
12. sur laquelle il revenait sans cesse
13. C'était si laconique.
14. téléphonai à
15. sur la façon de travailler de MVD
16. Je m'en occupe.

"I trusted him."

I was going to say I'm sorry or something equally hackneyed[1], but I decided to keep it to myself[2].

"You were right," she said.

"About?"

"Lonnie Berger was probably my closest[3] friend. I trusted him more than anyone. Well, except for Ira, who's got one arm locked in the straitjacket as it is[4]."

I tried to smile.

"By the way, how's my self-pity act[5]? Pretty attractive, right?"

"Actually," I said, "it is."

She turned away from the window and looked at me.

"Are we going to try again, Cope? I mean, after this is all done[6] and we figure out what happened to your sister. Are we going back to our lives[7] – or are we going to try to see what could happen here[8]?"

"I love when you beat around the bush[9]."

Lucy wasn't smiling.

"Yeah," I said. "I want to try."

"Good answer. Very good."

"Thanks."

"I don't always want to be the one risking my heart[10]."

"You're not," I said. "I'm there too."

"So who killed Margot and Doug?" she asked.

"Wow, that was a quick segue[11]."

"Yeah, well, the faster we figure out what happened..." She shrugged.

"You know something?" I said.

"What?"

"It's just so damn easy to remember why I fell for you[12]."

Lucy turned away. "I am not going to cry, I am not going to cry, I am not going to cry...."

"I don't know who killed them anymore," I said.

1. d'aussi banal
2. de ne rien dire
3. le plus proche
4. qui, à ce jour, a un bras dans une camisole de force
5. tu le trouves comment mon numéro d'apitoiement sur moi-même
6. quand tout ça sera fini
7. Allons-nous reprendre le cours de nos vies
8. entre nous
9. tu tournes autour du pot
10. qui met son cœur en danger
11. c'est sans transition
12. suis tombé amoureux de toi

"Okay. How about Wayne Steubens? Do you still think he did it?"

"I don't know. We do know[1] that he didn't kill Gil Perez."

"Do you think he told you the truth?"

"He said he hooked up with you."

"Yuck.[2]"

"But that he only got to second base."

"If he counts the time he intentionally bumped into me[3] during a softball game and copped a feel[4], well, then technically he's telling the truth. Did he really say that?"

"He did. He also said he slept with Margot."

"That's probably true. Lots of guys had[5] Margot."

"Not me."

"That's because I snagged you[6] as soon as you arrived."

"That you did. He also said that Gil and Margot had broken up."

"So?"

"Do you think it's true?" I asked.

"I don't know. But you know how camp was. It was like a life cycle in seven weeks. People were always going out and then breaking up[7] and then finding someone new[8]."

"True."

"But?"

"But the common theory was that both couples went into the woods to, uh, mess around[9]."

"Like we were doing," she said.

"Right. And my sister and Doug were still an item[10]. Not in love or anything, but you know what I mean. My point is, if Gil and Margot were no longer together, why would they have been sneaking into the woods?"

"I see. So if she and Gil were broken up[11] – and we know Gil didn't die in those woods..."

I thought about what Raya Singh had suggested – a woman who had clearly known and even been

1. Ce qu'on sait, c'est
2. Beurk.
3. la fois où il a fait exprès de me foncer dedans
4. pour me peloter
5. ont couché avec
6. t'ai alpagué
7. sortaient ensemble et rompaient ensuite
8. se trouvaient quelqu'un d'autre
9. coucher ensemble
10. sortaient encore ensemble
11. avaient rompu

close to Gil Perez, aka Manolo Santiago. "Maybe Gil killed Margot. Maybe Camille and Doug just stumbled across that[1]."

"So Gil silenced them."

"Right. Now he's in trouble. Think about it. He's a poor kid. He has a brother with a criminal record. He'd be under suspicion as it was[2]."

"So he faked like he died[3] too," she said.

We both sat there.

"We're missing something," she said.

"I know."

"We might be getting close."

"Or we might be way off[4]."

"One of the two," Lucy agreed.

Man, it felt good to be with her.

"Something else," I said.

"What?"

"Those journals. What were they talking about – you finding me covered with blood and me saying we can't tell anyone?"

"I don't know."

"Let's start with the first part – the part they got right[5]. About how we sneaked away."

"Okay."

"How would they know that?"

"I don't know," she said.

"How would they know you led me away[6]?"

"Or" – she stopped, swallowed – "how I felt about you[7]?"

Silence.

Lucy shrugged. "Maybe it was just obvious to anyone[8] who saw the way I looked at you."

"I'm trying hard to focus[9] here and not smile."

"Don't try too hard," she said. "Anyway, we got part one of the journal. Let's move on to[10] part two."

"The stuff about me covered in blood. Where the hell did they come up with that?[11]"

1. sont simplement tombés là-dessus par hasard
2. aurait fait un suspect tout trouvé
3. a fait croire qu'il était mort
4. complètement à côté
5. qui est conforme à ce qui s'est passé
6. m'as entraîné
7. ce que je ressentais pour toi
8. une évidence pour tous ceux
9. vraiment de me concentrer
10. Passons à
11. D'où est-ce qu'ils ont sorti ça ?

"No idea. But you know what really creeps me out[1]?"

"What?"

"That they knew we got separated. That we did lose sight of each other.[2]"

I had wondered about that too.

"Who would know about that?" I asked.

"I never told a soul[3]," she said.

"Neither did I."

"Someone could have guessed," Lucy said. She stopped, looked up at the ceiling[4]. "Or..."

"Or what?"

"You never told anyone about us getting separated, right?"

"Right."

"And I never told anyone about us getting separated."

"So?"

"So then there's only one explanation," Lucy said.

"That being?[5]"

She looked straight at me. "Someone saw us that night."

Silence.

"Gil maybe," I said. "Or Wayne."

"They're our two murder suspects, right?"

"Right."

"Then who murdered Gil?"

I stopped.

"Gil didn't kill himself and move his[6] body," she went on. "And Wayne Steubens is in a maximum security facility in Virginia."

I thought about that.

"So if the killer wasn't Wayne and it wasn't Gil," she said, "who else is there?[7]"

"Found her," Muse said, as she walked into my office.

Cingle Shaker followed. Cingle knew how to make an entrance[8], but I wasn't sure that was a conscious effort on her part[9]. There was something fierce[10] in

1. me fait vraiment froid dans le dos
2. Qu'on s'est perdus de vue.
3. ne l'ai jamais dit à qui que ce soit
4. leva les yeux au plafond
5. Laquelle ?
6. pour ensuite déplacer son propre
7. qui reste-t-il ?
8. faire son entrée
9. je ne pense pas que cela lui demandait un réel effort
10. de féroce

her movements, as if the air itself better make way[1]. Muse was no potted plant[2], but she looked like one next to[3] Cingle Shaker.

They both sat. Cingle crossed the long legs.

"So," Cingle said, "MVD is after you big-time[4]."

"Looks that way."

"It is that way. I've checked. It's a scorched-earth operation.[5] No expense spared. No lives spared[6] either. They destroyed your brother-in-law already. They sent a guy to Russia. They've put people on the street[7], I don't know how many. They had someone try to bribe your old buddy Wayne Steubens. In short, they're going to carve out any piece of your ass they can get their blade into[8]."

"Any word on[9] what they got?"

"Not yet, no. Just what you already know."

I told her about Lucy's journals. Cingle nodded as I spoke.

"They've done that before. How accurate are the[10] journals?"

"A lot is wrong. I never stumbled across blood or said we have to keep this secret or anything like that. But they know how we felt about each other. They know we sneaked away and how and all that."

"Interesting."

"How would they have gotten their information?"

"Hard to say."

"Any thoughts?"

She mulled it over for a few moments. "Like I said before, this is how they operate[11]. They want to stir something up[12]. It doesn't matter if it's the truth or not. Sometimes you need to shift reality[13]. Do you know what I mean?"

"No, not really."

"How to explain...?" Cingle thought about it a moment. "When I first got to MVD, do you know what I was hired to do[14]?"

I shook my head.

1. aurait intérêt à la laisser passer

2. n'avait rien d'une potiche

3. à côté de

4. à fond sur vous

5. Ils pratiquent la politique de la terre brûlée.

6. Aucune vie épargnée

7. lâché des gens dans la rue

8. vous réduire en chair à pâté

9. On a une idée de

10. Quel est la part de vérité de ces

11. leur mode de fonctionnement

12. soulever quelque chose

13. métamorphoser la réalité

14. quel était mon travail

"Catch cheating spouses.[1] It's big business[2] – adultery. My own firm[3] too. It used to be[4] forty percent, maybe more. And MVD is the best at it, though their methods are a tad unorthodox[5]."

"How?"

"Depends on the case, but the first step was always the same: Read the client.[6] In other words, see what the client really wants. Do they want the truth? Do they want to be lied to[7]? Do they want reassurance[8], a way to get a divorce, what?"

"I'm not following. Don't they all want the truth?"

"Yes and no. Look, I hated that end[9] of the business. I didn't mind surveillance or background checks – you know, following a husband or wife, checking out credit card charges[10], phone records, that kind of thing. That's all a tad seedy[11], but I get that[12]. It makes sense. But then there's this other side of the business."

"What other side?"

"The side that *wants* there to be[13] a problem. Some wives, for example, want their husbands to be cheating[14]."

I looked at Muse. "I'm lost."

"No, you're not. A man is supposed to be faithful forever[15], right? I know this one guy.[16] I'm talking to him on the phone – this is before we ever met face-to-face – and he's telling me how he would never, ever cheat, how he loves his wife, blah, blah, blah. But the guy is some ugly slob[17] who works as an assistant manager[18] at a CVS[19] or something – so I'm thinking to myself, 'Who is going to come on to him[20]?' Right?"

"I'm still not following."

"It is easier to be a good, honorable guy when there is no temptation. But in cases like that, MVD would shift reality. By using me as bait.[21]"

"For what?"

"For what do you think?[22] If a wife wanted to nail[23] her husband for cheating, my job would be to seduce

1. Coincer des conjoints infidèles.
2. Ça rapporte beaucoup
3. Dans ma propre société
4. Ça représentait
5. peu orthodoxes
6. Interpréter l'état d'esprit du client.
7. qu'on leur mente
8. être rassurés
9. partie
10. dépenses
11. un tantinet minable
12. ça passe encore
13. où il faut qu'il y ait
14. leur soient infidèles
15. fidèle à vie
16. Tiens, par exemple, prenons le cas de ce type.
17. un plouc hideux
18. est sous-directeur
19. [chaîne de pharmacies américaine]
20. pourrait bien le draguer
21. En se servant de moi comme appât.
22. À votre avis ?
23. coincer

him. That's how MVD worked. The husband would be at a bar or something. They would send me out as a" – she made quote marks with her fingers – "'fidelity test.'"

"So?"

"So I hate to sound immodest[1], but take a look." Cingle spread her arms. Even dressed down[2] in a loose[3] sweater, the sight was indeed impressive[4]. "If that's not unfair entrapment[5], I don't know what is."

"Because you're attractive?"

"Yep."

I shrugged. "If the guy's committed[6], it shouldn't make a difference how attractive the woman is."

Cingle Shaker made a face[7]. "Please."

"Please what?"

"Are you being intentionally dense?[8] How hard do you think it would be for me to get[9] Mr. CVS, for example, to look in my direction?"

"To look is one thing. To do more than that is another."

Cingle looked at Muse. "Is he for real?[10]"

Muse shrugged.

"Let me put it this way[11]," Cingle said. "I probably ran[12], oh, thirty or forty of these so-called fidelity tests. Guess how many married guys turned me down[13]?"

"I have no idea."

"Two."

"Not great stats[14], I admit – "

"Wait, I didn't finish. The two that turned me down? Do you know why?"

"No."

"They caught on.[15] They realized something had to be up[16]. They were both like, 'Wait, why would a woman who looks like this be coming on to me?' They saw the trap – that's why they didn't go through with it[17]. Does that make them better than the other guys?"

1. Donc, je ne veux pas avoir l'air de me vanter
2. habillée simplement
3. ample
4. le spectacle était effectivement impressionnant
5. se faire piéger de façon déloyale
6. est attaché à son épouse
7. fit une grimace
8. Vous faites exprès d'être bouché ?
9. de forcer
10. Non, sans rire ?
11. Je vais vous dire
12. ai sans doute fait passer
13. ont refusé mes avances
14. Pas géniales, les statistiques
15. Ils ont pigé.
16. qu'il se tramait un truc
17. ils n'ont pas franchi le pas

"Yes."

"How so?"

"They didn't go through with it."

"But shouldn't the why matter? One guy might say no because he's scared he'll get caught[1]. Does that make him any more moral than the guy who isn't scared? Maybe the guy who isn't scared loves his wife more. Maybe he's a better husband and more committed. Maybe the other guy wants to screw around like crazy[2] but he's so meek[3] and timid that he can't go through with it."

"So?"

"So fear – not love, not wedding vows[4], not commitment[5] – is the only thing keeping him honest. So which guy is better? Is it the act or the heart?"

"Heavy questions[6], Cingle."

"What's your take[7], Mr. Prosecutor?"

"Exactly. I'm a prosecutor. It's all about[8] the actions."

"The actions define us[9]?"

"In legal terms[10], yes."

"So the guy who is too scared to go through with it – he's clean[11]?"

"Yep. He didn't go through with it. The why is beside the point[12]. No one says he has to maintain his vow out of love[13]. Fear might be as good a reason as any[14]."

"Wow," she said. "I disagree."

"Fair enough.[15] But is there a point to this[16]?"

"The point is this[17]: MVD wants dirt[18]. Any way they can get it. If the current reality isn't providing any[19] – read[20]: if the husband isn't already cheating – they'll shift the reality – read: get[21] someone like me to hit on[22] the husband. Do you get it now?"

"I think so. I not only have to be careful about what I might have done, but what I look like I'm doing or appear to be doing[23] or might get entrapped into doing[24]."

"Bingo."

1. a peur de se faire prendre
2. se taper tout ce qui bouge
3. docile
4. les vœux de mariage
5. l'engagement
6. Ce sont des questions complexes
7. Quelle est votre position
8. Tout repose sur
9. font de nous ce que nous sommes
10. Sur le plan juridique
11. innocent
12. n'entre pas en ligne de compte
13. respecter ses vœux par amour
14. peut être une raison aussi valable
15. Je comprends.
16. où voulez-vous en venir
17. À ceci
18. a besoin de calomnies
19. la situation réelle n'en recèle aucune
20. c'est-à-dire
21. ils envoient
22. draguer
23. à ce que j'ai l'air d'être en train de faire
24. ou à ce qu'on pourrait me pousser à faire par ruse

"And you have no idea who provided them with the information in that journal?"

"Not yet. But hey, you've now hired me to do counterespionage. Who knows what I'll come up with?" She stood. "Anything else I can help you with?"

"No, Cingle, I think that covers it[1]."

"Cool. By the way, I have my bill[2] here for the Jenrette-Marantz case. Who should I give it to?"

Muse said, "I'll take it."

Cingle handed it to her and smiled at me. "I liked watching you in court, Cope. You nailed those sons of bitches but good.[3]"

"Couldn't have done it without you," I said.

"Nah. I've seen a lot of prosecutors. You're the real deal.[4]"

"Thanks. I wonder, though. Based on your definition, did we, uh, engage in reality shifting[5]?"

"No. You had me dig up honest information. No entrapment. Yes, I used my looks to extract the truth. But there's nothing wrong with that."

"I agree," I said.

"Wow. We should leave on that note[6] then."

I laced my hands at the fingers and put them[7] behind my head. "MVD must miss you."

"I hear they got a new hottie.[8] Supposedly she's very good.[9]"

"I'm sure she's not you."

"Don't count on it. Anyway, I might try to steal her from them. I could use[10] a second hottie, and she appeals to a slightly different demographic[11]."

"How's that?"

"I'm a blonde. MVD's new girl is dark skinned[12]."

"African-American?"

"No."

And then I felt the floor underneath me give way as[13] Cingle Shaker added, "I think she's from India."

1. qu'on a fait le tour
2. facture
3. Vous les avez bien eus, ces salopards.
4. Vous, vous êtes vraiment à la hauteur.
5. modifié la réalité
6. rester là-dessus
7. entrelaçai mes doigts et mis mes mains
8. Il paraît qu'ils ont une nouvelle bombe.
9. Et qu'elle serait très douée.
10. J'aurais bien besoin
11. plaît à un autre type d'hommes
12. a la peau foncée
13. sentis le sol se dérober sous mes pieds lorsque

Chapter 31

I called Raya Singh's cell phone. Cingle Shaker was gone, but Muse had stayed behind.

Raya picked up on the third ring. "Hello?"

"Maybe you're right," I said to her.

"Mr. Copeland?"

That accent was so phony[1]. How did I buy into it[2] – or had part of me known all along?

"Call me Cope," I said.

"Okay, uh, Cope." The voice was warm. I heard that knowing tease.[3] "What am I maybe right about?"

"How do I know you're not the one? How do I know you wouldn't make me deliriously happy?"

Muse rolled her eyes. Then she mimed sticking her index finger down her throat[4] and vomiting violently.

I tried to make a date[5] for tonight, but Raya would have none of it[6]. I didn't push it. If I pushed, she might get suspicious[7]. We set up a time to meet[8] in the morning.

I hung up and looked at Muse. Muse shook her head at me.

"Don't start."

"Did she really use that phrase? 'Deliriously happy'?"

"I said, don't start."

She shook her head again.

I checked the clock. Eight-thirty p.m.

1. bidon
2. Comment avais-je pu me faire avoir
3. Je sentis cette fois le ton délibérément allumeur.
4. fit semblant d'enfoncer l'index dans sa gorge
5. d'obtenir un rendez-vous
6. ne se laissa pas faire
7. avoir des soupçons
8. On fixa une heure pour se voir

"I better get home," I said.

"Okay."

"How about you, Muse?"

"I got some stuff to do."

"It's late. Go home."

She ignored that. "Jenrette and Marantz," Muse said. "They are really going after you hard."

"I can handle it[1]."

"I know you can. But it's amazing what parents will do[2] to protect their children."

I was going to comment that I understood, that I had a daughter, that I would do anything to keep her safe from harm[3]. But it sounded too patronizing.

"Nothing amazes me[4], Muse. You work here every day. You see what people are capable of doing."

"That's my point.[5]"

"What is?"

"Jenrette and Marantz hear that you're looking to seek higher office[6]. They figure it's a weak spot[7]. So they go after you, do all they can to intimidate you. It was smart[8]. Lots of guys would have caved[9]. Your case was only half-assed[10] anyway. They figured you'd see the information and settle[11]."

"They thought wrong. So?"

"So do you think they're just going to give up[12]? Do you think they'd just go after you? Or do you think there is a reason Judge Pierce wants to see you in chambers tomorrow afternoon?"

When I got home there was an e-mail from Lucy.

Remember how we used to make each other listen to[13] certain songs? I don't know if you've heard this one, but here. I won't be forward enough to say[14] think of me when you listen to it.
But I hope you do.
Love,
Lucy

1. gérer la situation
2. jusqu'où les parents peuvent aller
3. empêcher qu'on lui fasse du mal
4. ne m'étonne
5. C'est exactement ce que je veux dire.
6. envisages d'accéder à des fonctions plus élevées
7. point faible
8. rusé
9. auraient cédé
10. Ton affaire ne tenait pas vraiment la route
11. que tu te calmerais
12. vont laisser tomber
13. qu'on se faisait écouter
14. n'ose pas te dire

1. téléchargeai
2. en pièce jointe
3. standard assez rare
4. gâché
5. voudrait bien vivre à nouveau
6. se lamente et supplie qu'elle le reprenne dans ses bras
7. transférai
8. je m'endormis enfin
9. amérindien
10. [les Loups ou Delawares, peuple amérindien]
11. territoire
12. les Hollandais
13. irréfutable
14. ce qui n'empêche pas les vieux de la vieille
15. ses intentions
16. je m'étais fait avoir
17. pourtant
18. de m'en vouloir à cause de ça
19. n'arrivait pas à la cheville de Lucy
20. Je m'y accrochai.
21. drôle de sourire apparut sur
22. Ça me l'avait toujours fait, au contact de Lucy.
23. Ça recommençait.
24. Allez comprendre quelque chose à l'amour.

I downloaded[1] the attached[2] song. It was a fairly rare classic[3] from Bruce Springsteen called "Back in Your Arms." I sat there at my computer and listened to it. Bruce sang about indifference and regrets, about all he's thrown away[4] and lost and longs for again[5] and then he achingly begs to be back in her arms[6].

I started to cry.

Sitting there, alone, listening to this song, thinking about Lucy, about that night, I actually cried for the first time since my wife died.

I loaded[7] the song on my iPod and brought it into the bedroom. I played it again. And then once more. And after a while, sleep finally found me[8].

The next morning Raya was waiting for me in front of Bistro Janice in Ho-Ho-Kus, a small town in northeast New Jersey. No one is sure if the name is Hohokus or Ho Ho Kus or HoHoKus. Some people say that the name comes from a Native American[9] word used by the Lenni Lenape[10], who controlled this parcel[11] until the Dutch[12] started settling in 1698. But there is no definitive[13] proof one way or the other, though that never stops the old-timers[14] from arguing about it.

Raya wore dark jeans and a white blouse open at the throat. A killer. A total killer. Beauty has such an effect, even though I now knew what she was about[15]. I was angry and had been conned[16] and yet[17] I couldn't help feeling an attraction and hating myself for it[18].

On the other hand, as beautiful and young as she was, I couldn't help thinking that she wasn't in Lucy's league[19]. I liked feeling that. I held on to it.[20] I thought about Lucy and a funny smile crept onto[21] my face. My breathing grew a little shallow. It always had around Lucy.[22] It was again.[23]

Try to figure love.[24]

"I'm so glad you called," Raya said.

"Me too."

Raya bussed my cheek[1]. A subtle whiff[2] of lavender came off her[3]. We moved toward a booth in the back of the bistro. A striking mural[4] of life-size diners[5], painted by the owners' daughter, took up one entire wall. All the painted eyes seemed to follow us. Our booth was the last one, under a giant clock. I had been eating at Bistro Janice for the past four years. I have never seen that clock set to the correct time[6]. The owners' little joke, I guess.

We sat down. Raya gave me her best melt-'em smile[7]. I thought about Lucy. It knocked away[8] the effect.

"So," I said, "you're a private eye."

Subtlety[9] wasn't going to work here. I didn't have the time or the patience for it. I kept going[10] before she could start with the denials[11].

"You work for Most Valuable Detection of Newark, New Jersey. You don't really work for that Indian restaurant. I should have picked up on that[12] when the woman at the desk didn't know who you were."

Her smile flickered[13] but it stayed full wattage[14]. She shrugged. "How did you figure me out[15]?"

"I'll tell you later. How much of what you said to me was a lie?"

"Not much, actually."

"Are you still going to stick with that story about[16] not knowing who Manolo Santiago really was?"

"That part was true. I didn't know he was Gil Perez until you told me."

That confused me.

"How did you two really meet?" I asked.

She sat back and crossed her arms. "I don't have to talk to you, you know. This is work product by the attorney who hired me[17]."

"If Jenrette hired you through either[18] Mort or Flair, you could make that argument[19]. But here's your problem. You're investigating me. There is no way

1. m'embrassa sur la joue
2. subtil parfum
3. émanait d'elle
4. fresque hallucinante
5. clients attablés, grandeur nature
6. réglée à la bonne heure
7. son sourire le plus ravageur
8. cassa
9. La subtilité
10. poursuivis
11. à nier
12. dû percuter
13. vacilla
14. mais garda toute son intensité
15. m'avez-vous démasquée
16. maintenir votre version en prétendant
17. le résultat d'un travail pour lequel un avocat m'a engagée
18. par l'intermédiaire soit de
19. ça pourrait être un argument valable

you can claim[1] that Gil Perez could be work product on Jenrette or Marantz."

She said nothing.

"And since you feel no qualms about going after me[2], I will go after you. My guess is, you were not supposed to be found out[3]. There is no reason why MVD needs to know. You help me, I help you, win-win, please add your own cliché[4]."

She smiled at that.

"I met him on the street," she said. "Just like I told you."

"But not by accident[5]."

"No, not by accident. My job was to get closer to him[6]."

"Why him?"

John, the owner of Bistro Janice – Janice being his wife and chef – appeared at our table. He shook my hand, asked me who the lovely lady was. I introduced him. He kissed her hand. I frowned at him. He went away.

"He claimed[7] to have information on you."

"I don't understand. Gil Perez comes to MVD – "

"He was Manolo Santiago to us."

"Right, okay, Manolo Santiago comes up to you and says he can help you find dirt on me."

"Dirt is a bit strong, Paul."

"Call me Prosecutor Copeland," I said. "That was your task, right? Find something incriminating on me[8]? Try to get me to back off[9]?"

She did not reply. She didn't have to.

"And you don't have attorney-client privilege to hide behind[10], do you? That's why you're answering my questions. Because Flair would never let his client do this. And even Mort, as big a pain in the ass as he is[11], isn't this unethical[12]. EJ Jenrette hired you guys on his own[13]."

1. Vous ne pouvez en aucun cas affirmer
2. n'avez aucun scrupule à vous en prendre à moi
3. vous faire démasquer
4. ou quel que soit le cliché que vous souhaitez employer
5. pas par hasard
6. de devenir proche de lui
7. prétendait
8. qui me compromette
9. de m'obliger à faire marche arrière
10. ne pouvez pas invoquer le secret professionnel
11. aussi con soit-il
12. n'est pas aussi malhonnête
13. de son propre chef

"I'm not at liberty to say. And frankly, I wouldn't be in a position to know. I work out in the field. I don't deal with the client."

I didn't care about the inner workings[1] of her office, but it felt like she was confirming what I said.

"So Manolo Santiago comes to you," I went on. "He says he has information on me. Then what?"

"He won't say exactly what it is. He gets coy.[2] He wants money, lots of it."

"And you bring this message to Jenrette."

She shrugged.

"And Jenrette is willing to pay it. So go on from there.[3]"

"We insist on proof.[4] Manolo starts talking about how he still needs to nail down details[5]. But here's the thing.[6] We've checked up on him now. We know his name isn't really Manolo Santiago. But we also know that he's on to something big[7]. Huge[8] even."

"Like what?"

The busboy[9] put down our waters. Raya took a sip.

"He told us that he knew what really happened the night those four kids died in the woods. He told us that he could prove you lied about it."

I said nothing.

"How did he find you?" I asked.

"What do you mean?"

But I thought about it.

"You went to Russia to dig up stuff[10] on my parents."

"Not me."

"No, I mean, an investigator from MVD. And you guys also knew about those old murders, that the sheriff even questioned me. So..."

I saw it now.[11]

"So you questioned everyone involved in that case. I know you guys sent someone down to visit Wayne Steubens. And that means you went to the Perez family too, right?"

"I don't know, but that makes sense."

1. organisation interne
2. Il devient hésitant.
3. O.K., continuez.
4. On exige des preuves.
5. doit encore mettre la main sur certains éléments
6. Mais voilà.
7. tient quelque chose d'important
8. D'énorme
9. serveur
10. pour déterrer des trucs
11. Je comprenais mieux maintenant.

"And that's how Gil heard about it. You visited the Perezes. His mother or father or someone called you. He saw a way to score some money[1]. He goes to you. He doesn't tell you who he really is. But he has enough information that you're curious[2]. So they send you to, what, seduce him?"

"Get close to him. Not seduce."

"You say 'tomato,' I say 'tomahto.[3]' So did he take the bait?"

"Men usually do."

I thought about what Cingle said. This was not a road I wanted to travel down again.[4]

"And what did he tell you?"

"Almost nothing. You see, he told us you were with a girl that night. Someone named Lucy. That's all I knew – what I told you. The day after we met, I called Manolo on his cell phone. Detective York answered. You know the rest."

"So Gil was trying to get you proof[5]? In order to score this big payday?[6]"

"Yes."

I thought about that. He had visited Ira Silverstein. Why? What could Ira have told him?

"Did Gil say anything about my sister?"

"No."

"Did he say anything about, well, about Gil Perez? Or any of the victims?"

"Nothing. He was coy, like I said. But it was clear he had something big."

"And then he ends up dead[7]."

She smiled. "Imagine what we thought."

The waiter came over. He took our order. I got the salad special. Raya ordered a cheeseburger, rare[8].

"I'm listening," I said.

"A man says he has dirt on you. He is willing to give us proof for a price[9]. And then, before he can tell us all he knows, he ends up dead." Raya ripped a

1. un moyen de se faire de l'argent
2. pour attiser votre curiosité
3. Cela revient au même. [emprunté à une chanson de George Gershwin, Let's Call The Whole Thing Off]
4. Je ne voulais pas revenir sur ce sujet.
5. vous apporter des preuves
6. Pour toucher le pactole ?
7. on le retrouve mort
8. saignant
9. à un certain prix

tiny piece[1] of bread and dipped it[2] in olive oil. "What would you have thought?"

I skipped the obvious answer.[3] "So when Gil was found dead, your assignment[4] changed."

"Yes."

"You were supposed to get close to me."

"Yes. I thought my helpless[5] Calcutta story would get to you[6]. You seemed like the type."

"What type?"

She shrugged. "Just a type, I don't know. But then you didn't call. So I called you."

"That efficiency suite in Ramsey. The one you said Gil lived in – "

"We rented that room. I was trying to get you to admit to something[7]."

"And I did tell you some stuff[8]."

"Yes. But we weren't sure you were being accurate or truthful[9]. Nobody really believed that Manolo Santiago was Gil Perez. We figured that he was probably a relative[10]."

"And you?"

"I believed you, actually[11]."

"I also told you about Lucy being my girlfriend."

"We already knew about that. In fact, we'd already found her."

"How?"

"We're a detective agency, that's how. But according to Santiago, she was lying about something that happened back then too. So we figured a direct interrogation wouldn't work."

"You sent her journals instead[12]."

"Yes."

"How did you get that information?"

"That I don't know."

"And then it was Lonnie Berger's job to spy on her."

She didn't bother replying[13].

"Anything else?" I asked.

1. rompit un tout petit bout
2. le trempa
3. C'était si évident que je ne répondis même pas.
4. mission
5. complètement nulle
6. vous toucherait
7. de vous faire avouer quelque chose
8. certaines choses
9. que vous soyez précis ou que vous disiez la vérité
10. parent
11. en fait
12. à la place
13. ne prit pas la peine de répondre

“No,” she said. “Actually, this is kind of a relief[1], you finding out. It felt okay[2] when I thought you might be a killer. Now it just feels sleazy[3].”

I rose. “I might want you to testify.”

“I won’t.”

“Yeah,” I said. “I hear that all the time.[4]”

1. je suis presque soulagée
2. Ça allait
3. c'est plutôt sordide
4. C'est ce qu'on me dit tout le temps.

Chapter 32

Loren Muse was doing research on the Perez family. Funny thing she noticed right away.[1] The Perezes owned[2] that bar, the one where Jorge Perez had met up with Cope. Muse found that interesting. They'd been a family of poor immigrants, and now they had a net worth in excess of[3] four million dollars. Of course, if you start with close to a million nearly twenty years ago, even if you just invested reasonably well, that number would make sense[4].

She was wondering what that meant, if anything, when the phone call came in. She reached for the receiver and jammed it up[5] between her shoulder and ear.

"Muse here."

"Yo, sweetums[6], it's Andrew."

Andrew Barrett was her connection[7] at John Jay College, the lab guy. He was supposed to go out this morning to the old campsite and start searching for[8] the body with his new radar machine.

"Sweetums?"

"I only work with machines," he said. "I'm not good with[9] people."

"I see. So is there a problem?"

"Uh, not really."

1. Elle remarqua d'emblée une chose étrange.
2. étaient propriétaires de
3. avaient un patrimoine net de plus de
4. ce chiffre tenait la route
5. le coinça
6. ma douce [Sweetums est aussi le nom de l'ogre poilu dans « The Muppet Show »]
7. contact
8. à rechercher
9. ne suis pas trop à l'aise avec

There was a funny hum in his[1] voice.

"Have you gotten out to the[2] site yet?" she asked.

"You kidding? Of course we did. Soon as you gave me the okay[3], I was, like, so there[4]. We drove out[5] last night, stayed at some Motel 6[6], started working at first light[7]."

"So?"

"So we're in the woods, right? And we start searching. The XRJ – that's the name of the machine, the XRJ – was acting a little funny[8], but we got it revved up pretty good[9]. Oh, I brought a couple of the students with me. That's okay, right?"

"I don't care."

"I didn't think you would. You don't know them. I mean, why would you? They're good kids, you know, excited about getting some fieldwork. You remember how it is. A real case. They were Googling the case all night, reading up on the camp and stuff."

"Andrew?"

"Right, sorry. Like I said, good with machines, not so good with people. Of course, I don't teach machines[10], do I? I mean the students are people, flesh and blood[11], but still[12]." He cleared his throat. "So anyway[13], you know how I said this new radar machine – the XRJ – is a miracle worker[14]?"

"Yes."

"Well, I was right."

Muse switched hands[15]. "Are you saying...?"

"I'm saying you should get out here pronto[16]. The ME[17] is on her way, but you'll want to see this for yourself[18]."

Detective York's phone rang. He picked it up. "York."

"Hey, it's Max down at the lab[19]."

Max Reynolds was their lab liaison[20] on this case. This was a new thing down at the lab. Lab liaison. Every time you had a murder case, you got a new one. York liked this kid. He was smart[21] and knew to just

1. Il avait une drôle d'intonation dans la
2. As-tu pu aller jeter un coup d'œil au
3. ton feu vert
4. c'était comme si j'y étais déjà
5. On s'est mis en route
6. [chaîne d'hôtels économique]
7. dès l'aube
8. un peu bizarrement
9. on a réussi à la faire tourner rond
10. je n'enseigne pas à des machines
11. de chair et de sang
12. mais bon
13. Enfin bref
14. un miracle de technologie
15. changea le combiné du téléphone de main
16. rappliquer vite fait
17. médecin légiste
18. par toi-même
19. du labo
20. agent de liaison au laboratoire
21. intelligent

give him the information[1]. Some of the new lab guys watched too many TV shows and thought an explanation monologue was mandatory[2].

"What's up, Max?"

"I got the results back on the carpet-fiber[3] test. You know, the one on your Manolo Santiago corpse."

"Okay."

Usually the liaison just sent a report.

"Something unusual[4]?"

"Yes."

"What?"

"The fibers are old[5]."

"I'm not sure I follow."

"This test is usually a given[6]. Car manufacturers[7] all use the same carpet sources[8]. So you might find GM[9] and maybe a five-year window of when it might have been[10]. Sometimes you get luckier. The color was only used in one kind of model and only for one year. That sorta thing. So the report, well, you know this, the report will read[11] 'Ford-manufactured car, gray interior, 1999 through[12] 2004.' Something like that."

"Right."

"This carpet fiber is old."

"Maybe it isn't from a car. Maybe someone wrapped him up[13] in an old carpet."

"That's what we thought at first. But we did a little more checking. It is from a car. But the car has to be more than thirty years old[14]."

"Wow."

"This particular carpeting[15] was used between 1968 and 1974."

"Anything else?"

"The manufacturer," Reynolds said, "was German."

"Mercedes-Benz?"

"Not that upscale[16]," he said. "My guess? The manufacturer was probably Volkswagen."

1. savait lui passer les informations, sans en rajouter
2. se croyaient obligés de tout expliquer en long, en large et en travers
3. concernant les fibres du tapis
4. qui sort de l'ordinaire
5. anciennes
6. en général, est très sûr
7. Les constructeurs automobiles
8. fournisseurs
9. [General Motors]
10. établir les faits sur une plage de 5 ans, peut-être
11. stipule
12. à
13. l'a enveloppé
14. doit avoir plus de 30 ans
15. Ce modèle de tapis
16. si haut de gamme

Lucy decided to give it one more try with[1] her father.

Ira was painting when she arrived. Nurse Rebecca was with him. The nurse gave Lucy a look[2] when she entered the room. Her father had his back to her.

"Ira?"

When he turned, she almost took a step back[3]. He looked horrible. The color was gone from his face.[4] His shaving was spotty[5] so that there were spiky tufts[6] on his cheeks and neck. His hair had always maintained an unruly air[7] that somehow worked for him[8]. Not today. Today his hair looked like too many years of living among the homeless[9].

"How are you feeling?" Lucy asked.

Nurse Rebecca gave her an I-warned-you glare[10].

"Not so good," he said.

"What are you working on?"

Lucy walked over to the canvas[11]. She pulled up[12] when she saw what it was.

Woods.

It took her back. It was their woods, of course. The old campsite. She knew exactly where this was. He had gotten every detail right.[13] Amazing. She knew that he no longer had any pictures, and really, you'd never take a picture from this angle. Ira had remembered. It had stayed locked in[14] his brain.

The painting was a night view[15]. The moon lit up the treetops[16].

Lucy looked at her father. Her father looked at her.

"We'd like to be alone," Lucy said to the nurse.

"I don't think that's a good idea."

Nurse Rebecca thought that talking would make him worse[17]. The truth was just the opposite. Something was locked up there, in Ira's head. They had to confront it now, finally, after all these years.

Ira said, "Rebecca?"

"Yes, Ira?"

"Get out."

1. faire une nouvelle tentative auprès de
2. jeta un regard à Lucy
3. eut presque un mouvement de recul
4. Son visage était livide.
5. Il était mal rasé
6. des touffes de poils par endroits
7. toujours eu un aspect indiscipliné
8. mais d'une certaine manière, cela lui allait bien
9. les sans-abri
10. lui jeta un regard noir lui signifiant qu'elle avait pourtant été prévenue
11. toile
12. s'arrêta
13. Il ne manquait aucun détail.
14. gravé dans
15. vue de nuit
16. éclairait la cime des arbres
17. aggraverait son état

Just like that.[1] The voice wasn't cold, but it hadn't been inviting[2] either. Rebecca took her time smoothing her skirt[3] and sighing and standing.

"If you need me," she said, "just call. Okay, Ira?"

Ira said nothing. Rebecca left. She did not close the door.

There was no music playing today. That surprised Lucy.

"You want me to put some music on? Maybe a little Hendrix?"

Ira shook his head. "Not now, no."

He closed his eyes. Lucy sat next to him and took his hands in hers.

"I love you," she said.

"I love you too. More than anything. Always. Forever."

Lucy waited. He just kept his eyes closed.

"You're thinking back[4] to that summer," she said.

His eyes stayed closed.

"When Manolo Santiago came to see you – "

He squeezed his eyes tighter[5].

"Ira?"

"How did you know?"

"Know what?"

"That he visited me."

"It was in the logbook."

"But..." He finally opened his eyes. "There's more to it[6], isn't there?"

"What do you mean?"

"Did he visit you too?"

"No."

He seemed puzzled by this. Lucy decided to try another avenue[7].

"Do you remember Paul Copeland?" she asked.

He closed his eyes again, as though that hurt. "Of course."

"I saw him," she said.

The eyes popped open[8]. "What?"

1. Tel quel.
2. engageante
3. pour lisser sa jupe
4. repenses
5. ferma les yeux un peu plus fort
6. C'est plus compliqué que ça
7. d'aborder les choses sous un autre angle
8. s'ouvrirent d'un coup

"He visited me."

His jaw dropped.[1]

"Something is happening, Ira. Something is bringing this all back[2] after all these years. I need to find out what."

"No, you don't."

"I do. Help me, okay?"

"Why... ?" His voice faltered.[3] "Why did Paul Copeland visit you?"

"Because he wants to know what really happened that night." She tilted her head. "What did you tell Manolo Santiago?"

"Nothing!" he shouted. "Absolutely nothing!"

"It's okay, Ira. But listen, I need to know – "

"No, you don't."

"Don't what? What did you say to him, Ira?"

"Paul Copeland."

"What?"

"Paul Copeland."

"I heard you, Ira. What about him?"

His eyes almost looked clear. "I want to see him."

"Okay."

"Now. I want to see him now."

He was growing more agitated by the second[4]. She made her voice soft[5].

"I'll call him, okay? I can bring him – "

"No!"

He turned and stared at[6] his painting. Tears came to his eyes. He reached his hand[7] toward the woods, as if he could disappear into them.

"Ira, what's wrong?"

"Alone," he said. "I want to see Paul Copeland alone."

"You don't want me to come too?"

He shook his head, still staring at the woods.

"I can't tell you these things, Luce. I want to. But I can't. Paul Copeland. Tell him to come here. Alone.

1. Il parut estomaqué.
2. fait remonter tout ça à la surface
3. dit-il d'une voix faible.
4. était de plus en plus agité
5. prit une voix douce
6. regarda fixement
7. tendit la main

I'll tell him what he needs to hear[1]. And then, maybe, the ghosts will go back to sleep."

When I got back to my office, I had yet another shock[2].

"Glenda Perez is here," Jocelyn Durels said.

"Who?"

"She's an attorney. But she says you'll know her better as[3] Gil Perez's sister."

The name had slipped my mind[4]. I beelined into my waiting area[5] and spotted her right away. Glenda Perez looked the same as she had in those pictures[6] on the fireplace mantel.

"Ms. Perez?"

She rose and gave me a perfunctory handshake[7]. "I assume you have time to see me."

"I do."

Glenda Perez did not wait for me to lead the way[8]. She walked head high[9] into my office. I followed her and closed the door. I would have hit my intercom and said, "No interruptions," but I got the feeling Jocelyn understood from our body language[10].

I waved for her to take a seat.[11] She didn't. I moved around my desk and sat down. Glenda Perez put her hands on her hips[12] and glared down at me[13].

"Tell me, Mr. Copeland, do you enjoy[14] threatening old people?"

"Not at first, no. But then, once you get the hang of it[15], okay, yeah, it's kinda fun[16]."

The hands dropped from her hips.

"You think this is funny?"

"Why don't you sit down, Ms. Perez?"

"Did you threaten my parents?"

"No. Wait, yes. Your father. I did say that if he didn't tell me the truth I would rip his world apart[17] and go after him and his children. If you call that a threat, then yes, I made it."

1. doit entendre
2. un nouveau choc m'attendait
3. cela vous parlera plus si je vous dis que c'est
4. m'était sorti de l'esprit
5. fonçai tout droit dans ma salle d'attente
6. ressemblait exactement à la personne sur les photos
7. poignée de main machinale
8. que je lui montre le chemin
9. l'air décidé
10. rien qu'en voyant nos attitudes
11. Je lui fis signe de s'asseoir.
12. sur ses hanches
13. me jeta un regard noir
14. cela vous amuse
15. une fois que vous avez pris le coup
16. c'est plutôt marrant
17. lui pourrirais la vie

I smiled at her. She had expected denials[1] and apologies and explanations. I hadn't given her any, hadn't fueled her fire[2]. She opened her mouth, closed it, sat.

"So," I said, "let's skip the posturing[3]. Your brother walked out of those woods[4] twenty years ago. I need to know what happened."

Glenda Perez wore a gray business suit[5]. Her stockings[6] were that sheer white[7]. She crossed her legs and tried to look relaxed[8]. She wasn't pulling it off.[9] I waited.

"That's not true. My brother was murdered with your sister."

"I thought we were going to skip the posturing."

She sat and tapped[10] her lip.

"Are you really going to go after my family?"

"This is my sister's murder we're talking about. You, Ms. Perez, should understand that."

"I will take that as a yes."

"A very big, very nasty yes."

She tapped her lip some more. I waited some more.

"How about if I lay a hypothetical on you?[11]"

I spread my hands. "I'm all for[12] hypotheticals."

"Suppose," Glenda Perez began, "this dead man, this Manolo Santiago, was indeed my brother. Again just in terms of[13] this hypothetical."

"Okay, I'm supposing[14]. Now what?"

"What do you think it would mean to my family?"

"That you lied to me."

"Not just to you, though."

I sat back. "Who else?"

"Everyone."

She started with the lip tap[15].

"As you know, all of our families engaged in a lawsuit[16]. We won millions. That would now be a case of fraud[17], wouldn't it? Hypothetically speaking."

I said nothing.

1. des dénégations
2. je n'avais pas alimenté sa colère
3. arrêtons cette comédie
4. est sorti de ces bois
5. tailleur gris
6. bas
7. d'un blanc diaphane
8. essaya d'avoir l'air détendu
9. Elle avait du mal.
10. tapota
11. Que diriez-vous si j'avançais une hypothèse ?
12. Je n'ai absolument rien contre
13. uniquement selon
14. admettons
15. tapotait ses lèvres à nouveau
16. se sont lancées dans des poursuites judiciaires
17. deviendrait alors une affaire de fraude

"We used that money to buy businesses, to invest, for my education, for my brother's health. Tomás would be dead or in a home[1] if we hadn't won that money. Do you understand?"

"I do."

"And, hypothetically speaking, if Gil was alive and we knew it, then the entire case was based on a lie[2]. We would be open to fines[3] and perhaps prosecution[4]. More to the point[5], law enforcement investigated a quadruple homicide. They based their case on the belief[6] that all four teenagers died. But if Gil survived, we could also be accused of obstructing an ongoing investigation[7]. Do you see?"

We looked at each other. Now she was doing the waiting.[8]

"There is another problem with your hypothetical," I said.

"What's that?"

"Four people go into the woods. One comes out alive. He keeps the fact that he's alive a secret. One would have to conclude[9], based on your hypothetical, that he killed the other three."

Tapping the lip. "I can see where your mind might go in that direction[10]."

"But?"

"He didn't."

"I just take your word for that?[11]"

"Does it matter?"

"Of course it does."

"If my brother killed them, then this is over, isn't it? He's dead. You can't bring him back and try him[12]."

"You have a point."

"Thank you."

"Did your brother kill my sister?"

"No, he didn't."

"Who did?"

1. centre
2. toute l'affaire reposait sur un mensonge
3. exposés à des amendes
4. à des poursuites
5. Qui plus est
6. sur la conviction
7. d'obstruction à une enquête en cours
8. Cette fois, ce fut elle qui marqua une pause.
9. On peut en conclure
10. vers quelle conclusion vous pourriez vous orienter
11. Et je dois vous croire sur parole ?
12. le juger

Glenda Perez stood. "For a long time, I didn't know. In our hypothetical, I didn't know that my brother was alive."

"Did your parents?"

"I'm not here to talk about them."

"I need to know – "

"Who killed your sister. I get that."

"So?"

"So I'm going to tell you one more thing. And that's it. I will tell you this under one condition[1]."

"What?"

"That this always stays hypothetical. That you will stop telling the authorities that Manolo Santiago is my brother. That you promise to leave my parents alone."

"I can't promise that."

"Then I can't tell you what I know about your sister."

Silence. There it was. The impasse. Glenda Perez rose to leave[2].

"You're a lawyer," I said. "If I go after you, you'll be disbarred[3] – "

"Enough threats[4], Mr. Copeland."

I stopped.

"I know something about what happened to your sister that night. If you want to know what it is, you'll make the deal[5]."

"You'll just accept my word?[6]"

"No. I drew up a legal document.[7]"

"You're kidding."

Glenda Perez reached into her jacket pocket and pulled out the papers. She unfolded them[8]. It was basically[9] a nondisclosure agreement[10]. It also made clear that I would say nothing and do nothing about Manolo Santiago's being Gil Perez and that her parents would be immune from any prosecution[11].

"You know this isn't enforceable[12]," I said.

1. à une seule condition
2. se leva, prête à partir
3. radiée du barreau
4. Ça suffit, les menaces
5. vous acceptez cet accord
6. Vous vous contenterez de ma parole ?
7. J'ai rédigé un document à signer
8. les déplia
9. en gros
10. accord de confidentialité
11. ne pourraient faire l'objet d'aucune poursuite
12. n'est pas légal

She shrugged. "It was the best I could come up with[1]."

"I won't tell," I said, "unless I absolutely have to. I have no interest in harming you[2] or your family. I'll also stop telling York or anyone else that I think Manolo Santiago is your brother. I will promise to do my best. But we both know that's all I can do."

Glenda Perez hesitated. Then she folded the papers, jammed them back[3] into her pocket and headed to my door. She put her hand on the knob[4] and turned toward me.

"Still hypothetically speaking?[5]" she said.

"Yes."

"If my brother walked out of those woods, he didn't walk out alone[6]."

My whole body went cold[7]. I couldn't move. I couldn't speak. I tried to say something but nothing came out. I met Glenda Perez's eye. She met mine. She nodded and I could see her eyes were wet[8]. She turned away and turned the knob.

"Don't play games with me[9], Glenda."

"I'm not, Paul. That's all I know. My brother survived that night. And so did your sister[10]."

1. le meilleur moyen que j'ai trouvé
2. à vous faire du mal, à vous
3. les fourra à nouveau
4. sur la poignée
5. On se base toujours sur des hypothèses ?
6. il n'est pas parti seul
7. se glaça
8. étaient humides
9. Ne me faites pas marcher
10. votre sœur aussi

Chapter 33

Day was surrendering to the shadows[1] when Loren Muse reached[2] the old campsite.

The sign said[3] Lake Charmaine Condominium Center. The landmass was huge[4], she knew, stretching across[5] the Delaware River, which separates New Jersey and Pennsylvania. The lake and condos[6] were on the Pennsylvania side. Most of the woods were in New Jersey.

Muse hated the woods. She loved sports but hated the supposedly great outdoors[7]. She hated bugs[8] and fishing and wading[9] and taking hikes and rare antique finds[10] and dirt[11] and general posts[12] and lures[13] and prize pigs[14] and 4-H fairs[15] and everything else she considered[16] "rural."

She stopped at the little building that housed the rent-a-cop[17], flashed her ID[18], expected the gate to rise. It didn't. The rent-a-cop, one of those bloated weightlifter types[19], brought her ID inside and got on the phone.

"Hey, I'm in a hurry here."

"Don't get your panties in a bunch.[20]"

"My panties in a...?[21]"

She fumed[22].

1. Le jour baissait
2. arriva
3. panneau indiquait
4. Le territoire était immense
5. il s'étendait au-delà de
6. les résidences
7. les soi-disant grands espaces
8. les insectes
9. patauger
10. faire des randonnées et les brocantes
11. la boue
12. les bureaux de poste
13. les appâts
14. les cochons de concours
15. les festivals 4-H [mouvement pour la jeunesse du monde rural]
16. tout ce qui, pour elle, rentrait dans la catégorie
17. où se tenait l'agent de sécurité
18. présenta son badge
19. du genre balèze ayant abusé de la gonflette
20. Vous mettez pas la petite culotte au court-bouillon.
21. La petite culotte au quoi... ?
22. était furieuse

There were flashing lights up ahead[1]. A bunch of parked police cars, she figured. Probably every cop within a fifty-mile radius[2] wanted in on this one[3].

The rent-a-cop hung up the phone. He sat in his booth[4]. He didn't come back to her car.

"Yo," Muse called out.

He didn't respond.[5]

"Yo, buddy, I'm talking to you here."

He turned slowly toward her. Damn, she thought. The guy was young and male. That was a problem. If you have a rent-a-cop who is on the elderly side[6], well, it is usually some well-intentioned guy who's retired and bored[7]. A woman rental?[8] Often a mother looking to pick up some extra money[9]. But a man in his prime[10]? Seven out of ten[11] it was that most dangerous of muscle-heads[12], the cop wannabe[13]. For some reason he didn't make it onto a real force[14]. Not to knock[15] her own profession, but if a guy sets his sights on being[16] a cop and doesn't make it[17], there is often a reason, and it wasn't something you wanted to get anywhere near[18].

And what better way to atone for your own worthless life[19] than to keep[20] a chief investigator – a *female* chief investigator – waiting?

"Excuse me?" she tried, her voice an octave lower[21].

"You can't enter yet," he said.

"Why not?"

"You have to wait."

"For?"

"Sheriff Lowell."

"Sheriff Lobo[22]?"

"Lowell. And he said no one gets in without his okay[23]."

The rent-a-cop actually hitched up his pants.[24]

"I'm the chief investigator for Essex County," Muse said.

He sneered. "This look like Essex County to you?"

"Those are my people[25] in there. I need to go in."

1. des gyrophares au loin
2. rayon de 80 km
3. voulaient être sur ce coup
4. guérite
5. Il ne réagit pas.
6. plutôt âgé
7. s'ennuie à la retraite
8. Une femme agent de sécurité ?
9. qui veut arrondir ses fins de mois
10. dans la fleur de l'âge
11. Dans la plupart des cas
12. crétins
13. aspirant flic
14. les forces de l'ordre
15. Sans vouloir taper sur
16. si un type décide de devenir
17. échoue
18. mieux vaut ne pas rester dans les parages
19. Quel meilleur moyen de compenser votre vie de raté
20. que de faire poireauter
21. en baissant d'un ton
22. [comme dans la série télévisée The Misadventures of Sheriff Lobo]
23. son feu vert
24. Et là, l'agent rajusta son pantalon.
25. mes collaborateurs

"Hey, don't get your panties in a bunch."

"Good one.[1]"

"What?"

"The panties-in-a-bunch line.[2] You've used it twice now. It is very, very funny. Can I use it sometime, you know, when I *really* want to put someone down[3]? I'll give you credit.[4]"

He picked up a newspaper, ignored her. She considered driving straight through and snapping the gate[5].

"Do you carry a gun?[6]" Muse asked him.

He put down the paper. "What?"

"A gun. Do you carry one? You know, to make up for other shortcomings[7]."

"Shut the hell up.[8]"

"I carry one, you know. Tell you what. You open the gate, I'll let you touch it."

He said nothing. The heck with touching it.[9] Maybe she'd just shoot him.

Rent-A-Cop glared at her. She scratched her cheek[10] with her free hand, pointedly raising her pinkie[11] in his direction. From the way he looked at her she could tell it was a gesture that hit painfully close to home[12].

"You being a wiseass[13] with me?"

"Hey," Muse said, putting her hands back on the wheel, "don't get your panties in a bunch."

This was stupid, Muse knew, but damn if it wasn't also fun. The adrenaline was kicking in now[14]. She was anxious[15] to know what Andrew Barrett had found. Judging by the amount of flashing lights, it had to be something big.

Like a body.

Two minutes passed. Muse was just about to take out her gun and force him to open the gate when a man in uniform sauntered toward[16] her vehicle. He wore a big-brimmed[17] hat and had a sheriffs badge. His name tag read LOWELL.

"Can I help you, miss?"

1. Elle est bien bonne.
2. L'expression « petite culotte au court-bouillon ».
3. si je veux vraiment rabaisser quelqu'un
4. Je dirai que c'est de vous.
5. songea à passer en défonçant la barrière
6. Vous portez une arme ?
7. pour compenser d'autres défauts
8. Fermez-la.
9. Et puis merde, non, il n'y toucherait pas.
10. se gratta la joue
11. en levant ostensiblement le petit doigt [sous-entend un petit pénis]
12. qu'elle avait mis le doigt là où ça faisait mal
13. faites la maline
14. était en train de monter
15. Il lui tardait
16. s'approcha tranquillement de
17. à large bord

"Miss? Did he tell you who I am?"

"Uh, no, sorry, he just said – "

"I'm Loren Muse, the chief investigator for Essex County." Muse pointed toward the guardhouse. "Small Balls[1] in there has my ID."

"Hey, what did you call me?"

Sheriff Lowell sighed and wiped his nose with a handkerchief. His nose was bulbous and rather huge.[2] So were all his features[3] – long and droopy[4], as if someone had drawn a caricature of him and then let it melt[5] in the sun. He waved the hand holding the handkerchief at Rent-A-Cop.

"Relax, Sandy."

"Sandy," Muse repeated. She looked toward the guardhouse. "Isn't that a girl's name?"

Sheriff Lowell looked down the huge nose at her. Probably disapprovingly. She couldn't blame him.

"Sandy, give me the lady's ID."

Panties, then miss, now lady. Muse was trying very hard not to get angry. Here she was, less than two hours from Newark and New York City, and she might as well have been[6] in friggin' Mayberry[7].

Sandy handed Lowell the ID. Lowell wiped his nose hard – his skin was so saggy[8] that Muse half-feared some would come off[9]. He examined the ID, sighed and said, "You should have told me who she was, Sandy."

"But you said no one gets in without your approval."

"And if you told me on the phone who she was, I would have given it."

"But – "

"Look, fellas[10]," Muse interrupted, "do me a favor. Discuss your backwoods ways[11] at the next lodge meeting[12], okay? I need to get in there."

"Park to the right," Lowell said, unruffled[13]. "We have to hike up[14] to the site. I'll take you."

Lowell nodded toward Sandy. Sandy hit a button and the gate rose. Muse pinkie-scratched her cheek

1. Couille molle
2. Il avait un énorme nez en patate.
3. tous ses traits
4. allongés et tombants
5. l'avait laissée fondre
6. avait l'impression de se retrouver
7. [village de série TV, perdu et hors du temps]
8. pendait tellement
9. qu'un bout ne tombe
10. Eh, les mecs
11. des coutumes de votre bled
12. prochaine réunion de chasseurs
13. imperturbable
14. monter à pied

again[1] as she drove through. Sandy fumed impotently[2], which Muse found apropos[3].

She parked. Lowell met her. He carried two flashlights and handed her one. Muse's patience was running on the thin side[4]. She snatched it[5] and said, "Okay, already[6], which way?"

"You got a real nice way[7] with people," he said.

"Thanks, Sheriff."

"To the right. Come on."

Muse lived in a crapola garden apartment[8] of too-standard-to-be-standard brick[9] so she wasn't one to talk[10], but to her amateur eye, this gated community[11] looked exactly the same as every other, except that the architect had aimed for[12] something quasi-rustic and missed entirely[13]. The aluminum exterior was faux log cabin[14], a look beyond[15] ridiculous in a sprawling, three-level condo development[16]. Lowell veered off the pavement[17] and onto a dirt path[18].

"Sandy tell you not to get your panties in a bunch?" Lowell asked.

"Yes."

"Don't take offense.[19] He says that to everyone. Even guys."

"He must be the life[20] of your hunting group[21]."

Muse counted seven cop cars and three other emergency vehicles of one kind or another. All had lights flashing. Why they needed their lights on she had no idea. The residents, a mix of old folks and young families, gathered, drawn by[22] the unnecessary flashing lights, and watched nothing.

"How far is the walk?" Muse asked.

"Mile and a half maybe[23]. You want a tour as we go along[24]?"

"A tour of what?"

"The old murder site. We'll be passing where they found one of the bodies twenty years ago."

"Were you on that case?"

"Peripherally[25]," he said.

1. refit le coup du petit doigt
2. fulminait, impuissant
3. trouva fort à propos
4. était à bout de patience
5. la lui prit des mains
6. maintenant
7. Vous savez vous y prendre
8. rez-de-jardin pourri
9. d'un immeuble en pseudo-briques
10. était mal placée pour critiquer
11. résidence privée
12. avait voulu faire
13. qu'il était totalement passé à côté
14. imitait un chalet en bois
15. plus que
16. site résidentiel étalé sur trois niveaux
17. quitta le trottoir
18. et s'engagea sur un chemin de terre
19. Ne soyez pas vexée.
20. boute-en-train
21. groupe de chasseurs
22. étaient attroupés, attirés par
23. environ 2,5 km
24. visiter, en passant
25. En périphérie

"Meaning?"

"Peripherally. Concerned with relatively minor or irrelevant aspects.[1] Dealing with the edges or outskirts.[2] Peripherally."

Muse looked at him.

Lowell might have smiled, but it was hard to tell through the sags[3]. "Not bad for a hunting lodge backwoods hick[4], eh?"

"I'm dazzled[5]," Muse said.

"You might want to be a tad nicer to me[6]."

"Why's that?"

"First, you sent men to search for a corpse in my county without informing me. Second, this is my crime scene. You're here as a guest and as a courtesy[7]."

"You're not going to play that jurisdiction game with me, are you?"

"Nah," he said. "But I like sounding tough[8]. How did I do?"

"Eh. So[9] can we continue to the tour[10]?"

"Sure."

The path grew thinner[11] until it practically disappeared. They were climbing on rocks and around trees. Muse had always been something of a tomboy[12]. She enjoyed the activity. And – Flair Hickory be damned[13] – her shoes could handle it[14].

"Hold up," Lowell said.

The sun continued to dip[15]. Lowell's profile was in silhouette[16]. He took off his hat and again sniffled[17] into his handkerchief. "This is where the Billingham kid was found."

Doug Billingham.

The woods seemed to settle[18] at the words, and then the wind whispered[19] an old song. Muse looked down. A kid. Billingham had been seventeen. He had been found with eight stab wounds, mostly defensive. He had fought his assailant[20]. She looked at Lowell. His head was lowered, his eyes closed.

1. J'étais en charge des aspects assez mineurs ou insignifiants.
2. Je m'occupais de tout ce qui tournait autour de l'enquête.
3. à distinguer dans tous les plis
4. plouc arriéré dans sa cabane de chasseur
5. éblouie
6. devriez être un peu plus sympa avec moi
7. en tant qu'invitée et parce que je le veux bien
8. jouer les durs
9. Bon
10. la visite
11. devint plus étroit
12. un peu garçon manqué
13. au diable Flair Hickory
14. était adaptées
15. à décliner
16. se découpait contre le ciel
17. renifla
18. se figer
19. murmura
20. s'était battu contre son agresseur

Muse remembered something else – something from the file[1]. Lowell. That name. "Peripherally, my ass[2]," she said. "You were the lead.[3]"

Lowell did not reply.

"I don't get it. Why didn't you tell me?"

He shrugged. "Why didn't you tell me you were reopening my case?"

"We weren't really. I mean, I didn't think we had anything yet."

"So your guys hitting paydirt[4]," he said. "That was just dumb luck[5]?"

Muse didn't like where this was going.

"How far[6] are we from where Margot Green was found?" Muse asked.

"A half mile due south[7]."

"Margot Green was found first, right?"

"Yep. See, where you came in? The condos? That used to be where the girls' side of the camp was. You know. Their cabins. The boys were to the south[8]. The Green girl was found near there."

"How long after[9] you found Green did you locate[10] the Billingham boy?"

"Thirty-six hours."

"Long time."

"A lot of land to cover[11]."

"Still. He was just left out[12] here?"

"No, there was a shallow grave. That's probably why it was missed the first time through[13]. You know how it is. Everybody hears about missing kids and they want to be the good citizen[14] so they come out and help us cover ground[15]. They walked right over him[16]. Never knew he was there."

Muse stared down at the ground. Totally unremarkable[17]. There was a cross like those makeshift memorials[18] for car-accident deaths[19]. But the cross was old and nearly fallen over[20]. There was no picture of Billingham. No keepsakes[21] or flowers or stuffed bears[22].

1. qui était dans le dossier
2. mon cul
3. C'est vous qui dirigiez [l'enquête].
4. la trouvaille de vos gars
5. un coup de bol
6. À quelle distance
7. vers le sud
8. au sud
9. Combien de temps après
10. avez-vous trouvé
11. à parcourir
12. abandonné
13. on ne l'a pas vue au premier passage
14. agir en bons citoyens
15. à faire la battue
16. juste au-dessus de lui
17. ordinaire
18. semblable à ces petits monuments de fortune
19. pour les victimes d'accidents de la route
20. renversée
21. d'objet souvenir
22. d'ours en peluche

Just the beat-up[1] cross. Alone out here in the woods. Muse almost shivered[2].

"The killer – you probably know this – his name was Wayne Steubens. A counselor, as it turned out[3]. There are a lot of theories on what happened that night, but the consensus seems to be[4] that Steubens worked on the vanished kids[5] – Perez and Copeland – first. He buried them. He started to dig a grave for Douglas Billingham when Margot Green was found. So he took off[6]. According to the hotshot[7] down at Quantico[8], burying the bodies was part of what gave him his thrill[9]. You know Steubens buried all his other victims, right? The ones in the other states?"

"Yeah, I know."

"You know two of them were still alive when he buried them?"

She knew that too. "Did you ever question Wayne Steubens?" Muse asked.

"We talked to everyone at that camp."

He said that slowly, carefully. A bell rang in Muse's head.[10] Lowell continued.

"And yes, the Steubens kid gave me the creeps[11] – at least, that's what I think now. But maybe that's hindsight[12], I don't know anymore. There was no evidence linking[13] Steubens to the murders. There was nothing linking anybody, really. Plus Steubens was rich. His family hired a lawyer. As you can imagine, the camp broke up right away[14]. All the kids went home. Steubens was sent overseas[15] for the next semester. A school in Switzerland, I think."

Muse still had her eyes on the cross.

"You ready to keep moving?"

She nodded. They started hiking again[16].

Lowell asked, "So how long have you been chief investigator?"

"A few months."

"And before that?"

"Homicide[17] for three years."

1. déglinguée
2. en trembla presque
3. en l'occurrence
4. de l'avis général, il semblerait que
5. se soit occupé des gosses disparus
6. a déguerpi
7. pointures
8. [FBI]
9. des sensations fortes
10. Muse commença à être sur ses gardes.
11. me donnait la chair de poule
12. que je ressens ça avec le recul
13. reliant
14. a fermé immédiatement
15. à l'étranger
16. reprirent leur marche
17. La criminelle

He wiped the huge nose again. "It never gets easier[1], does it?"

The question seemed rhetorical, so she just kept trekking[2].

"It's not the outrage[3]," he said. "It's not the dead even. They're gone. Nothing you can do about that. It's what's left behind[4] – the echo. These woods you're walking through. There are some old-timers[5] who think a sound echoes forever in here[6]. Makes sense[7] when you think about it. This Billingham kid. I'm sure he screamed. He screams, it echoes, just bounces back and forth[8], the sound getting smaller and smaller[9], but never entirely[10] disappearing. Like a part of him is still calling out, even now. Murder echoes like that."

Muse kept her head down, watched her feet on the knotty ground[11].

"Have you met any of the victims' families?"

She thought about that.[12] "One is my boss, actually[13]."

"Paul Copeland," Lowell said.

"You remember him?"

"Like I said, I questioned everybody at that camp."

The bell in Muse's head sounded again.

"Is he the one who got you to look into the case[14]?" Lowell asked.

She didn't reply.

"Murder is unjust," he went on. "It's like God had this plan and there is this natural order He set up[15] and someone took it upon themselves to mess with that[16]. If you solve the case, sure, it helps. But it's like you crumpled up a piece of aluminum foil[17]. Finding the killer helps you spread it out again[18], but for the family, it never really regains its form[19]."

"Aluminum foil?"

Lowell shrugged.

"You're quite the[20] philosopher, Sheriff."

1. On ne s'y fait jamais
2. à avancer
3. l'indignation
4. C'est ce qui reste
5. des anciens
6. résonne à jamais, ici
7. Ça se tient
8. et se répercute
9. diminuant de plus en plus
10. vraiment
11. sol accidenté
12. Elle réfléchit avant de répondre :
13. en fait
14. vous a demandé d'examiner cette affaire
15. qu'Il a instauré
16. avait pris l'initiative de tout bouleverser
17. comme si vous aviez froissé une feuille de papier aluminium
18. l'étaler à nouveau
19. rien ne sera plus jamais comme avant
20. un vrai

"Look into your boss's eyes sometimes. Whatever happened in these woods that night? It's still there. It still echoes, doesn't it?"

"I don't know," Muse said.

"And I don't know if you should be here."

"Why's that?"

"Because I did question your boss that night."

Muse stopped walking. "Are you saying there's some kind of conflict of interest?"

"I think that might be exactly what I'm saying."

"Paul Copeland was a suspect?"

"It is still an open case.[1] It is still[2], despite your interference, my case. So I won't answer that. But I will tell you this. He lied about what happened."

"He was a kid on guard duty. He didn't know how serious it was[3]."

"That's no excuse."

"He came clean later[4], right?"

Lowell did not respond.

"I read the file," Muse said. "He goofed off[5] and didn't do what he was supposed to on guard duty. You talk about devastation[6]. How about the guilt[7] he must feel over that[8]? He misses his sister[9], sure. But I think the guilt eats at him more[10]."

"Interesting."

"What?"

"You said the guilt eats at him," Lowell said. "What kind of guilt?"

She kept walking.

"And it's curious, don't you think?"

"What is?" Muse asked.

"That he left his post that night. I mean, think about it. Here he is, a responsible kid[11]. Everyone said so. And suddenly, on the night that these campers sneak out[12], on the night that Wayne Steubens plans on committing murder[13], Paul Copeland chooses to slack off[14]."

Muse said nothing.

1. Le dossier n'a pas été classé.
2. Cela reste
3. à quel point c'était grave
4. a fini par tout dire
5. a tiré au flanc
6. de ravages
7. Et la culpabilité
8. à cause de ça
9. Sa sœur lui manque
10. le ronge encore plus
11. gosse fiable
12. filent en douce
13. projette de commettre un meurtre
14. décide de prendre du bon temps

"That, my young colleague, has always struck me as a hell of a coincidence[1]."

Lowell smiled and turned away.

"Come on," he said. "It's getting dark and you're going to want to see what your friend Barrett found."

After Glenda Perez left, I didn't cry, but I came awfully close[2].

I sat in my office, alone, stunned[3], not sure what to do or think or feel. My body was shuddering[4]. I looked down at my hands. There was a noticeable quake.[5] I actually did that thing when you wonder if you're dreaming[6]. I did all the checks.[7] I wasn't. This was real.

Camille was alive.

My sister had walked out of those woods. Just like Gil Perez had.

I called Lucy on her cell phone.

"Hey," she said.

"You're not going to believe what Gil Perez's sister just told me."

"What?"

I filled her in.[8] When I got to the part about Camille walking out of those woods, Lucy gasped out loud[9].

"Do you believe her?" Lucy asked.

"About Camille, you mean?"

"Yes."

"Why would she say that if it wasn't true?"

Lucy said nothing.

"What? You think she's lying? What would be her motive?[10]"

"I don't know, Paul. But we're missing so much here[11]."

"I understand that. But think about it. Glenda Perez has no reason to lie to me about that."

Silence.

"What is it, Lucy?"

1. j'ai toujours trouvé que c'était une sacrée coïncidence
2. n'en étais pas loin
3. assommé
4. parcouru de frissons
5. Elles tremblaient vraiment.
6. si vous ne rêvez pas
7. Je fis toutes ces vérifications.
8. Je la mis au courant.
9. laissa échapper un cri de surprise
10. Pour quelle raison le ferait-elle ?
11. il nous manque tellement d'éléments

"It's just odd, that's all. If your sister is alive, where the hell has she been[1]?"

"I don't know."

"So what are you going to do now?"

I thought about that, tried to settle my mind[2]. It was a good question. What next?[3] Where do I go from here?[4]

Lucy said, "I talked to my father again."

"And?"

"He remembers something about that night."

"What?"

"He won't tell me[5]. He said he'd only tell you."

"Me?"

"Yep. Ira said he wanted to see you."

"Now?"

"If you want."

"I want. Should I pick you up?[6]"

She hesitated.

"What?"

"Ira said he wanted to see you alone. That he won't talk in front of me."

"Okay."

More hesitation.

"Paul?"

"What?"

"Pick me up anyway[7]. I'll wait in the car while you go in."

Homicide detectives York and Dillon sat in the "tech room[8]," eating pizza. The tech room was actually a meeting space[9] where they wheeled in[10] televisions and VCRs[11] and the like[12].

Max Reynolds entered. "How are you guys?"

Dillon said, "This pizza is awful."

"Sorry."

"We're in New York, for crying out loud[13]. The Big Apple.[14] The home[15] of pizza. And this tastes like something that disobeyed a pooper-scooper law[16]."

1. bon sang, où est-elle passée
2. reprendre mes esprits
3. Et maintenant ?
4. Que devais-je faire à présent ?
5. refuse de me le dire
6. Je passe te prendre ?
7. quand même
8. local technique
9. salle de réunion
10. installaient
11. des magnétoscopes
12. et autres
13. nom d'un chien
14. [surnom de New York]
15. La patrie
16. ça a un goût de merde [pooper-scooper (pelle ramasse-crottes) law : loi obligeant les propriétaires de chiens à ramasser les déjections]

Reynolds turned on the television. "I'm sorry the cuisine does not measure up to your standards[1]."

"Am I exaggerating?" Dillon turned to York. "I mean, seriously, does this taste like hobo vomit[2], or is it me?"

York said, "That's your third slice[3]."

"And probably my last. Just to show I mean it."

York turned to Max Reynolds. "What have you got for us?"

"I think I found our guy. Or at least, his car."

Dillon took another riplike bite[4]. "Less talk, more show."

"There is a convenience store[5] on the corner two blocks from where you found the body," Reynolds began. "The owner has been having problems with shoplifters grabbing items[6] he keeps outside. So he aims[7] his camera out that way[8]."

Dillon said, "Korean?"

"Excuse me?"

"The convenience store owner. He's Korean, right?"

"I'm not sure. What's that got to do with anything?"

"Dollars to doughnuts, he's[9] Korean. So he points his camera outside because some asswipe[10] is stealing an orange. Then he starts screaming about how he pays taxes when he probably has like ten illegals working in the place[11] and someone should do something. Like the cops should comb through his cheap-ass, blurry-crap tapes[12] to find Mr. Fruit Stealer."

He stopped. York looked at Max Reynolds. "Go on."

"Anyway, yes, exactly, the camera gives us a partial[13] of the street. So we started checking for cars around that age – more than thirty years old – and look what we found here."

Reynolds already had the tape keyed up[14]. An old Volkswagen bug[15] drove by. He hit the freeze[16] button.

"That's our car?" York asked.

1. ne soit pas à la hauteur de vos exigences
2. du vomi de clochard
3. part
4. avala un autre morceau avec voracité
5. supérette
6. des voleurs à l'étalage qui ont piqué des articles
7. oriente
8. par là
9. Ma main à couper qu'il est
10. connard
11. emploie, allez, dix clandestins
12. se taper le visionnage des cassettes floues de ce radin
13. une vue partielle
14. avait déjà mis la cassette en route
15. Coccinelle
16. pause

"A 1971 Volkswagen Beetle. One of our experts says he can tell by the[1] MacPherson strut front suspension[2] and front luggage compartment[3]. More important, this type of car matches[4] the carpet fibers we found on Mr. Santiago's clothing."

"Hot damn[5]," Dillon said.

"Can you make out the license plate[6]?" York asked.

"No. We only get a side view[7]. Not a partial, not even the state."

"But how many original[8] Volkswagen Bugs in yellow can there be on the road?" York said. "We start with the New York motor vehicle records[9], move to[10] New Jersey and Connecticut."

Dillon nodded and talked while chewing like a cow[11]. "We should get some kind of hit[12]."

York turned back to Reynolds. "Anything else?"

"Dillon was right, the quality isn't great. But if I blow this up[13]" – he hit a button and the picture zoomed – "we can get a partial look at the guy."

Dillon squinted. "He looks like Jerry Garcia[14] or something."

"Long gray hair, long gray beard," Reynolds agreed.

"That it?[15]"

"That's it."

York said to Dillon, "Let's start checking the motor vehicles record. This car can't be that hard to find."

1. que ça se voit au
2. [bras de suspension transversal]
3. au coffre à l'avant
4. correspond
5. Bon sang
6. distinguer la plaque d'immatriculation
7. vue latérale
8. d'origine
9. service des immatriculations
10. on continue avec
11. en mâchant comme une vache
12. trouver quelque chose
13. grossis ça
14. [chanteur et compositeur de folk, rock et blues, chevelu et barbu]
15. C'est tout ?

Chapter 34

1. dans les bois silencieux
2. qui n'était pas bête
3. aucun doute
4. super patron
5. procureur sacrément doué
6. lui avaient fait se souvenir de quelque chose
7. affaire criminelle
8. Elle mènerait là où elle devait mener
9. remonter jusqu'à son patron
10. Pas de favoritisme.
11. broussailles
12. était l'archétype du dégingandé
13. tout en membres et coudes,
14. avec des gestes complètement désarticulés
15. traînait
16. landau
17. l'interpella
18. mécontent
19. s'illumina

Sheriff Lowell's accusations echoed in the still of the woods[1].

Lowell, nobody's fool[2], thought Paul Copeland had lied about the murders.

Had he? Did it matter?

Muse thought about that. She liked Cope, no question[3]. He was a great boss[4] and a damned good prosecutor[5]. But now Lowell's words had brought her back[6]. They reminded her of what she already knew: This was a homicide case[7]. Like any other. It led where it led[8], even if that meant back to her boss[9].

No favorites.[10]

A few minutes later a noise came from the brush[11]. Muse spotted Andrew Barrett. Barrett made lanky an art form[12], all long limbs and elbows[13] and awkward, jerky movements[14]. He was dragging[15] what looked like a baby carriage[16] behind him. It had to be the XRJ. Muse called out to him[17]. Barrett looked up, clearly displeased[18] with the interruption. When he saw who it was, his face lit up[19].

"Hey, Muse!"

"Andrew."

"Wow, great to see you."

"Uh-huh," she said. "What are you doing?"

"What do you mean, what am I doing?" He put the machine down. There were three young people in John Jay sweatshirts trudging along beside him[1] – students, she assumed. "I'm looking for graves."

"I thought you found something."

"I did. It's up ahead another hundred yards[2]. But I thought there were two bodies missing, so I figured, hey, why rest on my laurels[3], you know what I'm saying?"

Muse swallowed. "You found a body?"

Barrett's face had a fervor usually reserved for tent revivals[4].

"Muse, this machine. Oh my, it's just amazing. We got lucky, of course. There hasn't been any rain in this area in, I don't know, how long, Sheriff?"

"Two, three weeks," Lowell said.

"See, that helps. A lot. Dry ground. You know anything about how ground-penetrating radar works? I stuck an 800 MHz[5] on this baby. That lets me go down only four feet[6] – but what a four feet! Most of the time, they look too deep[7]. But very few killers dig beyond[8] three, four feet. The other problem is, the current machines have trouble differentiating[9] between like-size items[10]. Like, say, a pipe[11] or deep roots[12] versus[13] what we want – bones[14]. The XRJ not only gets you clearer cross-sectional underground images of the soil[15], but with the new 3-D enhancer[16] – "

"Barrett?" Muse said.

He pushed up[17] his glasses. "What?"

"Do I look like I give the smallest rat's buttock[18] *how* your toy[19] works?"

He pushed the glasses up again. "Uh..."

"I just care *that* your toy works.[20] So please tell me what you found before I shoot someone?"

"Bones, Muse," he said with a smile. "We found bones."

"Human, right?"

1. traînant des pieds à ses côtés
2. là-haut, à 100 mètres
3. me reposer sur mes lauriers
4. [réunions religieuses se tenant sous des chapiteaux]
5. [antenne]
6. Ça me fait descendre à 1,20 m seulement
7. explorent trop profond
8. creusent à plus de
9. ont du mal à faire la différence
10. des éléments de même taille
11. tuyau
12. des racines profondes
13. par opposition à
14. des ossements
15. des images souterraines du sol en coupe transversale plus nettes
16. correcteur 3-D
17. rajusta
18. d'en avoir quelque chose à foutre
19. joujou
20. Ce qui m'intéresse, c'est qu'il marche.

1. Absolument.
2. crâne
3. font les fouilles
4. chêne
5. coroner
6. projecteurs
7. scène de tournage
8. éclairage puissant
9. en plein jour
10. de la police scientifique
11. entre des impuretés et une pépite d'or
12. si une fille est sexy
13. que tu as décroché le gros lot
14. tu t'en mords les doigts
15. en caoutchouc
16. de longs cheveux d'un noir profond
17. qu'ils doivent être élus
18. qu'ils font campagne et tout ça
19. douée avec les morts
20. riposterais bien avec un bon mot
21. vous autres, citadins snobs
22. nous, les péquenots
23. un euphémisme
24. d'une beauté renversante
25. son physique perturbait l'équipe
26. jetait sans cesse des regards furtifs vers

"Definitely.[1] In fact, the first thing we found was a skull[2]. That's when we stopped digging. The pros are excavating[3] now."

"How old are they?"

"What, the bones?"

"No, Barrett, that oak tree[4]. Yes, the bones."

"How the hell would I know? The coroner[5] might have an idea. She's at the site now."

Muse hurried past him. Lowell followed. Up ahead she could make out big spotlights[6], almost like a movie set[7]. She knew that lots of excavation teams used powerful voltage[8] even when they were digging in the direct sunlight[9]. As one crime-scene-unit[10] guy had told her, bright lights help differentiate the dross from the gold[11]: "Without the bright lights, it's like judging how hot a chick is[12] by being drunk in a dark bar. You may think you have something[13], but in the morning, you want to bite your arm off[14]."

Lowell pointed toward an attractive woman wearing rubber[15] gloves. Muse figured it was another student – she couldn't have been thirty years old. She had long, cave black hair[16] perfectly pulled back, like a flamenco dancer.

"That's Doc O'Neill," Lowell said.

"She's your coroner?"

"Yep. You know it's an elected position[17] out here?'"

"You mean they have campaigns and stuff[18]? Like,'Hi, I'm Doctor O'Neill. I'm really good with the dead[19]'?"

"I'd make a witty comeback[20]," Lowell said, "but you city slickers[21] are too clever for us yokels[22]."

As Muse got closer, she could see that "attractive" may have been understating it[23]. Tara O'Neill was a knockout[24]. Muse could see that her looks were something of a distraction to the crew[25] too. The coroner is not in charge of a crime scene. The police are. But everyone kept sneaking glances at[26] O'Neill. Muse stepped quickly toward her.

"I'm Loren Muse, chief investigator for Essex County."

The woman offered the glove hand. "Tara O'Neill, coroner."

"What can you tell me about the body?"

She looked wary[1] for a second, but Lowell nodded[2] that it was okay. "Are you the one who sent Mr. Barrett out here?" O'Neill asked.

"I am."

"Interesting fellow[3]."

"As I'm well aware.[4]"

"That machine works, though. I don't know how on earth he found these bones. But he's good. I think it helped that they ran over[5] the skull first."

O'Neill blinked and looked away.

"There a problem?" Muse asked.

She shook her head. "I grew up in this area. I used to play right here[6], right over this spot[7]. You'd think, I don't know, you'd think I would have felt a chill[8] or something. But nope, nothing."

Muse tapped her foot[9], waited.

"I was ten when those teens vanished. My friends and I used to hike out here[10], you know? We'd light fires. We'd make up[11] stories about how the two kids who were never found were still out here, watching us, that they were the undead[12] or whatever, and that they were going to hunt us down[13] and kill us. It was stupid. Just a way of getting your boyfriend to give you his jacket and put his arm around you."

Tara O'Neill smiled and shook her head.

"Dr. O'Neill?"

"Yes."

"Please tell me what you found here."

"We're still working on it, but from what I can see we have a fairly[14] complete skeleton. It was found three feet down. I'll need to get the bones[15] to the lab to make a positive ID."

"What can you tell me now?"

1. méfiante
2. lui fit signe
3. gars
4. J'en sais quelque chose.
5. qu'ils soient tombés sur
6. jouais ici même
7. pile à cet endroit
8. on pourrait croire que j'aurais eu un frisson
9. tapant du pied
10. venions en randonnée par ici
11. On inventait
12. des morts-vivants
13. nous traquer
14. quasiment
15. envoyer les ossements

"Come this way."

She walked[1] Muse over to the other side of the dig[2]. The bones were tagged[3] and laid out on a blue tarp[4].

"No clothing?" Muse said.

"None."

"Did they disintegrate or was the body buried naked[5]?"

"I can't say for sure. But since there are no coins or jewelry[6] or buttons or zippers[7] or even footwear[8] – that usually lasts a very long time[9] – my guess would be[10] naked."

Muse just stared at the brown skull. "Cause of death?"

"Too early to tell. But there are some things we know."

"Such as?"

"The bones are in pretty bad shape[11]. They weren't buried all that deep[12] and they've been here awhile[13]."

"How long?"

"It's hard to say. I took a seminar[14] last year on crime-scene soil sampling[15]. You can tell by the way the ground has been disturbed[16] how long ago the hole was dug[17]. But that's very preliminary."

"Anything? A guesstimate?[18]"

"The bones have been here awhile. My best estimate would be at least fifteen years. In short – and to answer the question on your mind – it is consistent[19], *very* consistent, with the time frame[20] of the murders that took place in these woods twenty years ago."

Muse swallowed and asked the real question that she'd wanted to ask from the beginning.

"Can you tell gender[21]? Can you tell me if the bones belong to someone male or female?"

A deep voice[22] interrupted, "Uh, Doc?"

It was one of the crime-scene guys, complete with the prerequisite windbreaker[23] announcing such[24]. He was husky, with a thick beard and a thicker

1. guida
2. du site de fouille
3. étiquetés
4. disposés sur une bâche bleue
5. dénudé
6. ni pièces de monnaie, ni bijoux
7. ni fermetures Éclair
8. et pas même des chaussures
9. qui, normalement, ne se désagrègent pas avant longtemps
10. je dirais qu'il était
11. très mauvais état
12. si profond que ça
13. depuis un bon moment
14. J'ai suivi un séminaire
15. les prélèvements de terre
16. à la façon dont la terre a été remuée
17. depuis combien de temps le trou a été creusé
18. Une idée, au pifomètre ?
19. c'est compatible
20. avec la période
21. déterminer le sexe
22. Une voix grave
23. vêtu du coupe-vent réglementaire
24. arborant « police scientifique »

midsection[1]. He had a small hand shovel and was breathing the labored breath[2] of the out-of-shape[3].

"What's up, Terry?" O'Neill asked.

"I think we got it all."

"You want to pack it in[4]?"

"For tonight, yeah, I think. We might want to come out tomorrow, check for more[5]. But we'd like to transport the body now, if that's okay with you."

"Give me two minutes," O'Neill said.

Terry nodded and left them alone. Tara O'Neill kept her eyes on the bones.

"Do you know anything about the human skeleton, Investigator Muse?"

"Some."

"Without a thorough examination[6], it can be pretty difficult to tell the difference between the male and female skeleton. One of the things we go by[7] is the size and density of the bones. Males have a tendency to be thicker and larger, of course. Sometimes the actual height[8] of the victim can help – males are usually taller. But those things often aren't definitive."

"Are you saying you don't know?"

O'Neill smiled. "I'm not saying that at all. Let me show you."

Tara O'Neill got down on her haunches[9]. So did Muse. O'Neill had a thin flashlight[10] in her hand, the kind that casts a narrow but potent beam[11].

"I said, pretty difficult. Not impossible. Take a look."

She pointed her light toward the skull.

"Do you know what you're looking at?"

"No," Muse said.

"First off, the bones appear to be on the lighter side[12]. Second, check out the spot below where[13] the eyebrows would have been[14]."

"Okay."

"That's technically known as the supraorbital ridge[15]. It's more pronounced in males. Females have very vertical foreheads[16]. Now, this skull has been

1. ventre encore plus imposant
2. avait le souffle court
3. de ceux qui ne font pas assez d'exercice
4. qu'on arrête
5. regarder s'il y en a d'autres
6. Sans examen minutieux
7. sur lesquelles nous nous basons
8. taille réelle
9. s'accroupit
10. torche fine
11. du genre de celles qui émettent un rayon étroit mais puissant
12. plutôt légers
13. ce point au-dessous duquel
14. devaient se trouver les sourcils
15. arcade sourcilière
16. un front

worn down[1], but you can see the ridge is not pronounced. But the real key – what I want to show you down here – is in the pelvis area[2], more specifically, the pelvic cavity[3]."

She shifted[4] the flashlight. "Do you see it there?"

"Yeah, I see it, I guess. So?"

"It's pretty wide[5]."

"Which means?"

Tara O'Neill snapped off[6] the flashlight.

"Which means," O'Neill said, getting back to her feet[7], "that your victim is Caucasian[8], about five-foot-seven[9] – the same height as Camille Copeland, by the way – and yes, female."

Dillon said, "You're not going to believe this."

York looked up. "What?"

"I got a computer hit[10] on that Volkswagen. There are only fourteen in the tristate area[11] that fit the bill[12]. But here's the kicker[13]. One is registered to[14] a guy named Ira Silverstein. That name ring a bell[15]?"

"Isn't he the guy who owned that camp?"

"That's it."

"Are you telling me that Copeland might have been right all along[16]?"

"I got the address where this Ira Silverstein is staying[17]," Dillon said. "Some kind of rehab place.[18]"

"So what are we waiting for?" York said. "Let's haul ass.[19]"

1. érodé
2. zone du bassin
3. cavité pelvienne
4. déplaça
5. plutôt large
6. éteignit
7. en se relevant
8. qu'il s'agit d'une victime blanche
9. d'environ 1,70 m
10. des résultats
11. États de New York, du New Jersey et du Connecticut
12. pourraient correspondre
13. la cerise sur le gâteau
14. est immatriculée au nom d'
15. ne te dit rien
16. depuis le début
17. habite
18. Un genre de centre de désintoxication.
19. Allez, on se magne.

Chapter 35

When Lucy got into the car, I pressed the button for the CD player. Bruce's "Back in Your Arms" came on. She smiled. "You burned it already[1]?"

1. l'as déjà gravé

"I did."

"You like it?"

"Very much. I added a few others. A bootleg[2] from one of Springsteen's solo shows[3]. 'Drive All Night.'"

2. enregistrement pirate

3. concerts en solo

"That song always makes me cry."

"All songs make you cry," I said.

"Not 'Super Freak' by Rick James[4]."

4. [chanteur de funk et de soul]

"I stand corrected.[5]"

5. Mea culpa.

"And 'Promiscuous.' That one doesn't make me cry."

"Even when Nelly sings, 'Is your game MVP[6] like Steve Nash?'"

6. Est-ce que tu joues comme les meilleurs [Most Valuable Player : meilleur joueur]

"God, you know me so well."

I smiled.

"You seem calm for a man who just learned that his dead sister might be alive."

"Partitioning."

"Is that a word?[7]"

7. C'est un mot, ça ?

"It's what I do. I put things in different boxes. It's how I get through the craziness.[8] I just put it somewhere else for a while."

8. C'est ma façon de résister à la folie.

"Partitioning," Lucy said.

"Exactly."

"We psychological types have another term for partitioning," Lucy said. "We call it 'Big-Time Denial[1].'"

"Call it what you will.[2] There's a flow here now[3], Luce. We're going to find Camille. She's going to be okay."

"We psychological types have another term for that too. We call it 'Wishful or even Delusional Thinking[4].'"

We drove some more.

"What could your father possibly remember now?" I asked.

"I don't know. But we know that Gil Perez visited him. My guess is, that visit stirred[5] something in Ira's head. I don't know what. It might be nothing. He's not well. It might be something he imagined or even made up[6]."

We parked in a spot near Ira's Volkswagen Beetle. Funny seeing that old car. It should have brought me back. He used to drive it around the camp all the time. He would stick his head out[7] and smile and make little deliveries[8]. He would let cabins decorate it[9] and pretend it was leading a parade[10]. But right now the old Volkswagen did nothing for me[11].

My partitioning was breaking down[12].

Because I had hope[13].

I had hope that I would find my sister. I had hope that I was truly connecting[14] with a woman for the first time since Jane died, that I could feel my heart beating next[15] to someone else's.

I tried to warn myself. I tried to remember that hope was the cruelest of all mistresses[16], that it could crush your soul[17] like a Styrofoam cup[18]. But right now I didn't want to go there. I wanted the hope. I wanted to hold on to it[19] and just let it make me feel light for a little while.

I looked at Lucy. She smiled and I felt it rip open my chest[20]. It had been so long since I felt like this[21], felt

1. le grand déni
2. Appelle ça comme tu veux.
3. Il se passe quelque chose, ici et maintenant
4. prendre ses désirs pour des réalités ou même délirer
5. a éveillé
6. ou même inventé
7. passait sa tête par la vitre
8. nous disait quelque mots
9. laissait les groupes des cabanes la décorer à tour de rôle
10. faire comme si elle ouvrait un défilé
11. ne parvint pas à m'émouvoir
12. s'effritait
13. j'avais de l'espoir
14. de pouvoir nouer un vrai lien
15. que mon cœur puisse battre aux côtés
16. l'espérance était la plus cruelle des maîtresses
17. vous broyer l'âme
18. gobelet jetable
19. m'y accrocher
20. j'en fus tout chaviré
21. que je n'avais ressenti ça

that heady rush[1]. Then I surprised myself. I reached out with both my hands[2] and took her face in my hands. Her smile disappeared. Her eyes searched for mine. I tilted her head up[3] and kissed her so softly that it almost hurt. I felt a jolt.[4] I heard her gasp[5]. She kissed me back[6].

I felt happily shattered by her.[7]

Lucy lowered her head onto[8] my chest. I heard her sob softly. I let her. I stroked her hair and fought back the swirl[9]. I don't know how long we sat like that. Could have been five minutes, could have been fifteen. I just don't know.

"You better go in," she said.

"You're going to stay here?"

"Ira made it clear[10]. You, alone. I'll probably start up[11] his car, make sure the battery is still charged."

I didn't kiss her again. I got out and floated up the path[12]. The setting for[13] the house was peaceful and green. The mansion was Georgian brick, I guessed, almost perfectly rectangular with white columns in the front. It reminded me of an upscale fraternity house[14].

There was a woman at the desk. I gave her my name. She asked me to sign in. I did. She placed a call and spoke in a whisper[15]. I waited, listening to the Muzak version[16] of something by Neil Sedaka[17], which was a little bit like listening to a Muzak version of Muzak[18].

A redheaded[19] woman dressed in civilian clothes[20] came down to see me. She wore a skirt and had glasses dangling[21] on her chest. She looked like a nurse trying not to look like a nurse.

"I'm Rebecca," she said.

"Paul Copeland."

"I'll bring you to Mr. Silverstein."

"Thank you."

I expected her to lead me down the corridor, but we walked through the back[22] and straight outside[23].

1. élan grisant
2. tendis les deux mains
3. attirai à moi son visage
4. Je sursautai.
5. haleter
6. m'embrassa à son tour
7. J'étais bouleversé et comblé.
8. posa sa tête contre
9. tout en tentant de contrôler mes émotions
10. me l'a bien fait comprendre
11. ferai sans doute démarrer
12. remontai l'allée d'un pas léger
13. cadre autour de
14. résidence étudiante cossue
15. parla en chuchotant
16. l'adaptation en musique de fond
17. [crooner et pianiste américain]
18. c'était un peu comme écouter de la musique de fond édulcorée
19. rousse
20. habillée en civil
21. des lunettes se balançaient
22. on passa par l'arrière,
23. directement à l'extérieur

The gardens were well tended[1]. It was a little early for landscape lights[2], but they were on. A thick row of hedges[3] surrounded the premises[4] like guard dogs.

I spotted Ira Silverstein right away.

He had changed and yet he hadn't changed at all. You know people like that. They get older, they gray, they widen[5], they slump[6], and yet they are exactly the same. That was how it was with Ira.

"Ira?"

No one ever used last names[7] at camp. The adults were Aunt and Uncle, but I just couldn't see calling him Uncle Ira anymore[8].

He wore a poncho I'd last seen[9] in a Woodstock documentary. He had sandals on his feet. Ira stood slowly and put his arms out toward me[10]. Camp had been that way too.[11] Everyone hugged. Everyone loved each other. It was all very "Kumbaya[12]." I stepped into his embrace[13]. He held me tight, with all his strength. I could feel his beard against my cheek.

He let go of me and said to Rebecca, "Leave us alone."

Rebecca turned away. He led me to a park bench of cement and green wood[14]. We sat.

"You look the same[15], Cope," he said.

He'd remembered my nickname[16]. "So do you."

"You'd think the hard years would show on our faces more[17], wouldn't you?"

"I guess so, Ira."

"So what do you do now?"

"I'm the county prosecutor."

"Really?"

"Yes."

He frowned. "That's kind of establishment.[18]"

Still Ira.[19]

"I'm not prosecuting antiwar protesters[20]," I assured him. "I go after murderers and rapists. People like that."

1. bien entretenus
2. l'éclairage de jardin
3. épaisse rangée de haies
4. les lieux
5. grossissent
6. s'affaissent
7. les noms de famille
8. ne me voyais pas l'appeler encore Oncle Ira
9. vu pour la dernière fois
10. tendit les bras vers moi
11. Comme à la colonie.
12. [chanson traditionnelle afro-américaine répandue dans les camps de vacances]
13. m'avançai et il me prit dans ses bras
14. banc de jardin en ciment et bois vert
15. Tu n'as pas changé
16. surnom
17. que ces années difficiles nous auraient plus marqués
18. C'est un peu l'establishment, ça.
19. Il était toujours le même.
20. les manifestants pacifistes

He squinted. "Is that why you're here?"

"What?"

"Are you trying to find murderers and rapists?"

I didn't know what to make of that[1] so I went with the flow[2]. "In a way, I guess. I'm trying to learn what happened that night in the woods."

Ira's eyes closed.

"Lucy said you wanted to see me," I said.

"Yes."

"Why?"

"I want to know why you've come back."

"I never went anywhere."

"You broke Lucy's heart, you know."

"I wrote her. I tried to call. She wouldn't call me back."

"Still.[3] She was in pain."

"I never meant for that to happen.[4]"

"So why are you back now?"

"I want to find out what happened to my sister."

"She was murdered. Like the others."

"No, she wasn't."

He said nothing. I decided to press a little.

"You know that, Ira. Gil Perez came here, didn't he?"

Ira smacked his lips[5]. "Dry."

"What?"

"I'm dry.[6] I used to have this friend from Cairns. That's in Australia. Coolest dude[7] I ever knew. He used to say, 'A man is not a camel[8], mate[9].' That was his way of asking for a drink[10]."

Ira grinned.

"I don't think you can get a drink out here, Ira."

"Oh, I know. I was never much of a booze man[11] anyway. What they now call 'recreational drugs[12]' was more my bag[13]. But I meant water. They got some Poland Spring[14] in that cooler[15]. Did you know that Poland Spring[16] comes to you straight from Maine[17]?"

1. comment le prendre
2. continuai sur ma lancée
3. Peu importe.
4. Ce n'était pas ce que je voulais.
5. se passa la langue sur les lèvres
6. J'ai la bouche sèche.
7. Le mec le plus cool
8. chameau
9. mon pote
10. de demander un verre
11. L'alcool n'a jamais vraiment été mon truc
12. les drogues douces
13. c'était plus ma tasse de thé
14. [marque d'eau minérale]
15. glacière
16. source naturelle
17. [Poland est une ville de l'État du Maine]

He laughed and I didn't correct him[1] on that old radio commercial[2]. He stood and stumbled toward the right. I followed. There was a trunk-shaped[3] cooler with a New York Rangers logo on it. He opened the lid[4], grabbed a bottle, handed it to me, grabbed another. He twisted off the cap[5] and chugged[6]. The water spilled down[7] his face, turning the white of his beard into something darker gray.

"Ahhhh," he said when he finished.

I tried to get him back on track[8].

"You told Lucy that you wanted to see me."

"Yes."

"Why?"

"Because you're here."

I waited for more.

"I'm here," I said slowly, "because you asked to see me."

"Not *here* here. Here, as in back in our lives[9]."

"I told you. I'm trying to find out – "

"Why now?"

That question again.

"Because," I said, "Gil Perez didn't die that night. He came back. He visited you, didn't he?"

Ira's eyes took on that thousand-yard stare.[10] He started to walk. I caught up with him[11].

"Was he here, Ira?"

"He didn't use that name," he said.

He kept walking. I noticed that he limped[12]. His face pinched up in pain[13].

"Are you okay?" I asked him.

"I need to walk."

"Where?"

"There are paths[14]. In the woods. Come."

"Ira, I'm not here – "

"He said his name was Manolo something. But I knew who he was. Little Gilly Perez. Do you remember him? From those days[15], I mean?"

"Yes."

1. [allusion à une polémique concernant la provenance réelle de cette eau minérale et l'absence de source naturelle à l'endroit cité]
2. ancienne publicité à la radio
3. en forme de malle
4. couvercle
5. dévissa le bouchon
6. but d'un trait
7. coula le long de
8. lui faire reprendre le cours de la conversation
9. de retour dans nos vies
10. Le regard d'Ira se perdit alors dans le lointain.
11. le rattrapai
12. qu'il boitait
13. grimaçait de douleur
14. des sentiers
15. À cette époque

Ira shook his head. "Nice boy. But so easily manipulated[1]."

"What did he want?"

"He didn't tell me who he was. Not at first. He didn't really look the same but there was something in his mannerisms[2], you know? You can hide stuff. You can gain weight[3]. But Gil still had that soft lisp[4]. He still moved the same[5]. Like he was wary all the time.[6] You know what I mean?"

"I do."

I had thought the yard was fenced in[7], but it wasn't. Ira slipped past a break in the hedges[8]. I followed. There was a wooded hill[9] in front of us. Ira started trudging up the[10] path.

"Are you allowed to leave?"

"Of course. I'm here on a voluntary basis[11]. I can come and go as I please."

He kept walking.

"What did Gil say to you?" I asked.

"He wanted to know what happened that night."

"He didn't know?"

"He knew some. He wanted to know more."

"I don't understand."

"You don't have to."

"Yes, Ira, I do."

"It's over. Wayne is in prison."

"Wayne didn't kill Gil Perez."

"I thought he did."

I didn't quite get that one. He was moving faster now, limping along in obvious pain[12]. I wanted to call him to stop, but his mouth was also moving.

"Did Gil mention my sister?"

He stopped for a second. His smile was sad. "Camille."

"Yes."

"Poor thing.[13]"

"Did he mention her?"

1. manipulable

2. son attitude

3. prendre du poids

4. léger zézaiement

5. se déplaçait de la même façon

6. Comme s'il était constamment sur ses gardes.

7. que le jardin était clôturé

8. se glissa dans une trouée de la haie

9. colline boisée

10. à monter péniblement le long du

11. de mon plein gré

12. il boitait et, manifestement, avait mal

13. Pauvre petite.

"I loved your dad, you know. Such a sweet[1] man, so hurt by life[2]."

"Did Gil mention what happened to my sister?"

"Poor Camille."

"Yes. Camille. Did he say anything about her?"

Ira started to climb again[3]. "So much blood that night."

"Please, Ira, I need you to focus[4]. Did Gil say anything at all about Camille?"

"No."

"Then what did he want?"

"Same as you."

"What's that?"

He turned. "Answers."

"To what questions?"

"The same as yours. What happened that night. He didn't understand, Cope. It's over. They're dead. The killer is in jail. You should let the dead rest[5]."

"Gil wasn't dead."

"Until that day, the day he visited me, he was. Do you understand?"

"No."

"It's over. The dead are gone. The living are safe.[6]"

I reached out and grabbed his arm. "Ira, what did Gil Perez say to you?"

"You don't understand."

We stopped. Ira looked down the hill. I followed his gaze[7]. I could only make out[8] the roof of the house now. We were in the thick of the woods[9]. Both of us were breathing harder[10] than we should. Ira's face was pale.

"It has to stay buried."

"What does?"

"That's what I told Gil. It was over. Move on.[11] It was so long ago. He was dead. Now he wasn't. But he should have been."

"Ira, listen to me. What did Gil say to you?"

"You won't leave it alone[12], will you?"

1. adorable
2. si meurtri par la vie
3. recommença à grimper
4. que tu te concentres
5. laisser les morts reposer en paix
6. Les vivants sont en sécurité.
7. suivis son regard
8. ne distinguais plus que
9. au cœur des bois
10. plus fort
11. Passe à autre chose.
12. ne laisseras jamais tomber

"No," I said, "I won't leave it alone."

Ira nodded. He looked very sad. Then he reached underneath[1] his poncho and pulled out[2] a gun, aimed it[3] in my direction, and without saying another word, he fired at me[4].

1. passa la main sous
2. en sortit
3. qu'il pointa
4. il me tira dessus

Chapter 36

1. un mouchoir si grand qu'on aurait dit un accessoire de clown
2. poste de police
3. avait imaginé
4. elle ne s'attendait pas à grand-chose
5. épuré et impeccable
6. des écrans d'ordinateur
7. des box
8. Beaucoup de tons
9. Remarquable, vraiment.
10. trop fort, d'autres pas assez
11. sur le feu
12. bons citoyens
13. a offert une machine à café à capsules
14. Vous essayez de m'amadouer
15. en jouant de votre charme rustique et candide

"What we have here is a problem."

Sheriff Lowell wiped his nose with a handkerchief that looked large enough to be a clown's prop[1]. His station[2] was more modern than what Muse had expected[3], but then again her expectations weren't high[4]. The building was new, the design sleek and clean[5] with computer monitors[6] and cubicles[7]. Lots of[8] whites and grays.

"What you have here," Muse replied, "is a dead body."

"That's not what I mean." He gestured toward the cup in her hand. "How's the coffee?"

"Outstanding, actually.[9]"

"Used to be crap. Some guys made it too strong, some too weak[10]. It got left on the burner[11] forever. And then last year, one of the fine citizens[12] of this municipality donated one of those coffee pod machines[13] to the station. You ever use one of those things, the pods?"

"Sheriff?"

"Yes."

"Is this your attempt at wooing me[14] with your aw-shucks, homespun charm[15]?"

He grinned. "A little."

"Consider me wooed. What's our problem?"

"We just found a body that's been in the woods, by early estimates[1], a pretty long time. We know three things: Caucasian, female, height of five-seven. That's all we know for now. I have already combed through the records[2]. There were no missing or unaccounted girls within a fifty-mile radius[3] who match that description."

"We both know who it is," Muse said.

"Not yet we don't.[4]"

"You think, what, another five-foot seven-inch girl was murdered in that camp around the same time and buried near the other two bodies?"

"I didn't say that."

"Then what did you say?"

"That we don't have a definite ID. Doc O'Neill is working on it. We've ordered Camille Copeland's dental records[5]. We should know for sure in a day or two. No rush.[6] We have other cases."

"No rush?"

"That's what I said."

"Then I'm not following."

"See, this is where I have to wonder, Investigator Muse – what are you first and foremost[7]? Are you a law enforcement officer or a political crony[8]?"

"What the hell does that mean?"

"You're the county chief investigator," Lowell said. "Now, I'd like to believe a person, especially a lady your age, reached that level based on[9] her talent and skill[10]. But I also live in the real world. I understand graft[11] and favoritism and ass kissing[12]. So I'm asking – "

"I earned it.[13]"

"I'm sure you did."

Muse shook her head. "I can't believe I have to justify myself[14] to you."

"But, alas, my dear, you do. Because right now, if this was your case and I came waltzing in[15] and you

1. selon les premières estimations
2. épluché les archives
3. aucune jeune femme disparue dans un rayon d'environ 80 km
4. Non, pas encore.
5. le dossier dentaire
6. Rien ne presse.
7. avant tout
8. à la botte des politiques
9. a atteint cette position grâce à
10. ses compétences
11. suis conscient qu'il y a des magouilles
12. des lèche-cul
13. l'ai méritée.
14. Je n'en reviens pas de devoir me justifier
15. que je débarquais gaiement

knew that I was going to run right home and tell[1] my boss – someone who was, at the very least, involved[2] – what would you do?"

"You think I'd sweep his involvement under the rug[3]?"

Lowell shrugged. "Again: If I was, say, the deputy[4] here and I was given my job by the sheriff who was involved in your murder, what would you think?"

Muse sat back. "Fair enough," she said. "So what can I do to comfort you[5]?"

"You can let me take my time identifying the body."

"You don't want Copeland to know what we found?"

"He's waited twenty years. What's another day or two?[6]"

Muse understood where he was going with this.

"I want to do right by the investigation[7]," she said, "but I don't much relish lying[8] to a man I trust[9] and like."

"Life's tough, Investigator Muse."

She frowned.

"Something else I want too," Lowell went on. "I need you to tell me why that Barrett guy was out there with that little toy of his looking for long-dead bodies[10]."

"I told you. They wanted to test this machine in the field."

"You work in Newark, New Jersey. Are you telling me there are no possible burial sites[11] in that area you could have sent them to?"

He was right, of course. Time to come clean.[12]

"A man was found murdered in New York City," Muse said. "My boss thinks it was Gil Perez."

Lowell dropped the poker face[13]. "Come again?[14]"

She was about to explain when Tara O'Neill rushed in[15]. Lowell looked annoyed by the interruption but he kept his voice neutral. "What's up, Tara?"

"I found something on the body," she said. "Something important, I think."

1. tout raconter à
2. dans le meilleur des cas, y était impliqué
3. que je vais dissimuler son implication
4. l'adjoint
5. pour vous rassurer
6. Ça change quoi, un jour ou deux de plus ?
7. agir dans l'intérêt de l'enquête
8. ne suis pas enchantée de mentir
9. en qui j'ai confiance
10. les cadavres de gens morts depuis longtemps
11. aucun site où des corps pourraient être enterrés
12. Il était temps de tout lui dire.
13. changea d'expression
14. Pardon ?
15. entra en trombe

After Cope left the car, Lucy sat alone for a good five minutes[1] with the trace of a smile on her lips. She was still swimming from his kiss.[2] She had never experienced[3] anything like that, the way his big hands held her face, the way he looked at her... it was as though her heart had not only started beating again but had taken flight[4].

It was wonderful. It was scary.

She checked through[5] his CD collection, found one by Ben Folds[6], put on the song "Brick." She had never been sure what the song was about – a drug overdose, an abortion[7], a mental collapse[8] – but in the end, the woman is a brick and she's drowning him[9].

Sad music was better than drinking, she guessed. But not much.

As she turned off the engine[10], she saw a green car, a Ford with New York license plates[11], pull up[12] right to the front of the building. The car parked in the spot that read NO PARKING. Two men got out – one tall, one built like a square[13] – and strolled inside[14]. Lucy didn't know what to make of it. It was probably nothing.

The keys to Ira's Beetle were in her bag. She rummaged through the purse[15] and found them. She jammed a piece of gum[16] in her mouth. If Cope kissed her again, she'd be damned if bad breath was going to be a factor[17].

She wondered what Ira was going to say to Cope. She wondered what Ira even remembered. They had never talked about that night, father and daughter. Not once.[18] They should have. It might have changed everything. Then again it might have changed nothing. The dead would still be dead, the living still living. Not a particularly deep thought[19], but there you go[20].

She got out of the car and started toward the old Volkswagen. She held the key in her hand and pointed it toward the car[21]. Odd what you get used to.[22] No

1. cinq bonnes minutes
2. Le baiser lui tournait encore la tête.
3. vécu
4. s'était envolé
5. regarda dans
6. [chanteur américain, figure du piano rock]
7. avortement
8. dépression nerveuse
9. est un vrai boulet et il coule avec elle
10. coupait le moteur
11. immatriculée à New York
12. s'arrêter
13. avait une large carrure
14. entrèrent tranquillement
15. fourragea dans son sac
16. fourra un chewing-gum
17. il était hors de question qu'elle ait mauvaise haleine
18. Pas une fois.
19. Ce n'était pas une pensée très profonde
20. mais bon
21. la pointa en direction de la voiture
22. Curieux, les habitudes qu'on prend.

cars today open with a key. They all have the remote[1]. The Beetle didn't, of course. She put the key into the lock on the driver side[2] and turned it. It was rusted[3] and she had to twist hard[4] but the lock popped up[5].

She thought about how she had lived her life, about the mistakes she'd made. She'd talked to Cope about that feeling of being pushed that night, of tumbling down a hill and not knowing how to stop. It was true. He had tried to find her over the years, but she had stayed hidden. Maybe she should have contacted him earlier. Maybe she should have tried to work through[6] what happened that night right away. Instead you bury it. You refuse to face it. You're scared of confrontation so you find other ways to hide[7] – Lucy's being the most common[8], in the bottom of the bottle[9]. People don't go to the bottle[10] to escape.

They go to hide.[11]

She slid into the driver's seat and immediately realized that something was wrong.

The first visual clue[12] was on the floor of the passenger seat. She looked down and frowned.

A soda can.[13]

Diet Coke to be more exact.

She picked it up. There was still some liquid in it. She thought about that. How long had it been since she'd been in the Beetle? Three, four weeks at least. There hadn't been a can then[14]. Or if there had, she had missed it[15]. That was a possibility.

That was when the smell hit her.[16]

She remembered something that happened in the woods near camp when she was about twelve. Ira had taken her for a walk. They heard gunshots[17] and Ira had totally freaked[18]. Hunters had invaded their land. He found them and started yelling[19] that this was private property. One of the hunters had started yelling back. He got close to them, bumping Ira's chest[20], and Lucy remembered that he smelled horrible[21].

1. une télécommande
2. serrure, côté conducteur
3. rouillée
4. forcer
5. verrou finit par céder
6. affronter
7. moyens de se cacher
8. celui de Lucy étant le plus banal
9. au fond d'une bouteille
10. ne se tournent pas vers l'alcool
11. Ils s'y réfugient.
12. premier indice qu'elle vit
13. Une canette de soda.
14. à ce moment-là
15. elle ne l'avait pas vue
16. C'est alors que l'odeur l'assaillit.
17. des coups de feu
18. était devenu dingue
19. à hurler
20. Il s'était approché d'eux, bousculant Ira
21. sentait affreusement mauvais

She smelled that now.

Lucy turned and looked in the backseat[1].

There was blood on the floor.

And then, in the distance, she heard a crack of gunfire[2].

The skeletal remains[3] were laid out on a silver table with tiny holes in it[4]. The holes made it easier to clean by simply spraying it with a hose[5]. The floor was tile[6] and tilted toward a drain in the center[7], like the shower room at a health club, which also made it easier to get rid of debris. Muse didn't want to think what got caught up in such drains[8], what they used to clean it out, if Drāno[9] did any good at all[10] or if they had to use something stronger.

Lowell stood on one side of the table, Muse on the other with Tara O'Neill.

"So what's up?" Lowell asked.

"First off, we're missing some bones. I'll go out later and take another look. Small stuff, nothing major. That's normal in a case like this. I was about to run some X-rays[11], check the ossification centers[12], especially up at the clavicle[13]."

"What will that tell us?"

"It gives us an idea of age. Bones stop growing as we get older.[14] The last place of ossification is up there, pretty much where[15] the clavicle meets[16] the sternum. The process stops around the age of twenty-one. But that's not important right now."

Lowell looked at Muse. Muse shrugged.

"So what's the big thing you found?"

"This."

O'Neill pointed to the pelvis.

Muse said, "You showed me that before. That's the proof that the skeleton belonged to a female."

"Well, yes. The pelvis is wider, like I said before. Plus we have the less prominent ridge[17] and smaller bone density[18] – all the signs that she's female. There

1. à l'arrière
2. un coup de feu
3. restes du squelette
4. percée de minuscules trous
5. simplement à l'aide d'un tuyau d'arrosage
6. était carrelé
7. incliné vers une bouche d'évacuation, au centre
8. ce qui passait par ces canalisations
9. [marque de nettoyant pour canalisations]
10. était vraiment efficace
11. faire des radios
12. centres d'ossification
13. en haut, au niveau de la clavicule
14. Avec l'âge, les os cessent de se développer.
15. quasiment là où
16. rejoint
17. arcade moins saillante
18. densité osseuse plus faible

is no doubt in my mind. We are looking at the skeletal remains of a female."

"So what are you showing us?"

"The pubic bone[1]."

"What about it?"

"You see here? We call this notching[2] – or better, the pitting of the pubic bones[3]."

"Okay."

"Cartilage holds bones together.[4] That's basic anatomy. You probably know this. We mostly think of[5] cartilage in terms of the knee or elbow[6]. It's elastic. It stretches[7]. But you see this? The marks on the face[8] of the pubic bone? That's formed on the cartilaginous surface where the bones once met and then separated[9]."

O'Neill looked up at them. Her face was glowing[10].

"Are you following me?"

Muse said, "No."

"The notches[11] are formed when the cartilage is strained[12]. When the pubic bones separate[13]."

Muse looked at Lowell. Lowell shrugged.

"And that means?" Muse tried.

"That means that at some point in her life[14], the bones separated. And that means, Investigator Muse, that your victim gave birth[15]."

1. pubis
2. articulation
3. symphyse pubienne
4. Le cartilage maintient les os ensemble.
5. Le plus souvent, on associe le
6. au genou et au coude
7. s'étire
8. à la surface
9. se rejoignaient et se sont séparés
10. rayonnait
11. encoches
12. tendu
13. se séparent
14. qu'à un moment de sa vie
15. a accouché

Chapter 37

Things do not slow down[1] when you have a gun pointed at you.

To the contrary, they speed up[2]. When Ira pointed the gun at me, I expected to have time to react. I started to raise my hands, the primitive demonstration of being harmless[3]. My mouth began to open to try to talk my way through this[4], to tell him I would cooperate and do what he wanted. My heart raced[5], my breathing stopped, and my eyes could only see the gun, nothing but the opening of that barrel[6], the giant black hole now facing me.

But I didn't have time for any of that. I didn't have time to ask Ira why. I didn't have time to ask him what had happened to my sister, if she was alive or dead, how Gil had gotten out of the woods that night, if Wayne Steubens was involved or not. I didn't have time to tell Ira that he was right, I should have let it lie[7], I would let it lie now and we could all go back to our lives[8].

I had no time to do any of that.

Because Ira was already pulling the trigger[9].

A year ago I read a book called *Blink* by Malcolm Gladwell. I don't dare[10] simplify his arguments but part of what he says is that we need to rely on our

1. Rien ne se passe au ralenti
2. tout s'accélère
3. ce geste originel indiquant qu'on ne veut aucun mal
4. de m'en sortir en discutant
5. s'emballa
6. la bouche de ce canon
7. que j'aurais dû laisser tomber
8. reprendre le cours de nos vies
9. pressait déjà sur la détente
10. ne me permettrais pas de

instincts more[1] – the animal part of our brain[2] that will automatically jump out of the way if a truck is bearing down on us[3]. He also notes that we make snap judgments[4], sometimes seemingly based on little evidence, what we used to call hunches[5], and that they are often right. Maybe that was at work here. Maybe something in Ira's stance[6] or the way he pulled out the gun or whatever made me realize that there would indeed be no talking to him[7], that he was going to fire and that I was going to die.

Something made me jump right away.

But the bullet still hit me[8].

He had aimed for the center of my chest. The bullet hit my side[9], ripping across my waist[10] like a hot lance[11]. I fell hard on my side and tried to roll behind a tree. Ira fired again. He missed[12] this time. I kept rolling.

My hand found a rock. I didn't really think. I just picked it up and, still rolling, threw it in his direction. It was a pitiful move, born out of desperation[13], something a child lying on his stomach might try.

The throw had no power behind it.[14] The rock hit him but I don't think it mattered. I realized now that this had been Ira's plan all along. This was why he wanted to see me alone. This was why he had taken me into the woods. He wanted to shoot me.

Ira, that seemingly gentle soul[15], was a killer.

I looked behind me. He was too close. I flashed to that scene[16] in the original *In-Laws* movie[17], a comedy where Alan Arkin is told to avoid bullets by running "serpentine[18]." That wouldn't work here. The man was only six, eight feet away[19]. He had a gun. I was already hit, could feel the blood leaking out of me[20].

I was going to die.

We were stumbling down the hill, me still rolling, Ira trying not to fall, trying to gain enough balance to

1. devrions plus nous fier à notre instinct
2. cette partie reptilienne de notre cerveau
3. nous fait bondir instinctivement pour éviter le camion qui nous fonce dessus
4. des jugements hâtifs
5. intuitions
6. posture
7. comprendre qu'en réalité, je ne pourrais pas lui parler
8. me toucha quand même
9. m'atteignit au côté
10. traversant ma taille
11. lance chauffée à blanc
12. Il me manqua
13. un geste pitoyable, désespéré
14. Il n'y avait aucune énergie dans ce lancer.
15. cet être doux en apparence
16. revis cette scène
17. dans la version originale du film The In-Laws [Ne tirez pas sur le dentiste]
18. courir en zigzaguant pour éviter les balles
19. à 2 m
20. que je perdais du sang

take another shot[1]. I knew he would. I knew I only had a few seconds.

My only chance was to reverse direction[2].

I grabbed[3] the ground and made myself break[4]. Ira was caught off balance[5]. He tried to slow. I grabbed a tree with both hands and whipped my legs toward him[6]. It, too, was a pathetic move, I thought, a bad gymnast on a pommel horse[7]. But Ira was just within striking range[8] and just enough off balance[9]. My feet hit against the side of his right ankle[10]. Not all that hard. But hard enough.

Ira let out a shout[11] and tumbled to the ground.

The gun, I thought. Get the gun.

I scrambled[12] toward him. I was bigger. I was younger. I was in much better condition. He was an old man, his brain half-fried[13]. He could fire a gun, sure. There was still power in his arms and his legs. But the years and the drug abuse had slowed the reflexes down[14].

I climbed on top of him[15], searching for the gun. It had been in his right hand. I went for[16] that arm. *Think arm. Only arm.* I grabbed it with both my hands, rolled my body on it, pinned it down[17] and then bent it back[18].

The hand was empty.

I had been so preoccupied with the right hand that I never saw the left coming[19]. He swung in a long arc[20]. The gun must have dropped when he fell. He had it now in his left hand, gripping it like a rock. He crashed the butt[21] against my forehead.

It was like a lightning bolt had seared through my[22] skull. I could feel my brain jerk to the right, as though ripped from its moor[23], and start to rattle[24]. My body convulsed.

I let go of him.

I looked up. He had the gun pointed at me.

"Freeze[25], police!"

I recognized the voice. It was York.

1. retrouver assez d'équilibre pour tirer à nouveau
2. de changer de direction
3. J'agrippai
4. pour me freiner
5. perdit l'équilibre
6. balançai mes jambes vers lui
7. cheval d'arçons
8. à ma portée
9. et déjà un peu en déséquilibre
10. cheville droite
11. poussa un cri
12. rampai
13. au cerveau à moitié cramé
14. diminué ses réflexes
15. grimpai sur lui
16. me jetai sur
17. le plaquai au sol
18. le pliai
19. ne vis pas arriver la main gauche
20. décrivit un grand arc de cercle
21. frappa la crosse
22. la foudre s'était abattue sur mon
23. faire un bond vers la droite, comme s'il se détachait
24. vibrer
25. Ne bougez plus

The air stopped, crackled.[1] I moved my gaze from the gun to Ira's eyes. We were that close[2], the gun pointed straight at my face. And I saw it. He was going to shoot and kill me. They wouldn't get to him in time. The police were here now. It was over for him. He had to know that. But he was going to shoot me anyway.

"Dad! No!"

It was Lucy. He heard her voice and something in those eyes changed.

"Drop the gun now![3] Do it! Now!"

York again. My eyes were still locked[4] on Ira's.

Ira kept his eyes on me. "Your sister is dead," he said.

Then he turned the gun away from me, put it in his own mouth and pulled the trigger.

1. L'atmosphère se figea, il y eut comme un crépitement.
2. presque nez à nez
3. Lâchez tout de suite votre arme !
4. rivés

Chapter 38

I passed out.[1]

That was what I was told. I do have dim memories[2], though. I remember Ira falling on me, the back of his head gone[3]. I remember hearing Lucy scream. I remember looking up, seeing the blue sky, watching the clouds fly by me[4]. I assume I was on my back, on a stretcher[5], being taken to the ambulance. That was where the memories stopped. With the blue sky. With the white clouds.

And then, when I started to feel almost peaceful and calm, I remembered Ira's words.

Your sister is dead....

I shook my head. No. Glenda Perez had told me that Camille had walked out of those woods. Ira wouldn't know. He couldn't.

"Mr. Copeland?"

I blinked my eyes open.[6] I was in a bed. A hospital room.

"My name is Dr. McFadden."

I let my gaze travel[7] the room. I saw York behind him.

"You were shot in the side. We stitched you up.[8] You're going to be fine, but there will be soreness[9] – "

"Doc?"

1. Je perdis connaissance.

2. de vagues souvenirs

3. pulvérisé

4. filer au-dessus de moi

5. brancard

6. J'ouvris les yeux en clignant des paupières.

7. Mon regard balaya

8. On vous a recousu.

9. ce sera douloureux

McFadden had been using his best doctor sing-song[1], not expecting such an early interruption. He frowned. "Yes?"

"I'm okay, right?"

"Yes."

"Then can we talk about this later? I really need to speak to that officer."

York hid a smile[2]. I expected an argument[3]. Doctors are even more arrogant than attorneys. But he didn't give me one[4]. He shrugged and said, "Sure. Have the nurse page me[5] when you're done."

"Thanks, Doc."

He left without another word. York moved closer to the bed.

"How did you know about Ira?" I asked.

"The lab guys matched carpet fibers found on the body of, uh..." York's voice drifted off[6]. "Well, we still don't have an ID but if you want we can call him Gil Perez."

"That would be good."

"Right, anyway, they found these carpet fibers on him. We knew that they came from an old car. We also found a security camera that was near where the body was dumped. We saw it was a yellow Volkswagen, matched it to[7] Silverstein. So we hurried over[8]."

"Where's Lucy?"

"Dillon's asking her some questions."

"I don't get it. Ira killed Gil Perez?"

"Yep."

"No question?[9]"

"None. First off, we found blood in the backseat of the Volkswagen. My guess is, it'll match Perez. Two, the staff[10] at that halfway house confirmed that Perez – signing in as Manolo Santiago – visited Silverstein the day before the murder. The staff also confirmed that they saw Silverstein leave in the Volkswagen the next morning. First time he'd been out in six months."

1. avait pris sa voix la plus mélodieuse pour faire son rapport médical
2. dissimula un sourire
3. à ce qu'il proteste
4. ce ne fut pas le cas
5. Demandez à l'infirmière de m'appeler
6. s'interrompit
7. puis avons découvert qu'elle appartenait à
8. avons accouru
9. Il n'y a aucun doute ?
10. personnel

I made a face. "They didn't think to tell his daughter?"

"Staff who saw him weren't on duty[1] the next time Lucy Gold came in. Plus, hey, as the staff told me repeatedly[2], Silverstein has never been declared incompetent[3] or anything like that. He was free to come and go as he pleased."

"I don't get it. Why would Ira kill him?"

"The same reason he wanted to kill you, I guess. You were both looking into[4] what happened at that camp twenty years ago. Mr. Silverstein didn't want that."

I tried to put it together.[5] "So he killed Margot Green and Doug Billingham?"

York waited a second, as though expecting me to add my sister to the list. I didn't.

"Could be.[6]"

"And what about Wayne Steubens?"

"They probably worked together somehow, I don't know. What I do know is, Ira Silverstein killed *my* guy. Oh, another thing: the gun Ira shot you with? It's the same caliber as the one used to shoot Gil Perez. We're running a ballistic test[7] now, but you know it'll be a match. So you add that to the blood in the backseat of the Beetle, the surveillance tapes of him and the vehicle near where the body was dumped off... I mean, come on, it's overkill[8]. But hey, Ira Silverstein is dead, and as you know, it is very difficult to try[9] a dead man. As for[10] what Ira Silverstein did or didn't do twenty years ago" – York shrugged – "hey, I'm curious too. But that's someone else's mystery to solve[11]."

"You'll help, if we need it?"

"Sure. Love to.[12] And when you do figure it all out, why don't you come into the city and I'll take you for a steak dinner[13]?"

"Deal.[14]"

We shook hands.

"I should thank you for saving my life," I said.

1. de service
2. à plusieurs reprises
3. irresponsable
4. Vous vous intéressiez tous les deux à
5. J'essayai de procéder par recoupements.
6. C'est possible.
7. On fait une analyse balistique
8. c'est plus qu'il n'en faut
9. juger
10. Concernant
11. ce n'est pas moi qui résoudrai cette énigme
12. Avec plaisir.
13. et je vous paierai un steak un soir
14. Marché conclu.

"Yeah, you should. Except I don't think I did.[1]"

I remembered the look on Ira's face, his determination to kill me. York had seen it too – Ira was going to shoot me, consequences be damned[2]. Lucy's voice had been what saved me more than York's gun.

York left then. I was alone in a hospital room. There are probably more depressing places to be alone, but I couldn't think of one[3]. I thought about my Jane, how brave she was, how the only thing that really scared her, terrified her, was being alone in a hospital room. So I stayed all night. I slept in one of those chairs that can be made into the most uncomfortable bed on God's green earth[4]. I don't say that to get applause[5]. It was Jane's one moment of weakness[6], the first overnight[7] at the hospital, when she grabbed my hand and tried to keep the desperation out of her voice[8] when she said, "Please don't leave me alone here."

So I didn't. Not then. Not until much later, when she was back home, where she wanted to die because the thought of being back in a room like the one I was in now...

Now it was my turn. I was alone here. It didn't scare me too much. I thought about that, about where my life had taken me. Who would be here for me in a crisis[9]? Who could I expect to be at my bedside[10] when I woke up in a hospital? The first names that popped into my head[11]: Greta and Bob. When I cut my hand last year slicing open a bagel[12], Bob had driven me, Greta had taken care of Cara. They were family[13] – the only family I had left. And now they were gone[14].

I remembered the last time I was hospitalized. When I was twelve years old I came down with rheumatic fever[15]. It was pretty rare then, even rarer now. I spent ten days in the hospital. I remember Camille visiting. Sometimes she brought her annoying[16] friends because she knew that would distract me. We played Boggle a lot. Boys loved Camille. She used to bring the cassette tapes they made for her[17]

1. Sauf que je ne pense pas y être pour quelque chose.
2. en se fichant des conséquences
3. ne voyais pas lequel
4. au monde
5. pour qu'on me félicite
6. l'unique moment de faiblesse
7. nuit passée
8. masquer son désespoir
9. en cas de problème
10. à mon chevet
11. qui me vinrent à l'esprit
12. en coupant un bagel en deux
13. étaient ma famille
14. je les avais perdus
15. j'avais été atteint de rhumatisme articulaire aigu
16. agaçantes
17. cassettes qu'ils lui enregistraient

– groups like Steely Dan and Supertramp and the Doobie Brothers. Camille told me what groups were great, what groups were lame[1], and I followed her taste[2] as though it were biblical[3].

Did she suffer out in those woods?

That was what I'd always wondered. What did Wayne Steubens do to her? Did he tie her up and terrify her, like he did with Margot Green? Did she struggle[4] and suffer[5] defensive wounds like Doug Billingham? Did he bury her alive, like those victims in Indiana or Virginia? How much pain had Camille been in?[6] How terrifying were her last moments[7]?

And now... the new question: Had Camille somehow gotten out of those woods alive?

I turned my thoughts to Lucy. I thought about what she must be going through[8], watching her beloved father blow his head off[9], wondering about the whys and hows[10] of it all. I wanted to reach her, say something, try somehow to comfort her a little.

There was a knock on my door.

"Come in."

I expected it to be a nurse. It wasn't. It was Muse. I smiled at her. I expected her to smile back[11]. She didn't. Her face couldn't have been more closed[12].

"Don't look so glum[13]," I said. "I'm fine."

Muse moved closer to the bed. Her expression didn't change.

"I said – "

"I already talked to the doctor. He said you might not even have to stay overnight[14]."

"So what's with the face[15]?"

Muse grabbed a chair, pulled it next to the[16] bed. "We need to talk."

I had seen Loren Muse make this face before.

It was her game face.[17] It was her I'm-gonna-nail-da-bastard face.[18] It was her try-to-lie-and-I'll-spot-it face.[19] I had seen her direct this look[20] at murderers

1. nuls
2. goûts
3. c'était parole d'évangile
4. S'était-elle débattue
5. avait-elle subi
6. Est-ce que Camille avait beaucoup souffert ?
7. ses derniers instants
8. traverser
9. se tirer une balle dans la tête
10. s'interrogeant sur le pourquoi et le comment
11. à la voir sourire à son tour
12. était totalement fermé
13. sombre
14. jusqu'à demain
15. pourquoi tu fais cette tête
16. l'approcha du
17. Elle faisait sa tête de tueuse.
18. C'était son expression qui voulait dire « je vais te coincer, salaud ».
19. Ou celle qui disait : « si tu mens je le saurai illico ».
20. infliger ce regard

and rapists and carjackers and gangbangers[1]. Now she was aiming at me[2].

"What's the matter?"

Her expression didn't soften[3]. "How did it go with Raya Singh?"

"It was pretty much what we thought." I filled her in briefly because, really, talking about Raya felt almost beside the point at this stage[4]. "But the big news is, Gil Perez's sister came to see me. She told me Camille was still alive."

I saw something change in her face. She was good, no doubt, but so was I. They say that a true "tell[5]" lasts less than a tenth of a second[6]. But I spotted it[7]. She wasn't necessarily surprised by what I said. But it had jolted her nonetheless[8].

"What's going on, Muse?"

"I talked to Sheriff Lowell today."

I frowned. "He hasn't retired yet[9]?"

"No."

I was going to ask her why she'd reached out to him, but I knew Muse was thorough[10]. It would be natural for her to have contacted the lead from[11] those murders. It also explained, in part, her behavior toward me.

"Let me guess," I said. "He thinks I lied about that night."

Muse did not say yes or no. "It is odd, don't you think? You not staying on guard duty the night of the murder."

"You know why. You read those journals."

"Yes, I did. You sneaked off with your girlfriend. And then you didn't want to get her in trouble[12]."

"Right."

"But those journals also said that you were covered with blood. Is that true too?"

I looked at her. "What the hell is going on?"

"I'm pretending that you aren't my boss."

1. à des voleurs de voitures et des violeurs en bande organisée
2. c'était moi sa cible
3. ne se radoucit pas
4. paraissait presque insignifiant à ce stade
5. signe révélateur [terme de poker]
6. dure moins d'un dixième de seconde
7. je l'avais décelé
8. elle avait tout de même été secouée
9. n'est pas encore à la retraite
10. était minutieuse
11. qu'elle ait pris contact avec celui qui dirigeait l'enquête sur
12. qu'elle ait des problèmes

I tried to sit up[1]. The stitch[2] in my side hurt like hell[3].

"Did Lowell say I was a suspect?"

"He doesn't have to. And you don't have to be a suspect for me to ask these questions. You lied about that night – "

"I was protecting Lucy. You know this already."

"I know what you've already told me, yes. But put yourself in my position[4]. I need to handle this case with no agenda or bias[5]. If you were me, wouldn't you ask these questions?"

I thought about it. "I get it, okay, fine, fire away[6]. Ask me whatever you want."

"Was your sister ever pregnant[7]?"

I just sat there[8], stunned. The question had hit me like a surprise left hook[9]. Probably her intent[10].

"Are you serious?"

"I am."

"Why the hell would you ask that?"

"Just answer the question."

"No, my sister was never pregnant."

"Are you sure?"

"I think I'd know."

"Would you?" she asked.

"I don't understand. Why are you asking me that?"

"We've had cases where girls have hidden it from their families. You know that. Heck[11], we had a case where the girl herself didn't know until she delivered the baby[12]. Remember?"

I did.

"Look, Muse, I'm pulling rank here[13]. Why are you asking if my sister was pregnant?"

She searched[14] my face, her eyes crawling on me like slimy worms[15].

"Cut that out[16]," I said.

"You have to recuse yourself[17], Cope. You know that."

"I don't have to do anything."

1. me redresser dans mon lit
2. Les points de suture
3. me faisaient un mal de chien
4. mets-toi à ma place
5. sans arrière-pensée ni parti pris
6. vas-y
7. enceinte
8. restai sans rien dire
9. m'avait fait l'effet d'un crochet du gauche reçu par surprise
10. ce qu'elle recherchait
11. Nom d'un chien
12. avant d'avoir accouché
13. c'est ton supérieur hiérarchique qui parle
14. scruta
15. posant sur moi un regard pénétrant et inquisiteur
16. Arrête ça
17. te retires de l'enquête

"Yeah, you do. Lowell is still running the show[1]. It's his baby."

"Lowell? That hick[2] hasn't worked on this case since they arrested Wayne Steubens eighteen years ago."

"Still. It's his case. He's the lead."

I wasn't sure what to make of this. "Does Lowell know about Gil Perez being alive this whole time?"

"I told him your theory."

"So why are you suddenly ambushing me[3] with questions about Camille being pregnant?"

She said nothing.

"Fine, play it that way.[4] Look, I promised Glenda Perez that I would try to keep her family out of it[5]. But tell Lowell about it. Maybe he'll let you stay involved[6] – I trust you a lot more than the backwoods sheriff[7]. The key thing is[8], Glenda Perez said my sister walked out of those woods alive."

"And," Muse said, "Ira Silverstein said she was dead."

The room stopped.[9] The tell was more obvious on her face this time. I looked at her hard[10]. She tried to hold my gaze, but eventually she broke[11].

"What the hell is going on, Muse?"

She stood. The door opened behind her. A nurse entered. With nary a hello[12], she strapped a blood pressure collar[13] around my arm and started pumping[14]. She stuck[15] a thermometer in my mouth.

Muse said, "I'll be right back."

The thermometer was still in my mouth. The nurse took my pulse[16]. The rate had to be off the charts[17]. I tried to call out around the thermometer.

"Muse!"

She left. I stayed in bed and stewed[18].

Pregnant? Could Camille have been pregnant?

I couldn't see it. I tried to remember. Did she start wearing loose clothes[19]? How long was she pregnant for – how many months? My father would have no-

1. est toujours aux commandes
2. plouc
3. pourquoi est-ce que tu me tends tout d'un coup un guet-apens
4. Parfait, continue comme ça.
5. laisser sa famille en dehors de ça
6. rester sur l'affaire
7. le shérif de ce coin paumé
8. L'essentiel, c'est que
9. Une chape de plomb s'abattit sur la pièce.
10. avec insistance
11. elle finit par céder
12. Sans même un bonjour
13. sangla le tensiomètre
14. à pomper
15. fourra
16. pouls
17. pulsations devaient crever le plafond
18. en bouillonnant
19. des vêtements amples

ticed if she was showing at all[1] – the man was an ob-gyn. She couldn't have hid it from him[2].

But then again maybe she didn't.

I would say this was nonsense[3], that it was absolutely impossible that my sister had been pregnant, except for one thing. I didn't know what the hell was going on here, but Muse knew more than she was saying. Her question wasn't haphazard.[4] Sometimes a good prosecutor needs to do that with a case. You need to give the crazy notion[5] the benefit of the doubt. Just to see. Just to see how it could possibly fit[6].

The nurse finished up. I reached for the phone and dialed home to check up on[7] Cara. I was surprised when Greta answered with a friendly "Hello."

"Hi," I said.

The friendly fled[8]. "I hear you're going to be fine."

"That's what they tell me."

"I'm here with Cara now," Greta said, all business[9]. "I can have her stay at my place tonight, if you'd like."

"That would be great, thanks."

There was a brief lull.[10]

"Paul?"

She usually called me Cope. I didn't like that. "Yes?"

"Cara's welfare[11] is very important to me. She is still my niece. She is still the daughter of my sister."

"I understand that."

"You, on the other hand, mean nothing to me[12]."

She hung up the phone.

I sat back and waited for Muse to return, trying to turn it over in my aching head[13]. I went through it step by step.

Glenda Perez said my sister walked out of those woods alive.

Ira Silverstein said she was dead.

So who do I believe?

1. le moindre signe
2. n'aurait pas pu le lui cacher
3. Pour moi, c'était insensé
4. Elle n'avait pas posé cette question au hasard.
5. à une idée folle
6. si cela pourrait coller
7. pour prendre des nouvelles de
8. ton amical disparut
9. d'un ton ferme
10. Il y eut un petit blanc.
11. Le bien-être de Cara
12. par contre, tu ne représentes rien pour moi
13. remettre de l'ordre dans mes idées malgré ma migraine

Glenda Perez appeared to be somewhat[1] normal. Ira Silverstein had been a lunatic[2]. Point:[3] Glenda Perez.

I also realized that Ira had kept talking about wanting things to stay buried. He killed Gil Perez – and was about to kill me – because he wanted us to stop digging. He would have figured that as long as[4] I thought my sister was alive, I would search. I would dig and raze[5] and do whatever was necessary[6], consequences be damned, if I thought there was a chance I could bring Camille home. Ira clearly didn't want that.

That gave him a motive to lie[7] – to say she was dead.

Glenda Perez, on the other hand, also wanted me to stop digging. As long as I kept my investigation active, her family was in real danger. Their fraud and all the other quasi-crimes she'd listed could be exposed[8]. Ergo, she too would have realized that the best way to get me to back off was to convince me that nothing had changed from[9] twenty years ago, that Wayne Steubens had indeed killed my sister. It would have been in her interest to tell me my sister was dead.

But she didn't do that.

Point: Glenda Perez.

I felt the hope – there was that word again[10] – rise in my chest[11].

Loren Muse came back into the room. She closed the door behind her. "I just talked to Sheriff Lowell," she said.

"Oh?"

"Like I said, it's his case. I couldn't talk about certain things until I got his okay[12]."

"This is about your pregnancy question?"

Muse sat down as if she were afraid the chair might break. She put her hands in her lap[13]. That was weird for her.[14] Muse usually gestured[15] like an

1. relativement
2. dingue
3. Un point en faveur de
4. pensait certainement que, tant que
5. J'allais fureter encore et encore
6. tout ce qu'il fallait
7. Ce qui l'avait poussé à mentir
8. pouvaient être révélés
9. par rapport à
10. encore ce mot
11. renaître en moi
12. sans son feu vert
13. sur ses genoux
14. Ça ne lui ressemblait pas.
15. gesticulait

amphetamine-fueled[1] Sicilian who's nearly gotten clipped[2] by a speeding car. I had never seen her so subdued[3]. She had her eyes down. My heart went out to her a little bit.[4] She was trying so hard to do the right thing. She always was.

"Muse?"

She raised her eyes. I didn't like what I saw.

"What's going on here?"

"Do you remember my sending Andrew Barrett up to the campsite?"

"Of course," I said. "Barrett wanted to try out some new ground-penetrating radar gizmo[5]. So?"

Muse looked at me. That was all she did. She looked at me and I saw her eyes go wet[6]. Then she nodded at me. It was the saddest nod I have ever seen.

I felt my world drop with a splat.[7]

Hope. Hope had been gently cradling my heart[8]. Now it spread its talons and crushed it[9]. I couldn't breathe. I shook my head but Muse just kept nodding.

"They found old remains not far from where the other two bodies were found," she said.

I shook my head harder. Not now. Not after all this.

"Female, five-foot-seven, probably been in the ground between fifteen and thirty years."

I shook my head some more. Muse stopped, waiting for me to get my bearings[10]. I tried to clear my thoughts[11], tried not to hear what she was saying. I tried to block[12], tried to rewind[13]. And then I remembered something.

"Wait, you asked me if Camille was pregnant. Are you saying this body... that they can tell that she was pregnant?"

"Not just pregnant," Muse said. "She gave birth."

I just sat there. I tried to take it in[14]. I couldn't. It was one thing to hear that she'd been pregnant. That could have happened. She could have had an abortion or something, I don't know. But that she carried

1. carburant aux amphétamines
2. qui aurait failli se faire renverser
3. effacée
4. Je ressentis un peu de compassion pour elle.
5. gadget
6. se brouiller de larmes
7. Mon univers s'effondra avec fracas.
8. m'avait bercé le cœur avec douceur
9. il le foulait aux pieds
10. que je me ressaisisse
11. de me vider la tête
12. faire barrage
13. revenir en arrière
14. de digérer tout ça

1. ait mené sa grossesse à terme

2. dans la nature

to term[1], that she delivered a baby, and that now she was dead, after all this...

"Find out what happened, Muse."

"I will."

"And if there is a baby out there[2]..."

"We'll find that too."

Chapter 39

"I have news.[1]"

Alexei Kokorov was still an impressive, though hideous, specimen[2]. In the late eighties[3], right before the Wall came down[4] and their lives changed forever[5], Kokorov had been Sosh's underling[6] at InTourist. It was humorous[7] when you thought about it. They had been elite KGB men back home[8]. In 1974, they'd been in "Spetsgruppa A" – the Alfa Group[9]. The group was supposedly counterterrorism and crime[10], but on a cold Christmas morning in 1979, their unit had stormed[11] the Darulaman Palace in Kabul[12]. Not long after that, Sosh had gotten the InTourist job and moved to New York. Kokorov, a man Sosh had never particularly gotten along with[13], had gone too. They had both left their families behind. This was how it was.[14] New York was seductive.[15] Only the most hardened Soviet[16] would be allowed to go. But even the most hardened needed to be watched[17] by a colleague he didn't necessarily love or trust. Even the most hardened needed to be reminded[18] that there were loved ones back home who could be made to suffer[19].

"Go on," Sosh said.

1. J'ai du nouveau.
2. bien que hideux, restait impressionnant
3. À la fin des années 1980
4. la chute du Mur
5. et que leurs vies ne changent irrémédiablement
6. le sous-fifre
7. C'était drôle
8. dans leur pays
9. [forces spéciales russes]
10. censé lutter contre le terrorisme et la criminalité
11. pris d'assaut
12. Kaboul
13. un homme avec lequel Sosh ne s'était jamais vraiment bien entendu
14. Ça se passait comme ça.
15. Partir à New York était tentant.
16. les agents soviétiques les plus convaincus
17. devaient être surveillés
18. qu'on leur rappelle
19. à qui l'on pouvait s'en prendre

Kokorov was a drunk[1]. He had always been one, but in his youth, it almost worked to his advantage[2]. He was strong and smart[3] and drink made him particularly vicious[4]. He obeyed, like a dog. Now the years had crept up on him[5]. His children were grown and had no use for him[6]. His wife had left him years ago. He was pathetic, but again, he was the past[7]. They had not liked each other, true, but there was still a bond[8]. Kokorov had grown loyal to[9] Sosh. So Sosh kept him on the payroll[10].

“They found a body in those woods,” Kokorov said.

Sosh closed his eyes. He had not expected this and yet he was not totally surprised. Pavel Copeland wanted to unearth[11] the past. Sosh had hoped to stop him. There are things a man is better off not knowing[12]. Gavrel and Aline, his brother and sister, had been buried in a mass grave[13]. No headstone[14], no dignity. It had never bothered[15] Sosh. Ashes to ashes[16] and all that. But sometimes he wondered. Sometimes he wondered if Gavrel would rise up one day, point an accusing finger at[17] his little brother, the one who’d stolen an extra bite of bread more than sixty years ago. It was just a bite, Sosh knew. It hadn’t changed anything. And yet Sosh still thought about what he’d done, the stolen bite of bread, every morning of his life.

Was that how this was too? The dead crying out for vengeance[18]?

“How did you learn of this?” Sosh asked.

“Since Pavel’s visit, I’ve been watching the local news[19],” Kokorov said. “On the Internet. They reported it.[20]”

Sosh smiled. Two old KGB toughies[21] using the American Internet to gather information – ironic.[22]

“What should we do?” Kokorov asked.

“Do?”

“Yes. What should we do?”

“Nothing, Alexei. It was a long time ago.”

1. ivrogne
2. cela lui avait presque rendu service
3. intelligent
4. méchant
5. l’avaient rattrapé
6. étaient grands et n’avaient que faire de lui
7. représentait le passé
8. lien
9. était devenu loyal envers
10. à son service
11. déterrer
12. qu’il vaut mieux ne pas savoir
13. fosse commune
14. stèle
15. n’avait jamais dérangé
16. Tu es poussière et tu retourneras à la poussière
17. apparaîtrait, un jour, en pointant un doigt accusateur vers
18. réclamant vengeance
19. informations régionales
20. Ils en ont parlé.
21. gros durs
22. quelle ironie !

"Murder has no statute of limitations[1] in this country. They will investigate."

"And find what?"

Kokorov said nothing.

"It's over. We have no agency or country to protect anymore."

Silence. Alexei stroked his chin and looked off.

"What is it?"

Alexei said, "Do you miss those days[2], Sosh?"

"I miss my youth," he said. "Nothing more."

"People feared us[3]," Kokorov said. "They trembled when we passed."

"And what, that was a good thing, Alexei?"

His smile was a horrible thing, his teeth too small for his mouth, like a rodent's[4]. "Don't pretend. We had power. We were gods."

"No, we were bullies[5]. We were not gods – we were the dirty henchmen[6] of the gods. They had the power. We were scared, so we made everyone a little more scared. That made us feel like big men – terrorizing the weak[7]."

Alexei waved a dismissive hand[8] in Sosh's direction. "You're getting old."

"We both are."

"I don't like this whole thing coming back.[9]"

"You didn't like Pavel coming back either. It's because he reminds you of his grandfather, doesn't he?"

"No."

"The man you arrested. The old man and his old wife."

"You think you were better[10], Sosh?"

"No. I know I wasn't."

"It wasn't my decision. You know that. They were reported[11], we took action."

"Exactly," Sosh said. "The gods commanded you to do it. So you did. Do you still feel like such a big man?[12]"

"It wasn't like that.[13]"

1. Il n'y a pas de prescription en cas de meurtre
2. Tu regrettes cette époque
3. nous craignaient
4. comme celles d'un rongeur
5. des brutes
6. sales hommes de main
7. les plus faibles
8. fit un geste dédaigneux de la main
9. Ça ne me plaît pas que tout ça ressorte.
10. que tu valais mieux
11. ont été dénoncés
12. Tu te considères toujours comme un grand homme ?
13. Ça ne s'est pas passé comme ça.

"It was exactly like that."

"You'd have done the same."

"Yes, I would have."

"We were helping a higher cause[1]."

"Did you ever really buy that, Alexei?"

"Yes. I still do. I still wonder if we were so wrong[2]. When I see the dangers freedom has wrought, I still wonder[3]."

"I don't," Sosh said. "We were thugs[4]."

Silence.

Kokorov said, "So what happens now – now that they found the body?"

"Maybe nothing. Maybe more will die[5]. Or maybe Pavel will finally get the chance to face his past."

"Didn't you tell him that he shouldn't do that – that he should let the past stay buried?"

"I did," Sosh said. "But he didn't listen. Who knows which one of us will be proven right[6]?"

Dr. McFadden came in and told me that I was lucky, that the bullet went through my side without hitting any internal organs[7]. It always made me roll my eyes[8] when the hero gets shot and then goes on with his life as though nothing ever happened[9]. But the truth is, there are plenty of gunshot wounds that do heal like that[10]. Sitting in this bed wasn't going to make it any better[11] than resting[12] at home.

"I'm more worried about the blow to your head[13]," he said.

"But I can go home?"

"Let's let you sleep awhile, okay? See how you feel when you wake up. I think you should stay overnight."

I was going to argue but there was nothing to be gained by going home. I felt sore and sick and achy.[14] I probably looked like hell and would scare Cara with my appearance.

They had found a body in the woods. I still couldn't wrap my brain around that one[15].

1. étions au service d'une cause plus noble
2. avions tort à ce point
3. que la liberté a fabriqués, je me pose encore la question
4. des voyous
5. que d'autres mourront
6. qui de nous deux aura raison
7. sans toucher aucun organe
8. J'ai toujours trouvé ça peu vraisemblable
9. continue de vivre comme si de rien n'était
10. guérissent comme ça
11. n'apporterait rien de plus
12. me reposer
13. pour le coup que vous avez reçu à la tête
14. J'avais mal partout, j'avais la nausée et des courbatures.
15. n'arrivais toujours pas à me faire à cette idée

Muse had faxed the preliminary autopsy to the hospital. They didn't know much yet, but it was hard to believe that it wasn't my sister. Lowell and Muse had done a more thorough examination of[1] missing women from that area, seeing if there were any other women unaccounted for[2] who could possibly fit this bill. The search had been fruitless[3] – the only preliminary match for the computer records of the missing[4] was my sister.

So far[5] the coroner had come up with no cause of death[6]. That wasn't unusual in a skeleton of this shape[7]. If he had sliced her throat or buried her alive, they probably would never know. There would be no nicks[8] on the bone. The cartilage and internal organs were long gone, the victims of some parasitic entity that had feasted on them[9] long ago.

I skipped down to the key item[10]. The pitting of the pubic bone.

The victim had given birth.

I again wondered about that. I wondered if that was possible. Under normal circumstances, that might give me some hope that it wasn't my sister they'd dug up[11]. But if it wasn't, what could I conclude exactly? That around the same time[12] some other girl – a girl no one can account for[13] – had been murdered and buried in the same area as the ones at that camp?

That didn't make sense.

I was missing something.[14] I was missing a lot.

I took out my cell phone. There was no service[15] in the hospital but I looked up York's number on it. I used my room phone to make the call.

"Anything new?" I asked him.

"Do you know what time it is?"

I didn't. I checked the clock. "It's a few minutes after ten," I said. "Anything new?"

He sighed. "Ballistics[16] confirmed what we already knew. The gun Silverstein shot you with is the same one he used to kill Gil Perez. And while DNA will

1. recherche plus poussée sur
2. disparues
3. n'avait rien donné
4. première personne correspondant, d'après le fichier informatique des personnes disparues,
5. Jusqu'à présent
6. n'avait pas déterminé la cause du décès
7. avec un squelette dans cet état
8. n'y aurait pas d'entailles
9. victimes de parasites qui les avaient dévorés
10. passai directement à l'élément essentiel
11. déterrée
12. Qu'à peu près au même moment
13. inconnue de tous
14. Quelque chose m'échappait.
15. Il n'y avait pas de réseau
16. La balistique

take a few weeks, the blood type in the back of the Volkswagen Beetle matches Perez's. In sports terms[1], I'd call that game, set, match."

"What did Lucy say?"

"Dillon said she wasn't much of a help[2]. She was in shock. Said her father was not well, that he probably imagined some kind of threat."

"Dillon buy that?"

"Sure, why not? Either way our case is closed[3]. How are you feeling?"

"Peachy.[4]"

"Dillon got shot once[5]."

"Only once?"

"Good one. Anyway, he still shows every woman he meets the scar. Turns them on[6], he says. You remember that."

"Seduction tips from[7] Dillon. Thanks."

"Guess what line he uses[8] after he shows them the scar?"

"'Hey, babe[9], want to see my gun?'"

"Damn, how did you know?"

"Where did Lucy go after you finished talking to her?"

"We drove her back to her place on campus."

"Okay, thanks."

I hung up and dialed Lucy's number. The call went to her voice mail.[10] I left a message. Then I called Muse's mobile.

"Where are you?" I asked.

"Heading[11] home, why?"

"I thought maybe you'd be going to Reston U[12] to question Lucy."

"I already went."

"And?"

"She didn't open the door. But I could see lights on[13]. She's in there."

"Is she okay?"

"How would I know?"

1. En langage sportif
2. qu'il n' y avait pas grand-chose à en tirer
3. notre affaire est classée
4. J'ai la pêche.
5. s'est fait tirer dessus, une fois
6. Ça les excite
7. Quelques conseils en séduction selon
8. ce qu'il raconte
9. ma poule
10. Je tombai sur sa boîte vocale.
11. En route pour
12. université
13. j'ai vu qu'il y avait de la lumière

I didn't like it. Her father had died and she was alone in her apartment. "How far are you from the hospital?"

"Fifteen minutes."

"How about[1] picking me up?"

"Are you allowed out?[2]"

"Who's going to stop me? And it's just for a little while."

"Are you, my boss, asking me to drive you to your girlfriend's house?"

"No. I, the county prosecutor, am asking you to drive me to the home of a major person of interest[3] in a recent homicide."

"Either way," Muse said, "I'm so very there.[4]"

No one stopped me from leaving the hospital.

I didn't feel well, but I had felt worse[5]. I was worried about Lucy and I realized with growing certainty[6] that it was more than normal worry[7].

I missed her.

I missed her the way you miss someone you're falling in love with. I could run around that statement[8], soften it somehow[9], say that my emotions were on hyperdrive with[10] all that was going on, claim that this was nostalgia for a better time[11], a more innocent time, a time when my parents were together and my sister was alive, and heck, even Jane was still healthy and beautiful and somewhere happy. But that wasn't it.

I liked being with Lucy. I liked the way it felt[12]. I liked being with her the way you like being with someone you're falling in love with. There was no need to explain further.[13]

Muse drove. Her car was small and cramped[14]. I was not much of a car guy and I had no idea what kind of car it was, but it reeked of[15] cigarette smoke. She must have caught the look on my face because she said, "My mother is a chain smoker[16]."

1. Tu peux
2. Ils te laissent sortir ?
3. au domicile d'une personne très impliquée
4. c'est comme si j'étais déjà là.
5. j'avais connu pire
6. avec de plus en plus de certitude
7. qu'une inquiétude naturelle
8. tourner cette phrase dans tous les sens
9. l'édulcorer un peu
10. exacerbées par
11. d'une meilleure époque
12. ce que cela me faisait
13. Toute autre explication était superflue.
14. encombrée
15. puait la
16. grosse fumeuse

"Uh-huh."

"She lives with me. It's just temporary. Until she finds Husband Five. In the meantime[1] I tell her not to smoke in my car."

"And she ignores you[2]."

"No, no, I think my telling her that makes her smoke more. Same with my apartment. I come home from work, I open my door, I feel like I'm swallowing ashes[3]."

I wished that she'd drive faster.

"Will you be okay for court tomorrow?" she asked.

"I think so, yeah."

"Judge Pierce wanted to meet with counsel in his chambers."

"Any idea why?"

"Nope."

"What time?"

"Nine a.m. sharp.[4]"

"I'll be there."

"You want me to pick you up?"

"I do."

"Can I get a company car[5] then?"

"We don't work for a company. We work for the county."

"How about a county car?"

"Maybe."

"Cool." She drove some more. "I'm sorry about your sister."

I said nothing. I was still having a hard time[6] reacting to that. Maybe I needed to hear that the ID was confirmed. Or maybe I had already done twenty years of mourning[7] and didn't have that much left. Or maybe, most likely[8], I was putting my emotions on the back burner[9].

Two more people were dead now.

Whatever happened twenty years ago in those woods... maybe the local kids were right, the ones who said that a monster ate them or that the bogey-

1. En attendant
2. ne t'écoute pas
3. j'ai l'impression d'avaler des cendres
4. À 9 heures pile.
5. voiture de société [voiture de fonction]
6. J'avais encore du mal à
7. que j'étais en deuil depuis 20 ans
8. et c'était le plus probable
9. que je mettais mes émotions de côté pour l'instant

man took them away. Whatever[1] had killed Margot Green and Doug Billingham, and in all likelihood[2] Camille Copeland, was still alive, still breathing, still taking lives. Maybe it had slept for twenty years. Maybe it had gone somewhere new or moved to other woods in other states. But that monster was back now – and I'd be damned[3] if I was going to let it get away again[4].

The faculty housing at Reston University was depressing. The buildings were dated brick[5] and shoved together[6]. The lighting was bad, but I think that might have been a good thing.

"You mind staying in the car?" I said.

"I have to run a quick errand[7]," Muse said. "I'll be right back."

I headed up the walk. The lights were out, but I could hear music. I recognized the song. "Somebody" by Bonnie McKee[8]. Depressing as hell[9] – the "somebody" being this perfect love she knows is out there but she will never find – but that was Lucy. She adored the heartbreakers[10]. I knocked on the door. There was no answer. I rang the bell, knocked some more. Still nothing.

"Luce!"

Nothing.

"Luce!"

I knocked some more. Whatever the doctor had given me was wearing off[11]. I could feel the stitches in my side. It felt exactly like it was – as though my very movements were ripping my skin apart[12].

"Luce!"

I tried the doorknob[13]. Locked.[14] There were two windows. I tried to peer in[15]. Too dark. I tried to open them. Both locked.

"Come on, I know you're in there."

I heard a car behind me. It was Muse. She pulled to a stop[16] and got out.

"Here," she said.

1. La créature qui
2. vraisemblablement
3. que je sois pendu
4. si je la laissais s'en tirer encore une fois
5. Les bâtiments en brique étaient vieillots
6. regroupés n'importe comment
7. Il faut que je fasse un saut quelque part
8. [auteure-interprète américaine]
9. Horriblement déprimant
10. les chansons qui déchirent l'âme
11. ne faisait presque plus effet
12. chacun de mes mouvements était une torture
13. tournai la poignée
14. C'était fermé à clé.
15. voir à l'intérieur
16. arrêta la voiture

"What is it?"

"Master key.[1] I got it from campus security."

Muse.

She tossed it to me[2] and headed back to the car. I put the key in the lock, knocked one more time, turned it. The door opened. I stepped in and closed the door behind me.

"Don't turn on the light."

It was Lucy.

"Leave me alone, Cope, okay?"

The iPod moved on to[3] the next song. Alejandro Escovedo musically asked about what kind of love[4] destroys a mother and sends her crashing through the tangled trees[5].

"You should do one of those K-tel collections[6]," I said.

"What?"

"You know, like they used to advertise on TV. Time Life[7] presents *The Most Depressing Songs of All Time.*"

I heard her snort a laugh[8]. My eyes were adjusting[9]. I could see her sitting on the couch now. I moved closer.

"Don't," she said.

But I kept walking. I sat next to her. There was a bottle of vodka in her hand. It was half empty. I looked around her apartment. There was nothing personal, nothing new, nothing bright[10] or happy.

"Ira," she said.

"I'm so sorry."

"The cops said he killed Gil."

"What do you think?"

"I saw blood in his car. He shot you. So yeah, of course, I think he killed Gil."

"Why?"

She didn't answer. She took another long swig[11].

"Why don't you give me that?" I said.

"This is what I am, Cope."

"No, it's not."

1. C'est un passe-partout.
2. me le lança
3. passa à
4. s'interrogeait en musique sur la nature de cet amour qui
5. la pousse à foncer [en voiture] dans un bouquet d'arbres
6. [société proposant des compilations musicales]
7. [maison de disques]
8. pouffer de rire
9. s'habituaient à l'obscurité
10. rien de pimpant
11. longue gorgée

"I'm not for you. You can't rescue me."

I had a few replies to that[1] but every one reeked of cliché[2]. I let it go.

"I love you," she said. "I mean, I never stopped[3]. I've been with[4] other men. I've had relationships[5]. But you've always been there. In the room with us. In the bed even. It's stupid and dumb[6] and we were just kids, but that's the way it is."

"I get it," I said.

"They think maybe Ira was the one who killed Margot and Doug."

"You don't?"

"He just wanted it to go away[7]. You know? It hurt so much[8], caused so much destruction. And then, when he saw Gil, it must have been like a ghost was coming back to haunt him[9]."

"I'm sorry," I said again.

"Go home, Cope."

"I'd rather stay."

"That's not your decision.[10] This is my house. My life. Go home."

She took another long draw[11].

"I don't like leaving you like this."

Her laugh had an edge[12]. "What, you think this is the first time?"

She looked at me, daring me to argue[13]. I didn't.

"This is what I do. I drink in the dark and play these damn songs. Soon I'll drift off or pass out[14] or whatever you want to call it. Then tomorrow I'll barely have a hangover[15]."

"I want to stay."

"I don't want you to."

"It's not for you. It's for me. I want to be with you. Tonight especially."

"I don't want you here. It will just make it worse."

"But – "

1. J'aurais pu répondre de plusieurs façons

2. empestait le cliché

3. n'ai jamais cessé de t'aimer

4. ai connu

5. des liaisons

6. complètement débile

7. que tout ça disparaisse

8. Cela avait été si douloureux

9. était revenu le hanter

10. Ce n'est pas toi qui décides.

11. but à nouveau une longue gorgée

12. était tendu

13. me mettant au défi de lui répondre

14. Bientôt, je vais m'assoupir ou m'évanouir

15. c'est tout juste si j'aurai la gueule de bois

1. était implorante

"Please," she said, and her voice was a plea[1]. "Please leave me alone. Tomorrow. We can start again tomorrow."

Chapter 40

Dr. Tara O'Neill rarely slept more than four, five hours a night. She just didn't need sleep. She was back in the woods by six a.m., at first daylight[1]. She loved these woods – any woods, really. She'd gone to undergrad and medical school[2] in the city, at the University of Pennsylvania in Philadelphia. People thought that she'd love it. You're such a lovely girl, they said. The city is so alive[3], so many people, so much happening[4].

But during her years in Philadelphia, O'Neill had returned home every weekend. She eventually ran for[5] coroner and made extra money[6] working as a pathologist[7] in Wilkes-Barre. She tried to figure out her own life philosophy[8] and came up with something she once heard a rock star – Eric Clapton, she thought – say in an interview about not being a big fan of, uh, people. She wasn't either. She preferred – as ridiculous as it sounded – being with herself[9]. She liked reading and watching movies without commentary[10]. She couldn't handle[11] men and their egos and their constant boasting[12] and their raging insecurities[13]. She didn't want a life partner[14].

This – out in the woods like this – was where she was happiest.

1. dès six heures du matin, aux premières lueurs du jour
2. fait son premier cycle et la faculté de médecine
3. animée
4. il s'y passe tant de choses
5. Finalement, elle avait présenté sa candidature au poste de
6. arrondissait ses fins de mois
7. médecin légiste
8. philosophie de la vie
9. rester seule
10. sans [subir de] commentaires
11. ne supportait pas
12. vantardises
13. violent sentiment d'insécurité
14. compagnon

O'Neill carried her tool case[1], but of all the fancy new gizmos[2] that the public had helped pay for[3], the one she found most useful was the simplest: a strainer[4]. It was nearly the exact same[5] as the kind she had in her kitchen. She took it out and started in the dirt.

The strainer's job was[6] to find teeth and small bones.

It was painstaking[7] work, not unlike an[8] archaeological dig she had done after her senior year in high school[9]. She had apprenticed[10] in the Badlands of South Dakota[11], an area known as the Big Pig Dig because, originally, they had found an Archaeotherium[12], which was pretty much a huge ancient pig. She worked with pig and ancient rhinoceros fossils. It had been a wonderful experience.

She worked through this burial site with the same patience – work most people would find mind-deadeningly tedious[13]. But again Tara O'Neill thrived[14].

An hour later, she found the small piece of bone.

O'Neill felt her pulse quicken. She had expected something like this, realized that it was a possibility after the ossification X-rays. But still. To find the missing piece...

"Oh my..."

She said it out loud, her words echoing in the stillness of the woods. She couldn't believe it, but the proof was right there, right in the palm of her rubber-gloved hand[15].

It was the hyoid bone[16].

Half of it anyway. Heavily calcified, brittle[17] even. She went back to her search, sifting[18] as fast as she could. It didn't take long now. Five minutes later, O'Neill found the other half. She held up both pieces[19].

Even after all these years, the bone fragments still fit together like a jigsaw[20].

1. trousse
2. de tous les nouveaux gadgets fantaisistes
3. l'argent public subventionnait
4. passoire
5. presque identique
6. Elle utilisait la passoire
7. minutieux
8. un peu comme cette
9. sa terminale
10. avait fait un stage
11. [parc national]
12. [espèce éteinte de mammifère]
13. fastidieux à mourir
14. se régalait
15. main gantée de caoutchouc
16. l'os hyoïde
17. Très calcifié, fragile
18. en tamisant
19. elle plaça les deux fragments devant elle
20. s'emboîtaient comme les pièces d'un puzzle

Tara O'Neill's face broke into a beatific smile[1]. For a moment, she stared at her own handiwork[2] and shook her head in awe[3].

She took out her cell phone. No signal. She hurried back half a mile until two bars appeared. Then she pressed[4] Sheriff Lowell's number. He picked up on the second ring.

"That you, Doc?"

"It is."

"Where are you?"

"At the burial site," she said.

"You sound excited."

"I am."

"Why?"

"I found something in the dirt," Tara O'Neill said.

"And?"

"And it changes everything we thought[5] about this case."

One of those random hospital beeping noises[6] woke me. I stirred[7] slowly, blinked open my eyes, and saw Mrs. Perez sitting with me[8].

She had pulled the chair right next to my bed. The purse was in her lap. Her knees touched. Her back was straight. I looked into her eyes. She'd been crying.

"I heard about Mr. Silverstein," she said.

I waited.

"And I also heard that they found bones in the woods."

I felt parched.[9] I looked to my right. That yellow-brown plastic water pitcher[10], that one unique to[11] hospitals and specifically designed to make the water taste awful[12], sat[13] on the stand[14] next to me. I was about to reach for it[15], but Mrs. Perez was up before I could do so much as lift my hand[16]. She poured the water into a cup and handed it to me.

"Do you want to sit up[17]?" Mrs. Perez asked.

1. afficha un sourire béat
2. son œuvre
3. impressionnée
4. composa
5. pensions savoir
6. bips intempestifs propres aux hôpitaux
7. bougeai
8. assise à mon chevet
9. Je me sentais déshydraté.
10. pichet
11. qu'on ne trouve que dans les
12. qui semble spécialement conçu pour que l'eau ait un goût horrible
13. était posé
14. table de nuit
15. l'attraper
16. avant même que je n'aie soulevé la main
17. vous redresser

"That's probably a good idea."

She pressed the remote control and my back began to curl into a sit[1].

"Is that okay?"

"That's fine," I said.

She sat back down.

"You won't leave this alone," she said.

I didn't bother responding.

"They say that Mr. Silverstein murdered my Gil. Do you think that's true?"

My Gil. So the pretense was down.[2] No more hiding behind a lie[3] or a daughter. No more hypothetical.[4]

"Yes."

She nodded. "Sometimes I think Gil really did die in those woods. That was how it was supposed to be. The time after that, it was just borrowed[5]. When that policeman called me the other day, I already knew. I'd been expecting it, you see? Part of Gil never escaped from those woods."

"Tell me what happened," I said.

"I thought I knew. All these years. But maybe I never learned the truth[6]. Maybe Gil lied to me."

"Tell me what you do know[7]."

"You were at the camp that summer. You knew my Gil."

"Yes."

"And you knew this girl. This Margot Green."

I said that I did.

"Gil fell for her hard[8]. He was this poor boy. We lived in a burnt-out section[9] of Irvington. Mr. Silverstein had a program where[10] children of workers got to attend[11]. I worked in the laundry room. You know this."

I did.

"I liked your mother very much. She was so smart. We talked a lot. About everything. About books, about life, about our disappointments[12]. Natasha was

1. le matelas se recourba en position assise
2. Donc, on ne faisait plus semblant.
3. derrière un mensonge
4. On ne faisait plus d'hypothèses.
5. c'était juste un sursis
6. peut-être que je n'ai jamais vraiment su la vérité
7. vous savez vraiment
8. en est tombé amoureux fou
9. un quartier délabré
10. auquel
11. pouvaient participer
12. nos déceptions

what we call an old soul[1]. She was so beautiful but it was fragile. Do you understand?"

"I think so, yes."

"Anyway, Gil fell very hard for Margot Green. It was understandable. He was eighteen. She was practically a magazine model[2] in his eyes. That's how it is with men. They are so driven by lust[3]. My Gil was no different. But she broke his heart. That too is common. He should have just suffered for a few weeks and then moved on. He probably would have."

She stopped.

"So what happened?" I asked.

"Wayne Steubens."

"What about him?"

"He whispered in Gil's ear.[4] He told him that he shouldn't let Margot get away with it[5]. He appealed to Gil's machismo[6]. Margot, he said, was laughing at[7] Gil. You need to pay that tease back[8], Wayne Steubens whispered in his ear. And after a while – I don't know how long – Gil agreed."

I made a face. "So they slit her throat?"

"No. But Margot had been strutting all over camp[9]. You remember this, yes?"

Wayne had said it. She was a tease.

"There were many kids who wanted to knock her down a peg[10]. My son, of course. Doug Billingham too. Maybe your sister. She was there, but that might have been because Doug talked her into it[11]. It's not important."

A nurse opened the door.

"Not now," I said.

I expected an argument but something in my voice must have worked. She backed up[12] and let the door close behind her. Mrs. Perez had her eyes down. She stared at her purse as though afraid someone would snatch it.

"Wayne planned it all very carefully[13]. That's what Gil said. They were going to draw[14] Margot out to

1. vieille âme
2. mannequin photo
3. tellement influencés par le désir
4. Il a soufflé des idées à Gil.
5. s'en sortir comme ça
6. a joué sur le machisme de Gil
7. se moquait de
8. dois le lui faire payer, à cette allumeuse
9. se pavanait dans tout le camp
10. la remettre à sa place
11. l'en avait persuadée
12. se retira
13. a tout organisé minutieusement
14. attirer

the woods. It was going to be a prank.[1] Your sister helped with the lure[2]. She said that they were going to meet some cute boys. Gil put a mask on his head. He grabbed Margot. He tied her up. That was supposed to be the end of it.[3] They'd leave her there for a few minutes. She'd either escape from the rope[4] or they'd untie her[5]. It was dumb, very immature, but these things happen."

I knew that they did.[6] Camp was full of "pranks" back then. I remembered one time we'd taken a kid and moved his bed into the woods. He woke up the next morning alone, outside, terrified. We used to shine a flashlight in a sleeping camper's eyes[7] and make a train noise and shake them and yell[8], "Get off the tracks[9]!" and watch the kid dive off[10] his bed. I remembered that there were two bully campers[11] who used to call the other kids "faggots[12]." Late one night, when both were deep in sleep, we picked one up, took off his clothes, put him in bed with the other. In the morning, the other campers saw them naked in the same bed. The bullying[13] stopped.

Tying up a total tease[14] and leaving her in the woods for a little while... that wouldn't have surprised me.

"Then something went very wrong," Mrs. Perez said.

I waited. A tear escaped Mrs. Perez's eye. She reached into her purse and pulled out a wad of tissues[15]. She dabbed her eyes, fought the tears back[16].

"Wayne Steubens took out a razor blade[17]."

I think my eyes widened a little[18] when she said that. I could almost see the scene. I could see the five of them out in the woods, picture[19] their faces, their surprise.

"You see, Margot knew[20] what was going on right away. She played along[21]. She let Gil tie her up. Then she started mocking my son. Made fun of him[22], said he didn't know how to handle[23] a real woman. The same insults women have thrown at men throughout

1. Ils allaient lui faire une blague.
2. a participé à la ruse
3. Cela devait s'arrêter là.
4. Soit elle arriverait à se détacher
5. la libéreraient
6. J'étais bien placé pour le savoir.
7. d'éblouir à la lampe torche un des garçons de la colo endormi
8. de le secouer en criant
9. Sors des rails
10. plonger hors de
11. brutes au camp
12. pédés
13. brimades
14. Attacher une allumeuse invétérée
15. paquet de mouchoirs en papier
16. ravala ses larmes
17. a sorti une lame de rasoir
18. s'écarquillèrent légèrement
19. imaginer
20. avait compris
21. a joué le jeu
22. Elle riait de lui
23. s'y prendre avec

history[1]. But Gil didn't do anything. What could he do? But suddenly Wayne had the razor blade out. At first, Gil thought it was part of the act[2]. To scare her. But Wayne didn't hesitate. He walked over to Margot and slashed her neck from ear to ear."

I closed my eyes. I saw it again. I saw the blade going across that young skin, the blood spurting[3], the life force leaving her. I thought about it. While Margot Green was being slaughtered[4], I was only a few hundred yards away making love to my girlfriend. There was probably poignancy in that[5], in that most horrible of man's actions running adjacent to his most wondrous[6], but it was hard to see it now.

"For a moment no one moved. They all just stood there. Then Wayne smiled at them and said, 'Thanks for the help.'"

I frowned, but maybe I was starting to understand. Camille had drawn Margot out[7], Gil had tied her up...

"Then Wayne lifted the blade. Gil said they could see how much Wayne liked what he had done. How he stared at Margot's dead body. He had a thirst now[8]. He started toward them[9]. And they ran. They ran in different directions. Wayne chased them. Gil ran for miles and miles. I don't know what happened exactly. But we can guess. Wayne caught up to[10] Doug Billingham. He killed him. But Gil got away. And so did your sister."

The nurse returned.

"I'm sorry, Mr. Copeland. I need to take your pulse and blood pressure[11]."

I nodded for her[12] to come in. I needed to catch my breath[13]. I could feel my heart hammering[14] in my chest. Again. If I didn't calm down, they'd keep me in here forever.

The nurse worked quickly and silently. Mrs. Perez looked around the room as if she'd just entered it, as if she'd just noticed where she was. I was afraid I was going to lose her[15].

1. depuis la nuit des temps
2. mise en scène
3. jaillissant
4. se faisait massacrer
5. Il y avait probablement quelque chose de poignant dans tout ça
6. le fait que se déroulent, côte à côte, la plus horrible et la plus magnifique des activités humaines
7. avait attiré Margot dans les bois
8. était assoiffé [de sang] à présent
9. s'est dirigé vers eux
10. a rattrapé
11. votre tension artérielle
12. lui fis signe
13. reprendre mon souffle
14. cogner
15. qu'elle en reste là

"It's okay[1]," I said to her.

She nodded.

The nurse finished up. "You're being released[2] this morning."

"Great."

She gave me a tight smile[3] and left us alone. I waited for Mrs. Perez to continue.

"Gil was terrified, of course. You can imagine. So was your sister. You have to see it from their viewpoint. They were young. They were nearly killed[4]. They had watched Margot Green get slaughtered. But maybe most of all, Wayne's words haunted them[5]. 'Thanks for the help.' You understand?"

"He had made them a part of it.[6]"

"Yes."

"So what did they do?"

"They just hid. For more than twenty-four hours. Your mother and I were worried sick[7]. My husband was home in Irvington. Your father was at camp too. But he was out with the search parties[8]. Your mother and I were together when the call came in. Gil knew the number of the pay phone[9] in the back of the kitchen. He dialed it three different times[10] but he hung up when someone else answered. Then, more than a day after they went missing[11], I picked it up."

"Gil told you what happened?"

"Yes."

"You told my mother?"

She nodded. I was starting to see it.

"Did you approach[12] Wayne Steubens?" I asked.

"We didn't have to. He'd already approached your mother.

"What did he say?"

"Nothing incriminating.[13] But he made it clear[14]. He had set up[15] an alibi for that night. And you see, we knew already. Mothers are like that."

"You knew what?"

1. Ça va aller
2. On vous laisse sortir
3. m'adressa un sourire pincé
4. avaient failli se faire tuer
5. les poursuivaient
6. Il les avait impliqués.
7. étions folles d'inquiétude
8. équipes de recherche
9. téléphone payant
10. à trois reprises
11. qu'ils aient disparu
12. Êtes-vous allées voir
13. Rien de compromettant.
14. s'est fait clairement comprendre
15. s'était fabriqué

"Gil's brother, my Eduardo, was serving time[1]. Gil had a small arrest record[2] – he and some friends stole a car. Your family was poor, my family was poor. There would be fingerprints on the rope[3]. The police would wonder why your sister had led Margot Green into the woods. Wayne had gotten rid[4] of the evidence against him. He was rich and well liked[5] and could hire the best attorneys. You're a prosecutor, Mr. Copeland. You tell me.[6] If Gil and Camille came forward[7], who would have believed them?"

I closed my eyes. "So you told them to stay hidden."

"Yes."

"Who planted[8] their clothes with the blood[9]?"

"I did that. I met Gil. He was still in the woods."

"Did you see my sister?"

"No. He gave me the clothes. He cut himself, pressed his shirt against the wound. I told him to stay hidden until we came up with a plan. Your mother and I tried to figure a way to turn it around[10], to get the police to learn the truth[11]. But nothing came to us[12]. Days passed. I knew how the police could be. Even if they did believe us, Gil was still[13] an accomplice. So was Camille."

I saw something else.

"You had a handicapped son."

"Yes."

"And you needed money. To take care of him. And maybe to pay for Glenda to go to a decent[14] school." My eyes found hers. "When did you realize that you could cash in[15] with that lawsuit?"

"That wasn't part of our original thinking.[16] That came later – when Billingham's father started screaming about how Mr. Silverstein didn't protect his son."

"You saw an opportunity."

She shifted in her seat. "Mr. Silverstein should have watched them. They would have never gone in those woods. He wasn't blameless in this[17]. So yes, I saw an opportunity. So did your mother."

1. était en prison
2. un début de casier judiciaire
3. des empreintes sur la corde
4. s'était débarrassé
5. apprécié
6. À vous de le dire.
7. s'étaient présentés
8. a déposé
9. ensanglantés
10. d'arranger la situation
11. pour que la police apprenne la vérité
12. nous n'avons rien trouvé
13. malgré tout
14. bonne
15. toucher de l'argent
16. Nous n'y avons pas pensé au départ.
17. irréprochable dans cette affaire

My head was spinning.[1] I tried to make it stop just long enough to accept this new reality. "Are you telling me..." I stopped. "Are you telling me that my parents knew that my sister was alive?"

"Not your parents," she said.

And I felt the cold gust hit my heart[2].

"Oh no..."

She said nothing.

"She didn't tell my father, did she?"

"No."

"Why not?"

"Because she hated him."

I just sat there. I thought about the fights, the bitterness[3], the unhappiness. "That much?[4]"

"What?"

"It's one thing to hate a man," I said. "But did she hate my father so much that she'd let him think[5] his own daughter was dead?"

She didn't respond.

"I asked you a question, Mrs. Perez."

"I don't know the answer. I'm sorry."

"You told Mr. Perez, right?"

"Yes."

"But she never told my father."

No answer.

"He used to go out in those woods and search for her," I said. "Three months ago, as he lay on his deathbed, his last words were that he wanted me to keep looking[6]. Did she hate him that much, Mrs. Perez?"

"I don't know," she said again.

It started to hit me, like heavy raindrops. Big thuds.[7] "She bided her time[8], didn't she?"

Mrs. Perez didn't respond.

"She hid my sister. She never told anyone – not even... not even me. She was waiting until the settlement money came through[9]. That was her plan. And as soon as it did... she ran[10]. She took enough money and ran and met up with my sister."

1. La tête me tournait.
2. mon cœur se glaça
3. aux disputes, à l'amertume
4. À ce point ?
5. au point de lui faire croire
6. que je continue à chercher
7. Une idée jaillit en moi et se mit à marteler mon esprit.
8. a attendu le bon moment
9. l'argent de la transaction arrive
10. s'est enfuie

"That was... that was her plan, yes."

I blurted out the next question.[1] "Why didn't she take me?"

Mrs. Perez just looked at me. I thought about it. Why? And then I realized something. "If she took me, my father would never stop looking. He'd get[2] Uncle Sosh and all his old KGB cronies[3] on it[4]. He might let my mother go[5] – he had probably fallen out of love with her too[6]. He thought my sister was dead so that wouldn't be a draw[7]. But my mother knew that he'd never let me go."

I remembered what Uncle Sosh said, about her returning to Russia. Were they both there? Were they both there right now? Did that make sense?

"Gil changed his name," she went on. "He traveled around[8]. His life was less than spectacular.[9] And when those private detectives came around to our house and asked questions, he got wind of it[10]. He saw it as a way of cashing in again. You see, it was odd. He blamed you too[11]."

"Me?"

"You didn't stay on guard duty that night."

I said nothing.

"So part of him blamed you. He thought that maybe this was a good time for payback[12]."

It added up.[13] It fit in perfectly with[14] what Raya Singh had told me.

She stood. "That's all I know."

"Mrs. Perez?"

She looked at me.

"Was my sister pregnant?"

"I don't know."

"Did you ever see her?"

"Excuse me?"

"Camille. Gil told you she was alive. My mother told you she was alive. But did you ever see her yourself?"

"No," she said. "I never saw your sister."

1. La question suivante sortit toute seule.

2. aurait mis

3. camarades

4. sur le coup

5. pouvait peut-être se faire à l'idée de laisser partir ma mère

6. ne l'aimait probablement plus, lui non plus

7. alors il n'avait pas vraiment de raison de l'empêcher de partir

8. un peu partout

9. Sa vie fut loin d'être exaltante.

10. il l'a su

11. vous en voulait, à vous aussi

12. que c'était peut-être le moment de prendre sa revanche

13. Tout se recoupait.

14. Cela correspondait parfaitement à

Chapter 41

I didn't know what to think.

There was almost no time either.[1] Five minutes after Mrs. Perez left my room, Muse entered.

"You got court.[2]"

We checked out of the hospital without fuss[3]. I had an extra suit[4] in my office. I changed into it. And then I headed to Judge Pierce's chamber. Flair Hickory and Mort Pubin were already there. They had heard about my episode[5] the night before, but if they cared[6], they weren't about to show it today.

"Gentlemen," the judge said. "I'm hoping we can find a way of settling this case[7]."

I was in no mood[8]. "That's what this is about?[9]"

"It is."

I looked at the judge. He looked at me. I shook my head. It made sense. If they had tried to pressure me[10] by digging up dirt[11], what would have stopped them from doing the same with the judge?

"The People aren't interested in a deal[12]," I said.

I stood.

"Sit down, Mr. Copeland," Judge Pierce said. "There may be problems with your DVD evidence[13]. I may have to exclude it.[14]"

I started for the door.

1. Je n'en eus pas vraiment le temps non plus.
2. Tu dois aller au tribunal.
3. sans histoires
4. costume de rechange
5. aventure
6. s'ils compatissaient
7. régler ce dossier
8. n'étais pas d'humeur
9. Nous sommes là pour ça ?
10. m'intimider
11. en dénichant des casseroles
12. Le ministère public n'a aucune intention de passer un accord
13. votre preuve sur DVD
14. Elle pourrait ne pas être recevable.

"Mr. Copeland!"

"I'm not staying," I said. "It's on me[1], Judge. You did your part. Blame me.[2]"

Flair Hickory frowned. "What are you talking about?"

I didn't reply. I reached for the doorknob.

"Sit down, Mr. Copeland, or be in contempt[3]."

"Because I don't want to settle?"

I turned and looked at Arnold Pierce. There was a quiver in his lower lip.[4]

Mort Pubin said, "Will somebody explain to me what the hell is going on?"

The judge and I ignored him. I nodded to Pierce that I understood. But I wasn't about to give in[5]. I turned the knob and left. I started down the hallway[6]. My wounded side ached.[7] My head throbbed.[8] I wanted to sit down and cry. I wanted to sit down and ponder[9] what I had just learned about my mother and my sister.

"I didn't think it would work."

I turned. It was EJ Jenrette.

"I'm just trying to save my son," he said.

"Your son raped a girl."

"I know."

I stopped. He had a manila folder in his hand.

"Sit a second," Jenrette said.

"No."

"Imagine your daughter. Your Cara. Imagine that one day she grows up. Maybe she has too much to drink at a party. Maybe she drives and hits someone[10] with the car. Maybe they die. Something like that. She makes a mistake."

"Rape is not a mistake."

"Yeah, it is. You know he'd never do it again. He screwed up.[11] He thought he was invincible. He knows better now.[12]"

"We're not getting into this again[13]," I said.

1. C'est moi qui paie les pots cassés

2. Mettez-moi tout sur le dos.

3. je vous poursuis pour outrage

4. Sa lèvre inférieure tremblait.

5. n'allais pas céder

6. m'engageai dans le couloir

7. Ma blessure au côté me faisait souffrir.

8. J'avais très mal à la tête.

9. méditer sur

10. renverse quelqu'un

11. Il a fait n'importe quoi.

12. Il a compris la leçon maintenant.

13. On ne va pas encore revenir là-dessus

"I know. But everyone has secrets. Everyone makes mistakes, commits crimes, does whatever. Some people are just better about burying them[1]."

I said nothing.

"I never went after your child," Jenrette said. "I went after you. I went after your past. I even went after your brother-in-law. But I never went near your child. That was my own personal line.[2]"

"You're a prince[3]," I said. "So what do you have on Judge Pierce?"

"It's not important."

He was right. I didn't need to know.

"What can I do to help my son, Mr. Copeland?"

"That horse is out of the barn[4]," I said.

"You really believe that? You think his life is over?"

"Your son will probably serve five, six years tops[5]," I said. "What he does while he's in there and what he does when he gets out – that'll decide what his life is[6]."

EJ Jenrette held up the manila envelope. "I'm not sure what to do with this."

I said nothing.

"A man does what he can to protect his children. Maybe that was my excuse. Maybe that was your father's."

"My father's?"

"Your father was KGB. Did you know that?"

"I don't have time for this.[7]"

"This is a summary[8] of his file. My people translated it into English."

"I don't need to see that."

"I think you should, Mr. Copeland." He held it out[9]. I didn't take it. "If you want to see how far a father might go[10] to make a better life for[11] his children, you should read this. Maybe you'll understand me a little better."

"I don't want to understand you."

1. plus doués pour les enterrer
2. C'est la limite que je m'étais fixée.
3. êtes bon prince
4. Le mal est fait
5. effectuera sans doute une peine de cinq ou six ans maximum
6. cela déterminera ce que sera sa vie
7. Je n'ai pas de temps à perdre avec ça.
8. résumé
9. me le tendit
10. jusqu'où un père peut aller
11. offrir une vie meilleure à

EJ Jenrette just held the file out. Eventually I took it.[1] He walked away without another word.

I headed back to my office and closed the door. I sat at my desk and opened the file. I read the first page. Nothing surprising. Then I read the second page and yet again[2], just when I thought I couldn't hurt any more[3], the words tore open my chest and shredded me apart[4].

Muse came in without knocking.

"The skeleton they found at that camp," she said. "It's not your sister."

I couldn't speak.

"See, this Dr. O'Neill found something called a hyoid bone. That's in the throat, I guess. Shaped like a horseshoe.[5] Anyway, it was snapped in half[6]. That means the victim was probably manually strangled[7]. But see, the hyoid bone isn't this brittle in[8] young people – it's more like a cartilage, I guess. So O'Neill ran some more ossification tests with X-rays[9]. In short, it is much more likely that the skeleton belonged to a woman in her forties[10], maybe even her fifties[11], than someone Camille's age."

I said nothing. I just stared at the page in front of me.

"Don't you get it? It's not your sister."

I closed my eyes. My heart felt so damn heavy.[12]

"Cope?"

"I know," I said.

"What?"

"It's not my sister in the woods," I said. "It's my mother."

1. Je finis par le prendre.
2. une fois de plus
3. que plus rien ne pouvait me faire de mal
4. me déchirèrent le cœur et me brisèrent
5. En forme de fer à cheval.
6. cassé en deux
7. a sans doute été étranglée avec les mains
8. n'est pas si fragile chez les
9. a fait d'autres analyses aux rayons X sur l'ossification
10. d'une quarantaine
11. d'une cinquantaine d'années
12. Bon Dieu, que j'avais le cœur lourd.

Chapter 42

Sosh wasn't surprised to see me.

"You knew, didn't you?"

He was on the phone. He put his hand over the mouthpiece[1].

"Sit down, Pavel."

"I asked you a question."

He finished his call and put the phone back in the cradle[2]. Then he saw the manila envelope in my hand. "What's that?"

"It's a summary of my father's KGB file."

His shoulders slumped[3]. "You can't believe[4] everything in those," Sosh said, but there was nothing behind his words[5]. It was as though he'd read them off a teleprompter[6].

"On page two," I said, trying to quiet the tremor[7] in my voice, "it says what my father did."

Sosh just looked at me.

"He turned in[8] my Noni and Popi, didn't he? He was the source that betrayed them.[9] My own father."

Sosh still wouldn't speak[10].

"Answer me, dammit[11]."

"You still don't understand."

"Did my own father turn my grandparents in, yes or no?"

1. recouvrit le combiné de sa main
2. sur son support
3. s'affaissèrent
4. Il ne faut pas croire
5. ses mots sonnaient creux
6. comme s'il les avait lus sur un prompteur
7. tremblement
8. Il a dénoncé
9. C'est lui qui les a trahis.
10. ne disait toujours rien
11. nom de Dieu

"Yes."

I stopped.

"Your father had been accused of botching a delivery[1]. I don't know if he did or not. It makes no difference. The government wanted him[2]. I told you all the pressure that they can apply. They would have destroyed your entire family."

"So he sold out[3] my grandparents to save his own skin[4]?"

"The government would have gotten them anyway. But yes, okay, Vladimir chose to save his own children over[5] his elderly in-laws[6]. He didn't know it would go so wrong[7]. He thought that the regime would just crack down a little, flex a little muscle[8], that's all. He figured they'd hold[9] your grandparents for a few weeks at the most[10]. And in exchange, your family would get a second chance. Your father would make life better for his children and his children's children. Don't you see?"

"No, I'm sorry, I don't."

"Because you are rich and comfortable[11]."

"Don't hand me that crap[12], Sosh. People don't sell out their own family members. You should know better.[13] You survived that blockade. The people of Leningrad wouldn't surrender[14]. No matter[15] what the Nazis did, you took it and held your head high[16]."

"And you think that was smart[17]?" he snapped[18]. His hands formed two fists.[19] "My God, you are so naive. My brother and sister starved to death. Do you understand that? If we had surrendered, if we'd given those bastards[20] that damn city, Gavrel and Aline would still be alive. The tide still would have turned[21] against the Nazis eventually[22]. But my brother and sister would have had lives – children, grandchildren, grown old. Instead..."

He turned away.

"When did my mother find out about what he'd done?" I asked.

1. d'avoir raté un accouchement
2. voulait sa peau
3. balancé
4. pour sauver sa peau
5. au détriment de
6. beaux-parents âgés
7. que cela tournerait aussi mal
8. sévirait un peu, ferait une petite démonstration de force
9. pensait qu'ils détiendraient
10. tout au plus
11. que tu vis dans le confort
12. Épargne-moi ces conneries
13. Tu le sais bien.
14. n'ont jamais capitulé
15. Peu importe
16. l'avez subi en gardant la tête haute
17. malin
18. rétorqua-t-il
19. Il serra les poings.
20. à ces salauds
21. Le vent aurait quand même tourné
22. en fin de compte

"It haunted him. Your father, I mean. I think part of your mother always wondered[1]. I think that was why she had such contempt[2] for him. But the night your sister vanished, he thought that Camille was dead. He crumpled[3]. And so he confessed the truth."

It made sense.[4] Horrible sense. My mother had learned what my father had done. She would never forgive him for betraying her beloved parents. She would think nothing of making him suffer[5], of letting him think that his own daughter was dead.

"So," I said, "my mother hid my sister. She waited until she had enough money from the settlement. Then she planned on disappearing[6] with Camille."

"Yes."

"But that begs the central question[7], doesn't it?"

"What question?"

I spread my hands. "What about me, her only son? How could my mother just leave me behind?"

Sosh said nothing.

"My whole life," I said. "I spent my whole life thinking my mother didn't care enough about me[8]. That she just ran off and never looked back[9]. How could you let me believe that, Sosh?"

"You think the truth is better?"

I thought of how I spied on my father in those woods. He dug and dug for[10] his daughter. And then one day he stopped. I thought that he stopped because my mother ran off. I remembered the last day he had gone out to those woods, how he told me not to follow him:

"Not today, Paul. Today I go alone...."

He dug his last hole that day. Not to find my sister. But to bury my mother.

Was it poetic justice[11], placing her in the ground where my sister supposedly died, or was there also an element of practicality[12] – who would think to look in a place where they had already searched so thoroughly[13]?

1. qu'au fond d'elle-même, ta mère s'est toujours interrogée
2. un tel mépris
3. s'est effondré
4. C'était cohérent.
5. Pour elle, c'était normal de le faire souffrir
6. a décidé de disparaître
7. soulève cette question essentielle
8. ne m'aimait pas assez
9. sans se retourner
10. pour retrouver
11. Était-ce un juste retour des choses
12. aspect pratique
13. fouillé si méthodiquement

"Dad found out she planned to run."

"Yes."

"How?"

"I told him."

Sosh met my eye. I said nothing.

"I learned that your mother had transferred a hundred thousand dollars out of their joint account. It was common KGB protocol[1] to keep an eye on one another[2]. I asked your father about it."

"And he confronted her."

"Yes."

"And my mother..." There was a choke in my voice.[3] I cleared my throat, blinked, tried again. "My mother never planned on abandoning me," I said. "She was going to take me too."

Sosh held my gaze and nodded.

That truth should have offered me some small measure of comfort[4]. It didn't.

"Did you know he killed her, Sosh?"

"Yes."

"Just like that?[5]"

Again he went quiet.

"And you didn't do anything about it, did you?"

"We were still working for the government," Sosh said. "If it came out[6] that he was a murderer, we could all be in danger."

"Your cover would have been blown.[7]"

"Not just mine.[8] Your father knew a lot of us."

"So you let him get away with it."

"It was what we did back then[9]. Sacrifice for the higher cause.[10] Your father said she threatened to expose us all[11]."

"You believed that?"

"Does it matter what I believed? Your father never meant[12] to kill her. He snapped.[13] Imagine it. Natasha was going to run away and hide. She was going to take his children and disappear forever."

1. Cela faisait partie de la routine du KGB

2. de se surveiller mutuellement

3. Ma voix s'étrangla.

4. me réconforter un peu

5. Et c'est tout ?

6. Si cela venait à se savoir

7. Tu aurais été grillé.

8. Pas que moi.

9. à l'époque

10. Se sacrifier pour une noble cause.

11. avait menacé de révéler notre existence à tous

12. ne voulait certainement pas

13. Il a perdu les pédales.

I remembered now my father's last words, on that deathbed...

"Paul, we still need to find her...."

Did he mean Camille's body? Or Camille herself?

"My father found out my sister was still alive," I said.

"It's not that simple."

"What do you mean, it's not that simple? Did he find out or not? Did my mother tell him?"

"Natasha?" Sosh made a noise. "Never. You talk about brave[1], about being able to withstand hardships[2]. Your mother wouldn't speak[3]. No matter what your father did to her."

"Including strangling her to death?[4]"

Sosh said nothing.

"Then how did he find out?"

"After he killed your mother, your father searched through[5] her papers, through phone records. He put it together[6] – or at least he had his suspicions[7]."

"So he did know?"

"Like I said, it's not that simple."

"You're not making sense[8], Sosh. Did he search for Camille?"

Sosh closed his eyes. He moved back around his desk. "You asked me before about the siege of Leningrad," he said. "Do you know what it taught me? The dead are nothing. They are gone. You bury them and you move on."

"I'll keep that in mind[9], Sosh."

"You went on this quest.[10] You wouldn't leave the dead alone. And now where are you? Two more[11] have been killed. You learned that your beloved father murdered your mother. Was it worth it[12], Pavel? Was it worth stirring up the old ghosts[13]?"

"It depends," I said.

"On what?"

"On what happened to my sister."

I waited.

1. Là, on parle vraiment de courage
2. et de résistance face aux épreuves
3. n'a jamais parlé
4. En l'occurrence, la tuer par strangulation ?
5. a fouillé dans
6. Il a compris
7. a eu des soupçons
8. Je ne te comprends pas
9. m'en souviendrai
10. Tu t'es lancé dans cette quête.
11. Deux personnes de plus
12. Cela en valait-il la peine
13. de remuer les fantômes du passé

My father's last words came to me[1]:

"Did you know?"

I'd thought[2] he was accusing me, that he saw guilt on my face. But that wasn't it. Did I know about the real fate[3] of my sister? Did I know what he'd done? Did I know that he murdered my own mother and buried her in the woods?

"What happened to my sister, Sosh?"

"This is what I meant when I said it's not so simple."

I waited.

"You have to understand. Your father was never sure[4]. He found some evidence, yes, but all he knew for certain[5] was that your mother was going to run with the money and take you with her."

"So?"

"So he asked me for help. He asked me to look into his evidence[6]. He asked me to find your sister."

I looked at him.

"Did you?[7]"

"I looked into it, yes." He took a step toward me. "And when I was finished, I told your father that he got it wrong[8]."

"What?"

"I told your father that your sister died that night in the woods."

I was confused.[9] "Did she?"

"No, Pavel. She didn't die that night."

I felt my heart start to expand in my chest[10]. "You lied to him. You didn't want him to find her."

He said nothing.

"And now? Where is she now?"

"Your sister knew what your father had done. She couldn't come forward[11], of course. There was no proof of his guilt[12]. There was still the matter of why she had disappeared[13] in the first place[14]. And of course, she feared your father. How could she just return to the man who murdered her mother?"

1. me revinrent à l'esprit
2. J'avais cru
3. ce qu'il était réellement advenu
4. n'a jamais su vraiment
5. la seule chose dont il était sûr
6. d'examiner les indices qu'il avait rassemblés
7. Tu l'as fait ?
8. qu'il s'était trompé
9. J'étais perdu.
10. prêt à exploser
11. se présenter [à la police]
12. aucune preuve de sa culpabilité
13. y avait encore le problème du motif de sa disparition
14. en premier lieu

I thought about the Perez family, the charges of fraud and all that. It would have been the same with my sister. Even before you add my father into the equation[1], it would have been difficult for Camille to come home.

Hope again filled my chest.[2]

"So you did find her?"

"Yes."

"And?"

"And I gave her money."

"You helped her hide from him."

He didn't answer. He didn't have to.

"Where is she now?" I asked.

"We lost touch[3] years ago. You have to understand, Camille didn't want to hurt you. She thought about taking you away. But that was impractical[4]. She knew how much you loved your father. And then later, when you became a public figure, she knew what her return, what this scandal, would do to you. You see, if she came back, it would all have to come out[5]. And once that happened, your career would be over."

"It already is."

"Yes. We know that now."

We, he said. We.

"So where is Camille?" I asked.

"She's here, Pavel."

The air left the room.[6] I couldn't breathe. I shook my head.

"It took a while[7] to find her after all these years," he said. "But I did. We talked. She didn't know your father had died. I told her. And that, of course, changed everything."

"Wait a second. You..." I stopped. "You and Camille talked?"

It was my voice, I think.

"Yes, Pavel."

"I don't understand."

1. Avant même que ton père entre en ligne de compte
2. Mon cœur se remplit à nouveau d'espoir.
3. On s'est perdus de vue
4. irréaliste
5. tout éclaterait au grand jour
6. L'atmosphère devint asphyxiante.
7. Cela m'a pris un certain temps

"When you came in, that was her on the phone."

My body went cold.

"She's staying at a hotel two blocks away[1]. I told her to come over." He looked at the elevator. "That's her now. On her way up.[2]"

I slowly turned and watched the numbers climb[3] above the elevator. I heard it ding[4]. I took one step toward it. I didn't believe it. This was another cruel trick[5]. Hope was having its way with me again[6].

The elevator stopped. I heard the doors begin to open. They didn't slide. They moved grudgingly[7], as though afraid to surrender their passenger[8]. I froze.[9] My heart hammered hard against[10] my chest. I kept my eyes on those doors, on the opening.

And then, twenty years after vanishing into those woods, my sister, Camille, stepped back[11] into my life.

1. à deux pâtés de maisons

2. Elle monte.

3. regardai les chiffres annonçant les étages s'afficher

4. entendis le tintement de la sonnerie

5. encore un mauvais tour

6. se jouait à nouveau de moi

7. s'ouvraient de mauvaise grâce

8. laisser sortir la personne de la cabine

9. Je me pétrifiai.

10. battait à tout rompre dans

11. refit son entrée

Epilogue

One Month Later

Lucy does not want me to take this trip[1].

"It's finally over," she says to me, right before I head to the airport.

"Heard that before," I counter[2].

"You don't need to face him again[3], Cope."

"I do. I need some final answers."

Lucy closes her eyes.

"What?"

"It's all so fragile, you know?"

I do.

"I'm afraid you'll shift the ground again[4]."

I understand. But this needs to be done.

An hour later, I am looking out the window of a plane. Over the past month[5], life has returned to quasi-normal. The Jenrette and Marantz case took some wild and weird twists[6] toward its rather glorious ending[7]. The families did not give up. They applied whatever pressure they could[8] on Judge Arnold Pierce and he broke[9]. He threw out[10] the porno DVD, claiming we didn't produce it in a timely enough fashion[11]. We appeared to be in trouble. But the jury saw through it[12] – they often do – and came back

1. que je fasse ce déplacement
2. ripostai-je
3. n'es pas obligé de l'affronter à nouveau
4. que tu remettes tout en question
5. Au cours du dernier mois
6. a connu toutes sortes de rebondissements
7. avant de s'achever de manière assez épatante
8. ont exercé toutes les pressions en leur pouvoir
9. a cédé
10. a rejeté
11. assez tôt
12. n'a pas été dupe

with guilty verdicts[1]. Flair and Mort are appealing[2], of course.

I want to prosecute[3] Judge Pierce, but I'll never get him. I want to prosecute EJ Jenrette and MVD for blackmail[4]. I doubt I'll get that either. But Chamique's lawsuit is going well. Rumor has it[5] that they want her out of the way quickly. A seven-figure settlement is being bandied about.[6] I hope she gets it. But when I peer into my crystal ball[7], I still don't see a great deal of happiness for Chamique down the road[8]. I don't know. Her life has been so troubled.[9] Somehow I sense that money will not change that.

My brother-in-law, Bob, is out on bail[10]. I caved in on that one.[11] I told the federal authorities that while my recollections were "fuzzy,"[12] I do believe Bob told me that he needed a loan and that I approved it. I don't know if it will fly[13]. I don't know if I'm doing the right thing or the wrong thing (probably the wrong) but I don't want Greta and her family destroyed. Feel free to call me a[14] hypocrite – I am – but that line between right and wrong grows so blurry[15] sometimes. It grows blurry here in the bright sunshine of the real world[16].

And, of course, it grows blurry in the dark of those woods.

Here is the quick yet thorough update on[17] Loren Muse: Muse remains[18] Muse. And I'm thankful for that. Governor Dave Markie hasn't called for my resignation yet[19] and I haven't offered it. I probably will and I probably should, but as of right now, I'm hanging in[20].

Raya Singh ended up leaving Most Valuable Detection to partner up[21] with none other than Cingle Shaker[22]. Cingle says that they're looking for a third "hottie[23]" so they can call their new agency "Charlie's Angels[24]."

1. a prononcé des verdicts de culpabilité
2. ont fait appel
3. Je voudrais bien poursuivre
4. chantage
5. Il paraît
6. On parle d'une transaction de plus d'un million.
7. regarde dans ma boule de cristal
8. pour la suite
9. La vie l'a tellement malmenée.
10. en liberté sous caution
11. Là, j'ai cédé.
12. même si mes souvenirs étaient un peu vagues,
13. cela passera
14. Vous pouvez me traiter d'
15. devient si floue
16. à la lumière crue des réalités du monde
17. Et maintenant, un compte rendu rapide mais complet à propos de
18. sera toujours
19. n'a pas encore demandé ma démission
20. pour l'instant, je reste
21. pour s'associer
22. Cingle Shaker en personne
23. bombe
24. Drôles de dames

The plane lands. I get off. I check my BlackBerry. There is a short message from my sister, Camille:

Hey, bro[1] – Cara and I are going to have lunch in the city and shop. Miss and love you, Camille

My sister, Camille. It is fantastic to have her back. I can't believe how quickly she had become a full-fledged and integral part of our lives[2]. But the truth is, there is still a lingering[3] tension between us. It is getting better. It will get better still. But the tension is there and unmistakable[4], and sometimes we go over the top in our efforts to[5] combat it by calling each other "bro" and "sis[6]" and saying that we "miss" and "love" each other all the time.

I still don't have Camille's entire backstory[7]. There are details she is leaving out[8]. I know that she started with a new identity in Moscow, but didn't stay long. There were two years in Prague and another in Begur on the Costa Brava of Spain. She came back to the United States, moved around some more, got married and settled outside Atlanta, ended up divorced three years later.

She never had kids, but she is already the world's greatest aunt[9]. She loves Cara, and the feeling is more than reciprocated[10]. Camille is living with us. It is wonderful – better than I could have hoped – and that truly eases[11] the tension.

Part of me, of course, wonders why it took so long for Camille to come home – that's where the majority of the tension comes from, I think. I understand what Sosh said about her wanting to protect me, my reputation, my memories of my father. And I know that she understandably was afraid of Dad while he still breathed[12].

But I think that there is more to it[13].

Camille chose to keep silent about what happened in those woods. She never told anyone what Wayne

1. frérot
2. comme elle est rapidement devenue partie intégrante de nos vies
3. persistante
4. manifeste
5. on en fait des tonnes pour essayer de
6. sœurette
7. ne sais pas encore dans le détail tout ce qu'a été la vie de Camille
8. laisse de côté
9. meilleure tatie du monde
10. plus que partagé
11. apaise véritablement
12. tant qu'il était en vie
13. qu'il y a autre chose

Steubens had done. Her choice, right or wrong, had left Wayne free to[1] murder more people. I don't know what would have been the right thing to do – if coming forward would have made it better or worse. You could argue that Wayne still would have gotten away with it[2], that he might have run off or stayed in Europe, that he would have been more careful about his killings, gotten away with more[3]. Who knows? But lies have a way of festering[4]. Camille thought that she could bury those lies. Maybe we all did.

But none of us got out of those woods unscathed[5].

As for my romantic life, well, I am in love. Simple as that. I love Lucy with all my heart. We are not taking it slow[6] – we plunged right in, as if trying to make up for lost time[7]. There is a maybe unhealthy desperation there[8], an obsession, a clinging-as-though-to-a-life-raft quality in what we are[9]. We see a lot of each other, and when we're not together I feel lost and adrift[10] and I want to be with her again. We talk on the phone. We e-mail and text-message[11] incessantly.

But that's love, right?

Lucy is funny and goofy and warm and smart and beautiful and she overwhelms me in the best way[12]. We seem to agree on everything.

Except, of course, my taking this trip[13].

I understand her fear. I know all too well[14] how fragile this all is. But you can't live on thin ice either[15]. So here I am again, in Red Onion State Prison in Pound, Virginia, waiting to learn a few last truths.

Wayne Steubens enters. We are in the same room as our last meeting. He sits in the same place.

"My, my," he says to me. "You've been a busy boy[16], Cope."

"You killed them," I say. "After all is said and done[17], you, the serial killer, did it."

Wayne smiles.

"You planned it all along[18], didn't you?"

"Is anyone listening in to this?"

1. avait permis à Wayne de
2. s'en serait quand même tiré
3. aurait tué encore en toute impunité
4. une façon bien à eux de s'envenimer
5. indemne
6. On n'y va pas en douceur
7. rattraper le temps perdu
8. On peut peut-être y voir une forme de désespoir malsain
9. du genre « on s'accroche l'un à l'autre comme à un radeau »
10. à la dérive
11. On s'envoie des e-mails et des textos
12. me comble à tous points de vue
13. sur le fait que j'entreprenne ce voyage
14. ne sais que trop bien
15. sur le fil du rasoir non plus
16. T'as pas arrêté
17. En fin de compte
18. Tu avais tout prévu depuis le début

"No."

He puts up his right hand. "Your word on that?"

"My word," I say.

"Then, sure, why not. I did, yes. I planned the killings."

So there it is.[1] He too has decided that the past needs to be faced[2].

"And you carried it out[3], just like Mrs. Perez said. You slaughtered Margot. Then Gil, Camille and Doug ran. You chased them. You caught up to Doug. You murdered him too."

He raises his index finger. "I made a miscalculation[4] there. See, I jumped the gun[5] with Margot. I meant her to be last[6] because she was already tied up. But her neck was so open[7], so vulnerable... I couldn't resist."

"There are a few things I couldn't figure out at first," I say. "But now I think I know."

"I'm listening."

"Those journals the private detectives sent to Lucy," I say.

"Ahh."

"I wondered who saw us in the woods, but Lucy got that one right[8]. Only one person could have known: the killer. You, Wayne."

He spreads[9] his hands. "Modesty prevents me[10] from saying more."

"You were the one who gave MVD the information they used in those journals. You were the source."

"Modesty, Cope. Again I plead modesty."

He is enjoying this.

"How did you get Ira to help?[11]" I ask.

"Dear Uncle Ira. That addle-brained hippie.[12]"

"Yes, Wayne."

"He didn't help much. I just needed him out of the way.[13] You see – and this might shock you, Cope – but Ira did drugs[14]. I had pictures and proof. If

1. Alors nous y voilà.
2. qu'il fallait affronter le passé
3. as exécuté ton plan
4. mauvais calcul
5. j'ai brûlé les étapes
6. Elle aurait dû être la dernière
7. offert
8. avait vu juste, là-dessus
9. écarte
10. La modestie m'interdit
11. Comment as-tu obtenu l'aide d'Ira ?
12. Ce hippie à l'esprit embrumé.
13. Je ne voulais pas qu'il soit dans mes pattes.
14. se droguait

it came out[1], his precious camp would have been ruined. So would he."

He smiles some more.

"So when Gil and I threatened to bring it all back[2]," I say, "Ira got scared. Like you said, he was somewhat addle-brained then – he was a lot worse now. Paranoia clouded his thinking[3]. You were already serving time – Gil and I could only make things worse by bringing it all back. So Ira panicked. He silenced Gil and tried to silence me."

Another smile from Wayne.

But there is something different in the smile now.

"Wayne?"

He doesn't speak. He just grins. I don't like it. I replay[4] what I'd just said. And I still don't like it.

Wayne keeps smiling.

"What?" I ask.

"You're missing something, Cope."

I wait.

"Ira wasn't the only one who helped me."

"I know," I say. "Gil contributed. He tied Margot up. And my sister was there too. She helped get Margot into those woods."

Wayne squints and puts his forefinger and thumb half an inch apart[5]. "You're still missing one teensy-weensy thing[6]," he says. "One itsy-bitsy secret[7] I've kept all these years."

I am holding my breath.[8] He just smiles. I break the silence.

"What?" I ask again.

He leans forward and whispers, "You, Cope."

I can't speak.

"You're forgetting your part[9] in this."

"I know my part," I say. "I left my post."

"Yes, true. And if you hadn't?"

"I would have stopped you."

"Yes," Wayne says, drawing out the word[10]. "Precisely."

1. on l'apprenait
2. tout faire ressortir
3. avait altéré son raisonnement
4. repense à
5. plisse les yeux, tout en écartant le pouce et l'index d'un centimètre
6. Un tout petit truc t'échappe encore
7. secret de rien du tout
8. Je retiens mon souffle.
9. rôle
10. en insistant longuement sur le mot

I wait for more. It doesn't come.[1]

"Is that what you wanted to hear, Wayne? That I feel partially responsible?"

"No. Nothing that simple."

"What then?"

He shakes his head. "You're missing the point.[2]"

"What point?"

"Think, Cope. True, you left your post. But you said it yourself. I planned it all out.[3]"

He cups his hands around his mouth[4] and his voice drops to a whisper again[5].

"So answer me this: How did I *know* you wouldn't be at your post that night?"

Lucy and I drive out to the woods.

I already got permission from Sheriff Lowell, so the security guard, the one[6] Muse had warned me about, just waves us through[7]. We park in the condo lot[8]. It is strange – neither Lucy nor I had been here in two decades. This housing development[9] hadn't existed back then, of course. But still, after all this time, we know just where we are.

Lucy's father, her dear Ira, had owned all this land. He had come up here all those years ago, feeling like Magellan discovering a new world. Ira probably looked out at these woods and realized his lifelong dream[10]: a camp, a commune[11], a natural habitat free from the sins of man[12], a place of peace and harmony, whatever, something that would hold his values[13].

Poor Ira.

Most crimes I see start with something small. A wife angers[14] her husband over something inconsequential[15] – where the remote control[16] is, a cold dinner – and then it escalates[17]. But in this case, it was just the opposite. Something big got the ball rolling[18]. In the end, a crazy serial killer had started it all. Wayne Steubens's lust for blood[19] set everything in motion[20].

1. J'attends la suite. En vain.
2. T'es à côté de la plaque.
3. J'avais tout prémédité.
4. Il place ses mains autour de sa bouche
5. redevient un murmure
6. celui contre lequel
7. m'a mis en garde, nous fait simplement signe de passer
8. parking
9. zone résidentielle
10. pris conscience du rêve de sa vie
11. communauté
12. exempt des péchés de l'homme
13. représenterait ses valeurs
14. provoque la colère de
15. d'insignifiant
16. télécommande
17. c'est l'escalade
18. d'énorme avait tout déclenché
19. La soif de sang
20. a tout mis en branle

Maybe we all facilitated him[1] in one way or another. Fear ended up being Wayne's best accomplice. EJ Jenrette had taught me the power of that too – if you make people fearful enough[2], they will acquiesce[3]. Only[4] it hadn't worked in his son's rape case. He hadn't been able to scare Chamique Johnson. He hadn't been able to scare me either.

Maybe that was because I had already been scared enough.

Lucy carries flowers, but she should know better[5]. We don't place[6] flowers on tombstones in our tradition. We place stones. I also don't know who the flowers are for – my mother or her father. Probably both.

We take the old trail[7] – yes, it is still there, though it's pretty overgrown[8] – to where[9] Barrett found my mother's bones. The hole where she lay[10] all these years is empty. The remnants of yellow crime-scene tape[11] blow in the breeze[12].

Lucy kneels down. I listen to the wind, wonder if I hear the cries. I don't. I don't hear anything but the hollow of my heart[13].

"Why did we go into the woods that night, Lucy?"

She doesn't look up at me[14].

"I never really thought about that. Everyone else did. Everyone wondered how I could have been so irresponsible. But to me, it was obvious. I was in love. I was sneaking away with my girlfriend. What could be more natural than that?"

She puts the flowers down carefully. She still won't look at me.

"Ira didn't help Wayne Steubens that night," I say to the woman I love. "You did."

I hear the prosecutor in my voice.[15] I want him to shut up[16] and go away. But he won't[17].

"Wayne said it. The murders were carefully planned[18] – so how did he know I wouldn't be at

1. lui avons-nous tous facilité les choses
2. effrayez suffisamment les gens
3. obtempèrent
4. Mais
5. c'est curieux de sa part
6. ne déposons pas
7. l'ancienne piste
8. bien qu'elle soit envahie de végétation
9. menant là où
10. a reposé
11. restes du ruban de signalisation jaune délimitant la scène de crime
12. s'agitent dans la brise
13. le vide de mon cœur
14. ne lève pas les yeux vers moi
15. C'est le procureur qui parle.
16. qu'il se taise
17. il n'y a rien à faire
18. soigneusement préparés

my post? Because it was your job to make sure that I wasn't[1]."

I can see her start to grow smaller, wither[2].

"That's why you could never face me," I say. "That's why you feel like you're still tumbling down a hill and can't stop. It's not that your family lost the camp or their reputation or all the money. It's that you helped Wayne Steubens."

I wait. Lucy lowers her head. I stand behind her. Her face drops in her hands.[3] She sobs. Her shoulders shake[4]. I hear her cries, and my heart breaks in two. I take a step toward her. The hell with this, I think. This time, Uncle Sosh is right. I don't need to know everything. I don't need to bring it all back.

I just need her. So I take that step.

Lucy holds up a hand[5] to stop me. She gathers herself a piece at a time.[6]

"I didn't know what he was going to do," she says. "He said he'd have Ira arrested if I didn't help. I thought... I thought he was just going to scare Margot. You know. A stupid prank."

Something catches in my throat.[7] "Wayne knew we got separated."

She nods.

"How did he know?"

"He saw me."

"You," I say. "Not us."

She nods again.

"You found the body, didn't you? Margot's, I mean. That was the blood in the journal. Wayne wasn't talking about me. He was talking about you."

"Yes."

I think about it, about how scared she must have been, how she probably ran to her father, how Ira would have panicked too.

"Ira saw you covered in blood. He thought..."

She doesn't speak. But now it makes sense[8].

1. tu devais faire en sorte que je n'y sois pas
2. la vois qui se recroqueville et se décompose
3. Elle enfouit son visage dans ses mains.
4. tremblent
5. lève la main
6. Elle se reprend peu à peu.
7. Ma gorge se serre.
8. tout s'explique

"Ira wouldn't kill Gil and me to protect himself," I say. "But he was a father. In the end, with all his peace, love and understanding, Ira was first and foremost[1] a father like any other. And so he'd kill to protect his little girl."

She sobs again.

Everyone had kept quiet. Everyone had been afraid – my sister, my mother, Gil, his family, and now Lucy. They all bear some of the blame[2], and they all paid a stiff price[3]. And what about me? I like to excuse myself by claiming youth[4] and the need to, what, sow some wild oats[5]. But is that really any excuse? I had a responsibility to watch the campers that night. I shirked it.[6]

The trees seem to close in on us[7]. I look up at them and then I look at Lucy's face. I see the beauty. I see the damage[8]. I want to go to her. But I can't. I don't know why. I want to – I know it is the right thing to do. But I can't.

I turn instead and walk away[9] from the woman I love. I expect her to call out for me to stop.[10] But she doesn't. She lets me go. I hear her sobs. I walk some more. I walk until I am out of the woods and back by the car. I sit on the curb[11] and close my eyes. Eventually[12] she will have to come back here. So I sit and wait for her. I wonder where we will go after she comes out. I wonder if we will drive off together[13] or if these woods, after all these years, will have claimed one last victim[14].

1. avant toute chose

2. Ils portent tous une part de responsabilité

3. l'ont tous payé très cher

4. en invoquant ma jeunesse

5. faire les quatre cents coups

6. J'ai failli à mon devoir.

7. se refermer sur nous

8. les ravages

9. Au lieu de ça, je fais demi-tour et m'éloigne

10. Je m'attends à ce qu'elle m'appelle pour me supplier de rester.

11. rebord du trottoir

12. Tôt ou tard

13. repartirons ensemble

14. auront fait une dernière victime

La collection Yes you can!

Faux débutants

Ken Follett *The Modigliani Scandal*

Mary Higgins Clark *A Stranger is Watching*

Mary Higgins Clark *Loves Music, Loves to Dance*

Mary Higgins Clark *Where are the Children?*

Anthony Horowitz *The House of Silk*

Yann Martel *Life of Pi*

Nicholas Sparks *Message in a Bottle*

Intermédiaires

Harlan Coben *Play Dead*

Harlan Coben *Stay Close*

Harlan Coben *Tell No One*

Harlan Coben *The Woods*

Michael Connelly *The Black Box*

Michael Connelly *The Drop*

Ken Follett *Paper Money*

Mary Higgins Clark *A Cry in the Night*

P.D. James *A Mind to Murder*

Douglas Kennedy *The Big Picture*

John le Carré *A Most Wanted Man*

Avancés

Paul Auster *Oracle Night*

Julian Barnes *The Sense of an Ending*

Michael Cunningham *By Nightfall*

Michael Cunningham *The Hours*

Helen Fielding *Bridget Jones's Diary*

Elizabeth George *A Great Deliverance*

Stephen King *Misery*

Imprimé en Italie par La Tipografica Varese Srl
Dépôt légal : mai 2015
313702-01/11025879-mai 2015